KT-167-672

New York Times bestselling author **Christine Feehan** has over 30 novels published and has thrilled legions of fans with her seductive and sensual 'Dark' Carpathian tales. She has received numerous honours throughout her career including being a nominee for the Romance Writers of America RITA, and receiving a Career Achievement Award from *Romantic Times*, and has been published in multiple languages and in many formats, including audio book, e-book, and large print.

For more information about Christine Feehan visit her website: www.christinefeehan.com

700043237413

Christine Feehan's
'Dark' Carpathian Series:

Dark Prince
Dark Desire
Dark Gold
Dark Magic
Dark Challenge
Dark Fire
Dark Legend
Dark Guardian
Dark Symphony
Dark Melody
Dark Destiny
Dark Secret
Dark Demon
Dark Celebration
Dark Possession
Dark Curse
Dark Slayer
Dark Peril
Dark Predator
Dark Storm
Dark Lycan
Dark Wolf
Dark Blood

Dark Nights
Darkest at Dawn (omnibus)

Also by Christine Feehan

Sea Haven Series:
Water Bound
Spirit Bound
Air Bound

GhostWalker Series:
Shadow Game
Mind Game
Night Game
Conspiracy Game
Deadly Game
Predatory Game
Murder Game
Street Game
Ruthless Game
Samurai Game
Viper Game

Drake Sisters Series:
Oceans of Fire
Dangerous Tides
Safe Harbour
Turbulent Sea
Hidden Currents
Magic Before Christmas

Leopard People Series:
Fever
Burning Wild
Wild Fire
Savage Nature
Leopard's Prey

The Scarletti Curse

Lair of the Lion

Mind Game

Christine Feehan

piatkus

PIATKUS

First published in the US in 2004 by The Berkley Publishing Group,
A division of Penguin Group (USA) Inc., New York
First published in Great Britain in 2008 by Piatkus Books
This paperback edition published in 2008 by Piatkus Books

7 9 10 8

Copyright © 2004 by Christine Feehan

The moral right of the author has been asserted.

*All characters and events in this publication, other than those
clearly in the public domain, are fictitious and any resemblance
to real persons, living or dead, is purely coincidental.*

All rights reserved.
No part of this publication may be reproduced, stored in a
retrieval system, or transmitted, in any form or by any means, without
the prior permission in writing of the publisher, nor be otherwise circulated
in any form of binding or cover other than that in which it is published
and without a similar condition including this condition being
imposed on the subsequent purchaser.

A CIP catalogue record for this book
is available from the British Library.

ISBN 978-0-7499-3878-9

Data manipulation by Phoenix Photosetting, Chatham, Kent
Printed and bound in Great Britain by
Clays Ltd, St Ives plc

Papers used by Piatkus are from well-managed forests
and other responsible sources.

MIX
Paper from
responsible sources
FSC   FSC® C104740
www.fsc.org

Piatkus
An imprint of
Little, Brown Book Group
100 Victoria Embankment
London EC4Y 0DY

An Hachette UK Company
www.hachette.co.uk

www.piatkus.co.uk

For my beloved sister Mary, with much love.
Hope always shines eternal, even in our darkest hour.
Somehow, you always have known that.

ACKNOWLEDGMENTS

Without two wonderful men, this book would never have been written. I would like to thank Morey Sparks for all of his help and the many hours he spent talking to me about his experiences in the military. It wasn't always easy, and I appreciate it.

Special thanks to Dr. Christopher Tong, coeditor of the "state of the art" series, *Artificial Intelligence in Engineering Design (volumes I, II, and III)*. He has also published books with such titles as *Beyond Believing, You CAN Take It With You,* and *Beyond Spiritual Correctness*. He has been a manager, consultant, teacher, and researcher at many well-known institutions including Rutgers, MIT, IBM Thomas J. Watson Research Center, Xerox Palo Alto Research Center, and Siemens Research. He was invaluable to me with his help on this book.

THE GHOSTWALKER CREED

We are the GhostWalkers, we live in the shadows
The sea, the earth, and the air are our domain
No fallen comrade will be left behind
We are loyalty and honor bound
We are invisible to our enemies and we destroy them
    where we find them
We believe in justice and we protect our country and those
    unable to protect themselves
What goes unseen, unheard, and unknown are
    GhostWalkers
There is honor in the shadows and it is us

We move in complete silence whether in jungle or desert
We walk among our enemy unseen and unheard
Striking without sound and scatter to the winds before
    they have knowledge of our existence
We gather information and wait with endless patience for
    that perfect moment to deliver swift justice
We are both merciful and merciless
We are relentless and implacable in our resolve
We are the GhostWalkers and the night is ours

Nox noctis est nostri

CHAPTER
ONE

"She's obviously not cooperating again," Dr. Whitney grumbled and scribbled fiercely in his notebook, clearly somewhere between total exasperation and frustration. "Don't let her have her toys again until she decides to work. I've had enough of her nonsense."

The nurse hesitated. "Doctor, that isn't a good idea with Dahlia. She can be very. . ." She paused, clearly searching for the right word. "Difficult."

That caught his attention. He looked up from his papers, the impatience on his face changing to interest. "You're afraid of her, Milly. She's four years old, and you're afraid of her. Why?" There was more than scientific interest in his tone. There was eagerness.

The nurse continued to watch the child through the glass window. The little girl had shiny black hair, thick and long and falling down her back in an unkempt, untidy mass. She sat on the floor rocking back and forth, clutching a small blanket to her and moaning softly. Her eyes were enormous, as black as midnight and as penetrating as steel.

Milly Duboune winced visibly and looked away when the child turned those black, ancient eyes in her direction.

"She can't see us through the glass," Dr. Whitney pointed out.

"She knows we're here." The nurse dropped her voice to a whisper. "She's dangerous, Doctor. No one wants to work with her. She won't let us brush her hair or tell her to go to bed, and we can't punish her."

Dr. Whitney lifted an eyebrow, sheer arrogance crossing his face. "You're all *that* afraid of this child? Why wasn't I informed?"

Milly hesitated, fear etched on her face. "We knew you'd demand more from her. You have no idea what you'd unleash. You don't pay any attention to them after you make your demands. She's in terrible pain. We don't blame her when she throws her tantrums. Ever since you insisted we separate the children, many are showing signs of extreme discomfort or, as in Dahlia's case, a high level of pain. She can't eat or sleep properly. She's too sensitive to light and sound. She's losing weight. Her pulse is too rapid, her heart rate up all the time. She cries even in her sleep. Not a child's cry, but a cry of pain. Nothing we've tried has helped."

"There's no reason for her to be in pain," Dr. Whitney snapped. "All of you coddle those children. They have a purpose, a much bigger purpose than you can imagine. Go back in there and tell her if she doesn't cooperate, I'll take all of the toys and her blanket away from her."

"Not her blanket, Dr. Whitney, it's all she clings to. It's all the comfort she has." The nurse shook her head forcefully and stepped back from the window. "If you want that blanket, you go take it away from her yourself."

Dr. Whitney studied the desperation in the woman's eyes with clinical detachment. He indicated for the nurse to reenter the room. "See if you can coax her to cooperate. What does she want the most?"

"To be put back in the same room with either Lily or Flame."

"*Iris.* The child's name is Iris, not Flame. Don't indulge her personality simply because she has red hair. She already is more trouble than she's worth with that temper of hers. The last thing we want is for Iris and this one," he indicated the dark-haired little girl, "to get together. Go tell her she can spend time with Lily if what she does pleases me."

Milly took a deep breath and pushed open the door to the small room. The doctor flicked a switch so he could hear the conversation between the nurse and the little girl.

"Dahlia? Look at me, honey," Milly wheedled. "I have a surprise for you. Dr. Whitney said if you do something really good for him, you can spend time with Lily. Would you like that? To spend the rest of the evening with Lily?"

Dahlia clutched the raggedy blanket to her and nodded her head, her eyes solemn. The nurse knelt beside her and reached out her hand to smooth Dahlia's hair away from her face. Immediately the little girl ducked, clearly unafraid, simply avoiding physical contact with her. Milly sighed and dropped her hand. "Okay, Dahlia. Try something with one of the balls. See if you can do something with them."

Dahlia turned her head and looked directly at the doctor through the one-way glass. "Why does that man stare at us all the time? What does he want?" She sounded more adult than child.

"He wants to see if you can do anything special," the nurse answered.

"I don't like him."

"You don't have to like him, Dahlia. You just have to show him what you can do. You know you have all sorts of wonderful tricks you can do."

"It hurts when I do them."

"Where does it hurt?" The nurse glanced at the glass too, a small frown beginning to form.

"In my head. It hurts all the time in my head and I can't make it go away. Lily and Flame make it go away."

"Just do something for the doctor and you can spend all evening with Lily."

Dahlia sat silent for a moment, still rocking, her fingers

curled tightly in the blanket. Behind the one-way glass, Dr. Whitney sucked in his breath and scribbled across the page of his notebook hastily, intrigued by the child's demeanor. She seemed to be weighing the advantages and disadvantages and making a judgment call. Finally she nodded, as if bestowing a great favor on the nurse.

Without further argument, Dahlia placed her tiny hand over one ball and began to make small circles above it. Dr. Whitney leaned close to the glass to study the lines of concentration on her face. The ball began to spin on the floor then rose beneath her palm. She moved the ball along her index finger, keeping it spinning a few inches above the floor in an amazing display of her phenomenal ability to control it with her mind. A second sphere joined the first in the air beneath her hand, both balls spinning madly like tops. The task appeared almost effortless. Dahlia seemed to be concentrating, but not wholly. She glanced at the nurse and then at the glass, looking nearly bored. She held the balls spinning in the air for a minute or two.

Abruptly she let her hand fall, clapping both hands against her head, pressing her palms tightly against her temples. The balls fell to the ground. Her face was pale, white lines around her mouth.

Dr. Whitney swore softly and flicked a second switch. "Have her do it again. This time with as many balls as she can handle. I want the action sustained this time so I can time her."

"She can't, Doctor, she's in pain," Milly protested. "We have to take her to Lily. It's the only thing that will help her."

"She's only saying that so she can get her way. How could Lily or Iris take her pain away? That's just ridiculous, they're children. If she wants to see Lily she can repeat the experiment and try a little harder."

There was a small silence. The little girl's face darkened. Her eyes grew pitch-black. She stared fiercely at the glass. "He's a bad man," she told the nurse. "A very bad man." The glass began to fracture into a fine spider's web. There were at least ten balls of varying size on the floor near the child. All of them began to spin madly in the air before slamming again and again against the window. Glass fragments broke off and rained onto the floor. Chips flew wildly in the air, until it appeared to be snowing glass.

The nurse screamed and ran from the small room, slamming the door behind her. The walls swelled outward with the terrible rage on the child's face. The door rocked on its hinges. Flames raced up the wall, circled the doorjamb, bright crackling orange and red, spreading like a storm. Everything that could move was picked up from the floor and spun as if in the center of a tornado.

Through it all, Whitney stood watching, mesmerized by the power of her rage. He didn't even move when the glass cut his face and blood ran down into the collar of his immaculate shirt.

Dr. Lily Whitney-Miller snapped off the video and turned to face the small group of men who had been watching the tape with the same mesmerized enthrallment the doctor in the film had exhibited. She took a deep breath and let it out slowly. It was always hard to watch her father behaving in such a monstrous fashion. No matter how often she viewed the tapes of his work, she could not equate that man with the one who had been so loving to her. "That, gentlemen, was Dahlia at age four," she announced. "She would be a couple of years younger than me now, and she's the one I believe I've located."

There was an awed silence. "She was that powerful at the age of four? A four-year-old child?" Captain Ryland Miller put his arm around his wife to comfort her, knowing how she felt when she delved into the experiments her father had performed. He stared at the picture of the black-haired child on the screen. "What else do you have on her, Lily?"

"I've found more tapes. These are of a young woman being given advanced training as some kind of field operative. I'm convinced it's Dahlia. My father's code is different in these books, and the subject under training is referred to as *Novelty White*. I didn't understand it at first, but my father called each of the missing girls he experimented on by the name of a flower. Dahlia is often referred to as a novelty. I think he interchanges the name *Dahlia* with *Novelty* in these experiments. These tapes cover preteen and teen years. She's an exceptional young woman, high IQ, very talented, tremendous psychic ability, but the tapes are difficult to watch because she is wide open to assault from the outside world and no one has taught her how to protect herself."

"How could she possibly exist in the outside world without being taught shields?" one of the men sitting in the shadows asked. Lily turned her head to look at him, sighing as she did so. Nicolas Trevane always seemed to be in the shadows, and he was one of the GhostWalkers who made her nervous. He sat in such stillness he seemed to blend in with his surroundings, yet when he went into action, he exploded, moving so fast he seemed to blur. For part of his childhood he was raised on a reservation with his father's people, and then he spent ten years in Japan with his mother's relatives. His face never seemed to give anything away. His black eyes were flat and cold and frightened her almost as much as the fact that he was a sniper, a renowned marksman capable of the most deadly and secret of missions.

Lily bowed her head to avoid looking into his icy eyes. "I don't know, Nico. I have fewer answers now than I did a few months ago. I'm still having trouble making myself understand how my father could have experimented on children and then again on all of you. As for this poor girl, this child he virtually tortured, if I'm reading these notes correctly, she was eventually trained as a government operative, and I think it's possible they're still using her."

"That's not possible, Lily," Ryland objected. "You saw what happened to us when we tried to operate without an anchor. You said your father had tried using pulses of electricity on all of you. You know the results of that. Brain bleeds, acute pain. Strokes. It just isn't possible. She'd go insane. The experiment Dr. Whitney conducted opened all our brains, leaving us without barriers or our natural filters.

We're grown men, already trained, yet you're talking about a child trying to cope with impossible demands."

"It should have driven her over the edge," Lily agreed. She held up the notebook. "I've discovered a private sanitarium in Louisiana that the Whitney Trust owns. It is run by the Sisters of Mercy. And it has one patient—a young woman." She looked at her husband. "Her name is Dahlia Le Blanc."

"You aren't going to tell me your father bought out a religious organization," Raoul "Gator" Fontenot protested. He hastily crossed himself. "I won't believe nuns could possibly be a part of Whitney's cover-up."

Lily smiled at him. "Actually, Gator, I think the nuns are fictitious, as is the sanitarium. I think it's really a front to hide Dahlia from the world. As the sole director of all the trusts, I was able to dig fairly deep and it seems she's really the only patient, and aside from the Trust picking up all her bills, she has a sizable trust in her own name with regular deposits. The deposits coincide with entries seemingly indicating my father had become suspicious she was being used as an operative for the United States government. Apparently he allowed her to be trained and then when he realized it was too difficult for her, he moved her to the sanitarium and, as always, when things went wrong, he left her without following up." There was an edge of bitterness to her voice. "I think my father tried to create a safe place for her there, just as he created this house for me."

Ryland bent his head to Lily's, his chin rubbing the top of her sable hair. "Your father was a brilliant man, Lily. He had to learn about love, it wasn't shown to him as a child." It was a refrain he reminded her of often since it had come to light that not only had Dr. Whitney experimented on Lily, removing the filters from her brain in order to enhance psychic ability, she wasn't his biological child, as he'd led her to believe, but one of many children he'd "bought" from foreign orphanages.

There was another silence. Tucker Addison whistled softly. He was a tall, stocky man with dark skin, brown eyes, and an engaging smile. "You did it, Lily. You actually found her. And she's a GhostWalker like all of us."

"Before we get too excited, I think you should watch some of the other training tapes I found. Each of these is labeled *Novelty*." She signaled to her husband to press Play on the machine to start the video running.

Lily found herself holding her breath. She was certain the child Novelty and Dahlia were one and the same. "According to the records, Novelty is eight years old here." The child's hair was thick and as black as a raven's wing. She wore it in a clumsy braid that hung to her waist in a thick rope. Her face was delicate, matching the rest of her, and the thick hair seemed to overpower her. "I'm certain this is the same child. Look at her face. Her eyes are the same." Lily felt the child was hiding from the world behind the mass of silken strands. She looked exotic, her origins Asian. Like all the missing girls, Dr. Whitney had adopted her from a foreign country and brought her to his laboratory to enhance her natural psychic abilities.

In the video, the little girl was on a balance beam. She didn't walk carefully. She didn't even look down. She ran across it as if it was a wide sidewalk instead of a narrow piece of wood. She didn't hesitate at the end of the beam, but did a flip off of it, landing on her feet, still running without breaking stride. She was far too small to leap up and catch the bars over her head, but she didn't seem to notice. She launched herself skyward, her hands outstretched, her small body tucked as she connected with the bars and swung over them with ease.

A collective gasp told Lily the men were all watching. She let the tape play through. All the while the little girl performed amazing skills. At times the child laughed aloud, bringing home to them the fact that she was alone in the room with only the cameras catching her incredible performance. Lily waited for the end of the tape and the reaction it would bring. As many times as she viewed it, she could not believe what she was seeing.

The child went up and over a two-story-high cargo net

and then raced across the floor toward the last obstacle. A cable stretched across the length of the room, sagging in the middle, several feet above ground level. Novelty stared at the cable as she ran, concentration apparent on her face. The cable began to stiffen and by the time she leapt onto the steel wire, it was woven into a thick rope, with no sag whatsoever in the middle, allowing her to run lightly across it to the end and jump off laughing.

There was another silence when Ryland switched off the tape. "Can any of you do that?"

The men shook their heads. "How did she do it?"

"She has to be manipulating energy. We all do it to a much smaller extent," Lily said. "She's able to take it a step further and at little expense to herself. I'm willing to bet that she's generating an antigravitational field to levitate the cable. It could be done by psychokinetically converting the underside of the cable into a superconductor, and applying the Li–Podkletnov technique of spinning the nuclei in the atoms of the underside to generate a sufficiently powerful antigrav field to lift it. And that would explain how she just danced across it *as if she were floating!*" Lily turned to look at the men, her eyes alight with excitement. "She *was* floating! Her own weight was reduced to almost nothing by the same antigrav field."

"Lily." Ryland shook his head. "You're doing it again. Try speaking normal English."

"I'm sorry. I get carried away when I'm excited," Lily admitted. "It's just so incredible. I've been scouring the research literature, and what's amazing to me is that she's doing with her mind what a couple of scientists are only beginning to be able to do in labs: generate antigravity. Only she does it much better, and she seems to be able to generate antigravity whenever she likes. She turns it on and off in a way that the scientists aren't even close to at this point. Plus scientists, and I as well, would give anything to know how she is doing it at room temperature. They currently need to lower the temperature to several *hundred* degrees below zero in order to create their superconductors."

"Antigravity?" Gator echoed, "isn't that just a little far-fetched?"

"And what we do isn't?" Nicolas asked.

"Well, actually I thought it was impossible at first, too," Lily conceded. "But if, like me, you've watched these tapes several hundred times, you begin to notice little details. Here, let's rewind it to where she's crossing the cable. Now let's watch it in slow motion. See? Right there when the cable starts to straighten out?" She touched the screen to indicate where they should look. "Look here, at the ceiling above the cable—see that electrical wire connecting the two overhead lights? Look, it's moved up, about half an inch! Do you see that? And then it falls back right when Dahlia jumps off the other end of the cable. That's *exactly* what you'd expect to see if there was an antigrav field extending upward from the cable."

Lily pointed to the image of the young girl frozen on the screen. "Look at her, she's laughing, not grabbing her head in pain." She pushed in another tape. "In this one, she moves locks so fast, at first I thought a machine had to be involved." The tape showed a huge vault with a complex lock system. The bolts slid so fast, the tumblers spun and clicked as if a large pattern was predetermined. The camera had focused completely on the heavy door so that it wasn't until they heard a child's laughter as the door swung open that they even realized Dahlia was there, opening locks with her mind.

Lily regarded the men. "Isn't that incredible? She never even touched the vault. I considered a few theories— clairaudition for one, but I just couldn't account for the sheer *speed* with which she opened the vault. Finally it hit me. She was directly intuiting and taking pleasure in the state of lowest entropy in the tumbler–lever system of the vault!"

Lily looked so triumphant Ryland hated to crush her joy. "Sweetheart, I'm so excited for you. Really, I am. It's just that I didn't understand a damn thing you said." He looked around the room with a raised eyebrow. The other men shook their heads.

She tapped her finger on the table, frowning. "All right, let's see if I can come up with a way to explain it to you. You know those movies where the burglars put their stethoscope up against the safe as they're turning the dial?"

"Sure," Gator said. "I watch that stuff all the time. They're listening for the tumblers to click into place."

"Not exactly, Gator," Lily corrected. "They're actually listening for a *drop* in the amount of sound. You're hearing clicking with each number you pass, and then you hear just a little *less* clicking when one of the tumblers has fallen into place. That's why I first thought of clairaudition, which as you know, is like clairvoyance, seeing things at a distance in your mind, but this would be hearing things at a distance in your mind."

"But you don't think that's what she's doing?" Nicolas asked.

Lily shook her head. "No, I had to throw that theory out. It doesn't explain her incredible speed. Plus, I found out that the vault in the videotape—like most safes made since the 1960s—has all kinds of safeguards like nylon tumblers and sound baffles that make them pretty much impenetrable from lock-picking of this sort."

"So Dahlia doesn't do it through sound," Nicolas said.

"No, she doesn't," Lily agreed. "I was stumped for a while. But in the middle of the night a much simpler explanation occurred to me; she literally 'feels' each lever falling into place. But there's more. I think she has an emotional distaste for entropy in systems that gives her speed."

"You've lost me again, Lily," Ryland said.

"Sorry. The second law of thermodynamics says that the amount of entropy, or disorder, in the universe, tends to increase unless it is prevented from doing so. You can see the second law in action everywhere. A vase breaks into pieces. You never see a bunch of pieces assemble themselves into a vase. Left to itself, a house always gets dustier, never cleaner. And tumblers, because they're spring-loaded, always spring *out* of place, not into place, when left to themselves. That's the second law of thermodynamics in action—disorder keeps increasing if things are left to themselves. The closest I can figure it is that Dahlia is a part of nature that runs *counter* to the second law. In other words, she loves order and despises entropy."

"That's true of a lot of people. Rosa is a nut about the house being tidy," Gator said, referring to their housekeeper. "And her kitchen has to be just so. We don't dare move anything around."

Lily nodded. "That's true, but with Dahlia it runs much deeper. Because she's psychic, she actually takes pleasure when she intuits the tumblers falling into place. It's because she's doing her lock-picking at the level of feeling and intuition, motivated by pleasure—that gives her speed. Think of how quickly we take our hand off a hot stove when we start to feel pain, or how the knee jerks up when you hit it with a hammer. These are reflexive responses; they don't involve any thinking, which is a good thing for that hot hand, because thinking is much slower."

"I can open small locks," Ryland admitted. He glanced at Nicolas. "You can too. But I admit, I'm definitely thinking about it. I have to concentrate."

"And neither of us can open locks on that scale or at that speed," Nicolas commented. His gaze remained riveted to the screen. "She's amazing."

"I'd have to agree, Nico," Lily said. "So as near as I can tell, she's psychokinetically moving the tumblers into place in the same kind of reflexive fashion. It doesn't get slowed down by her thinking mind; she's getting *instantly* rewarded by a jolt of pleasure from her nervous system every time she moves one of the tumblers into place. And when all the tumblers are in place . . . well, that's why she laughed with such exuberance when the door swung open. That was the real rush for her." She swallowed and looked away from them. "I'm that same way with mathematical patterns. My mind continually has to work on them, and I get a rush when the patterns all click into place."

Nicolas whistled softly. "I can see why the government would want her working for them."

Lily stiffened. "She's still a child who deserved a childhood. She should have been playing with toys."

Nicolas turned his head slowly, looking at her with his cold, black eyes. "That's exactly what she appears to be doing, Lily. Playing with toys. You're angry with your father and rightly so. But he tried to do for this child what he did for you. Your brain had to work on mathematical problems and patterns all the time; this girl required a different type of work, but she obviously needed it just as much. Why wasn't she adopted out?" His voice was flat, almost a monotone, but it carried weight and authority. He never raised his voice, but he was always heard.

Lily repressed a shiver. "Maybe I'm too close to the problem," she agreed. "And you very well could be right. She does seem to be able to do all this without pain. I'd like to know why. Even now, with all the work I've done, the exercises to make myself stronger, I still get violent headaches if I use telepathy too much."

"But maybe you weren't a natural telepath. You have other talents that are amazing. When I use telepathy, it doesn't bother me at all," Nicolas said.

"Lily, you said the tapes of the child were difficult to watch," Tucker pointed out, "but she seems fine in that one."

Lily nodded. "The tapes involving operative training were difficult for me to watch. The one you're about to see really covers both her tremendous skills and how dangerous she can be—and the cost of her gifts."

The hallway depicted on the screen was very narrow, an obvious maze set up to represent various rooms in a house. A dozen other rooms were seen as smaller images along the left side of the screen. A small, black-haired woman came into view, stalking silently along the wall. She took several steps into the maze and stopped. She seemed to be listening or concentrating internally. The watchers could see a large man crouched behind a curtain in one of the rooms and a second man in the beams along the ceiling waiting in ambush almost directly above the first man.

The woman was tiny, her black hair straight and shiny,

swept back in a careless ponytail. She wore dark clothes and moved with graceful, fluid, stealthy steps. When she stilled, she seemed to become part of the shadows, a vague, blurred image, so slight as to be a part of the wall. The watchers blinked several times to keep her in focus.

"She's able to blur her image enough to trick anyone watching," Ryland said in awe. "That would be useful for us to learn."

"The focus and concentration required is incredible," Lily pointed out. "But it's costing her. She's rubbed her temples twice, and if you look closely at her face, she's already sweating. She obviously can feel the emotions of those waiting to attack her. I observed her training in martial arts. She was reading the mind of her opponent, anticipating everything he did before he did it. She utilized her psychic abilities as well as her physical ones."

"She's not armed," Nicolas pointed out.

"No, but she doesn't need to be," Lily assured.

They watched the woman called Novelty continue unerringly to the right room, not even bothering to check the various empty rooms between her and the two men waiting to ambush her. She trusted her instincts and her highly evolved psychic senses.

"She's so damned small," Gator said. "She looks like a child. She can't weigh even a hundred pounds."

"Maybe," said Lily, "but watch her. She's lethal."

The woman moved with confidence until she was against the wall nearest where one man crouched behind the curtains covering the opening to a closet. "She's laying her hand against the wall, almost as if she's feeling for something," Lily said. "Energy perhaps? Could she be that sensitive? Could a human being's energy pass through the wall in sufficient force to allow her to feel his presence, or is she reading his thoughts?"

Novelty stepped back from the wall in total silence, but remained staring at it for several minutes, slowly sweeping her gaze upward as if she could see the ceiling in the other room as well. The walls slowly blackened. Smoke poured into the hall. Angry flames leapt through the wall to the inside of the room and raced up toward the ceiling, reaching hungrily for both men. Almost immediately the entire room was engulfed in flames, which triggered a sprinkler system. It was the only thing that saved the two ambushers from a terrible death.

"She generates heat," Ian McGillicuddy said. He was a giant of a man, with wide shoulders and a heavy muscular body. His dark brown eyes were fixed on the screen, watching the flames in awe. "I wouldn't mind that particular gift."

"Or curse," Nicolas interjected.

Ian nodded. "Or curse," he agreed.

The young woman slipped from the house and moved back into the trees, pressing both hands to her head. She sank to her knees, fell backward, and went immediately into a violent seizure. The cameras remained focused on her as blood trickled from her mouth. In several seconds she lay unmoving on the ground.

Ryland swore and turned away. His gaze collided with Nicolas's. They stared at one another for a long moment of understanding.

Lily paused the tape, leaving the distressing picture of the woman lying in a heap on the ground. "What's causing this pain? I've checked through my father's notes and viewed the other training tapes. Every tape where she's left completely alone, she's able to perform all sorts of incredible and nearly unbelievable feats, but if there is a human being close by, she suffers tremendous pain and often passes out."

"Emotions swamping her?" Gator guessed. "With no anchor she's left wide open to all the emotions. The men in the room would have been scared and angry and feeling betrayed by their handlers. I would imagine they didn't like being put in the position of nearly being roasted alive."

"Maybe," Lily mused, "but I think it's more complicated than what we go through. I'm not certain she reads emotions, or at least not how most of us do."

Nicolas stared at the screen for a long time, studying the

image of the unconscious woman. "She didn't sense the presence of her adversaries in the way we do, did she? It isn't emotions, it's something else."

"I think it could be energy," Lily said. "My father didn't understand about anchors, not really. When he first performed the experiment on all of us children, he thought we just had close friendships. He didn't understand that some of us trapped the overload of emotion away from the others, allowing them to function. Novelty, or Dahlia, is *not* an anchor—she needs one in order to function without pain. If you notice, in the majority of the training tapes, she's alone. They built a home for her, much like my home was built for me, and she was shielded from people. Dr. Whitney believed she could read minds in the same way many of us can, and he thought he was shielding her from emotions."

"You're getting all this from his notes?" Ryland asked. "How dangerous does he say she is?"

Lily shrugged. "He talked about the necessity of removing her from society several times, yet he continued to allow this training to take place. I studied the tapes as he must have, and she doesn't attack unless she believes she is forced to defend herself. So certainly, during her teenage years, she's gained some semblance of control over her abilities."

Lily put on the remaining tapes, one after the other. She had watched them already, the heartbreaking scenes of the woman she was certain was the missing Dahlia doing martial arts, anticipating every move before it was made, defeating every opponent in spite of her small size and lack of weight, but inevitably collapsing in a heap of muscle spasms, with a retching stomach and blood trickling from her mouth and even her ears at times. She never cried out; she merely rocked back and forth, pressing her hands to her head before her ultimate collapse. The tapes depicted training that could possibly be used for undercover work, and each time the woman called Novelty ended up the same way, curled up in a ball in the fetal position.

Watching it made Lily sick. Once her father discovered Dahlia couldn't work under the conditions they were expecting, he should have pulled her from the training immediately. Unfortunately, she always performed the given task before she collapsed. Remembering the earlier tapes of the stubborn and vengeful child in the laboratory, Lily wondered what they held over her head to get her to work for them when she was so clearly strong-willed enough to refuse.

Instead of watching the tapes she watched the reactions of the men. She wanted to send the most sympathetic after Dahlia. The woman had suffered trauma for years. She needed the safety of the Whitney home, with the protection of the thick walls and a compassionate and kind-hearted staff, all of whom had natural barriers so they couldn't project emotions to the GhostWalker team. Her father had provided the safe house for her, and she had, in turn, chosen to share it with the men her father had experimented on.

Lily looked at their faces and for the first time felt the urge to laugh. Why had she thought she'd be able to read them? They hid their thoughts behind expressionless masks. They were well prepared by the military, each of them receiving special training long before they were ever recruited for duty in the GhostWalker squad.

She waited until the last tape had been played and the impact on the men was the most profound. Dahlia Le Blanc was the kind of woman most men would want to protect. Very small, very slight, with enormous sad eyes and flawless skin. She looked like a doll with her skin and eyes and wealth of jet-black hair. Lily knew Dahlia needed help, a tremendous amount of help, to adjust to living in the world again. She was determined to give Dahlia everything Dr. Whitney had failed to provide. A home, a sanctuary, people she could call family and count on. It wouldn't be easy to convince Dahlia to come back to the very place where the original damage had been done to her.

Ryland swept his arm around Lily and bent his head to hers. "You have tears in your eyes."

"Everyone else should, too," Lily said and blinked rapidly. "My father took away her life, Ryland. No one would adopt her and give her a home. No one *could* adopt her. I don't even know if we can help her. And why would she trust me?"

"I'll go after her," Nicolas said suddenly. Unexpectedly. And unwanted.

Lily tried not to gape in horror. She took a deep breath and let it out. "You just came back from that mission in the Congo, Nico. I know it wasn't pleasant. You need rest, not another mission. I can't ask you to go."

"You didn't ask me, Lily." His black eyes pinned her. Held her. "And you wouldn't ask me, but it doesn't matter. I'm an anchor, and I can handle her. I'm here and on extended leave. I'll go."

Lily wanted to protest but couldn't think of reasons to stop him. It annoyed her that she was so transparent that Nicolas could see she was uneasy around him. It wasn't that she didn't like him, but he frightened her with his too cold eyes and his implacable resolve. It didn't help that she knew his expertise. "I thought Gator would know the area better and find it easier." It was the best excuse she could come up with.

Nicolas simply looked at her. "I'm going after her, Lily. If you need to give me papers to authorize me to get her out of there and bring her here, get them done. I'll leave in an hour."

"Nico," Ryland protested. "You haven't had more than a couple of hours of sleep. You just got home. At least rest tonight."

Lily knew none of the men would argue with Nicolas. They just never did. And she had no good reason to argue with him. Dahlia would be safe with him. She glanced at Gator in the hopes he'd volunteer to go along. He wasn't looking at her. Of course, the men would stand solidly behind Nicolas. She sighed and capitulated. "I'll have Cyrus Bishop draw up the papers giving you the authority to remove her. We know we can trust Cyrus to stay quiet." Lily had taken her time trusting the family lawyer after learning the extent of her father's hidden secrets, uncertain just how deeply Cyrus Bishop had been involved. Experimenting on people, especially children was monstrous, yet Peter Whitney had provided her with a loving home life and a wonderful childhood. She was still struggling to understand the two sides of her father.

Ryland waited until his wife left the room before turning to Nicolas. "If she knew about that little scratch that almost ended your life, she'd be up in arms, Nico."

I have to go, Rye. Nicolas indicated the others as he spoke telepathically to insure privacy. It had taken long months of practice to be able to direct telepathic communication to only one subject and keep the others from hearing, but it was a useful tool, and Nicolas had worked hard to learn the skill. *Lily has them all bleeding in sympathy for this woman. Anyone capable of generating an antigravity field or the kind of heat it takes to start a fire or of changing the structure of a cable is dangerous. Every one of the men would hesitate to do whatever was necessary if she turned on them. I won't.*

Ryland let his breath out slowly. Nicolas always sounded the same. Calm, unemotional—logical. He wondered what it would take to ever stir Nicolas up and destroy his tranquil nature. *I trust you, Nico, but Lily is afraid for this woman. She feels her father robbed Dahlia of everything she deserved. Parents, a home, a family, essentially a life.*

He did. Lily takes on his blame, and she shouldn't. She's every bit as much a victim as this poor woman, but none of that changes the danger to anyone trying to persuade Dahlia to leave her only known sanctuary. Don't you see what they've done, Rye? If they're using her as an operative as Lily suspects, they keep her in line because she needs that home out in the swamp. She has no choice but to return to it. She can't live outside of that environment, so she does what they tell her and returns to it. They wouldn't even need to watch her; they'd know she'd have to come back.

Nicolas stood up and stretched, suppressing the wince when his body protested. The bullets had come a little too close to his heart for comfort, and he was still recovering.

He had looked forward to some downtime. His team immediately got to their feet. Ian MacGillicuddy, Tucker Addison, and Gator were all tired and needed rest. He knew they expected to accompany him. Nicolas scowled at them. "Do the lot of you think I can't handle that little woman all by myself?"

The men exchanged grins. "I don't think you can handle any woman, Nico," Tucker answered. "Least of all that little stick of dynamite. We have to go along and make certain she doesn't kick your ass."

"I've gotta agree," Gator said. "She looks like she could do some real damage to a pushover like you."

Ian snorted in derision. "She might run if she saw your sorry face looking at her through the swamp. She'd think you were some swamp monster sent to drag her into the black depths. She needs to see a good-looking man coming to take her home."

"And that wouldn't be you, would it?" Gator nudged him. "I'm familiar with the bayou, Nico, and I know how you get so turned around."

Ryland watched the men laughing and joking with Nicolas. All of them knew Nicolas could be sent out alone into the deepest jungle or the broadest expanse of desert for months and always return with the job done. It didn't matter—they could throw everything they could think of at him, and Nicolas would take it all good-naturedly, but in the end, he would leave his team behind.

All of them had pulled duty in the Congo and had spent weeks infiltrating the enemy both in the villages and camps to gain vital information. Using psychic talent for extended periods of time, especially shielding themselves from large groups, was extraordinarily draining. All of them needed rest. Nicolas would see to his men first, and he would protect them from Dahlia Le Blanc in spite of any sympathy they might feel toward her.

Do your best to reassure Lily. Ryland found it much easier to use telepathy these days. The exercises Lily insisted the men do daily had added not only to their control, but to reconstructing a semblance of the barriers her father had brought down in his experiment to enhance them all. Lily worked hard at conditioning them, hoping to give them the necessary tools to be able to live in the world with families and friends. In the meantime, she generously shared her home and her time, working with them all. It only made him love her more. He wanted Nicolas to find a way to reassure Lily. Nicolas wasn't the type of man to lie even to make Lily feel better.

If it's at all possible, I'll bring Dahlia back to her. That's the best I can do.

Ryland nodded to him and left the men to their teasing. He glanced up at a camera and waved in case Arly, their security man, was watching as he went in search of his wife. He found her in their bedroom, staring out the large bay window at the rolling lawns below.

"Lily, he promised he'd bring her home to you."

She didn't turn around. "It isn't that I don't like him, Ryland. I hope you know that. I hope he knows it. It's just that he can be so unemotional. She needs someone to love her and care about all the things she's been through. I don't think Nicolas is capable of that kind of compassion."

"So you think the reason he's leaving his men behind is duty? He looks out for them, watches over them. He takes every dangerous job himself, Lily, and believe me, what you're asking is very dangerous, very high risk."

"He's capable of killing her," she protested.

"And she's just as capable of killing him."

Lily looked at him with sorrow in her eyes. "What did my father do?"

CHAPTER

TWO

The boat pushed through the green sludge of the Louisiana bayou, the motor chugging slowly and steadily. The sky had turned from blue to an incredible collage of pinks, reds, and oranges. Night closed in fast, and the swamp was already stirring to life. Snakes plopped into the water and alligators roared to one another before sliding into the algae-covered bogs. The air was heavy with moisture, so hot the heat seeped through Nicolas's clothes. Sweat trickled down his skin and beaded on his chest and belly. Insects swarmed in clouds over the waters so that the fish jumped at them and bats swooped low. The boat continued the journey through the maze of canals toward the small island Nicolas was searching for.

A variety of birds inhabited the swamp and most ignored his presence, but a few larger species shook wings and flew off in a huff as if disturbed by the sight of him. Egrets, cormorants, herons, and ibises took to the air, flying over the swamp to a new location. Frogs took up a chorus of croaking, the sound swelling in volume. Gray moss

hung in strands from the branches of trees, looking like
macabre stickmen in the gathering darkness. Nicolas found
a certain beauty in the unusual surroundings. He noted several species of turtles and lizards, some swimming, but
most on logs or in trees.

As the boat moved up the channel, Nicolas peered down
at the water, fascinated at how it appeared to be a black mirror, reflecting the trees and the violent colors of the sky. He
had always enjoyed the solitude of his profession. He found
peace in nature, and the bayou offered a startling glimpse
into another world. He had been reared in a world apart, ac-
companying his grandfather into the mountains for weeks,
even months. Those were joyous times, a young boy learning from an elder wise in the ways of the land, even as he
could run free and play like the child he was. Nicolas smiled
at the memories and offered up a silent thanks to his grandfather, long gone from him, but always held close.

Nicolas knew he belonged in the wilderness. It was
where he felt most at home. He often thought he belonged
in another era when there were fewer people and much
more wilderness. He was grateful to Lily for the use of her
home and for the work she did to enable all of them to live
in the outside world. Her father's experiment had opened
their brains to continuous assaults from the people around
them, and they needed the home and training Lily provided. But Nicolas still had trouble being in such close
proximity to so many others—it had little to do with the
enhancement and everything to do with his background
and nature. Volunteering to retrieve the woman in the sanitarium was not just about saving his teammates from their
own compassion. It was necessary to be able to get away
on his own where he felt he could breathe.

Twice Nicolas consulted the map Lily had provided for
him. In the maze of channels and canals, it was easy to lose
one's way. Some of the channels were so narrow the boat
barely scraped through, while others were wide enough to
be considered a lake.

Lily's father, Dr. Whitney, had deliberately hidden the

sanitarium on an island, mostly marshland, overgrown and still primitive. It was so deep in the labyrinth of canals that even the local hunters had only a vague idea of where it was located. Lily had found the detailed map in the Trust papers, but even with the map and his unerring sense of direction, Nicolas was having a difficult time finding the right island. He was still searching when night fell, darkening the swamp and complicating his mission. Twice he had to pull the boat through waist-deep, reed-choked channels, and even with the occasional sliver of light from the moon, it was difficult to see if the dark shapes in the water were alligators or floating logs.

As the boat rounded a small island he caught sight of several birds lifting into the sky from somewhere behind a thick stand of trees. At once his skin prickled and his belly churned. Nicolas shut off the boat's motor. He drifted, waiting in silence, listening to the sounds of the wetlands. Insects had been humming and frogs croaking. They went silent now. Nicolas immediately slid low in the boat so that his body would be much more difficult to detect. He could slide into the water if necessary—he had been close to alligators on more than one occasion—but he wanted to keep his weapons dry if at all possible.

Nicolas avoided the pier and dock and the worn ribbon of a trail leading toward the center of the island. He knew most of the island was spongy and probably filled with sinkholes an unwary traveler could fall into, but it was safer there than being on a path where someone might be waiting in ambush. And he was very certain someone was waiting in the heavy shrubbery.

He eased the boat into a small inlet several hundred yards from the dock and around a bend, out of sight. Nicolas slipped into knee-deep water, pulling the boat behind him to tie up to a tree. It was a slow process, taking care not to splash as he slogged through the mire until he was on higher ground. It was still a bog. Grass grew wild and tall and a multitude of shrubbery and flowers filled in spaces the trees didn't take up.

Nicolas moved in silence, as he had most of his life. He had grown up on the reservation and spent much of his childhood with his shaman grandfather who believed in the old ways. He automatically avoided dry twigs and leaves, and with his enhanced abilities, he was able to keep wildlife from giving away his presence as he made his way across the spongy marsh toward higher ground where the sanitarium was located.

He heard gunshots in the distance. Birds screeched and rose like a cloud into the air. Nicolas ran toward the sound, closing in on the building. The bushes and trees grew much thicker on the high ground, obviously planted and coaxed into wide fences, obscuring vision of the large structure. As he pushed through a thick hedge of saw grass, he heard the distinct crackle of a radio and instantly dropped down, remaining motionless until he could determine the exact position of the guard.

Sound carried at night, especially on water. The guard was more interested in the action taking place in the building then he was in watching the water. His gaze kept straying toward higher ground and twice he swore under his breath, stroking his gun.

Nicolas let his breath out slowly. This was no amateur hit. No drug addicts looking for money. This was a professional cleanup crew, moving with military precision, hitting hard and fast and leaving only the dead behind. Lily had made inquiries in the wrong places, and a team must have been sent out to dispose of all evidence. Dahlia Le Blanc was on a hit list and the squad was taking her out. His warning radar was shrieking at him. He had stumbled into the middle of a high-level operation.

Nicolas had no way of knowing if Dahlia had been caught inside the sanitarium or if by some miracle she had been outside. She had training and skill and was obviously quite dangerous. The fact that there were fires breaking out inside the building might mean she was still alive and fighting back. Whatever the case, he couldn't afford to waste time. He had to get past the guard and go to her aid.

It took maneuvering to get within striking distance of his prey. Nicolas lay in the open, only feet from the guard. He wished he had Dahlia's ability to blur her image. Instead, he counted on his talent to persuade his enemy to look the other way. He whispered the suggestion even as he "pushed" at the guard's mind to stay focused on the water. The guard was vibrating with excitement, impatient to make a kill. Any kill.

Nicolas rose up out of the bog like a giant shadow, enveloping the man, swallowing him, his hands fast and his blade sharp. He murmured to the earth and sky his plea for forgiveness and offered the universe his regret at taking a life even as he lowered the body silently to the marshy water and moved on.

He went across the spongy ground as fast as he could without chancing sinking into the bog. If Dahlia was in the building, the team would be overrunning even her capabilities. The double doors to the main entrance were open as if in invitation. Tendrils of smoke drifted out, along with the smells of gasoline and blood. Nicolas exploded through the doorway, rolling into a ball and coming up on his feet, tracking the room with his gun, eyes adjusting to the darker interior. Two bodies lay sprawled on the floor. Keeping a wary eye on the door leading into the sanitarium, Nicolas approached the bodies.

He recognized them from the pictures and dossier on each woman. Bernadette Sanders and Milly Duboune lay dead, each executed with a single bullet to the forehead. It particularly bothered him, the sight of them lying lifeless, their blood soaking into round balls of wool half unraveled on the floor. There was nothing he could do for them. The office was destroyed, files already saturated with accelerant and burning. Nicolas moved on quickly, knowing he had little time.

He found himself in what was obviously a gymnasium with every kind of exercise and training equipment money could buy. There was little damage to the room, but he smelled the gasoline splashed on the walls. There was nothing to be gained in the room so he chose a door that led into a large hallway.

The door was ajar, an open invitation, but his survival instincts were screaming. He stayed to the side of the door and took a cautious look. Flames licked up the walls and smoke billowed from several places along the floor. A table and several chairs were overturned and glass was smashed everywhere. Several men were in the room, all armed. Several splashed gasoline over the walls and floor, soaking the table and chairs. One was yelling at a man on the floor. Twice he kicked the downed man and once slammed the butt of his gun into the man's ribs.

"Where the hell is she, Calhoun? She should have been here."

"Go to hell, Dobbs." Blood poured down Calhoun's face and soaked his shirt. He spit a mouthful of blood on the floor. "She's long gone, and you're never going to find her."

Dobbs reacted to the taunt instantly, turning his gun on the man's outstretched leg and pulling the trigger. Calhoun screamed. Blood spattered the walls. A man out of Nicolas's sight laughed.

Nicolas took aim and fired, one shot, dead center, and melted away before Dobbs could fall to the floor in a lifeless heap. At once a rain of bullets spat through the walls and doorway, seeking Nicolas as the death crew fired blindly in retaliation.

Nicolas had already gone up, choosing to use the high ceiling as a refuge, waiting for the first man to come through the door, knowing they would believe he had fled into another room. He sprawled like a spider above their heads, motionless, a shadow in the dark interior. Even the flickering orange and red of the flames didn't reach him. They would fan out and search for him and that would divide them into a much more manageable enemy. He waited as he always did. Calm. Patient. Certain of his enemies' next move.

Nicolas heard them talking. Heard Calhoun scream in agony as someone obviously moved him with more haste than care. Two men nudged the door open and slipped into the room with him. They split up, one going right, the other left in a standard search pattern, checking every corner of the room. Nicolas remained utterly still, only his eyes moving, watching, measuring the distance beneath him to his prey.

Dahlia? Nicolas heard the name clearly in his head. Heard the pain etched into the voice, the thoughts. He glimpsed a swirling eddy of fear and shock, of determination. *You can't save me. Get the hell out of here. Disappear. That's an order.*

Nicolas recognized Calhoun's voice. He had to be Dahlia's handler. There was no doubt in Nicolas's mind she had been used as an operative, but by whom? For whom? And how was Calhoun able to speak telepathically? Nicolas had witnessed many interesting and unexplainable phenomena with each of his grandfathers, but other than the GhostWalkers, psychically enhanced individuals, he had never heard of such strong telepathy being natural and genuine. He could only surmise Calhoun was a Ghost-Walker. And that meant Dr. Whitney had performed his experiment on others at some other time.

Who are you? He reached out to Calhoun carefully. One of the men searching the room was directly beneath him. Nicolas dropped down like a spider, his hands grasping the head and twisting with tremendous force. The second man whirled around, gun coming up, but all he could see was his partner slumping, almost in slow motion. The rifle, falling from nerveless hands, clattered loudly when it hit the floor, and the man shot toward the sound, a wild hail of bullets that thumped into the floor and wall and into his dead partner.

Nicolas, already a part of the deepest shadows, was half-way on the other side of the room. He returned a single shot, whispering the death chant as he did so. His grandfathers had taught him the value of life—all lives, not just the ones he approved of—and that taking a life was no small matter. There could be no hesitation, but there must be regret. Each life belonged to the universe, and Nicolas believed each had purpose.

There had been no answer from Calhoun. Nicolas could

no longer feel his presence and that meant one of two things. Calhoun was dead, or he'd lost consciousness. Had Calhoun deliberately withdrawn, Nicolas was confident he would still be able to feel him. Nicolas entered the room where Calhoun had been shot and found only blood and flames. The blood trail told him Calhoun had been dragged from the room. He hurried through the building, searching to find anyone else alive or dead. Searching for a clue where Dahlia Le Blanc might be.

He found her apartment. Or wing. The place was large and obviously built exclusively for Dahlia. Just as Dr. Whitney had built a house for Lily, he had done the same for Dahlia and hired Bernadette and Milly to take care of her needs. Dahlia's walls were lined with books. Books in every language. Textbooks, reference books on every subject. There were sets of small round balls in various gemstones on nearly every surface. Nicolas scooped up several and put them inside his pack. There were too many of the small balls not to matter to Dahlia. He knew many Eastern people used similar balls for stress relief.

On the nightstand were four books stacked neatly atop a small, folded, raggedy child's blanket. He scooped them up and stuffed them into a pillowcase, looking quickly around to see what else might be of value to Dahlia. She would keep the things that mattered close. If she survived the purge, and he managed to get her to Lily Whitney, she would need familiar things around her. The room was extraordinarily neat, even the books alphabetized on the shelves. He found a light sweater made of the same wool that had been beside the two dead women. Obviously they had knitted it for Dahlia. It was folded neatly and kept beside the bed on her nightstand. He tucked that inside the case as well. The only other item close to the bed was a stuffed teddy bear dressed in a kimono. It had been propped up on the pillow before he had thrown it aside. He bent to pick it up. A bullet thunked into the wall where his head had been.

Nicolas hit the floor and rolled, using the bed for cover, coming up on one knee and firing, laying down a shield of bullets while he located his enemy. He caught a brief glimpse of a man running down the hall. And then he saw the cluster of explosives, obviously C-4, a plastic explosive that would obviously destroy not only the evidence of murder, but the very building itself. He sucked air into his lungs, forcing calm. He had no idea how long he had before the sanitarium went up, but he doubted if it was more than a couple of minutes. Catching up the pillowcase, he shoved it in his waterproof pack as he ran, following behind the man who had tried to ambush him.

As Nicolas approached the door to the room where Calhoun had been shot, he caught a glimpse of movement and threw himself to one side, firing from the hip, rolling across the floor in a somersault and coming up smoothly onto his feet only a scant distance from his assailant. He saw his assailant's eyes widen in desperation, but the man was already falling backward, his gun spraying the ceiling with bullets. Nicolas murmured his chant as he raced toward the door, a silent bid to the gods of his grandparents to lend wings to his feet.

"JUST a few more minutes," Dahlia consoled herself aloud. It didn't matter how many deep breaths she took, she was on serious overload and shards of glass seemed to be stabbing through her head. Her tired eyes could barely make out the dangerous terrain. One misstep and she would sink into the bogs of the swamp. The ground beneath her feet was spongy, matted with thick grasses. The foul stench of stagnant water permeated the air.

There was no more than a sliver of moon to spill light across the swamp. In the darkness, the cypress trees looked macabre, as if they stretched long stick arms instead of branches. Grayish moss hanging like streamers looked like tattered clothes fluttering occasionally above the blackened water. The breeze barely stirred, so that the muggy air seemed barely breathable.

Dahlia pressed her fingers to her temple and paused, her

body swaying, rocking back and forth to console herself. Stars exploded in front of her eyes. Her stomach lurched. She lifted her head, suddenly wary. She should be feeling better, not worse, out in the swamp, far from the human emotions breaching the walls of her unprotected brain. She went still, a shadow in the darkness, blurring her image further to keep prying eyes from spotting her.

There was something or someone stalking her, waiting for her to come into its web. Her heart accelerated with fear for those she called family. Her nurses, or guards, she had never really defined them, but they were all she'd known most of her life. Milly and Bernadette. They were mother and sister and friend and nurse to her, women who insisted she learn to do things she always pretended to dislike. She often teased them that crocheting and knitting were for old women, that the sewing they did made them squint.

No one knew about her or her home. She was human, yet not normal, so different she could never be accepted in the world. Nor could she ever fit in and live comfortably. She had a vague idea of her childhood, but mostly she remembered pain. It lived and breathed in her body as if alive. The only way to turn it off was to go to her sanctuary, her home. And someone hunted her, using her home as a trap.

The knowledge blossomed, nearly consuming her brain, a stark reality she couldn't avoid. Her mission had had unexpected complications, but she'd made it out and knew no one followed her. Had they found another way to find her home? Everything that could go wrong had certainly gone wrong, but she knew absolutely she hadn't been followed. Jesse Calhoun, her handler, was certain to be waiting for her. He was lethal and fast when he needed to be. Jesse interested her because he was the only other human being she knew of with capabilities close to hers. And he was also telepathic, so why wasn't he warning her of the danger?

Dahlia knew how to be patient. She pushed the pain aside and waited there in the swamp, inhaling to try to catch a scent. Listening for a sound. There was only the occasional plop of a snake dropping from overhead branches into the murky waters. Still, she waited, knowing movement drew the eye. The faint smell of smoke drifted to her on the breeze.

Her breath caught in her throat. There was only one building that could feed a fire. She *needed* her home. She couldn't survive without it. If they took her residence, they might as well put a bullet in her head. Dahlia took two steps to her right. She doubted anyone knew the way through the swamp. Anyone waiting for her would be expecting her to be coming in by boat. Most likely they would be watching the dock. She stepped carefully on the trail, knowing she could sink into the bog if she took one misstep. An alligator growled somewhere close. Dahlia merely glanced in the direction of the sound, a quick acknowledgment of the creature's presence.

She took another cautious step forward. She counted ten steps and stepped to her right again. Moving through the swamp was nearly automatic. She counted steps in her mind, but was really concentrating on the smell drifting on the slight breeze. Dahlia peered through the night, her instincts sharp and alert. Something waited for her, something terrible, and a dark dread was taking hold.

She approached her home from the north, the only real safe passage through the swamp. Twice she had to wade knee-deep through the black water, using the cypress trees to guide her progress. Dahlia was careful to make no sound, blending with the night creatures, tuning to them so the insects continued in harmony and the frogs croaked with annoying repetition. The last thing she wanted was to give her position away by having the animals go abruptly silent. It took stealth and calm to move in their world and not disturb them. Dahlia could do it, but it required all of her concentration when her heart was pounding in alarm.

The smell of something smoldering choked her as she approached the sanitarium. She could make out the cloud of black smoke rising and orange-red flames pouring from inside the building. The sanitarium was built on solid ground in the center of the small island. A walkway led from the dock over spongy marsh to the higher terrain where the building was located. Dahlia had taken two steps toward her home when the first wave of energy hit her so hard it drove her to her knees.

Violence—dark, malevolent. It poured from the building and rolled off the walls. Something terrible had happened. The energy was living, left behind by the aftermath of what had created it. Death. She smelled it. Knew it waited just inside the building.

Dahlia fought to breathe her way through the pain. She avoided violent energy whenever possible, but she could force herself to endure it if necessary. She'd done it before. She had to go inside. She had to know what happened, and she had to get to Milly and Bernadette and maybe even Jesse. Resolutely, she drew air into her lungs and stood up. Her tongue moistened her suddenly dry lips. It was difficult to concentrate with so much pain, but she'd learned to push it to the back of her head. And she had to see what happened. What was left. It was the only home she could remember. The only people she had contact with lived there with her. Her books. Her music. Her entire world was in that building.

She kept to the trees, running lightly through the tall grass, moving with the breeze rather than against it. She knew there was someone left behind. Someone waiting for her arrival. Energy flowed toward her and it confused her. There was the violence, hot angry waves rolling in to swamp her and a secondary source, completely different. Calm, centered—patient. The contrast was shocking. She'd never experienced it before, and it made her all the more wary.

As she approached her home, she could see several men dragging Jesse Calhoun down the well-worn path to the boat docks. Jesse appeared unconscious and covered in blood. His legs dragged uselessly and she could see the damage, raw and ugly even in the night. "Jesse." She whispered his name and switched directions, hurrying toward him, using the natural cover, uncertain how she could help him. She never carried a gun. She had long ago realized she couldn't survive the deliberate taking of a life.

There were too many men slipping through the night toward the waterway. A purge. The men had come to kill her, to wipe out her existence. Why? She'd completed her mission. She tried to maneuver closer, thinking she might be able to scare them away from Jesse with heat and fire. The sound of gunfire erupted from within the building.

"Milly. Bernadette." She'd never felt so helpless or torn in her life.

Shouts broke out as Jesse woke, struggling and fighting. Dahlia immediately followed the group of men, reaching out to Jesse as she did so. She wasn't particularly telepathic, but Jesse was, and he would feel her energy and know she was present. *Jesse. Tell me what to do.*

A man's voice answered in a hard, authoritative voice. . . . And it wasn't Jesse. *Don't do anything. Stay away from here.*

She froze, sinking into the tall grass. Other than Jesse, no one had ever spoken to her like that. The world was crashing down around her and nothing made sense. The overload of violent energy made her sick, her stomach rebelling as the waves rushed over her, wanting to consume her. Her head was throbbing with pain. She kept her eyes on Jesse, hoping he would reach out to her, tell her what was going on. She saw one of the men deliberately reach down and slam the butt of his gun into the raw mess that was Jesse's leg. Jesse screamed, a terrible sound that would echo in her dreams for a long time.

The rush of violence hit her hard, swamping her so that she sagged backward, but she kept her gaze focused on the man who had struck Jesse so viciously. Flames rushed up and over him, huge leaping streaks of orange and red, as high as a bonfire, flames she couldn't possibly control. Chaos erupted. Several men fired shots in scattered directions, uncertain where the attack was coming from. One man rolled his partner in a jacket to put out the flames.

A third man simply shot Jesse a second time, in his other leg. Dahlia had never heard so much agony in a scream. She was sick, over and over, the power of the violent energy swirling around her and beating at her with more force than she'd ever endured before.

"We'll keep shooting him. You can't get all of us," the

man who shot Jesse shouted. They kept moving, a tight unit now, Jesse in the middle, being dragged away while the men faced outward with their guns.

Dahlia was too sick to move, to think. She cursed her inability to do more than sit there, hiding like a rabbit in the grass while they tortured Jesse and took him away from her. Jesse, who had taught her to play chess and gave her more relief than she'd ever imagined possible by just his presence. Jesse with his easy, engaging smile. He was the only person who ever teased her. She hadn't even known what teasing was until Jesse had come into her life.

She should have carried a gun. She knew how to use one. She could only watch helplessly until they were out of sight and she heard the boat motor start up. Dahlia rushed down to the docks to see two boats disappearing down the channel. The only evidence of Jesse was the terrible bloodstain. The red puddle looked shiny black in the darkness.

Dahlia turned back toward her home. Smoke poured from the windows and doors, drifted toward the sky. She could see the flames licking at the walls. Jesse was gone. They'd taken him. *I'll find you. Stay alive, Jesse. I'll come for you.* She made it a vow. Just using telepathy without him creating the bond sent shards of glass into her brain, but she was far beyond caring.

That's what they want, Dahlia. I'm the bait. Don't let them kill us both.

Jesse's voice was weak, tinged with pain. Her heart turned over. *I'll find you, Jesse.* She vowed it with determination. Dahlia knew Jesse was aware she was stubborn and would do exactly what she said. She prayed it gave him the necessary hope to stay alive in the worst of circumstances. Knowing there was nothing she could do for him, she made her way up the path to the house.

She staggered at the entrance. The energy was much stronger close to the source of the violence. Her body was rebelling, and she could feel the reaction building despite her attempts to keep control. She had only a few minutes to discover whether Bernadette and Milly had survived the purge.

Dahlia curled her fingers into a tight fist, nails digging into her palm. There was only one person whose energy she could feel emanating from her home. Male. A stranger. She couldn't get a direction on him, the energy level was too low and too spread out, almost as if he could disperse it deliberately across a vast area. She gained the wide verandah, her soft soles making no noise on the wood. "Be alive." She heard the whisper of breath and knew she said it, although she didn't remember the actual thought. She already knew otherwise; her senses told her the truth, but her mind wouldn't accept it.

Smoke poured out the open door leading to the entryway and offices. No one ever manned the offices, they were there mostly for show if anyone visited. No one ever did . . . until now. She glanced inside and saw the file cabinets overturned and folders spilled onto the floor smoldering or already succumbing to the flames. Her heart began to pound loudly. She could see a ribbon of wool, a pale blue splashed with a bright red.

Tears swam in her eyes, blurred her vision. She swallowed hard and brushed at her cheeks and lashes. There was a strange roaring in her head. She didn't want to look, but she couldn't prevent her terrified gaze from following the blue string to the blood-soaked ball of wool and the outstretched hand beside it.

Milly lay sprawled on the floor. Dahlia heard a noise escape her throat, a high keening sound of grief. She knelt by Milly, stroked back her hair. She'd been shot in the forehead. Dahlia couldn't bear to have her lying on the floor with the horrible mess around her and smell of gasoline heavy in the room. Bernadette lay only a few feet away. Dahlia sat between them, rocking back and forth, a keening sound that she was certain was not really coming from her throat sounding loud in her ears.

Dahlia could barely contain her grief. It built in her, fed by the voracious appetites of the violence embedded deep in the waves of energy rolling through her burning home. These two women were her only family. Jesse had been her only friend. She reached out to touch Bernadette, a silent apology for being late. She stroked a caress down her arm and tried to weave her fingers through Bernadette's, needing to hold her hand, to simply have the contact. There was something in Bernadette's hand.

Dahlia leaned over her to pry the object from her fingers. It was a heart-shaped amethyst. Dahlia had brought it to her a few years earlier. Bernadette's eyes had brightened as she took it, murmuring something about a waste of money for Dahlia to buy her such trinkets. She had worn it around her neck every day since.

Grief clawed at Dahlia's insides, raked hard so that she felt raw and wounded. She took the small heart and pressed it to her face. Tears poured down her face, and her chest hurt so bad she was afraid it would explode. Heat seared the air around her, shimmering in the room. Papers ignited only a scant few inches from where she sat.

Without warning she heard a door to the nearby gymnasium bang open. Startled, she glanced at the open door to see a man sprinting toward her.

"Run!" She heard the command, a sharp imperious demand that cut through the terrible pain burning in her chest. He seemed to flow across the floor, a sinuous movement of muscle and power. Immediately she had the impression of a great tiger bearing down on her.

"Run. Get out of here."

As he bore down on her, she felt the first flutter of fear. It blossomed immediately into a panic attack. For the first time in her life, Dahlia was frozen, unable to move or think. She could only watch as the heavily muscled man closed the distance between them with his long strides. He reached down without missing a step and scooped her up effortlessly, as casually as he would have retrieved a ball, and continued running from the building.

Dahlia found herself upside down over his shoulder, a package much like his rifle and gear. She'd never experienced grief before, not the mind-numbing kind that pervaded her body and left her pliant in a stranger's arms.

She'd never been in any man's arms. She'd never been this close to a man before in her life.

"Keep your head down. The building's rigged with explosives. When it goes off we want to be far away." Nicolas gave Dahlia the explanation although he hardly thought it necessary to explain his actions. It was just that she was so pale and shell-shocked. He could feel her heart pounding, threatening to come right through her chest. He didn't expect her to be so fragile and to feel so feminine against his body. He didn't expect to notice her much at all, yet he was acutely aware of her, even in the life-threatening situation.

"I can't just leave them." The words slipped out, choked with grief, when she knew it was silly to say it. To think it. Who would be stupid enough to go back into a burning building that might blow up any moment to retrieve two dead bodies?

"You're in shock, Dahlia. Let me get us to safe ground."

There was no safe ground. He didn't understand that. No one was safe, least of all the man trying to save her life. She clung to his back, a dizzying ride as he raced across the bog to save their lives.

Nicolas counted to himself, judging the time they had, knowing it couldn't be long, but wanting to use every second to put distance between them and the blast. Dahlia was making the most heartbreaking noise he'd ever heard and it was twisting his insides and tearing at his heart, a first for him. He wanted to hold her in his arms and comfort her as he would a child. Worse, he was certain she wasn't even aware she was making the noise. Her fingers were clutched in his jacket, and she didn't fight him at all. The Dahlia he had seen in the tapes had been a fighter all the way and that told him how shocked she really was.

Well into the tree line, he dragged her from his shoulder and pushed her into the waterlogged ground, following her down, pinning her there with his much heavier body. Almost at once the ground shook and the force of the explosion rocked the entire island.

CHAPTER

THREE

Dahlia lay trapped beneath the large stranger, water soaking her clothes, her chest tight and burning while the ground trembled with the force of the horrendous explosion. The stranger's body helped muffle the sound, but she knew her home, her only sanctuary, was gone from her. Overhead birds shrieked in protest and the world was filled with chaos, but deep inside her, she felt absolute stillness. The eye of the hurricane. Dahlia sucked in her breath and began to struggle, pushing at his heavier body. It was like trying to move a large tree trunk.

"You're in danger, you have to get away from me." Desperation edged her voice. He was immovable and there was no way to make him understand. She still didn't understand and she lived with it every day of her life. The energy from the explosion swamped her, filled her, mixed with her grief and her own wild rage. She couldn't contain it much longer, and anything and everything in close proximity to her was in deadly peril.

"We're fine," he said, his voice soothing, calm even.

There was a cadence to his voice that caught at her—touched her. For a brief second the energy seemed to pause, to stop its swirling madness, but then the pressure surged. "*We* are not fine. Get away from me before I hurt you." She pushed at the wall of his chest, trying to get him off of her. Already the heat was flowing out of her, washing over both of them, filling the air around them with something unnatural. Something wrong. Dahlia struggled to contain it.

His chest shook, and it took a moment to realize he was amused at her concern. Dahlia hissed at him. "You are an utter idiot. Get off of me right now." He was laughing. Damn the man, she was desperately trying to save his worthless life and he was laughing at her. She hadn't wanted to hurt him, but he didn't deserve her concern. She drove her thumbs hard into the pressure points just above his groin. He sucked in his breath and his hands caught her wrists like a vise.

"I'm not going to hurt you, Dahlia, I'm trying to save your life." There was no laughter in his voice. None at all. His voice made her shiver. Maybe she'd been mistaken about his amusement. He didn't look like the kind of man who ever laughed.

"I'm trying to save *your* life," she countered in a low tone. She could hear the note of desperation she couldn't quite stifle. "I can't explain to you what's going to happen, but you have to believe me. If you don't get away from me immediately, you'll be in terrible danger."

He had been looking away from her, back toward the collapsed building, his gaze moving constantly, taking in their surroundings, the flight of the birds and bats, everything but her. He looked down at her for the first time, his black eyes meeting hers. Dahlia felt the impact like a blow. Hard. Penetrating. Deep. She couldn't read anything at all in his expression, but his gaze seemed to burn her as it moved over her face. He eased his body from hers, getting to his feet in one lithe movement, pulling her up with him. "You're afraid of the energy you create, aren't you?"

It wasn't that she created energy, but how to explain the unexplainable? *She* didn't create the energy—*it* found *her*.

It craved her. Raced to her. Dahlia had never experienced grief or rage at such an unrestrained level. That alone would have been enough of a danger to anyone close to her, but with the violence of death, with the explosion and fire, the energy was far beyond her capabilities to contain it. It was volatile. Unstable. And any moment it would explode in a fiery ball, destroying everything near her.

Dahlia stepped away from him, putting as much distance between them as she could manage while the energy raged and swirled and demanded to be used. The moment she did, the vortex of heat consumed her, burning her from the inside out, robbing her of her ability to speak, to breathe, to even function. The raw heat shimmered in the air, crackling with electricity. She wanted to cry out to him to run, to save himself. She couldn't bear to be responsible for another death, but he just stood there looking down at her with his ice-cold eyes.

He deliberately stepped close to her, so close their skin nearly touched. "Look at me, Dahlia. Don't be afraid of what will happen to me. Just keep looking at me." His tone hadn't changed. It was still as calm and as tranquil as a pool of water.

The moment he closed the distance between them, the temperature went down. The energy ceased roiling. Her lungs worked properly. She found herself staring into the black depths of his eyes. Cold eyes—cooling her skin, cooling the energy. Dahlia sucked in her breath. "Who are you?"

"Nicolas Trevane. I'm a GhostWalker, the same as you are."

She wanted to step away from him, but she didn't dare. He was trapping the energy, or more precisely, he was cooling the raging aftereffects of violence. She'd never been able to do it, no matter how hard she tried. She could channel it, aim it, and send it, but she couldn't defuse it. His words caught at her, she wanted, no *needed,* to know more. "I've never heard of a GhostWalker."

"I know you haven't. Keep looking at me. Breathe with me. Find your center. Think of it as a pool of water. Don't try to control it; let the water take the brunt of the energy. The waves can rage and reach higher and higher, but the walls will contain it for you. Visualize it, Dahlia."

"How do you know me?"

"Just do this for me and then we'll talk. They'll come back. They know you're here and they're not going to go away without making a try for you. They're pros, and they've got weapons that can reach us from a long distance. We need to move fast and that means you have to get rid of the energy so you're not so sick."

Sick wasn't the word she would have used. The overflow of violence incapacitated her. It was only his presence that prevented a seizure and unconsciousness. She knew her body, knew the load it could take, and she was far, far over the limit.

Nicolas took her hand. She immediately felt panic-stricken and yanked it away, rubbing her tingling palm along her jeans. "Don't touch me. People never touch me."

"They don't touch me either. I'm sorry, I should have warned you what I was doing." His tone was very patient and made her feel like a desperate child. "I want you to feel the beat of my heart. We have to slow yours down. I know you have no real reason to trust me, Dahlia, but if we don't get this under control, we're going to have to fight our way out of here and we're outgunned and outmanned."

Looking down at her, into her enormous black eyes, Nicolas felt like he was falling forward into a labyrinth, a trap, somewhere deep and beautiful he'd never managed to travel in all of his wanderings. Dahlia was a surprise, and few things surprised him. There was immense power in her small body. He could feel it swirling around the two of them, feel it *inside* of her. Dahlia Le Blanc was all about energy.

He reached for her hand again, this time slowly, gently, letting her get used to the idea. His fingers slid over hers, almost in a caress. Her gaze locked with his. Her body reacted, shuddering, wincing. He kept eye contact, not letting her look away as he brought her palm over his heart. "We're all part of the universe. Each of us shares energy. Slow your heart rate down. Think about it, concentrate on it."

Dahlia swallowed hard and blinked up at him, all too aware of his muscles beneath his shirt. Aware of his heart, slow and steady. Aware of the heat of his skin. Heat was everywhere, surrounding them. Welling up inside of her like a deadly volcano. But she was also puzzled by the way he was keeping the violent energy at bay. "I've tried meditation, it doesn't work for me. The energy consumes me. It gathers like a force inside of me. I attract it the way a magnet attracts things. And then I can't contain it and people get hurt."

"You can harness the energy though, can't you?" Nicolas kept his voice very calm. They were running out of time. She had to get back in control so they could move fast. At least she was listening to him. It was most likely the shock and grief and the sheer surprise of finding someone who could contain the energy for her.

"Not when it's like this. There's too much energy, and it's too powerful. It finds me—I don't make it happen. It comes from an outside source. Actions. Emotions. Who even cares? I've studied meditation, Eastern philosophy. It can't be controlled. It has to dissipate some way." Why was she listening to him? Letting him touch her? She felt almost mesmerized by him. All the while the energy churned and boiled and waited, lurking like some terrible monster looking for a victim.

There was a strange push and pull effect on her with Nicolas Trevane. She never stayed long in anyone's company, and already she needed her space. She was sick and dizzy and overwhelmed with grief and fearful of his safety. Yet he held the energy at bay. She recognized power in him. It was far subtler than her raw strength, but it was enormous for all its subtlety. And she couldn't look away from the intensity of his gaze, no matter how hard she tried, or how much she wanted to.

"If you have to find a way to disperse the energy, Dahlia, we'll do it together. Energy, even violent energy, can be directed." Nicolas could see the signs of overload.

Grief was living and breathing in her. Taking her well past the point of thinking rationally for herself.

"Can you do that?" She didn't altogether trust him. She didn't trust anyone. Not Jesse, not even Milly and Bernadette, but that hadn't stopped her from loving them. She felt lost and alone and had no idea what to do, but there was something solid about Trevane. Perhaps his calm. Or the power he so obviously was comfortable wielding.

"*We* can do it. Follow my lead." Nicolas kept all anxiety from his voice. His skin was prickling, a sure sign of trouble. The hit team was probably dropping men back into the swamp and coming at them from all directions. There would be more violence and more death before he managed to get her away safely.

Dahlia did as he said simply because she couldn't think of anything else to do. She concentrated on his breathing. Listened to the sound of his voice, the deep timbre, velvet soft and captivating, almost hypnotic. He built the picture of a deep, clear pool in her mind. The waves raged, wild and out of control, reaching endlessly to escape, but he kept building the walls of the pool higher and higher.

Dahlia felt better, less sick, but she knew he was fighting a losing battle. The energy was alive and looking for a target. Trevane was definitely holding the energy within the walls of the pool, but it was growing in strength, continually seeking a way to harm someone.

"No it isn't. The energy isn't alive, Dahlia. It may have the aftermath of violence within it, but it doesn't have personality. It needs an escape, like water boiling in a kettle. We just have to provide it."

"You're reading my thoughts?" The idea was terrifying. She didn't have the kind of thoughts fit for public reading.

"I'll explain later." Now the hair on the back of his neck was standing up. "We're in trouble, Dahlia. We're being hunted. If you want to live, you're going to have to trust me to get us out of this."

Her gaze moved over his face, assessing him. Assessing her choices. Slowly. A long inspection. "You're a killer."

She made the judgment just like that. Harsh, without any softening.

Nicolas refused to wince. Refused to look away. He met her steady gaze with one of his own. The ice was there. The distance between him and the rest of the world. He damn well wasn't going to apologize for what he did. "Yes." If she wanted to name him a killer, he would accept it. Let her deal with what he was if she wanted to live.

"Why would you risk your life to save mine?"

"What difference does it make? I don't make casual conversation. Let's do this and get out of here."

"I didn't realize the conversation was casual. It isn't to me."

He wanted to swear—and he wasn't a swearing man. She stared up at him with her dark, enormous eyes and her exotic, Asian beauty and somehow slipped past his guard and got under his skin. There was something about her he couldn't quite grasp, something important, elusive, something that floated in his mind but refused to be caught. It had to do with feelings, and the one thing Nicolas wasn't good at was dealing with emotion.

He let his breath out, determined not to let her get to him. He had to keep them alive and that was all that mattered. "Focus away from us. Think of the energy like a charge. Something you're detonating. Direct it to a specific area."

She shook her head. Her heartrate might be following his, but her lungs were starved for air, the energy choking her with wanting to get out. "I can't."

"Focus out there." He indicated the bog several hundred yards away from them. "Think of it as an arrow. You're sending it right there. Picture a target and get as close to the center of the bull's-eye as you can and send the energy there."

"It will burn everything."

"There isn't much to burn." His gaze shifted restlessly, examining the areas around them. Instinctively he was crouching now, pulling her down with him so that the trees and bushes gave them more cover. "Send it." This time, deliberately, there was hard authority in his tone. They were out of time. He didn't mention that he had seen shadows move in the bog.

Dahlia sent up a silent prayer that it would work. She stared out into the night, wishing the moon didn't keep going behind clouds so she could actually see an image. She felt the force of the energy moving within her. And she felt something more. *Nicolas Trevane.* His strength, his determination. *His* focus.

The energy poured out of her, dark and terrible, raging and churning as it leapt toward the bog. The night exploded into flame, everything turning red and orange and burning blue-black. Screams erupted, horrible, agonizing. Gunfire burst through the night, like angry red bees streaking out of the heavy swamp.

Nicolas heard a distinct thump. "Incoming." He knew the sound of a M203 when he heard one. They were in for trouble.

Dahlia was backing away from him, a horrified expression on her face. He simply caught her smaller body and slammed her down into the muck, his body covering hers as the grenade hit somewhere behind them, spreading destruction in all directions. The force of the blast rushed over them. Nicolas was up, dragging her with him, hurrying now, heading away from the water back toward the interior.

"Head west," Dahlia said. She kept her head down while hell erupted around them. "The ground is firmer and we can move faster." Her stomach was churning, but her mind was blessedly numb. The backwash of energy was already racing to find her, but it didn't matter. Nothing mattered. She worked at keeping her brain from functioning past survival. If she allowed the energy to find her too quickly, she had no hope, and perhaps Nicolas would die as well.

"We're going to have to go into the water, Dahlia." He wanted to prepare her. Alligators and snakes called the bayou home. He had to know if she was going to balk. Again he heard the distinctive thump of a grenade fired and pressed her to the earth. She made no protest and didn't fight him. It was the most he could hope for under the circumstances. The blast landed to their left, a distance away.

Nicolas never questioned himself. He made decisions fast, under life and death conditions and didn't believe in second-guessing himself. It was a useless and detrimental trap, yet he found himself regretting using her abilities against their enemies. He glanced at her as they ran again. She was impossibly pale, her eyes enormous. Her body trembled beneath his and she winced, shrinking from the contact each time he took them to the ground to avoid the blast from the scattered grenade shells.

He tried to tell himself it was the shock of losing her home and the people she loved, but he knew it was more. He knew the repercussions of harming their attackers had somehow turned back on her. She was game enough, forcing her body to move, to keep from slowing him down, but she was in trouble and he was responsible. It was the one problem the GhostWalkers faced and would continue to face. They were living in untried territory. The backlash of using psychic talents was enormous, and they often had no idea what could happen until the aftermath of the results reared up to bite them.

Dahlia was a GhostWalker with all the extraordinary gifts and, unfortunately, the terrible penalties that often occurred with the use of those gifts. She was dangerous, perhaps even more so than any of them had considered, but not by her nature. The danger came from the energy that raced to her and crammed inside of her as if her body were an empty vessel waiting to be filled. The leftover energy she couldn't take inside of her surrounded her so that she had no peace. It was no wonder she lived as solitary a life as possible.

Nicolas steered them first toward the interior, staying to the west and higher ground as she'd indicated, but eventually began to work toward the outer edge of the island. They had to get off. They could play hide-and-seek for a short while, but if they remained on the island, they would be found. He was certain the perimeters would be more heavily guarded, but the team had to be spread thin and they'd lost a few men.

"Dahlia, can you hang on until we're off the island?" he asked, more to get her to stay focused on him than for any other reason.

She stopped running abruptly, going down on one knee to be violently sick. Her skin beaded with sweat that had nothing to do with the heat. She looked up at him and nodded as she wiped her mouth. "I can make it."

He had an insane desire to pull her close and wrap her safely in his arms. She was gutsy and he was certain he could count on her in the water. "Stay close. Hopefully if I'm close to you, it will help keep the energy at bay."

Dahlia winced at the sound of grenade fire, ducking as he pushed her toward the ground. She took a cautious look around. "It seems like the entire world is on fire. Do you really think we can get out of this?" Her vision was blurred and her head pounded until she wanted to scream, but she was determined to keep going until she couldn't walk any longer. The closer she stayed to Nicolas the easier it was to bear the burden of the energy rushing at her from the grenades.

Nicolas handed her his canteen, urging her to drink the water. "We'll get out," he assured. "This island is crawling with men though." He took the canteen back and dragged a shirt from his pack. "Put this on. The sleeves will cover your arms and you'll blend better. I want to darken your face as well. It's going to take a little skill to get past them."

Dahlia sank down into the marsh. The island was mostly spongy surface. Even hunters and trappers knew to avoid it. The center had been raised by bringing in soil to build up an area for the sanitarium. Dahlia had never questioned why, but she'd heard Milly and Bernadette talking about the flooding during heavy rains and how ridiculous it was to build on the island when there was enough money to go anywhere and worse, not using stilts. One of the biggest dangers was falling through the thin layer of ground to the waters below. Sinkholes were abundant on the island and the only truly safe places were the narrow path leading to and the actual grounds surrounding her home. She realized that it had been built that way for a specific purpose.

"Did they plan all along on killing me?" She was soaked, but she put his shirt on over her own clothes. It was far too big and she tied the tails around her hips.

"My guess is yes, once you were discovered or you'd outlived your usefulness to them," he replied honestly. He wasn't looking at her, but out into the night, his rifle rock steady in his hands.

"It occurred to me a couple of years ago when I started asking Jesse too many questions, and he didn't want to answer or didn't know the answers, that maybe I was in trouble." She tried to hold still and not wince away from Nicolas as he blackened her face with some tube he carried in his pack. She looked up at him with solemn eyes. "Who are they? Why do they want me dead?"

"These men are military-trained, but I think they're mercenaries. No combat unit would do this. Which agency do you work for?"

Before she could answer, he clapped his hand over her mouth, pressing her body into the trunk of a tree and crouching lower to stay in the shadow of the trunk. He looked directly into her eyes, slowly removed his hand, and held up three fingers. She nodded to indicate she understood, turning her head as slowly as she could in the direction his rifle was aimed. She noted his hands were steady and his eyes like ice. Dahlia was unable to prevent the continual shivering that shook her body. Nicolas was pressed tight against her, dwarfing her, caging her between his hard frame and the tree. She hated that he was so stone cold calm and she was shaking like a leaf.

The vegetation all around them was on fire, red and orange flames reaching to the sky. The fire lit up the areas closest to it and cast macabre shadows over the rest of the shrubbery and trees. The leaping flames were reflected in Nicolas's eyes. Her heart leapt. She was trusting him, yet she knew nothing about him. She had never met anyone that gave off such a low energy reading and yet was capable of such extreme violence. There seemed to be an endless arc of electricity that leapt from his skin to hers. She could feel a strange tingling in her bloodstream. The heat between them was tremendous . . . and frightening.

Nicolas brought his hand up and pressed her face against his chest, stroking her hair with his palm in an effort to comfort her. If she shook any harder, he feared she might break her little bird bones. He bent his head over hers, holding her there while the world burned and their enemy slipped by. He put his mouth against her ear. "Are you ready for this?"

Dahlia nodded, not certain she was, but knowing she had no other choice if she wanted to live. He put a finger to his lips, indicating the need for silence, and then walked his fingers in the air. Dahlia took a deep breath as he stepped away from her. The respite from the violent energy assaulting her had been so complete, the force of the wave hitting her nearly drove her to her knees. She steadied herself by reaching out to him, the first time she'd ever voluntarily touched him. The moment her fingers touched him, rested on him, the force battering at her lessened.

Nicolas put his hand over hers. He bent his head to hers again. "I can carry you if you think it will help." Dahlia almost smiled. For the briefest of moments the terrible sorrow weighing her down lifted, and he caught sight of a mischievous Dahlia, but she was gone almost immediately.

"Hold my hand if you can while we make our way out of here." It cost her to ask him, but she had no choice. "I can take your pack."

Nicolas didn't bother to respond. His fingers linked with hers and he took her with him, moving away from the direction the three men had taken, around the wall of fire, weaving their way closer to the reed-choked channel. Nicolas didn't hesitate at the edge of a stagnant pool, but waded in, pulling Dahlia in after him. Insects, birds, snakes, lizards, and frogs were making a mass exodus into the water right along with them, trying desperately to escape the fire. He kept a wary eye out for alligators.

Somewhere behind them, guns went off.

"AKs," he identified. "They aren't close, so they aren't

shooting at us. They're either spooked or ran into alligators."

"There are alligators all around this island," Dahlia confirmed.

The moon crept back behind the clouds. Nicolas suddenly stopped, his head up alertly. Dahlia remained silent, waiting. If there was one thing she was certain of, it was that he knew what he was doing. She was far safer with him than without him. When he abruptly froze, not moving a muscle, she followed his lead. Dahlia found herself holding her breath, her fingers clinging to his. The water soaked into the jeans she was wearing and something live bumped against her leg, but she stood, just waiting, trying to see into the darker shadows of the bayou.

Nicolas bent his head to hers. "We are hunted." He mouthed the words against her ear, his breath warm, sending butterflies skittering through her stomach.

"Tell me something new." She whispered it, knowing the night carried sound easily.

"He's like me."

She knew what Nicolas meant. She had named him a killer, and he was telling her another of his profession followed them through the swamp. She wanted to ask how he knew but he signaled for silence and pointed to the low strip of embankment leading to the open channel. Her breath caught in her throat. The bank was stripped bare of all shrubbery. A few scattered plants grew low to the ground, but there was no cover to speak of. If they chose that entrance to the channel, anyone following them would see them immediately.

Nicolas touched her face to bring her attention back to him. She was staring in horror at the bank. He flattened his hand and slid it forward, indicating they would creep forward on their bellies simulating an alligator going into the water.

Dahlia peered at the bank as Nicolas began to submerge most of his body, holding his rifle just above the waterline. There was definitely an alligator slide. She wasn't afraid of alligators, but she was smart enough to have a healthy respect for them. Playing in their territory seemed a drastic solution.

"You must have a boat hidden somewhere. Can't we make our way to that?"

He shook his head. "We can't take the chance they found it already. If they have, they'll use it as a trap. Someone will be waiting. It's best to do the unexpected."

Dahlia pressed her hands against her churning stomach. "I don't suppose you have an affinity for animals."

"I'm afraid not," Nicolas admitted as he moved away from her. Two steps only but the energy reached for her, a greedy monster, slipping past her guard, seeping into her pores, filling her stomach until she staggered with the weight of it. Keeping his rifle well above the surface of the water, he reached back and caught the neck of her shirt, pulling her against him, almost as if he could feel the sickness invading. He guided her hand to his waistband, tucking her fingers into the edge. Her knuckles brushed his skin.

It was ridiculous to crouch in muddy water with fires surrounding them, her home burning, her world gone, her family dead, hunted by a killer and have the thought that touching Nicolas Trevane in such a way was intimate. Dahlia snatched her hand away, shocked at the passing thought, shocked at her awareness of Nicolas as a man, not simply a human being. She had the sudden urge to run and find a place to hide on her own. She didn't belong with people. Nothing made sense to her anymore.

"Dahlia." He said her name softly. His tone was impossibly gentle. "Don't panic on me. We're almost out of here. You can do this."

Ashamed, she realized she was backing away from him, shaking her head like a child. She forced her brain to work again, nodding to show she was in control. She had no idea what happened, only that the moment she could safely get away, she would put as much distance between Nicolas and herself as possible. To keep the violent swirls of energy at bay, she kept her hand on Trevane's broad back, and her mind carefully blank.

They made their way slowly through the water, staying low and moving carefully to prevent splashing. As they reached the bank, Nicolas eased his body, belly down, into the mud and began to inch his way over bare ground. Dahlia swallowed convulsively and followed his example. It was impossible to keep physical contact with Nicolas while she crawled in the muck, easing her body over the strip of bare ground to get to the alligator slide. The sickness slammed into her hard, burning through her body, roaring through her head. White spots danced in front of her eyes. She bit down hard on her lip, determined not to lose consciousness.

Nicolas knew they were fully exposed as they inched their way over bare ground. It required patience to move in the open. The natural inclination was to run, get past an open area, but movement always drew the eye. He had deliberately chosen this section as an exit because it was open and they wouldn't expect him to use it.

He could hear Dahlia fighting to breathe. The heat shimmered around her, waves of energy so strong he could actually feel them battering at her. Tuned to her now, he felt her level of exhaustion, knew she was nearing the end of her endurance. It didn't stop her from following him, inching her way through the mud, across the bare ground to the slide. His respect for her grew. She didn't complain even though her world had been torn apart.

She made a small choking sound. He knew she was fighting off the waves of sickness rolling over her. He breathed, air in and out, in an effort to help her. As he slid into the water of the channel, he kept his rifle above water, using his legs to keep him up. He turned back to wait for her. It was going to be impossible to keep his weapon dry, but until they were away safely, his rifle might be the difference between life and death.

Dahlia slipped into the water. There was a measure of comfort in seeing him waiting. In the dark, his striped face should have appeared frightening, yet she only felt relief looking at him. She touched his arm, needing the contact, trying to breathe down the rising bile. "There's a small island no one uses, if we swim in that direction." She pointed the way. "It isn't far and there's a boat we can use. I know of a trapper's cabin that's usable a few miles from there."

Nicolas nodded and laid out across the water on his back, low so that most of his body was submerged. He propelled himself using his legs beneath the water in a strong frog kick so that no sound could be carried in the night. Dahlia followed his lead, turning over, looking up at the smoke-filled sky and then over to the burning island. Everything seemed on fire. Her vision blurred and she blinked rapidly to clear it.

Nicolas didn't make a sound as he moved through the water. It should have been awkward as he kept his rifle out of harm's way, but he moved efficiently as if he'd done the maneuver a hundred times. Dahlia did her best to swim in silence and look like a log. She splashed a few times but was too sick to care.

"Just a little longer," he encouraged. "You're doing great."

"You do know there are snakes in this water."

"Better than bullets. We'll make it, Dahlia."

They were out in the middle of the channel now, and Nicolas wanted to put some distance between them and the island in case the moon came out from under the clouds. Exhaustion lined Dahlia's face. Her breathing was ragged. He noted her swimming was becoming clumsy as they made their way through the open water. "Don't quit on me," he said, a deliberate goad. He couldn't imagine Dahlia quitting anything.

She wanted to glare at him, but couldn't muster up the strength. It took every ounce of self-discipline she had to keep going. She followed him across the channel and through a short, weed-choked canal. Dahlia lost track of time. The water helped to dissipate the energy surrounding her, but she didn't dare allow what was inside of her to escape and give their position away. Her churning stomach helped her to stay awake.

After a while it felt like a terrible dream, one she struggled to wake from. She drifted, closing her eyes part of the time, trying to keep her mind from replaying the sight of Milly and Bernadette lying motionless on the floor. Had they felt pain? Had they been afraid? Dahlia had been delayed by no more than two hours. She was nearly always on time, but things hadn't gone exactly as planned. Had she returned earlier, could she have prevented the deaths of the two women and the burning of her home? And Jesse. He had screamed in pain. It had been a terrible thing to hear, to witness. She hadn't stopped them from taking him away. She'd made her promise to him and she intended to keep it. She would find him and somehow, if he were still alive, she would get him back.

Dahlia was certain she was swimming, moving through the water, yet suddenly Nicolas yanked her up by her collar and she was choking, fighting for air. She tried to push him away, but her arms no longer obeyed her, hanging limply at her sides. "I'm drowning."

"No you aren't, you're falling asleep." His voice never changed, calm and gentle and so irritating she wanted to scream. She was beginning to suspect he had no real emotions. And that made it all the more difficult to be showing weakness in front of him. It wasn't that he tried to act superior, but she *felt* he was.

"Keep going. I'll catch up." She was going to float. Just lie on the water and float. If an alligator wanted her for a late dinner, he could have her and she would just hope the energy inside of her, pushing so hard to get out, would be her revenge.

Nicolas gave up on keeping his weapon dry. He had a choice, the rifle or Dahlia, and he wasn't going to lose her now. He put the strap around his neck and reached for her, drawing her close. She felt small and light and his heart did a curious jump before settling back to a steady rhythm.

CHAPTER

FOUR

Nicolas dragged his weary body out of the channel onto the muddy bank, cradling Dahlia against his chest. He lay looking up at the night sky. Clouds churned over his head, an ominous warning of a coming storm. He had covered several miles swimming and few more wading waist-deep in the reeds and swamp. Tree trunks rose out of the water, silent sentinels everywhere, guarding narrow strips of land. He was exhausted and his side throbbed. He hoped it didn't mean he'd reopened the wound. Not a good thing when he was in the water.

He glanced down at the woman lying motionless on top of him. They were both covered with streaks of black mud. He pushed strands of her dark hair aside. "Dahlia. Wake up." She had finally lost consciousness out in the channel after fighting every step of the way, holding back the wash of energy to keep from giving away their position and gamely keeping up with him until her body said *enough*. "You're beginning to worry me." It was the truth, and he objected to worrying on principle. It was a useless pastime and one he avoided at all costs. He shook her gently. "Come on, Sleeping Beauty, wake up for me."

Nicolas sat up, ignoring the shrieking protest his body made. She looked vulnerable, starkly white beneath the mud. Just looking at her caused a curious shift in his belly. He was a man very much in control of himself, and yet, Dahlia had awakened something long dormant and apparently strong within him. It was uncomfortable not recognizing exactly what he was feeling.

Thunder boomed directly overhead, rattling the trees and shaking the ground. Rain poured down on them, a heavy deluge soaking them within minutes. Dahlia stirred, her slight body shrinking away from the impact of the stinging rain. She turned her head to try to escape the onslaught. Her lashes fluttered, drawing his attention to their length. She looked up at him. He caught a glimpse of fear quickly masked. She looked around her, slipping off his lap to break physical contact.

"I guess I passed out. The overload gets me every time." Her gaze touched his face, jumped away. "It can be a liability."

He shrugged, the gesture casual. "I'm a GhostWalker too, remember? I know what it's like." He got to his feet and reached down, offering his hand.

Dahlia hesitated a moment before she put her hand in his. "I still don't know what a GhostWalker is." She took a careful look around. "You got us to the right place. The trapper's cabin is that way." She indicated an area to their right.

Nicolas shouldered his pack. "Do you remember Dr. Whitney? Dr. Peter Whitney?" He watched her closely. Her face changed—her expression went blank. There was instant withdrawal, not only physically; she distanced herself from him in her mind. He could feel the separation and it was almost a blow. That stunned him. Uncertain if he could cover his rare inner turmoil, he was the one to look away, studying the direction she indicated before setting out.

"I remember him." Her voice was low and filled with distaste.

"Did you figure out what he did to you?" Nicolas kept his voice neutral and continued to walk ahead of her, keeping his back to her so she wouldn't have to hide her expression from him. Or maybe he needed to hide his expression, he wasn't entirely certain which it was. Before he'd started off on the trail, he noticed she was shivering, her body reacting to the harsh conditions. In spite of the deluge of rain, the air was still warm. It made him want to gather her up and hold her close. He shook his head in an effort to rid himself of his extraordinary thoughts.

Dahlia listened to the sound of the rain. She always found it soothing. Even now, with it pouring down on top of her, she felt she could lose part of herself in it. The part that hurt people. The part she could never control. When she sat out in the rain, it washed her clean. "I feel as if Whitney stole my life. Yet at the same time, I feel as if I should be grateful to him. He built my home and he hired Milly and Bernadette. He also provided me with everything I could need or want. My brain requires. . ." She broke off and stared at the silent trees on either side of them, afraid she might shame herself with tears. She was exhausted and vulnerable, filled with such grief she could barely breathe. She couldn't even look at Nicolas's broad back while they walked, not if he wanted to talk about Dr. Whitney.

"You aren't alone, Dahlia. Whitney brought over a number of children, most infants, from various foreign countries. He found the little girls in orphanages, and he was very wealthy so he didn't have much opposition. No one wanted the children, so when he paid for them, the authorities closed their eyes and asked no questions."

Her heart accelerated with every word he spoke. She forced herself to listen to the cadence of his voice. He might not have an inflection, but there was a carefulness, a way he had of speaking that told her volumes. Nicolas was not as unaffected as he seemed. "I was one of those children." She made it a statement.

"Yes." He stopped on the small strip of solid ground and

surveyed the grove of trees growing in knee-deep water straight ahead. "We're going to have to cross this."

Dahlia sighed. "I told you it was difficult. I'm sorry."

Nicolas turned his head and grinned at her. It was fleeting and barely lit his eyes, but it warmed her. "I think we're already soaked."

A reluctant smile touched her mouth briefly. "I guess we are."

"Is the rain getting the mud off of me?"

She tilted her head. A hint of laughter crept into her eyes. "Actually it's running down your face in a rather dramatic fashion. I think you'd even manage to scare an alligator."

"Before you start laughing at me, you might take a look at yourself." Nicolas made the mistake of reaching out to brush at a streak of mud on her face. At once her amusement vanished and she moved her head to escape his touch. His hand dropped to his side.

"Were you one of those children Whitney took out of the orphanage?" She met his gaze, a dark, almost belligerent challenge.

Nicolas stepped into the water. It was deeper than he thought. He reached back and shackled Dahlia's wrist, not giving her time to pull away from the contact. She initially resisted, a slight instinctive pull away from him, but he saw her set her jaw and step into the black water right beside him. "I came much later," he answered matter-of-factly, pretending not to notice her aversion to being touched. The water was over her breasts, nearly to her shoulders.

"What did he do?"

"He had an idea that he could enhance psychic abilities. He thought if he could find children with some signs of talent, he could boost their capabilities and improve on their ability to serve their country. He took the children to his laboratory, hired nurses for them, and conducted his experiments."

"What exactly did he do to us?"

"Do you remember Lily?" He stopped walking to look down at her.

Her breath caught in her throat. "I didn't think she was real."

"She's very real. Whitney kept her when he got rid of all the others. He told her she was his biological daughter and raised her as such. She had no knowledge of the enhancements, only that she was different and couldn't be around people for very long. She lived a fairly solitary life. When some of the men in my unit were killed and Whitney suspected murder, he brought her in on the project to try to help him figure out what was happening to us. Peter Whitney was murdered before he could tell her anything. Lily figured it out and helped us all. She's been looking for all the other girls he brought over from the orphanages ever since. That's how she discovered the sanitarium and you."

Dahlia rubbed her temple. "I actually feel sick for her. It must have been a terrible blow to find out the truth about Whitney. I remember her as being so nice. I always felt better if I was with her."

"She's an anchor. Like I am. We trap emotions, and to some extent energy, away from the others so they can function better. Is Jesse an anchor?" He slipped the question in deliberately as he turned away from her, tugging her through the water with him.

"I don't know. He must have been. It was easier to be in his presence. I never really questioned why. I felt calmer and more in control when he was around."

Nicolas felt a strange burning in the region of his belly. His chest grew tight. "Were you and Jesse close?" His tone was strictly neutral.

She glanced at him, suddenly nervous and not knowing why. "I guess we were. Closer than I am to most people. I don't know many people. I counted Jesse as family, the same way I did Milly and Bernadette."

There was honesty in her voice. Innocence. He let his breath escape slowly, not liking himself very much in that moment. He was learning things about himself he had never considered a part of his character before. It wasn't pleasant. "I'm sorry about the two women, Dahlia. They were already dead when I got there. I managed to take out the man who shot Jesse, but then things got a bit hot."

"I know you would have saved them if you could have." And she did know. "Tell me more about Whitney. What did he do to us?" Just the dreaded name conjured up memories she had worked to suppress.

"Lily can give you all the technical data if you want it. I listened to it and understood about a third of what she was saying. But basically, he removed all the filters in our brains. We're always on sensory overload. Of course he went a bit further and used electric pulses and designer drugs, but you get the idea. We feel things and hear things and can do things most people can't, but the cost is enormous. At least I volunteered. You had no choice. Whitney has a lot to answer for."

"Yes he does." Dahlia closed her eyes against the flood of bleak memories. Sounds of crying children. Pain that raged in her head night and day. The shadowy figure always watching, never smiling, never pleased. Not human. She thought of him that way. A tormenter, devoid of all feeling. He was a monster from her nightmares, something she pushed far away and tried never to think about.

"Dahlia?" Nicolas drew her under his shoulder. It was a measure of her distress that she didn't notice. She had such an aversion to physical contact, yet she remained close to his body. He could feel her shivering right through the soaked clothes. "I don't want to upset you. You've had a rough day. We can have this conversation another time."

Dahlia looked up at the rain, nearly stumbled in the water. The night sky was dark and cloudy and felt very much like her weeping heart. "I have to be careful." She tried to keep her voice as expressionless as his. "If I feel too much of anything, bad things can happen." She looked up at his face. In the night he looked made of granite, not flesh, a beautiful stone carving with amazing eyes. "Did he do that to me?"

"Yes." There was no reason to deny it. Peter Whitney was dead, murdered by a man far more unscrupulous and far more lethal than Peter had ever been. "I'm sorry. I wish I could say we've found a cure, but we haven't. We've found a way to make it easier to live among other people, but so far, there is no way to reverse the process."

The water was becoming shallow. Dahlia waited until they were back on solid ground before looking around to try to get her bearings. "It's over there, just through that grove of trees. The cabin is small and doesn't have hot water, but we can improvise. It sits right on the bank of a canal that runs like a ribbon through the island. Very few locals come out here because accessing it so difficult. A few of the older trappers come once in a while." She talked fast, trying to keep his words from sinking in. She hadn't realized until that moment, until he said there was no way to reverse the process, how she'd hoped he'd tell her they had a miraculous cure for her.

She forced herself to shrug. "I'm alive. Did I thank you for that? I doubt I would have made it away safely by myself. I would have tried to rescue Jesse right then, with all of them there. Do you think they tortured him to get him to tell them where I was?"

Nicolas wrapped his arm around her waist and lifted her over a rotted tree trunk, setting her smoothly down without missing a stride. "These type of men torture for the thrill of it. They don't need excuses."

They rounded a slight bend and found the shack. It sat on the edge of a canal, just as Dahlia had said, one wall sagging ominously. Cracks showed through the wood in places. A burlap sack covered a window, but the crooked door was locked.

"I'm going to get Jesse back," Dahlia said, staring at the lock.

It was a simple combination lock. As Nicolas reached for it, the center spun, first one way and then the other. Tumblers clicked into place, and the lock sprang open. It happened fast and smooth and Nicolas realized Dahlia had opened the lock without really thinking about doing it. She reached around him and took it from the latch and shoved the door open. "I'm not leaving him with those men."

"I wouldn't expect you to leave him behind." He looked around the small room. A mattress stuffed with moss lay on the floor. "He's like us."

Dahlia looked at him sharply. "Whitney experimented on him?"

"He's telepathic. I've never come across a natural telepath that strong. I'd say he was enhanced, and as far as I know, no one else had Whitney's formula." Nicolas took out this canteen and handed it to Dahlia. "We have plenty left. Drink as much as you need." He looked around him. "It isn't a five-star hotel, is it?"

Dahlia wrapped her arms around her waist, desperate to control the continual shivering. More than anything she wanted to be alone. She hadn't spent so much time with another human being in as long as she remembered, not even Milly and Bernadette. She forced a small smile. "I'm going outside for a while, so if you need to do anything private like dry off, the place is yours."

"There's no need to keep watch yet. I'll know if someone comes up on us. You're the one needing to dry off. My pack is waterproof. At least it's supposed to be." He placed his rifle on the rickety table before dragging out a shirt. "Wear this and we can spread your clothes out to dry."

Dahlia took the shirt with reluctance and watched him as he took apart the rifle. He dried each part of the weapon carefully and oiled it. She looked around the small room. There was no hope of privacy, so she moved to the corner as far from him as possible and turned her back on him.

"You have to be prepared for your friend to be dead, Dahlia."

She threw her wet clothing aside. "His name is Jesse, Jesse Calhoun." She glanced back to see if he was watching, but he kept his back to her. She stripped off the thin, pale blue bra and tossed it on the heap of soaked, muddy clothes and pulled the dry shirt on quickly. "It wouldn't make any sense to kill him. If they were going to kill him, they would have done it back at the sanitarium. They're using him as bait to draw me to him. What other possible motive could they have?" She peeled off her jeans and underwear, trying not to be embarrassed, trying to act as though it didn't matter to her.

"I'd have to agree. They took him for insurance. They figured if they didn't get you, they'd take him and you'd follow."

"Which is exactly what I'm going to do." She glared belligerently at his back. Not that he'd told her it was a stupid idea, but his neutral tone was becoming irritating. Of course she had to go to Jesse's aid. Jesse would never leave her in the enemy's hands.

Nicolas kept his head down and his eyes on his rifle as he wiped it with a cloth. He could feel her mounting agitation and guessed, from his experience as a GhostWalker, that her rising anxiety stemmed from being in such close and continual proximity to another human being. Added to her grief and shock, it was a dangerous combination. "I don't see any other recourse," he agreed. "Since they know we're coming after them, and we can't forget they've put an assassin on our trail, we'll have to outsmart them."

"I'm glad you understand." She rinsed the mud from her clothes before spreading them out to dry. She turned to watch as Nicolas set his rifle aside and pulled a few more items from his pack. One was a pillowcase she recognized from her room.

Nicolas opened a small tin and pulled out a tablet, setting it on a box. In spite of needing to keep her own distance, Dahlia moved closer, her eyes alive with curiosity. "What is that?"

"I've got waterproof matches in here. Some things are a bit damp. We were in the water a long time." He shielded the flare of the match with his hand and lit the tablet. "It's called a Sterno tab and it should give us enough heat to stop you from shivering."

Dahlia could already feel the heat flaring from the small object. "What else do you have in that bag? I don't suppose you brought food with you."

"Well, of course I did. Men don't go anywhere without food."

His eyes sparkled with brief amusement. Warmth washed over her. It was a small thing, but it had never happened before. Dahlia crossed her arms beneath her breasts and turned toward the warmth of the tablet, refusing to look at temptation. It didn't last long.

Nicolas began to deposit weapons on the wooden box that served as a table. Two boot knives. Two knives that had been tucked into a harness lying flat against his ribs. Another knife produced from a sheath between his shoulder blades. A nine mm Beretta and a belt filled with ammunition. She stared at it all. "Good grief. You certainly believe in having an edge."

"A person can never have too many weapons."

She studied him, the fluid way he moved, his watchful eyes. Everything about him screamed lethal. "You are a weapon."

He gave a small, fleeing grin that didn't quite reach his eyes. "There you go. It's called being prepared."

She was all too aware of him stripping off his wet clothes and tossing them aside. The man had absolutely no modesty, and her gaze kept straying to him in spite of her resolve. His size dwarfed the room, and her. He was tall with wide shoulders and obvious muscles. He turned slightly and she caught sight of the nasty wound on his side, up high, near his heart.

"You're hurt."

He shrugged. "A few weeks ago. It's almost healed." He dragged the first aid kit from his pack.

The wound didn't look healed or several weeks old to her. It looked raw and painful. "You should have told me." His black eyes moved over her face. She couldn't tell what he was thinking but something in his gaze disturbed her.

"What could you have done about it?"

"I would have tried harder to keep from passing out." She watched him apply a powder and ointment before he pressed a large pad over the area.

"Can you do that?"

She shrugged. "Sometimes. I pushed my limit this time,

but maybe with more incentive I could have forced myself to keep going." Even now her arms and legs ached from the long swim. She rubbed her hands over her biceps. "At least you wouldn't have had to drag me along with your pack and rifle."

"You don't weigh enough to notice."

She turned away from him, back to the warmth of the tablet. She knew she was small. Even Jesse teased her about needing to grow. It was a sore subject, but she tried never to show it bothered her.

"Here's some face wipes. Instant cleanup and then we can eat."

Dahlia turned just as he tossed the small box of wipes to her. She snagged them out of the air and knew immediately he was testing her reflexes. "I'm fine, Nicolas. I passed out from the overload of energy, not because I wasn't strong enough to continue. It happens a lot. I stay away from situations that can cause it. Really, you don't have to worry, I'm perfectly fine now. As a matter of fact, because I can utilize most energy, I last longer at physical things than most people."

He studied her averted face as he pulled on a much drier pair of jeans. She didn't look fine. She looked pale and sad. He had no idea how to comfort her. Women weren't his forte. She was doing a lousy job wiping off the streaks of mud. He took the wipe from her hand and awkwardly did it for her.

Dahlia's survival instincts shrieked at her to pull away, but she stood her ground. Nicolas was never awkward, not in any situation she'd seen him in. Yet she could feel how uncomfortable he was and recognized that he was trying to soothe her.

"Whitney's dead. He was murdered trying to protect the men in my unit after he experimented on us. After his death, several tapes were found. You were in them, that's what led us to you. In all the tapes of you learning martial arts you attacked or defended ahead of your partner. You felt the energy coming at you before they moved, didn't you?" He brushed more mud from her face, his touch so gentle she could barely feel it, yet electricity crackled in the air between them.

There was admiration in his voice and respect. Dahlia tried not to show it affected her, but her heart did its funny little flip at the unexpected comment. She nodded. "That's pretty much how it works. Everything gives off energy, including emotion. So when I'm practicing with someone, I can feel the force of the attack before it actually reaches me. And I can take that same energy and use it myself."

"That's pretty incredible, even for a GhostWalker. But you aren't telepathic?"

"Not strong. I can't ordinarily initiate, even with Jesse, and he's a very strong telepath. You warned me, didn't you? I heard your voice warning me off. You must be a very strong telepath as well." She glanced at him, at the shadows in his eyes. "Why do you call yourselves GhostWalkers?" She didn't object to the title, in fact, there was something very comforting in knowing others were like her. That she wasn't entirely alone, but part of a group, even if she didn't know them.

"We call ourselves GhostWalkers because we were put in cages and no longer considered human, or alive. And we knew we could escape into the shadows, into the night, and the night would belong to us." He tilted her face up for his inspection, two fingers beneath her chin. "There, I think I've got it all." His hand slipped away, taking his warmth with him. She watched him scrub the mud from his own face.

"Who are we?"

"Whitney thought his experiment failed because all of you from the orphanage were children and you weren't old enough or disciplined enough to cope with the effects of what he'd done. He waited a few years, believed he refined the process, and drew from a military pool, thinking highly trained and disciplined men would fare better."

"I take it they didn't." She took the wipe from his hand and gestured until he bent down. Dahlia wiped the streaks of mud from his face.

Nicolas felt the breath leave his body. She wasn't touching him, not with her fingers, not skin to skin, but it felt as if she were. His lungs burned for air, or maybe his body burned for something else. Something far more intimate. He didn't dare move or breathe in case she stopped. Or didn't stop. He was uncertain which would be safer. His reaction was so unexpected, so foreign to his nature, he stilled beneath her hand, a wild animal gathering itself for a strike. He could feel himself coiling, waiting. The strange part was, he had no idea what he was waiting for.

For a moment the room crackled with tension, with arcing electricity. It jumped from her skin to his and back again. "Stop it." She said it in a low voice.

His black gaze collided with hers. Air rushed into his body and took her scent with it. He should have smelled the swamp, but instead he smelled woman. *Dahlia.* He would always know when she walked into the room. He would always know whenever she was near. It had to be a chemistry thing. "I didn't realize I was the one doing it. I thought it was you."

"It's definitely you." She handed him the dirty wipe and stepped back, putting space between them.

She was giving them both the opportunity to drop the subject. She wanted to let it alone. Nicolas wasn't so certain he wanted the same thing. Her moving away from him didn't stop the flood of awareness. He rubbed his hand over his arm. She was there, under his skin, and he had no idea how she got there.

"Do you really have food in that pack?" Dahlia asked.

Nicolas let the heat in his gaze burn over her face. She stood her ground, but he felt her tense. He let the air escape his lungs. Dahlia was not prepared to accept any part of him. He relaxed and smiled at her. A quick, deliberate, male grin that said all kinds of things and yet said nothing. "And coffee or cocoa."

"I think you're a magician." Dahlia eased away from him even farther, moving around the makeshift table to put the rickety piece of furniture between them as if that would stop the strange awareness that was growing with every moment. Her heart was beating loudly, a hard, steady rhythm that told her she was in trouble.

What happened between them? She didn't know. She didn't want to know, but she wanted it to go away. Dahlia didn't trust anyone enough to share such a moment of total awareness. And there had been something proprietary in the energy rolling off of him. An element that was both male and very confident. Very determined. Extremely sexual. She glanced at him, then away. He was a hunter, a man who took months to single-mindedly follow a target and never missed. Dahlia shivered. She didn't want him to focus on her.

"I think cocoa would be perfect. A hot cup so I can sleep." She doubted she could do so even with the warm drink. She couldn't remember ever sleeping with someone in the same room with her. The idea made her feel slightly ill.

Nicolas pulled out the MRE, a sealed bag of prepared food the military provided for troops in the field. "There's plenty of food, Dahlia."

"Is it edible?"

"I eat it all the time."

A faint smile tugged at the corners of her mouth. "That isn't saying much. You probably would eat lizards and snakes."

"They can be quite tasty, cooked the right way. I often ate snake with my grandfather on the reservation where I grew up."

He didn't look at her, but kept busy preparing their meal. Dahlia had a better sense of him now. The conversation seemed casual enough, yet something in his voice told her he was imparting information he rarely shared with anyone. He was wearing only a pair of jeans. His bare chest was bronzed and heavily muscled. She couldn't help her gaze straying occasionally in his direction.

She cleared her throat. "Your grandfather raised you?"

"I never knew my parents. They died shortly after I was

born. Grandfather was a spirit guide and believed in the old ways. It was fun growing up with him. We spent months in the mountains tracking animals and learning to be a part of nature. He was a good man and I was lucky to grow up with him."

"You must have learned a lot from him."

"Everything but the one thing that mattered."

The regret in his voice was genuine and it tugged at her. "What would that be?"

"How to heal. I know all the chants and the right herbs and plants, but I just don't have the gift the way he did." Nicolas divided some of the food and put the rest away. He had the feeling they might need it later, and he believed in being prepared. "He taught me that all lives are important and before we learn to take life away, we should learn to give life back. And he could. You should have seen him. He was a good man, highly educated. He also knew the history of my people and the old ways. He respected nature and life and he could bring harmony to a chaotic situation just by being there."

Dahlia sighed. "He sounds like a very intriguing man. I had Milly and Bernadette. Bernadette was the medicine woman in the bayou. Quite a few of the locals would come to ask her to help them. She delivered babies and treated all sorts of things, mostly with plants and herbs. She was a trained nurse, but she told me her early and best education was here in the bayou with another woman who knew medicine. She taught me quite a bit. I liked being in the bayou, out in the open, away from everyone."

She had to turn away from him, away from grief and anger. She had to be in control at all times, as long as she was in his company. He helped ease the bombardment of energy, but more than once, Dahlia had lost control and others had suffered the consequences. "I'm very tired. Do you think we should take turns being on guard?"

"I doubt it's necessary. There are enough natural alarms around us. We'd both probably wake up immediately. I sleep light."

She didn't doubt that he slept light. There was something very self-contained about Nicolas Trevane. He exuded confidence and authority. "I'm going outside for a few minutes. If something does happen tonight or tomorrow, there's a boat tied up just around the bend. It's old and it leaks, but it has gas in the motor and will get you out of here." It was one of the many avenues of escape she kept out of necessity.

"We're sticking together, Dahlia. I hope you don't think you're going to hightail it out of here and go after Jesse on your own."

She shrugged. "We're adults, Nicolas. I have to do what's right for me, and I guess you have to do the same. I'm not leaving Jesse behind, and I'm not about to ask you to risk your life going after these people to get him back."

"My job is to keep you alive and escort you back to Lily. I guess we're going in the same direction."

"There's a small condo in the French Quarter Jesse showed me once. We can go there. There are clothes and money and ID stashed for me." She opened the door, let the sound of the rain into the small cabin, pausing in the open doorway to stare out into the bayou. "Do you think they know who you are?"

"I doubt they'll ever find out," Nicolas said.

Dahlia took a deep breath as she stepped outside, closing the door behind her. The rain had lessened in strength, falling in a light drizzle. The moment she was alone, she sagged against the wall of the cabin and pressed her hand to her mouth, afraid she might choke. She'd never been so off balance in her life. The man had risked his life to save hers. He'd hauled her through the swamp and provided clothes and food for her. She couldn't very well run off like a rabbit because she didn't know how to be in the company of people.

Maybe it was his company she was afraid of. She'd never had such a reaction to anyone before. She wanted to put it down to extreme circumstances, but Dahlia knew herself far better than that. She'd lived most of her life under difficult conditions, and she'd never had such an awareness of a man before.

Determined to get through the rest of the night without making a fool of herself, Dahlia went back inside quickly. Nicolas was the type of man who would come looking, and she didn't want that. There was dignity in returning on her own, unafraid, or at least giving the illusion of being unafraid.

Dahlia went directly to the mattress. She wasn't going to be a baby about sharing the only place he could stretch out in either. That, too, was beneath her dignity.

"You want the wall or the outside?" He didn't look at her, giving her space.

Her first inclination was to take the outside, but he was far better with weapons, and she was smaller. She could easily crawl off the mattress without disturbing him, whereas he didn't have a hope of doing the same. "I'll take the wall." She hoped she didn't suddenly develop claustrophobia.

Nicolas waited until she was lying on the thin mattress. He knew what it took for her to allow him to have the outside. It was more practical, but she had spent her life away from people, living a solitary existence, talking only to a couple of older women and Jesse Calhoun. Nicolas wanted a long talk with Calhoun. The man had to have been working for the same people who had used Dahlia as an operative. Just what had they been using her for?

Nicolas felt Dahlia shrink away from his body when he settled his weight beside her, stretching out fully. "Are you going to be able to do this, Dahlia?"

She closed her eyes, wishing he hadn't asked her. Wishing his tone wasn't so gentle, almost tender. Wishing the warmth of his body didn't envelope her and drive away the shivering she hadn't been able to stop since she'd found Milly and Bernadette dead. Murdered, execution style. "What did you bring in the pillowcase?"

"The pillowcase?"

"From my room. I saw you had a pillowcase from off of my bed."

"I picked up as many things that looked like they might

be of sentimental value to you and shoved them in it. A few books, a sweater, a stuffed animal. I didn't have much time."

Dahlia turned her head to look at him. "That was very considerate. I doubt if too many people would have thought of it under the circumstances."

Her drowsy voice conjured up images of satin sheets. He'd never laid on a satin sheet in his life, but he suddenly had visions of her looking up at him, naked, her dark hair spread out on the pillow, candlelight playing lovingly over her body. He didn't trust himself to answer. And he didn't trust his body to behave, even as uncomfortable and as tired as he was.

He turned away from her, on his side, giving her as much room as he could and took command of his breathing, slowing it down so he could fall asleep. Once he touched the rifle that lay beside him and the Beretta that was next to his hand. He could feel the outline of his knife, sheathed, but unhooked in case of quick need. He was ready should her enemies find them.

CHAPTER

FIVE

In his youth, Nicolas spent weeks alone, fasting in the mountains, waiting for the vision to come to him, to tell him of his special gifts. His Lakota grandfather said he needed patience, and Nicolas had done everything required of him, yet he could not interpret his dream. The prophecy came to him when he swayed with weariness, when he was sick or wounded, but it had never come to him while he actually slept before. The vision made no sense. There was nothing tangible to hold on to. It left him frustrated and feeling inadequate, unable to live up to the potential his grandfather had "seen."

In his dream, there was the steady beat of the drum. He smelled the smoke of the sacred fires. The healing lodge opened for him, waited for him. He knew the words of the healing chants, and he recited them over a man with the great wound in his chest. He passed his palms over the wound, felt the cold breath of death against his own skin.

Small hands covered his. Warmed his hands with the breath of life. The small fingers held an object he couldn't see, but knew was important. His voice rose in the prayer of life. He sang softly to the spirits, asking them to aid him in healing the terrible wound. He felt the object pressed into his palm, felt it grow warm as if gathering heat from an outside source to pass to him. He saw the red-orange flames dance through his fingers. The object was gone before he could identify it. Once again he placed his palms directly over the gaping wound. The smaller hands slid over his. A thousand butterflies took flight, wings brushing against his stomach at the touch of skin against skin. His singing rose with the smoke and drifted upward toward the sky. Beneath their joined hands, all around the wound, flames danced a ballet, and the wound slowly closed until the chest was unmarred.

He tried to see who aided him in the healing, but he could never see beyond the smoke. He could never see whom he healed. He felt the caress of those small hands sliding over his bare skin and looked down to see a wealth of shiny black hair sliding over his belly, gleaming like strands of silk, teasing and taunting him until his body hardened with urgent demands.

Nicolas frowned and reached for her, determined to know who she was this time. His fingers tunneled into the mass of hair. He came awake instantly, aware his fists were bunched in Dahlia's hair and his body was as hard as a rock. Her head lay on his stomach and she moved restlessly, fighting nightmares. He suppressed an aching groan of sheer frustration. If he woke her, she would be embarrassed. If he didn't, her nightmare and his discomfort would more than likely escalate. He lay motionless, his hands in her hair when her breathing changed abruptly. He knew instantly she had awakened.

Dahlia woke in the dark with fear choking her. It was a familiar nightmare, one that never quite faded away. Shadowy figures watching her. Always watching her. She needed open spaces where she could breathe, and at the sanitarium she often crawled out onto the roof. She lay perfectly still, listening to the steady sound of Nicolas's breathing, yet she knew he was awake. He lay in the darkness, probably awakened by the movement of her body, the way she tensed, the way her breathing had quickened. She was certain he was that attuned to her. And she was that aware of him.

It was only then that she realized she was wrapped around him, her thigh carelessly between his, her head on his abdomen. She moved away from him and felt her hair slip from between his fingers. She lay in silence, unable to think properly, wanting to apologize but not knowing how. In the end she took the coward's way out. Uncomfortable, Dahlia slipped off the moss-filled mattress, careful not to touch him, not to make physical contact. It was only an hour or so until dawn. She knew the night sounds of the bayou. She was awake more often than asleep after midnight so she knew each hour that insects, birds or frogs serenaded one another.

Nicolas didn't move, but she knew his eyes were open, watching her as she padded on bare feet across the floor and opened the door. She could feel the intensity of his gaze as it burned over her. She was immediately aware of the thinness of the shirt she was wearing. The tails covered her body, even went to her knees, but she wore nothing beneath it. Her body felt hot and achy, completely foreign. The cool night air rushed over her. She hoped her face wasn't glowing as hot as it felt.

Dahlia climbed onto the roof with the ease of long practice. Few physical activities were difficult for her. She sat carefully, tucking the shirt beneath her and looking up at the clouds floating above her. So many times she'd spent the nights looking up at the stars and wishing she could grab on to the clouds as they passed overhead. The rain had ceased sometime in the night. She loved the sound of rain, the continuous rhythm a lullaby that sometimes aided her in sleeping. The roof was damp, the bayou clear and crisp and fresh after the cleansing rain.

She refused to dwell on the fact that she had awoken with her body tangled with his. It happened. There was nothing she could do about it anymore than she could change what Whitney had done to her. "Lily." She whispered the name softly. Her secret, pretend friend. Lily had kept her sane on more than one occasion, yet Dahlia had been told there was no Lily. There never had been a Lily. Lily was a figment of her imagination. Milly had been her nurse for as long as she could remember. Milly had to have known Lily if she were real. It was a small thing, but it was a betrayal. Dahlia thought of Milly as family, as a mother. If she couldn't trust the things Milly told her, whom could she trust? What could she trust?

"I should have searched for you, Lily. And Flame and all the others. I shouldn't have stayed here, a prisoner really, and believed them all. I really thought maybe I was crazy." She stared out over the water and her vision blurred. "I should have been there to stop them from killing Milly and Bernadette. They never hurt anyone or anything in their lives. It just doesn't make sense."

She didn't hear the opening or closing of the door. She didn't even hear a noise as Nicolas gained the roof, but she was aware of his presence the moment he came up behind her. She rested her head on her knees, not turning as he stepped carefully to the spot beside her, avoiding the cracks in the roof.

"I was late. I should have been there."

Nicolas watched as Dahlia rubbed her face against the collar of the shirt she was wearing. His shirt. It enveloped her completely. He settled close to her. Close enough so that his thigh touched hers. He felt waves of grief pouring off of her, surrounding her. "Your being late is what saved your life, Dahlia. They were there to kill you. That was a hit squad."

"Maybe. Maybe not. But they were there to kill Milly and Bernadette and to destroy my home." She looked at him. "Why? After all this time, why would they decide to do that? Don't you think the timing is a bit coincidental?"

Her eyes gleamed with unshed tears. He felt a claw tearing at his gut. "I considered that immediately. I think it's more than likely that Lily dug in the wrong places and tipped someone off that she found you. She inherited everything.

The paperwork is enormous. She found the trust for the sanitarium buried in a lot of legal mumbo jumbo only the lawyer understood."

"Is she happy?"

"She seems very happy. She's married to a friend of mine. Ryland Miller. They're never very far apart."

"I'm glad." She looked up at the moving clouds. "Someone needs to have come out of this sane and happy. I'm glad it was Lily."

"Don't give up, Dahlia. There are things we can do to minimize the effects of what Whitney did to you."

She turned her head to look at him. "If there were things anyone could do for me, why was I kept apart from the rest of the world? Why was I raised alone in what was virtually a prison? I could walk away, everyone always reminded me of that, but I really couldn't, because in the end, it was the only place I had that gave my brain respite from the sensory overload. Now I don't have it anymore."

Nicolas felt awkward. If she needed him to shoot someone for her, he was her man, but comforting her was something altogether different. He didn't like feeling uncertain; it was foreign to his nature. Men didn't pat women like dogs, did they? He put his arm around her, drew her closer to him. She seemed so fragile he was afraid he might break her. She stiffened immediately, but she didn't pull away. "You might not have your home, Dahlia, but you have the GhostWalkers. Not just Lily, but an entire family of people just like you. We'll work through it together."

Dahlia kept her face averted. She sensed how Nicolas was struggling to find a way to help her and it was endearing, the only reason she didn't pull away from him and put distance between them. She knew he was trying to comfort her, but the thought of being around people she didn't know, in a house that was unfamiliar, was terrifying. Dahlia knew no other way of life. The sanitarium and the bayou were her home. She forced down grief and fear.

"I steal things."

"You do what?"

She wanted to smile at the incredulous tone. "Is stealing worse than killing? I thought it was all bad."

"You just surprised me." He didn't flinch at her candid assessment of what he did, but it bothered him—and people's opinions didn't bother him. He had his own moral code, a code of strict honor. It shouldn't matter what she said . . . but it did. She wasn't accusing or even judgmental, just matter-of-fact and perhaps that was what got under his skin. That she just accepted what he was. One-dimensional, as if that was *all* he was. And all he would ever be.

"That's what I do. I 'recover' things. Is that a better way of putting it? Data that has been stolen. I slip into offices and retrieve data from private corporations or even small businesses or anyone else that takes things they shouldn't."

"Whom do you work for?"

"Do you think all this time I've been working against the government instead of for it?" She turned her head and looked at him from beneath the impossibly long fringe of dark lashes.

"It's possible." He tried to assess her tone, but there was little inflection in her voice. She was very closed off to him, making it impossible to read her thoughts. "If it's a splinter branch, they're working outside the parameters. What about Jesse? What did he say about them? He must have been in direct contact with them."

"His orders always came from someone in the military. Jesse was a Navy SEAL. He would never, under any circumstances, betray his country. He's the ultimate patriotic gung ho male."

"If he's military and was a SEAL, we'll be able to find out about him. I know he's enhanced, yet he wasn't part of our unit when we trained together. I'd like to know where he came from and where he trained. Lily suspects Whitney performed the experiment first with the children from the orphanages, with us, and with some others. She's been working to find all the children. Of course, they'd all be grown by now, and she's looking for information on whether or not Whitney experimented on others."

"It would make sense, wouldn't it?" Dahlia looked down at her bare feet. She bent to rub at a smudge on her toenail. "If he believed in what he was doing so much, which he obviously did, would he really allow so many years to go by between experiments? He must have tried it on others."

Nicolas was listening to the sounds of the bayou. Frogs called to one another. Each group croaked louder than the other, trying to outdo one another, calling for mates. The frogs around the cabin were particularly loud, making a strange, off-key music. Abruptly, the group somewhere out near the strip of land leading to the channel went silent.

Nicolas immediately clapped his hand over Dahlia's mouth and pulled her backward over the side of the roof. He lay flat, preventing them from being sky-lined. She didn't struggle. She was familiar with the sounds and knew immediately that something had disturbed the frogs. Nicolas put his mouth against her ear. "Slide down to the window and go in that way. I won't let you fall. Hand me my rifle. The pack is ready, just get your clothes and be ready to move."

Dahlia nodded and inched her way down the slope of the roof. Her heart pounded overloud in her ears. The wood scraped her bare thighs and dragged the shirt up over her skin as she slid to the window. She tried not to think about her bare bottom exposed to Nicolas. Surely he had better things to look at or think about. She felt the color rising in her face as she managed to crawl into the cabin through the window.

The rifle lay on the table beside the pack. Everything was exactly as it had been before they entered with the exception of her scattered clothes. She handed the rifle to Nicolas through the window, careful to make no sound. Her jeans were damp and uncomfortable, but she pulled them on just the same. She was not traipsing naked through the bayou with only Nicolas's shirt to cover her skin. She didn't bother with the wet underwear, instead stuffed them in the pack. She picked up the belt of ammunition. It was heavy, and the pack was even heavier. Dahlia eased both through the window and onto the ground, hanging out so far she nearly fell headfirst to keep from making a sound. She made a grab at the windowsill, frantically trying to throw herself backward.

Nicolas caught her by the shirt and hauled her up beside him before the weight of the pack had a chance to pull her out. Dahlia closed her eyes in humiliation. She had rare abilities when it came to physical stunts, yet so far, she'd looked an incompetent ninny. Did women become helpless around men? If so, she preferred a solitary existence.

Nicolas made no sound as he moved to the ridge of the roof, rifle to his shoulder, his eye to the scope. Dahlia thought she was quiet in her work, but it wasn't just that he made no noise, it was the *way* he moved. Almost as if he flowed like water, so easily he couldn't possibly draw the eye to him. She watched his hands—rock steady. There was no change of expression, no quickening of breath, no animosity. And then she realized what she must be observing. Nicolas Trevane underwent a metamorphosis with the rifle in his hands and his eye to the scope. He was not completely human, yet not a machine, but something somewhere in between. He closed off emotion and his brain and body functioned at a rapid rate of speed.

He gave off such low levels of energy because he didn't feel anger when doing his job. He turned everything off. It wasn't an act of violence, it was something far deeper. Dahlia struggled to understand. Controlling energy was everything to her. Violence *always* created energy. Even the buildup of anger in a person created the violent waves that often made her ill. Nicolas didn't have those harsher emotions roiling inside of him. There was no fear. She didn't even catch a stray swirl slipping toward her. He waited calmly, his heart and lungs working steadily.

Dahlia knew the moment Nicolas spotted the assassin stalking them. She was so aware of him, she could almost catch his thoughts. There was no sudden spike in his breathing, but his finger moved along the trigger. One stroke, almost as if testing to insure it was exactly where it was supposed to be. The movement was slow and deliberate and it fascinated her. Although she was watching him, she was still shocked when he pulled the trigger and immediately slid down the side of the roof. He reached out and caught the back of her shirt, taking her with him.

He dropped her to the ground, signaling for her to run in the direction of the boat. She did as he indicated, sprinting through the swamp, staying low as she followed the path. The boat was tied up to a cypress tree. Dahlia waded out into the water to ready the boat. She couldn't help the way her heart pounded when she saw Nicolas coming toward her out of the heavier foliage. He looked a warrior of old, tall and strong and fierce. He didn't hesitate, but waded straight into the water, pushing the boat into the channel where the reeds grew the highest and could shield them as they made their getaway.

Dahlia expected a rush of violent energy to overtake her. She even braced herself for it, but there was nothing but cool morning air as Nicolas took the oars and drove through the water with long, smooth strokes. "You missed him," she said. Somehow it didn't seem possible. He was so sure of himself, almost invincible in his manner.

"I hit what I was aiming at," he answered quietly. "We have to keep moving. I'm hoping I slowed them down, but we can't count on it." He forced the oars through the water with his powerful arms and the boat shot through the channel toward open water.

"I didn't feel anything."

His gaze brushed her face, an odd little caress she felt all the way through her body, just as if he'd touched her with his fingers. "I wasn't aiming at you."

She caught the fleeting glint of his white teeth in what could have been a brief smile. One dark eyebrow rose in response. "Has anyone ever told you your sense of humor needs a little work?"

"No one's ever accused me of having a sense of humor before. You keep insulting me. First you accuse me of missing, and then you try to tell me I have a sense of humor."

His face was made of stone, his tone devoid of all

expression. His eyes were flat and ice cold, but Dahlia *felt* him laughing. Nothing big, but it was there in the boat between them, and the terrible pressure in her chest lifted a bit. "*And* it needs work," she pointed out. "Get it right." She even managed a brief smile of her own to match his.

The boat moved silently through the water, taking them through a labyrinth of channels until they were in open water. At once Nicolas started the motor. "You know the area much better than I do. Keep us away from the island where your home was and away from the cabin. You need a route that takes us under cover if possible. They'll have spotters. We don't know how well equipped they are, but if we hear a helicopter or small plane, I think it best to avoid them."

"I may steal things for them," Dahlia admitted, "but I've spent my entire life in a sanitarium. Even if this all came out, how much damage could I do to them? I'd be labeled crazy. And the sad truth is, I couldn't go into a courthouse and be in close proximity with so many people and not have a meltdown. None of this makes sense to me." She pinned him with her dark gaze. "Does it to you?"

"I'm giving it some thought," he replied mildly.

She shook her head in exasperation at his steady, unshaken manner and turned her attention to guiding them, at top speed, through the bayou.

Nicolas looked at her. She was very small-boned, but perfectly proportioned. The more he was around her, the more of a woman she seemed to him instead of the child he first thought her. And that was becoming a problem. He wanted his mind fully on keeping them alive, not on the fascinating fact that the shirt she was wearing was soaked and nearly transparent. Although small, she had beautiful breasts, and he couldn't keep himself from looking at them. He could see the darker outline of her nipples through the wet material. She had knotted the shirttails around the waistband of her jeans, and it called his attention to the curve of her hip and the memory of the brief, enticing glimpse of her bare butt as she slid down the roof. He had to admit, the glimpse had distracted him and he'd thought far too much about that particular part of her anatomy, not the smartest thing when on the run.

Nicolas couldn't stop looking at her with her head thrown back, her thick, black hair streaming in the wind, her body perfectly balanced as she guided the boat. With her head back, he could see her neck and the outline of her body beneath the shirt, almost as if she wore nothing at all. His body stirred, hardened. Nicolas didn't bother to fight the reaction. Whatever was between them, the chemistry was apparent and it wasn't going to go away. He could sit in the boat and admire the flawless perfection of her skin. Imagine the way it would feel beneath his fingertips, his palm.

Dahlia's head suddenly turned and her eyes were on him. Hot. Wild. Wary. "Stop touching my breasts." She lifted her chin, faint color stealing under her skin.

He held up his hands in surrender. "I have no idea what you're talking about."

"You know *exactly* what I'm talking about." Dahlia's breasts ached, felt swollen and hot, and deep inside her, a ravenous appetite began to stir. Nicolas was sitting across from her, looking the epitome of the perfect male statue, his features expressionless and his eyes cool, but she *felt* his hands on her body. Long caresses, his palms cupping her breasts, thumbs stroking her nipples until she shivered in awareness and hunger.

"Oh, *that.*"

"Yes, *that.*" She couldn't help seeing the rigid length bulging beneath his jeans, and he made no effort to hide it. His unashamed display sent her body into overtime reaction so that she felt a curious throbbing where no throbbing needed to be. She grit her teeth together. "I can still feel you touching me."

He nodded thoughtfully. "I consider myself an innocent victim in this situation," Nicolas said. "I've always had control, in fact I pride myself on self-discipline. You seem to have destroyed it. Permanently." He wasn't exactly lying to her. He couldn't take his eyes or his mind from her body. It was an unexpected pleasure, a gift.

He was devouring her with his eyes. With his mind. A part of her, the truly insane part—and Dahlia was beginning to believe there really was one—loved the way he was looking at her. She'd never experienced a man's complete attention centered on her in a sexual way before. And he wasn't just any man. He was . . . extraordinary.

"Well, stop all the same," she said, caught between embarrassment and pleasure.

"I don't see why my having a few fantasies should bother you."

"I'm *feeling* your fantasies. I think you're projecting just a little too strongly."

His eyebrows shot up. "You mean you can actually *feel* what I'm thinking? My hands on your body? I thought you were reading my mind."

"I told you I could feel you touching me."

"That's amazing. Has that ever happened before?"

"No, and it better not happen again. Good grief, we're strangers."

"You slept with me last night," he pointed out. "Do you sleep with many strangers?" He was teasing her, but the question sent a dark shadow skittering through him. Something dark and dangerous stirred deep inside of him.

Her eyes jumped to his face. "What is it? What's wrong?" She looked around quickly. "Should I cut the engine?"

Nicolas sat up a little straighter. She was so tuned to him, even that smoldering jolt of jealousy was noticed. "We're fine." But he was uncertain if it was the truth. He was beginning to be alarmed at how they seemed so aware of one another. Nicolas didn't experience emotions such as anger and jealousy. He had fine-tuned his mind to filter out such things, yet Dahlia was shattering an entire lifetime of conditioning.

"Tell me what's wrong. I know I'm not the average person, but I'm an adult, and despite having lived in a sanitarium and having a nurse raise me, I'm not completely insane. I don't want you treating me as less than an equal."

Nicolas studied her expression. Her dark eyes were spitting fire at him. Maybe that was the problem. She was melting the ice everyone said flowed in his veins. "When I figure it out, you'll be the first to know. I don't believe I've treated you as a child or as if you were insane, nor less than an equal. And it wouldn't matter what you thought, if you care to know the truth. I do what I think is right, and I'm not going to worry about what you're thinking." His words surprised him more than they did her. Was he stating a hard fact or striking out at her? Nicolas rubbed his jaw with the heel of his hand. Facing death was easier than talking to women any day of the week.

"Well that's good, because I'm *exactly* the same way. I guess we understand each other." She turned her head away from him, nose in the air, looking a bit like a drowned princess.

The sun was climbing into the sky and definitely providing a backlight. His gaze once again dropped to her breasts thrust against the thin material of his pale blue shirt. The shirt had become an instant favorite. He ran his tongue over his teeth, wishing he could do the same to her nipple.

Dahlia's breath hissed out of her throat. Slowing the boat, she swung back toward him, glaring. "*What* is so damned fascinating about breasts? If I show them to you will you stop?" Her hands went to the buttons of the shirt as if she might really rip the material open. There was color in her face and her breath came too fast. "I once heard that men thought about sex every three minutes but you must be setting some sort of record."

"It isn't just any breasts, Dahlia." He reached for the canteen of water. His hand was shaking. Actually shaking. Just the thought of her opening her shirt sent his body into a painful, hard, unrelenting ache.

"Well I have them, okay? Just like any other woman. They're there. I can't do much about it."

Nicolas took a long pull of water and nearly choked as she angrily unbuttoned the shirt and allowed the edges to gape open all the way to her waist. Her breasts were fuller than he'd first thought, jutting forward to tempt him more.

She was beautiful. Her skin was amazing. He swallowed hard. "I don't think that was a good idea."

Dahlia realized instantly she'd made a terrible mistake. His black eyes went from ice cold to a raging fever. His hand gripped the canteen until small dents appeared. Energy leapt between them, fierce and passionate, feeding on him, feeding on her, threatening to consume them both. At once she was hot, her clothes too heavy, too cumbersome, her skin too sensitive. She wanted to rip the shirt away, feel his hands, his mouth, sliding over her skin. She wanted things she'd never dreamed or thought of. Had no idea she even knew of.

The distance between them melted away. His body touched hers, his bare chest rubbing against the tips of her breasts. His hands tunneled in the wealth of her silken hair, fisted, holding her still while he bent down, his gaze as fierce and intent as the energy surrounding them, holding them captive in its burning center. He dragged her head toward his. His mouth fastened on hers, took possession. Fire leapt from her to him, raged between them. The kiss went on and on. It wasn't enough. It would never be enough.

His tongue slid into her mouth, danced a long, sensual tango. His mouth moved over hers, demanding. Urgent and wild. The back of her head fit nicely in his palm and he held her to him, kissing her soft mouth, her chin, her throat and back to her mouth again. The roaring in his head grew. His body hardened and grew until he thought his clothes might split. He *had* to have her. Had to make her his.

Her skin drew him. Soft, softer than anything he'd ever touched. It was impossible to think or reason with her tongue teasing his, her teeth biting at his lips and his chin, her breath moving in his lungs. He tasted her neck again. Nibbled his way to her throat. Felt the gasp as he lapped at her nipple. Heard her breath explode from her lungs as he fastened his mouth on her breast. She made a single sound, inarticulate, but her hands came up to cradle his head.

He feasted, devoured her. Something in his gut clawed for more. Heat rose until he thought he might catch fire. He did catch fire, somewhere in his belly—it roared, a conflagration out of control. He yanked at the knot on the shirt, desperate to get to her, desperate to have all of her.

Dahlia felt his mouth slip off of her breast, felt his tongue lap at her skin, teasing her every nerve ending. Both of his hands went to the knot at her waist. Her head was spinning, dizzy with need, with hunger. There was so much heat and pressure, she could barely stand with wanting him. Dahlia drew in a deep breath of air, closed her eyes, and shoved him away from her—hard. She turned and dove into the water, away from the boat. It was the only way she could save them both. He had no idea what was consuming him, but she knew. She'd dealt with it all of her life.

She went deep, letting the water cool her heated skin. It hadn't occurred to her that such a thing could happen. She'd never been physically attracted before. Jesse certainly wasn't attracted to her, nor had she been attracted to him. She hadn't been prepared at all for the explosive chemistry between Nicolas and her and she handled it all wrong. She'd actually kissed him back. Not just kissed him, she'd practically eaten him for dinner. The thought of facing him was more than she could bear.

Dahlia surfaced a distance from the boat, treading water while she fumbled for the buttons on her shirt. She was still so sensitive even brushing against her skin sent shock waves through her body. She didn't want to think how he'd be feeling. The boat was headed her way, and he didn't look very happy. She waved him off. "Go. Get away from here, Nicolas. Take the boat and go." She was trying hard to save him, but she could see from the harshness on his face that he didn't want to be saved.

Nicolas stopped the boat beside her. There was no ice at all in his eyes, rather a raging fury. "Get in the boat," he said, his voice grim.

"Get away from me. Do you think it's going to stop?" Angry, she hit the water, sending a plume splashing over him. He didn't even wince as the droplets settled over his head and chest and ran down to the waistband of his jeans.

She ducked her head beneath the water on the pretense of slicking back her hair. Dahlia used the brief moment to force her mind away from where those drops were heading. What the droplets would touch as they raced down his belly to his groin. She broke the surface, her heart pounding. "I know the bayou. I'll be fine. Take the boat and get out of here."

"Damn it, Dahlia, I'm not asking you again. Get in the damned boat. I'm not a filthy rapist. You were right there along with me, feeling the same thing."

She saw it then, his shame at his lack of control. His fear that he'd frightened her. His sexual frustration that must be every bit as bad or worse than her own. She reached for the rim of the boat and held herself there, tightening her fingers until her knuckles turned white. "Nicolas, it wasn't you or me. Not like you're thinking. I'm all about energy. Even sexual energy. You were throwing it out there. I was too. We were both feeding it, and it swallowed us. We can't be together. We just can't take the chance."

Nicolas sat very still just watching her. What he wanted to do was yank her back into the boat and weld their mouths together. Their bodies. He *craved* her like he would a drug. He made himself breathe. In and out. He could read the desperation in her eyes, the fear. Not of him, but *for* him. The tight coil in his belly began to relax. Not giving her time to argue or think, he simply caught her small wrists and lifted her into the boat. "We're adults, remember? Now that we know it can happen, we'll be more careful." He managed a quick, teasing grin. "Until we don't want to be careful."

Dahlia swallowed hard. She had courage, he had to give her that. Respect for her grew with every moment in her company. She didn't back away from him, but held her ground. They were both standing up, and she had a long way to look up. "It could happen, Nicolas. You've never seen what pure energy can do, but I have. I generate heat when it happens and fires start. People get hurt."

"Have you ever made love to someone, Dahlia?"

His voice was so low she had to strain to hear him. She

felt the surge of darkness, of danger, something lethal and deadly emanating from him.

"No, I've never wanted to get that close to anyone."

"Until now." He wanted to hear her say it. At least give him that much. He *needed* that much.

"Until now," she agreed.

Nicolas stepped away from her, sank back into position. "Thanks for not pushing me into the water. You must have thought about it."

"Don't give me too much credit." She made her way to the motor. "I wasn't certain if I shoved, you'd fall." She sent him a quick grin before turning to the task of speeding across the water.

Nicolas stared toward the thick brush and heavy trees and tried not to think about the taste and feel of Dahlia. He made it a mental exercise, clearing his mind, allowing the thoughts to enter without dwelling on them and letting them go out again on a tide. He was certain of only one thing. He knew Dahlia was part of him. How and why didn't matter. Nothing, no one, had ever thrown him before. She mattered to him. What she thought, how she felt. And he wanted her.

It was nearly noon when Dahlia eased the boat along a rickety pier. "This is where we get off. We'll have to catch a bus or hire a taxi from here."

"I'll have to break the rifle down. Even so, the two of us look memorable in these clothes. And your shirt is transparent. I don't think I can take a bunch of men ogling you." He didn't look up as he took his rifle apart and carefully wrapped it before putting it in his pack. The ammunition belt followed, along with every other visible weapon.

Dahlia gasped and crossed her arms over her breasts. "You could have said something."

"I didn't want to embarrass you." This time he did look up, only a small glance.

She had the impression of a fleeting smile. She caught the shirt he threw her and hastily put it on. "Next time, I'm pushing you in," she vowed.

CHAPTER

SIX

Nicolas walked through the large condo, checking all the exits, learning where the windows were and which made good escape routes. The main entrance opened out onto the street corner so they could choose either direction if they had to leave in a hurry. He noted there was also a street entrance through the locked wrought iron courtyard gate. The courtyard was large with overgrown plants, shrubbery, and large shade trees. It provided excellent cover should they need it. The condo had an upstairs with a balcony that also gave them access to the roof. Calhoun had chosen the location with care. They had cover, escape routes, and were near the river as well.

Dahlia opened a vault, hidden in the wall behind a picture of wild horses racing through waves. Inside were weapons, ammunition, and a great deal of cash. There were also a number of identity cards. Driver's licenses, Social Security, and other forms of ID in various names with pictures of both Jesse Calhoun and Dahlia Le Blanc.

Nicolas thumbed through the papers Dahlia had taken

from the safe earlier. All the while, he was conscious of the sound of water. Dahlia was taking a shower. No matter how hard he tried to prevent it, his imagination insisted on conjuring up a vivid picture of Dahlia naked, wet, her hair slick and her face turned up to the hot spray. He closed his eyes against the image and groaned softly. Where had all his self-discipline gone? His tremendous control? He couldn't blame energy, sexual or otherwise, for his fantasies. It was the glimpse of her bare bottom, the curve of her hip. Her bare breasts gleaming at him in the sun. Or maybe it was her smile. She didn't smile often, but when she did, Nicolas could swear it was for him alone, no one else. And then there was her skin. . . .

"Hey! Lover boy! Stop mooning around and hit the shower. You smell like a swamp rat, and it just doesn't do a thing to put me in the mood." Dahlia stood in the doorway, a towel wrapped around her like a sarong. Her hair was up in a towel and she was dripping water all over the floor. She'd obviously come downstairs straight from her shower to scold him for his indiscretions, but changed her mind.

"You're not helping me with my overactive imagination," he pointed out as he walked toward her. He paused beside her, close, trapping her body between his larger frame and the doorjamb. Deliberately, slowly, he reached out and touched her face. He thought it a small victory that she didn't automatically pull away. She braced herself for his touch, but she didn't wince as he drew his finger down her cheek to the side of her mouth. "You have incredibly beautiful skin."

Her eyes went black. Wary. He felt her tense, but she still didn't flinch away.

"I want to kiss you again, Dahlia."

Her eyes were huge. She lifted her chin, but didn't break eye contact. "I want to kiss you too, but that doesn't mean we should. It's dangerous. And we don't even know each other."

A faint smile came out of nowhere. "I'm willing to get to know you intimately. *Very* intimately. That would solve the problem quickly." His thumb slid over her velvet-soft lower lip, stroked small caresses there. He was fascinated by the shape of her lips. He could actually taste her in his mouth—haunting, feminine. Addicting.

Heat flared between them, smoldered there. Dahlia inhaled sharply. "Nicolas." There was an ache in her voice.

His fingers curved around the nape of her neck. He knew better. It wasn't that he didn't understand the consequences. It was just that nothing mattered but touching her. Getting close to her, skin to skin. Burying his body deep inside hers. The rest of it was just details. He had a primitive need to leave his mark on her, so that she would always be his. Always want him in the way he wanted her.

Dahlia could feel the heat swamping both of them. It would take so little to just wrap her arms around his neck and burn in the fire, but it wouldn't be fair to Nicolas. He had no idea what he'd be getting into, nor how dangerous it might be. She took a deep breath and pushed one hand against Nicolas's chest. "Go take a shower. Use cold water, it will help."

It took him a moment to control the urgent demands of his body. As he stepped away from her, the pad of his finger slipped down her throat and trailed over the swell of her breast before he dropped his hand to his side.

Dahlia shivered at his touch. She remained still, only inches from him, refusing to back away . . . or move forward. "Fortunately, Jesse stashed some clothes here for me. He's a thoughtful man."

"Is that what you call him? I think interfering busybody would just about say it all. I like you without clothes."

"Nicolas," she cautioned. "I'm hanging on by a thread. You're supposed to help."

"Tell me why again, and I'll work on it."

"We don't know what can happen." He was still standing close enough that she could feel the heat of his body. His need was urgent and evident and he made no effort to hide his arousal. "And," she held up her hand before he could speak, "I'm not completely comfortable with you yet."

He sighed softly. "You managed to think of the one thing to say that gives me no other recourse." He went up the stairs, his body aching for relief.

Nicolas would normally revel in the hot shower after such uncomfortable conditions, but he found he was different. Soaping the mud from his hair, he contemplated his uneasiness. As a rule, he enjoyed solitude. He *needed* seclusion. Isolation was his chosen way of life, so much so that he normally avoided people, yet he felt reluctant to be away from Dahlia.

He was a methodical man, one who thought things through logically. As he showered, he forced his mind to regain discipline and control. He should have been the one controlling the situation, not Dahlia, and yet she had stopped them both times. His lack of discipline when he was all about discipline confused him. Determined to recover his normal tranquility, he used the training ingrained in him by his maternal grandfather, Konin Yogosuto. Automatically he began deep breathing. He concentrated on his teachings, beliefs that were a part of his life, a part of who he was. Unification of mind and body. Complete harmony in the universe. One with the universe. Where there is chaos, there must also be calm. He repeated the soothing mantra, allowing the familiar teachings to center him.

Energy, sexual or violent, even normal energy, swarmed to Dahlia. He created the energy simply by thinking of her. By wanting her. If he was to find a path with her, he needed to find a measure of control. Dahlia was a unique woman, one who had lived a life of solitude and betrayal. She wouldn't trust him until he earned that trust, no matter how attracted they were physically. Dahlia needed friendship and she needed to feel "normal," whatever that might be. Whatever it was, he was determined he would find a balance that would work for them.

It felt good to be clean and dry again. He dragged on a pair of jeans and thought about what Dahlia's life had to have been like. While he was hunting and fishing and learning martial arts, she was alone in rooms filled with one-way glass and silent watchers. His grandfathers loved him and often hugged him, beaming with approval when he succeeded. There had been two women in Dahlia's life, and their loyalty had not been entirely hers. She needed time. Even if a sexual relationship bound them together, Nicolas knew it would never be enough for him. He knew he wanted *all* of Dahlia Le Blanc, not just her body.

DAHLIA dressed slowly, grateful for the clothes Jesse had stored in the closet for her. As she pulled on a pair of jeans, she listened to the sound of the shower. Nicolas had power now, and he knew it. Dahlia had never let another human being have true power over her since Dr. Whitney had when she'd been a child. Others might believe they had control, but it was never so. She should never have blurted out the truth, telling him she wanted to kiss him.

Jesse had always told her she should have a backup plan and not to trust anyone entirely. It had never seemed a problem before. Even Milly and Bernadette, the two people she'd really loved, had reported to someone else about her. It hadn't been just Dr. Whitney they'd reported to. Whitney had lost interest in her around the age of seventeen or eighteen. He had provided the money for her home and the specialized gymnasium equipment, but once he had made a decision that she would never be able to work as an operative, he never returned. Had he checked, even once, he would have found she'd proved him wrong, perhaps out of sheer stubbornness.

Dahlia wandered into the kitchen and opened cupboards. They were stocked only with the bare necessities. She made a pot of coffee, mainly for the aroma and something to do with her hands while she tried to puzzle out who wanted her dead. Who knew about her, and why would they want her dead? Was it possible those she'd worked with didn't want it known that she did recovery work for them and sent out a team to kill not only her, but Milly and Bernadette as well? It didn't make sense. None of it made sense.

She rubbed at her damp hair with the towel, taking out the excess moisture. There was no need to kill any of them. No one would ever believe Dahlia Le Blanc, a woman raised in a sanitarium. It was the perfect cover and the perfect protection. If she were caught, she was simply a madwoman unhinged by her own conspiracy theories.

She looked up as Nicolas sauntered into the room. His hair was damp from his shower and he wore only a pair of soft blue jeans. He was barefoot and shirtless, showing a broad, bronzed chest that robbed her of her ability to think clearly. She tried not to stare, but it was a losing proposition. In a lame attempt to cover her reaction to his presence, she settled into one of the kitchen chairs. "I'm just making coffee. I thought we both could use a cup."

"It smells great." Automatically, he glanced at the windows, making certain no one could see them from any angle.

"Tell me a little bit about how you got into recovery work," Nicolas suggested.

Dahlia leaned back and allowed herself a long look at him. "I think I only said I'd do it because Dr. Whitney said I couldn't do it. I really detested that man."

"So you're contrary on top of everything else."

She watched the way his muscles rippled as he made his way to the coffeepot. He reached easily into the cupboard and pulled out two mugs. "Very contrary when it's needed. The man who recruited me wore a uniform, and both Milly and Bernadette were afraid of him. More than just nervous, you know? I think he had a couple of stars on his uniform. Whitney was there at the time." She shrugged. "I was about seventeen, I think, and deliberately didn't pay much attention."

"What about his sleeve? Did you see an anchor alongside the stars?"

"Now that you say that, yes he did."

"Curious. So he presented himself as part of the military. This could have started as a black ops. Covert. Whitney had a lot of ties to the military. Most of his contracts were with the government, and he had a high security clearance. But if Whitney later became suspicious that you were being used by someone who didn't have his approval, why didn't he take you out of there?"

"Whitney and I didn't get along very well. When he was around, there were a few accidents." Dahlia studied her fingernails. "And yes, they were true accidents. I don't hurt people on purpose. The repercussions are brutal. I just hadn't learned to control my feelings. Teenagers have such intense emotions." She shrugged. "I think he preferred to forget I existed."

"He remembered you enough to leave a letter to Lily asking her to find you and the other women he experimented on."

"I suppose I should be grateful."

"I wouldn't go that far," Nicolas said. "If Jesse Calhoun is a Navy SEAL and the man you saw had the uniform of an officer, and it sounds as if he could be rear admiral, then we should probably start with any Navy connections to a high-level security splinter group. Before we found you, the GhostWalker program was slated to be wiped out by a splinter group of military. We thought we got all of them, but maybe we missed somebody. And if that's the case, they'd know about Lily and the rest of us."

"Are Lily and the others in danger?" Dahlia asked quickly. "Call them and warn them to be careful. I don't want anything to happen to Lily, especially because of me."

"It wouldn't be because of you, Dahlia. Lily is committed to the GhostWalkers, and she's very committed to finding each of the women Dr. Whitney experimented on and helping them recover."

Dahlia resumed towel drying her hair, wishing she had a brush. "How did you get involved with the experiment?"

Nicolas hesitated, choosing his words carefully. He had never told anyone the reasons for his involvement. "I needed my psychic abilities enhanced."

Dahlia waited for more. When it wasn't forthcoming she looked across the table at him with a raised eyebrow. "Nicolas, no one *needs* their psychic ability enhanced.

Why would you even consider doing such a thing?" His very body language screamed at her to drop the subject, but Dahlia couldn't imagine anyone wanting the life she'd led. "I've never known anything different, but you must have had a wonderful life prior to meeting Whitney."

He shrugged. "I wanted to be able to heal people. Both of my grandfathers seemed to think I was born with the gift, but I've never been able to utilize it."

"And you were willing to trade your entire life for a chance to try?"

"Obviously."

"But it didn't work," she guessed.

"The experiment worked, but not for healing," he said.

Dahlia studied his face, noting the sadness in his eyes. "It enhanced your natural abilities and made you a better hunter, didn't it?" she guessed. "And there isn't really a way to reverse the process, is there?"

Nicolas shook his head. "No, but there are ways to better live with it, ways Lily can help you so you might be able to live among people and at least have a chance at something resembling normal. She's helped all of us."

Dahlia shrugged. "Meeting her will be enough. A part of me did think I was losing my mind to believe she existed." She pushed her hands through her hair, lifting the wet mass from her neck. "I've been giving it some thought. I don't think it's going to be all that hard to find Jesse. They want me to come after him. They must have left a trail of some sort for me to find."

Nicolas poured a cup of coffee for her and handed it across the table. His fingertips brushed hers. His belly did an annoying ripple and his groin tightened. If he were a cursing man, now would be the best time. "I'd have to agree with you." He kept his voice calm and even.

Dahlia took a sip of coffee, looking serene. She sat tailor-fashion in the large kitchen chair, comfortable in jeans and a T-shirt. Her long hair spilled down to her waist, a cascade of black silk. The mass left damp spots on the shirt.

Nicolas shifted his gaze to the numerous IDs. "Did you find anything in there that will help us?"

"Not really. What about your people? Do they have the connections to check on Jesse's background? We could use a little help."

"Lily has top security clearance and she can hack her way around any security system. I called her while you were in the shower." He scrubbed his hand over his jaw. "She said to tell you she was very happy we found you, and it made her feel as if she weren't quite so alone."

Dahlia ducked her head, unable to hide her expression from his probing gaze. Lily had always meant so much to her, even when Dahlia was certain Lily was no more than a figment of her imagination. She couldn't readily identify how she felt knowing that Lily was real, that she was alive and was happy to have found her. It felt as if a long-lost family member had surfaced. She struggled to contain her emotions.

"Dahlia, it's okay to show your feelings. You know everything *I'm* thinking."

He thought she might smile, but she didn't. She sat in the oversized kitchen chair with tears on her lashes and looked up at him. "No I don't. I'm not like you. I told you, I'm not telepathic. I can reach out if the energy is right, and I can answer if the other person sustains the contact. Jesse was strong. We could talk together. You're strong, you maintain the bridge, but I'm not reading your thoughts. I *feel* your hands on my body, or your mouth. Whatever you're thinking, somehow transfers into a strong sensation. You're broadcasting, but my brain doesn't hear it. My body feels it."

Nicolas sat down slowly. "It's hard to take this in. Most of the GhostWalkers work off telepathy, at least to a great extent. The concept of using energy is different. It seems impossible for me to think something, you not hear my thoughts, but feel what I'm thinking."

"We all give off energy. Emotions give off energy. You have a particularly strong sexual attraction for me. The energy is strong, and it finds me."

"Has it ever happened with anyone else on any other level? You felt what they were thinking?" He stayed very calm, breathing in and out, but now he was tuned to his own mind and body, and the ripple of unease, of dark, dangerous violence, was acknowledged as part of him and let go.

She shook her head. "Lucky you. It's only been you."

He kept his expression blank, not showing the relief sweeping through him. "I do consider myself to be lucky, even privileged, being as I'm the only one. This never happened to you, even as a child? Maybe with Lily or one of the others?"

Dahlia shook her head. "Never."

"But you can't be around people," he probed gently.

"Strong emotions make me sick. Violence makes me extremely sick. I've had seizures before. I hurt someone a couple of times, accidentally. It looks as if I do it on purpose, but when I'm in the midst of violent energy, especially raw anger or the aftermath of death, such as we experienced at my home, I generate heat along with my own emotions and things happen. My own emotions can make it happen."

"The flames. It appears as if you throw them out there, but it's just the opposite, it's lack of control."

"Exactly, but it can be useful when people think I do it on purpose." Again that faint smile touched her soft mouth. Nicolas tried not to stare at her mouth or allow his mind to dwell for too long on the possibilities of kissing her.

She put her coffee cup on the table and leaned back. "Do you realize I know nothing at all about where I came from? I don't even have a family. You must feel very lucky knowing your grandfather. Tell me something about him."

"Actually I was lucky enough to know both of my grandfathers. My paternal grandfather was Lakota, a great shaman, a great man. He could do things I've never seen anyone do. He used to say each thing has a spirit, a breath of life, and he could talk to the spirits. Once I saw a small boy who had fallen from a cliff and lay broken, so many bones crushed he screamed in agony. While we waited for the rescue helicopter to come, my grandfather began to chant to the spirits, the sixteen who are one. He laid his hands over the boy, and I could feel the heat he generated. By the time the helicopter arrived, the boy was no longer screaming and his bones were perfectly fine. My grandfather was taken in the helicopter instead as his heart nearly failed."

"That's incredible. No wonder you wanted to be able to heal people. I've read about such things, but certainly never witnessed it. What was his name?"

Nicolas smiled. "Just Grandfather to me. *Nicolas* was one name he went by, but he had many."

"You really loved him, didn't you? You must love having his name."

Nicolas watched her fingers, the strange little rhythm she tapped in the air. She seemed unaware of it. He remembered feeling the rhythm as she tapped her fingers against the mattress in the cabin in the bayou. It obviously was a habit. "Yes I did, Dahlia. Growing up with him was a humbling experience. You can't imagine how perfect a childhood it was for a young boy. My grandfather taught me to track and to survive in any kind of condition, but most of all he taught me to respect life and nature." Her fingers fascinated him. There was something hypnotic about the way she spun her fingers in the air. "What are you doing?"

She looked startled. Her mouth formed a question, but she followed his gaze to her fingers. Faint color crept under her skin and she closed her hand into a fist. "I do exercises with small balls. It helps to alleviate the constant bombardment of energy. I had a collection of balls made out of mineral stones, mostly crystals. The different properties help with various types of energy." She shrugged as if it didn't matter. Nicolas could see it clearly did.

"I may have saved a few of your favorites. I tossed the ones I saw in your bedroom into the pillowcase right before I noticed the explosives."

Her entire face lit up. Nicolas felt as if he'd just been

handed a Christmas present. She nearly jumped at him, and he braced himself for her touch. At the last moment she changed her mind and simply brushed her soft lips over his face.

Heat seared his cheek. That brief, wisp of gesture seemed shockingly intimate. He reached up and touched the spot with his fingertips.

Dahlia's color deepened even more. "I'm sorry, that was thoughtless of me. I know you don't like to be touched anymore than I do. I'm acting out of character around you. I honestly don't throw myself at people on a regular basis."

"I think we've established I don't mind your touch, Dahlia," he said. He drew the pillowcase from his pack and fished around for the peculiar balls made of varying crystal and stones. They were cool to the touch, smooth and hard. His fingers brushed hers as he handed them to her. At once he felt the warmth, as if the spheres took on life when transferred to Dahlia. He looked down to see their hands together, his large, hers small, and something immediately tugged at his brain. The memory of his spirit vision came rushing over him.

"Thank you, Nicolas." She took the small spheres from him. One set was amethyst. Her fingers caressed them immediately, rubbing and rolling them together. Another set was made of rose quartz and still another was made of aquamarine.

It was a small thing, but it brought her pleasure, and that was all that mattered to him. "Do you believe crystals aid in healing?" he asked curiously.

"I don't know about healing, although they're reputed to be able to focus the energy and help. I do know they help me tremendously. When I need to be calm, any of these three sets really work, some of the others to a lesser degree."

"Both of my grandfathers used crystals," Nicolas said.

"What was your other grandfather like?"

"He was from Japan, and his name was Konin Yogosuto. After Grandfather Nicolas died, I went to stay with him. I was ten. He lived simply. He was a master in martial arts and had a great number of students."

"And you became one of them?"

Her black gaze teased him. At once he felt his body's reaction, the tightening of his muscles. That was easy enough to accept. It was the way his heart warmed, seemed to swell in his chest, that bothered him. He made every effort to appear serene, as he had spent so many years learning to do. "Not right away. Interestingly enough, like Grandfather Nicolas, Grandfather Yogosuto also believed in healing first and had as many people come to him for ailments as to learn the way of life. He was a very quiet man. When he said something, I listened."

"So you had two grandfathers raise you and no women. I had two nurses raise me and no men. Interesting that we turned out somewhat similar." She raised her gaze to his. For a moment there was silence.

Pain. An aching loneliness. Nicolas was beginning to understand what she meant about energy. He could feel a sadness emanating from her, and it touched him in places he hadn't known existed. If there was tenderness in him, it seemed to be reserved for Dahlia. He watched her swallow, the line of her throat delicate. She looked vulnerable in the large chair, sitting with her legs tucked up.

She forced a small smile. "Did you ever have a dog? I always wanted a dog. It wasn't that they wouldn't let me have one, it was a matter of control." She looked down at the table, anywhere but at him. What had ever possessed her to blurt out such intimate details to a perfect stranger?

"You were afraid they'd control you through the dog?"

Dahlia was silent for a moment, undecided whether to keep going or to end the conversation. Finally she nodded. "Everyone seemed to be in control of me, and I didn't want it to go any further."

"How could they control you?"

She shrugged. "I needed the house and the remoteness of the location."

"You have money, Dahlia. A lot of money. You could get your own house in a remote location."

She ducked her head; the amethyst spheres swirled in her fingers. He watched as they spun in her palm with remarkable precision. In minutes they were no longer in her palm but floating beneath her fingers, continuing the smooth action of rotating just as if her fingers were doing the manipulating.

"Dahlia." He said her name to get her attention and waited until she reluctantly looked up at him. "You *allowed* them to control you. Why did you do that?"

She was silent so long he thought she might not answer him. "I wanted a family. Milly and Bernadette and Jesse were the only people I had. I stayed to keep them. It was a trade-off."

Nicolas bit off a word he rarely used and turned his head away from her to stare out the window. For a moment his vision blurred and he blinked rapidly to clear it. "It was a hell of a trade-off, Dahlia. You might have been better off with the dog." The moment the words were out he wished he could take them back.

Dahlia stood up and shoved back her chair. Her hands were shaking. She put them behind her back. "I need a little space if you don't mind." If she burst into tears she would never forgive him . . . or herself.

"Wait." He took one step toward her. Glided silently. It felt more predatory than anything else and her heart pounded in alarm. She gave ground, taking a step back even though she knew better. *Step to the side, never back up, they just keep coming.* A standard training rule.

"Dahlia, I know I'm making mistakes with you. With us." He set his coffee cup on the table and rubbed the bridge of his nose, frowning when he noted she immediately went into a fighter's stance. "I'm not used to being with other people any more than you are. I don't know how to talk to women any more than you know how to talk to men." He grit his teeth for a moment, feeling like he was making an ass of himself, but he pressed on. "I don't always know the right thing to say. I'm bound to say something that hurts occasionally. Work with me here. Professionally, there's no problem, I know exactly what to do, but personally . . ."

She shook her head. "I don't know how to be personal

about anything, Nicolas. You're not going to get any real help from me."

"So we have to learn together. Is that so bad? We have common ground. We're both GhostWalkers. There are only a few of us in the entire world. I saw your books. We read the same books."

"What books?" She challenged.

There was a small silence. "I'm sure we have the same dictionary." Nicolas watched her mouth soften and shape into a small smile. He snapped his fingers. "*Zen Mind Beginner Mind.* There you go, I wore out two copies. You had one on your bed. I brought it with me in the pillowcase."

"You can't have my copy—I love that book." Dahlia was ready to forgive him, mostly because he tried so hard to put her at ease. "You must be hungry. We'll need groceries. I thought maybe if I walked around a bit and let myself be seen, they'll come to us and we won't have to work so hard looking for them."

"That was a sniper out in the swamp, Dahlia. If they sent a sniper, they were looking for a kill." There was no way to soft-soap it. He wasn't prepared to have her wandering the French Quarter, setting herself up as a target.

She nodded. "I figured that out. When you said he was like you, I thought at first you meant another GhostWalker, but you would have said like *us.* You didn't, so he had to be a sniper. How did you know he was following us?"

"Instinct, a sixth sense, my grandfather's spirit whispering in my ear. I don't know. When I'm out there, it comes to me and I know."

"Does he do that? Does your grandfather whisper to you?"

There was no amusement in her voice. She wasn't making fun of his beliefs. There was interest and perhaps a little envy, but Dahlia found nothing strange about his comment. She accepted people for who and what they were. She accepted him. Nicolas realized at that moment that Dahlia had led such a different life, so apart, she would never feel the need or desire to judge another for their peculiarities.

He doubted if she would ever feel completely at ease with others.

Nicolas knew he preferred a life apart. But it was a choice. He knew who he was and what he stood for. He never felt the need to apologize or explain, not even to Lily. He respected Lily and even felt a rare affection for her, as he did the members of the GhostWalker team, but the emotion was more about family than anything else. Whatever emotion Dahlia stirred in him ran hot and passionate and deep. She stirred up a dark violence he hadn't known was inside of him, and she brought out laughter, something infrequent in his life.

"Nicolas, you don't have to answer if you don't want to. I didn't mean to pry." Dahlia touched the back of his hand. A stroke of her fingertip. She left a streak of fire on his skin. "If I had a grandfather like yours, I might want to keep him to myself."

"Both of my grandfathers were meant to be shared with the world. They did their best to bring peace into other people's lives. Grandfather Nicolas does whisper to me when I need to hear him. To warn me, or to remind me. I feel him close to me. And *bousofu* is also near when I need him."

"That would mean?" she prompted.

"*Grandfather, deceased grandfather,*" he interpreted for her.

"How many languages do you speak?"

"Too many. My grandfathers both had many of the same beliefs. A man should gain as much knowledge as possible."

Dahlia nodded in agreement. "I read a lot and listened to tapes. All of my schooling was done with tutors. None of them stayed long, but I didn't need them. And I didn't want them. They were impatient or afraid or angry because of my strange personality. All of it became negative energy I had to cope with the entire time they were here. Often, it wasn't even me. They were upset before they ever got there."

"You learned several forms of martial arts."

"Yes, and for the most part, because I was doing something physical and most of my instructors enjoyed what they were doing, it was fun. Later, as I got older and they were serious about training me, I was faster than the instructors, and some of them would get angry."

"Honey, that's entirely understandable. You're barely five feet tall, and you can't weigh a hundred pounds. To make matters worse, you're a girl. Kicking some man's butt is not ladylike."

Dahlia heard the teasing note in his voice and for the first time didn't bristle at his pointing out her diminutive size. "I'm a good eater, in spite of my size. You might be able to live on that stuff in your backpack, but I want real food. I'm volunteering to go grocery shopping."

"I'll call in an order. There must be someone who's willing to earn a delivery fee. That's what cell phones are for."

"Aren't you afraid your name is on a hit list right alongside mine?"

"They have no idea who I am. No one got a good look at my face, and the only one who might have been able to identify me was the sniper they set on our trail. He's not in any condition to tell them who I am."

"How would he know?"

He shrugged. "Maybe he didn't know. Most likely he didn't, but we have a feel for one another. How we walk a path, that sort of thing."

"I see." She didn't, but she was becoming restless. "I need to walk around outside, Nicolas. It isn't you, really, you're being really supportive, but even Milly and Bernadette never spent more than fifteen or twenty minutes with me unless we were outdoors."

"Am I projecting sexual energy?" He was watching her hands again. She was whirling the amethyst spheres beneath her fingertips, never touching them, keeping them afloat in the air just beneath her palm.

"There's always energy, but that's not it. You're amazingly low-key. Most of the time, unless it is sexual, I don't feel anything. You're a very restful person to be with."

"How about going out into the courtyard, Dahlia? You can sit out there and relax. I'll make a list of things we need and call in the order and then make us something to eat."

She nodded. "Thanks for being understanding. I really appreciate it."

"Dahlia." He stopped her before she made it to the door. "Is it something I can help you with?"

She should have known he would see beyond mere words. Dahlia shook her head. "I've always relieved the buildup by physical activity. You saw my gym. I can wait until dark and use the rooftops. I get a little shaky is all."

"Are you hurting?"

"It isn't bad—and don't offer pain meds. I don't take them. I have a fairly high tolerance, and I get by."

He waved her toward the courtyard. Dahlia didn't hesitate. She needed to be alone. Part of it was she didn't want him to see her as she really was. She put her hands out, fists clenched around the spheres. Both hands were shaking. She was used to her routine, the sanctuary of her home. Interacting with Nicolas was exhilarating, but it took its toll. She began to jog around the courtyard, all the while keeping the spheres moving beneath the fingers of both hands.

CHAPTER

SEVEN

Dahlia paced back and forth in the small bedroom, her mind refusing to give her peace. Something was wrong. She'd walked the entire parameters of the house several times. She jogged in the courtyard. Her dinner, a traditional Cajun dish, wasn't sitting well in her stomach despite having been cooked to perfection. She missed something. Granted, she'd lost everything, and she'd been distracted by running through the bayou and practically sleeping with a man, but she *never* had so much trouble figuring things out. It was right there, within her grasp, yet she couldn't quite reach it.

She leapt onto the bed and raced halfway up the wall, taking refuge in physical activity. Someone wanted her dead. They shot Jesse. Was it possible the very people she worked for had sent a team to kill her? Her bare feet beat a small tattoo on the lower part of the wall as she ran lightly around it, circling several times before attempting to race up the wall to the ceiling. Why did they shoot Jesse and not kill him? They would know he didn't know where she was. She was late. She never had contact with Jesse until she reached her house. It was always set up that way. It never varied. She didn't carry a cell phone or a pager or anything else. Once he gave her the mission, she planned it and carried it out alone. Why did they shoot Jesse? Just to torture him? It didn't make sense. It wasn't the first time a recovery had taken a wrong turn, though she always completed the assignment, but there was a strong possibility the attack on her home and family was connected.

Dahlia raced up the side of the wall until she was upside down, hanging from the ceiling. It took a great deal of concentration. Her mind was not sufficiently following the process and she fell like a rag doll, hitting the bed and bouncing slightly, the breath slammed from her lungs at the jolt.

"What the hell are you doing?" Nicolas stood in the door looking disheveled and shaken from his usual calm. "Are you out of your mind?"

Dahlia sucked in air, enough to allow a smooth somersault that brought her upright and sitting tailor-fashion in the middle of the bed. She shook back her hair and looked at him. "I missed something important."

He couldn't help staring at her. Drinking her in. Dahlia wasn't shy or vain, or even modest. She didn't seem to notice her personal appearance. She sat on the bed, the covers rumpled, in a tank top that bared her shoulders and midriff and a loose pair of cotton drawstring pants. With her hair tumbling around her and pooling on the sheets she looked mysterious and feminine and all too sexy when she clearly wasn't trying.

A frown slipped across her face. "Quit fixating on my breasts. You cannot do whatever it is you're thinking right through my shirt, thank you very much. For heaven's sake, do you ever think of anything besides sex?"

"Apparently not," he admitted wryly. "I've never had the problem before I met you." He was damned if he'd be embarrassed. He could see the darker outline of her nipples through the thin white tank top, an intriguing shadow that tempted and beckoned and begged to be suckled. It wasn't his fault the woman never wore adequate clothing.

"What were you doing? People don't walk on ceilings."

Dahlia studied his face. His long black hair cascaded to his shoulders and looked as if he'd rubbed his hands through it over and over until he was completely rumpled. He wore a thin pair of sweats and nothing else. Heat radiated off of him, nearly shimmered in the air so that the temperature in the room rose several degrees. He was so beautiful he took her breath away. She stared at him, dazzled. Starry eyed. Idiotic.

Dahlia pressed her lips together. She was no better than he was at controlling the sexual awareness leaping between them. The moment they were together, it spread until it enveloped them and burned them up. She tilted her head. "Why is it that you emit such incredibly low energy, even in the most violent circumstances, but when you're with me the energy becomes a tidal wave?"

"You don't censor, do you, Dahlia?"

She shrugged her shoulders, drawing his eye to the line of her neck. He could plant little kisses right along her neck. Take small bites to the curve of her breasts.

Dahlia pressed her hands to the aching swell of her breasts and heaved a sigh. "You just aren't going to stop, are you?" She frowned. "Should I be censoring? I don't have a lot of experience in conversing like this. Do you want me to censor the things I say? Milly told me once that I was too outspoken."

Nicolas rubbed at his pounding temples. There was a strange roaring in his head. He always wondered what the proverbial walking hard-on meant and decided it was a person . . . him. No matter how much he meditated, the moment he went to sleep, he dreamt of Dahlia. Erotic, sexy dreams of her soft skin rubbing against his. Of her mouth sliding over his chest, his belly, edging lower until he thought he'd go out of his mind. Her hand wrapped around his erection, fingers slipping over him, dancing and teasing and stroking long silken caresses. As hard as he tried to control his wayward thoughts, she crept into his mind. He transferred his hand to the back of his neck, rubbing hard to ease the tension. "This is worse than basic training ever was, Dahlia, and no, I don't want you to censor."

"What's worse than basic training?"

"Wanting you. I even want you in my sleep. What the hell is that? I am completely disciplined at all times. What have you done to me?"

Unexpectedly, Dahlia laughed. She lifted the thick mass of her blue-black hair off the back of her neck and let it fall in a cloak around her. "I'm a voodoo queen, of course. I've cast my spell, and it's too late for you to get away from me."

He wanted to swear. He wanted to cross the room and pin her down on the bed and see if she dared laugh at him then. She'd melted whatever ice had run in his veins, and now she was sitting there in the middle of the damned bed laughing.

The smile faded slowly from her face, from her eyes. She pulled the pillow to her chest protectively. "It wasn't you, this time, Nicolas, it was me." Color crept under her skin as she made her confession. "I thought it was safe to indulge in a few fantasies. You didn't say you were affected when I was thinking about you."

He counted to ten silently to give himself time to collect his scattered control. "You didn't tell me you had fantasies about me. Especially erotic fantasies."

She sighed. "You don't have to throw it in my face. I am human after all. I may have been raised in a sanitarium, but I do have the usual hormones."

A slow, very male, smile of satisfaction settled on his face, relieving the grim lines. "For which I'm grateful. Why did you stop? It left me frustrated. I wouldn't be complaining if you'd finished what you started."

Her flush deepened, and her gaze shifted away from his face. When he stirred as if to take a step toward her, her eyes widened in alarm and he immediately regained her full attention. "We don't really need to talk about that. I've thought of something else important."

"If I'm going to survive the night, we definitely need to talk about it." He folded his arms across his bare chest.

To Dahlia, he looked like a statue, lovingly carved of

stone. Someone had paid attention to each detail of his body, of his face. She sighed as she pressed the pillow tighter against her midsection. "I didn't know exactly what to do."

He had to strain to hear her confession. He stood looking down at her, wondering how he could be such an idiot when he was reputed to have a high IQ. His smile widened, until he was grinning like an ape. She was just so beautiful, looking flustered and embarrassed, caught with her erotic fantasies just as he had been.

Dahlia threw the pillow at him—hard. "Go away. I'm thinking about very serious matters and you're not helping."

He caught the pillow in midair and stalked her across the room, looking every inch the prowling tiger. "I think sex is a *very* serious subject." He sat on the edge of the bed.

Dahlia glared at him. "You take up a lot of space. And air. I can't breathe with you in the room."

"I'm teasing you, Dahlia." His voice was so gentle, almost tender, and her heart did a funny little flip. She wished she had the pillow back.

"Are you going to tell me how you managed to run across the ceiling?" he asked.

"I didn't manage it. Only partway, and then I fell. It's a matter of bending gravity." She shrugged her shoulders again, and he tried not to stare at her flawless skin.

"Bending gravity?" She would never cease to amaze him.

Dahlia nodded, her face brightening. "Not exactly bending it, more like shielding it or modifying it. Basically, I have to gather a tremendous amount of energy in one place, which for me isn't all that difficult, and then I turn myself into a kind of energy superconductor."

He nodded. "I've noticed, but that doesn't explain how."

"I began playing with energy when I was child. I build a strong magnetic field around me, and as the energy builds up, it causes the nuclei of the atoms, in whatever part of my body I choose, to spin very fast. If I manage to align the nuclei with each other and get them spinning fast enough, then I can create a gravity field and aim it so it counteracts the earth's gravity field."

"And then what happens?"

She grinned at him. "Every woman's dream. I lose weight and can utilize the field to play in. I can run up walls and do all sorts of things. I'm not actually running up the wall, you know. I'm moving my feet to give the illusion, but I'm actually floating. Like an astronaut. It isn't the same thing I use out in the field when I'm working. This requires a tremendous amount of concentration actually. Going onto the ceiling is extremely difficult because I have to be upside down and use the top of my head as the superconductor. Which is why I take a few falls now and then. To make it look as if I'm running up the walls I have to make minute adjustments in the gravity field strength of various parts of my skin." She waved her hands to dismiss the subject. "It keeps me mentally balanced to try new things. It's just fun."

He smiled at her. She had no idea how special she really was. She was more embarrassed to be caught running up the walls and falling from ceilings than she was to be naked in a towel in front of him. *Because she found it fun.* The knowledge burst over him like the rays of the sun. She was embarrassed to be caught playing.

"It's amazing, Dahlia. You must have put in a tremendous amount of study time on antigravity fields and how they work. What made you decide to try?"

"When I was little, I didn't know what I was doing, but energy gathered around me, rather than dispersing as it normally would seek to do, so I played with it. I prefer to keep my mind and body active, and since I'm all about energy, I do my best to learn as much as I can about both. There are a few physicists who are working on superconductors, and I think they'll discover very soon that controlling gravity is possible on a much larger scale than they first thought." She frowned and rubbed her chin. "Though they'll first have to figure out how to create organic, room-temperature superconductors. And they'll have to realize that they can direct the effect several different ways, not just upward."

Nicolas shook his head. "You're using various parts of your own body as a superconductor?"

"Well, yes. If I used the entire surface of my skin, the front would cancel out the back. If I'm lying on the floor and I turn the skin of my entire backside into a superconductor, then the antigrav field generated by it will levitate my entire body. If I move my feet, I look as if I'm walking up the wall. That's fairly basic though and not much fun." She sent him a quick grin. "Hanging upside down is a lot tougher because I have to just use the top of my head to generate a much stronger antigravitational field capable of floating my entire body from that one spot."

"Which is why you fall."

She nodded. "Exactly."

"Lily will be so thrilled to hear you talk about this. She was going on about how you do what you do when we were watching the tapes of you in training, but I'm not certain any of us understood a single word she said. She mentioned the gravity field and superconductor. She noticed a wire above you moving as you ran across a cable and that tipped her off."

Dahlia felt a surge of anticipation, of excitement. "Everything above me is going to be caught in the antigrav field as well. You were too busy looking at me, but there were pens floating in the air as well as my amethyst spheres."

"Lily will want you to show her how to do it," he warned.

She shrugged, trying to look casual, but her eyes were bright, giving away her pleasure at the thought of showing Lily. "I have so many theories I've developed trying things out. I'd love to discuss them with her. I've spent a great deal of time reading the latest discoveries and seeing if my work matched closely with anyone else's. I'd love a chance to talk with her."

"She'll love the chance to talk to you." He could see how much it meant to her that she and Lily had something in common. "Speaking of which, what were you going to tell me before I distracted you with all the superconductor questions? Or was that you, hopping from one subject to another? I can never keep up."

She knew he was teasing. His tone was nearly the same,

but she felt the little flutter of butterfly wings brushing against her stomach, something that seemed to happen when he was bantering with her. "What I wanted to tell you, before you so *rudely* brought sex into the conversation, is, I don't know that this is all about me. The killings. Why did they shoot Jesse right there? In the leg that way?"

"They thought he would tell them where you were."

She shook her head. "If they were Jesse's people, they'd know I *never* tell Jesse anything. He has no idea where I am at any given time, nor can he contact me. It's always worked that way. Jesse could tell them the target, but not much else."

"You're certain his people know this?"

She nodded. "I've done recovery work for them for several years. We've always done it the same way—always. His people have to know that he would never know where I was or how to find me. Other than at the target location. They didn't hit me there, they hit me at home."

"What are you saying, Dahlia?"

"You thought they were destroying all the evidence of my existence by killing Milly and Bernadette and burning down my home."

"I don't believe in coincidence," Nicolas said. "Lily made inquiries and probably raised a red flag somewhere. If they aren't legitimate they would have to destroy all evidence, anything that might lead back to them."

"True, *if* they aren't legitimate, but Jesse Calhoun is no traitor. He believed in what he was doing. We had quite a bit of contact over the years, and even though I'm not telepathic, I still have a good feel for people through energy. He wasn't betraying his country. And he was no mercenary either."

"He might have been duped, Dahlia. I volunteered for the GhostWalker program. The contract was a military one and a colonel was overseeing it. The rot went all the way up the chain to a general. Calhoun could very well believe that his superior officers are telling him the truth. We believed—until people started dying."

"That doesn't make it the same situation. In fact, that only adds more doubt. If they were operating outside the government, they would have made sure they kept tabs on the relationship between Jesse and me. They'd know he couldn't tell them where I was."

"Do you have another contact for these people? I'm not convinced, but it's worth investigating."

Dahlia drew up her knees and rubbed her chin back and forth. "I could find them. I have contact numbers, but I've never used them. Jesse is always the contact."

"Dahlia, how could you be so careless when you were working with these people? You seem like someone who pays attention to details." Her behavior seemed out of character to him. He didn't know her that well, but she didn't seem like a woman who would work for an agency without knowing exactly what she was doing.

"I knew Milly worked for them. She watched over me, and she could contact them if needed. I've spent my entire life staying away from people. Separated from them. I didn't trust them, but it was something to occupy my mind and use my skills, so I did it. And I felt it was important."

"I think we need to have Lily run a check on both Milly and Bernadette." He said it carefully, knowing it would bother her. "She's looking into Calhoun now, and I hope she has something for us."

Dahlia shook her head, ignoring the reference to Milly and Bernadette. The moment he mentioned their names her chest burned with grief. "I just don't buy it, Nicolas. Jesse was too squeaky clean. And he's intelligent. Really, really smart. I think if something was off-kilter, even a little bit, he'd begin to suspect."

"Maybe he did suspect something and they wanted to get rid of him."

"Then they would have killed him."

"Not if they needed him as bait for you to follow," he said patiently.

"Then why shoot him in the leg so he can't walk? They had a long way to go to get him out of the bayou. It doesn't add up."

"I hate to disillusion you, but some men torture others for

the sheer pleasure of it." Nicolas reached out and tucked the curtain of hair behind her ear, his fingers lingering in the silky strands. Touching her seemed as necessary as breathing. Electricity sizzled in his bloodstream. He forced his mind to think of something else. Something besides petal-soft satin skin and a sexy, intriguing mouth. "Something with teeth. A big cat. Really large, maybe a saber-tooth."

"What in the world are you talking about?"

"I'm occupying my mind with things other than sex."

She glared at him. "We are discussing something *very* important here. You might want to participate and then you won't be thinking about sex."

"As long as you're sitting in front of me, Dahlia, I'm afraid sex is going to be uppermost on my mind. The saber-toothed tiger was to keep all other images out of my head," he added piously.

She bared her teeth at him. "How's this for an image?"

He closed his eyes and groaned, vividly picturing her small white teeth nipping over his skin. "That wasn't nice."

Dahlia smiled at him, a soft, feminine smile. Sheer poetry. Nicolas was certain she didn't need many other weapons. "I suppose it wasn't, but you deserved it." The smile faded and she rubbed her chin against her knees again. "Follow me on this for a minute. Let's say Jesse is really working for the government. If we've been doing our job, and it was all aboveboard, then there would be no reason for the destruction of my home and family." She could feel the anger begin to coil inside of her, to wrap itself around the tight knot of sorrow. The emotions were dangerous both to her and to anyone near her if she allowed them to rise out of control.

Nicolas was so tuned to Dahlia he could feel the energy gathering around her, generated by her own intense emotions, no longer sexual, but turbulent. He reached out and circled her ankle with his fingers, making a loose bracelet, but maintaining contact. At once the energy lessened, gave her breathing room.

"I'm sorry, it just happens sometimes."

"It's normal to feel grief and rage over the loss of your people and your home, Dahlia. The energy doesn't invade me the way it does you. I don't know why it can't really connect with me. I almost wish it could, especially if it meant I could run across the ceiling."

Dahlia took a deep breath and let it out. "I'm fine again. Thank you." It amazed her that just by touching her, Nicolas could ease the burden of the continual assault of energy, even when it was her own.

"So, what you were saying is, it may have been someone else who attacked you. Do you have that kind of enemy, Dahlia?" Nicolas tried to keep the conversation moving. Each time they stuttered to a halt, sensations seemed to overwhelm them both. The awareness was acute and intense and threatened to consume them at every turn.

"I don't know about enemies. I don't know people well enough to accumulate enemies, but I do steal things from companies. Mostly things that have to do with submarines and new weapons, things they shouldn't have in the first place. I only go in at night and slip past the guards and the security system, copy the data, and get out, or, more often, I go in and recover the stolen work so no one else has access to it. I could have been caught on a security camera, although it's highly unlikely. Or maybe I was traced through Jesse. There very well could be a traitor in the group I'm working for who sells that kind of information to others. There's big money in new weapons on the open market."

"You copied or stole back sensitive data and turned it over to Calhoun?"

Dahlia nodded. "In the last three years, that's just about all I've been doing."

"Dahlia, don't hedge. What the hell are you talking about?"

"There's a reason for a high-security clearance, Nicolas. I don't even know you."

"You know me. And for the record, you don't even exist, let alone have a high-security clearance. If you got caught, they would hang you out to dry."

"Well, of course. That was understood. I'm the poor girl raised in the sanitarium, as batty as they come, seeing conspiracy theories everywhere. They'd put me back in the sanitarium."

"Only if you were arrested. The kind of thing you're talking about can get people killed." Nicolas felt the first stirrings of a black, swirling anger in his gut. She was risking her life, and Jesse Calhoun and whatever agency he worked for knew it. As far as he could see, they did nothing to help her. They simply used her.

"Nicolas." She swept her hand lightly down his face. A mere brush of her fingertips. Her touch jolted through his body, set his heart pounding, and heated the blood in his veins. "Don't get upset over my life. I enjoy my work. It's an outing and a chance for me to utilize the skills I've developed. I *wanted* to do it. The thing that's important to understand about me is, I don't do anything unless I want to do it. Not anything. Not even when I was a child. I may seem impulsive, but I'm actually not. I think things over and weigh the pros and cons and make a decision. Once I make it, I make the best of it, no matter how it turns out, because it was *my* choice and ultimately, I'm responsible. I like it that way. The rear admiral or whoever he was, couldn't talk me into anything I didn't want to do. Neither could Jesse or Milly or even Bernadette. I'm just not like that."

"They used you, Dahlia." There was ice-cold rage in his voice.

Dahlia was grateful for the bracelet of fingers around her ankle keeping the shimmering energy already radiating violence away from her. "Is that how you see yourself, Nicolas? A victim? They send you out into a jungle or a desert and you have no backup, no one to help you if you did something so simple as to break a leg. If you were captured or shot, how much help would you have?"

"It isn't the same thing, Dahlia."

She tilted her chin at him. A small thing, but the gesture told him a great deal without words. He was tramping on some idiotic feminine code she had, and if he didn't back down, he was in serious trouble. He held up his free hand. "Don't attack me—I can't change who I am any more than you can. Regardless of whether or not we agree on this, it was dangerous. If Calhoun suspected there was something going on that was a threat to national security, he should have pulled the plug."

"With no proof?"

"So what do you think was going on? You must have looked at the data."

"I think Jesse was right. I think the three professors given a grant by the defense department came up with an idea for a stealth torpedo that would really work, and someone stole it from them. An investigation was launched, by Jesse's people, and when they thought they knew who stole the research, they sent me in to recover it." She watched his face closely as she deliberately mentioned the stealth torpedo.

Nicolas was silent, fear and anger washing through him. The anger deepened into full-blown rage. "They had no right involving you in something like this."

Dahlia tried to repress the relief flooding through her. If Nicolas was a plant looking for information, she doubted he was a good enough actor to conjure up the violent energy his anger was generating. "Are you going to listen or not?"

"I'm listening, and then I'm going to hunt down the bastards who sent you into a minefield while they sat back risk-free in their comfortable offices."

She blinked, her gaze riveted to his face. He was made of stone, perfectly expressionless. She couldn't read him at all, but the energy rolling off of him was not as low level as it usually was. It was furious and purposeful. In spite of his fingers shackling her ankle, the violence struck her hard, taking her breath, pounding at her head, building until she was afraid she would explode.

Dahlia threw herself sideways, away from him, rolling off the bed, breaking the light grip Nicolas had on her ankle. He made a grab for her, but she caught him off guard.

Glass fragmented in the windows, the sound loud in the night. Spiderweb cracks raced across the windows and mirror. The lightbulbs shattered, the pieces exploding like a bomb and raining down in slivers onto the floor. The room itself seemed to shift, the walls flexing, bubbling outward as if something pressed against them, then receding abruptly as if the invisible force could not find an escape. The temperature soared in the room. Nicolas peered over the edge of the bed. He couldn't see Dahlia's body, but a red glow burst from the floor, casting her small shadow on the wall briefly before the flickering color died down and winked out.

"Dahlia? Are you hurt?"

She coughed. "No. Are you?"

She sounded hurt, her voice shaky. Nicolas reached down and picked her up, dragging her against him. "Nothing touched me. Are you certain?" Her skin was hot to the touch, searing his fingers and palm.

"I'm going to be sick." Dahlia pushed away from him and staggered on bare feet toward the bathroom.

Nicolas caught her up and carried her, unwilling to take the chance that she might cut herself on the shattered glass. He held back her hair while she was violently sick, over and over. "This is my fault, isn't it?" Grimly he handed her a towel.

Dahlia rinsed her mouth repeatedly. "It's Whitney's fault, if we're going to blame anyone." She shrugged and looked at him. "It's my life."

"I'm sorry, honey, I should have been more careful."

She flashed a wan smile. "You can't stop feeling, it doesn't work that way. And who would really want it to? I'll be fine. Let me brush my teeth. It's gone now, a flash fire so to speak."

Nicolas turned away from her to pace restlessly across the floor. "Where's the broom? I'll clean this up." He couldn't think about what her life must be like. How difficult being around people would actually be.

"I'll get it. I don't bother with brooms. It's easier to just use whatever energy happens to be handy to collect it. And right now, there's plenty of energy in the room."

Nicolas turned back to look at her. She made the announcement so casually, as if what she said and did wasn't truly exceptional. She was busy brushing her teeth. He took a moment to really study her. She was all flowing grace and soft movement. Very feminine. Why hadn't he noticed it when he had watched the training tapes? He had viewed her as a potential enemy and looked for strengths and weaknesses. Everything was so different. Just looking at her warmed him.

"Dahlia, what did you mean by a stealth torpedo?"

"A silent torpedo. One that can't be detected before, during, or after being fired from a submarine." She tossed her hair over her shoulder and moved to stand beside him. She bent low, her palm just above the glass, and began to move her fingers in the same rhythm she often used with the spheres.

"That's impossible. You can hear the outer doors open. You can hear the burst into the water, and you can hear the motor of a torpedo." He couldn't take his eyes off of the glass shards as they began to spin in a circle, pulling together and rising beneath her palm. She amazed him with her control. "They've tried and failed over and over."

"I don't think they failed this time," Dahlia said and walked very carefully to the wastebasket. When her hand was over the top of it, she stopped all movement and watched the glass drop into the basket. Only then did she turn and look at him. "I think someone figured it out, or at least was close to figuring it out."

"And you know this how?"

"I don't *know* it, I just think there's enough data to be suspicious. Prior to being asked to go in for a recovery, I was asked to duplicate the information at the university where the professors were working together with their teams. I looked at the information I was bringing out over the last few months. The original research read nothing at all like the findings sent to the government."

"So it didn't work, and they've dropped it and gone to something else."

"They're dead. All of them. The first professor to die was a woman. She was in a car accident about four months ago. She had one assistant. He died while hiking in the national forest. That happened about three weeks after the first death. The second professor died when he fell from a balcony in what the police said was a 'freak' accident. The head of the team was walking along the street when he suddenly fell to the ground, clutching his chest in an apparent heart attack. That was a couple of weeks before I was sent out. Granted, they all died weeks apart from what could truly have been accidents, but if you put that with a couple of other deaths of minor assistants, all dying in similar ways, it means to me that they succeeded in their research and that someone wants to cover it up and sell it elsewhere."

"So the government was officially notified that it couldn't be done."

Dahlia nodded. "The report came in just a few weeks before they all started dying."

Nicolas studied her face before crossing the room to stand in front of the window where he examined the spiderweb fragmenting the glass. "You're not an innocent woman working out of a sanitarium, are you?" He stared out the window into the darkness. "You know exactly who you work for."

Dahlia crossed the room to stand beside him. Close, but not touching him. "I'm sorry, yes. I work for the NCIS, the Naval Criminal Investigative Service. So does Jesse. I didn't know who you were, Nicolas, or whom you worked for. You showed up the same time my home and my family was destroyed. I'm investigating something that has probably killed several people. Jesse Calhoun has been taken prisoner and is probably being tortured for information. If I were a member of the other side, I'd probably put someone like you in place. I had to be sure you were really who you said you were. It was such a coincidence for you to show up at exactly the right moment."

"All the time we talked, out in the bayou, you never really answered a single question I asked. It didn't add up at all. You aren't the kind of woman not to know *exactly* who you work for." He shook his head. "You've been feeding me just enough to test me, haven't you? You really know how to make a fool out of a man, don't you?"

There was no rancor in his voice, not even a note of bitterness. He just said it and turned and walked out. His bare feet made no noise on the floor as he left.

Dahlia stood quietly at the window for a long time, watching the night, watching the clouds spin across the dark sky. Feeling like the lowest creature on the face of the earth. She shouldn't have felt low. She was doing her job, just as he did his job, but she still felt as if she had betrayed him in some way. He knew what a security clearance was, and a need to know basis.

Her heart hurt. Ached. It was silly. She wasn't the kind of woman a man could ever take home to his mother. She could imagine sitting at a dinner table with one of his family members smoldering over the loss of their favorite football team and accidentally catching the dining room on fire. No matter how much she might want to get to know someone, or have a friend or be in a relationship, the bottom line was always the same—it was not possible. She would not feel sorry for herself.

She'd been careful, cautious, just as she'd been taught. Just as life had taught her to be. No one in her world was ever what they claimed to be. Nicolas Trevane was probably no different. He could still very well be an assassin sent to kill her the moment she turned over the documents she'd been sent to recover. She sighed and pushed her hair back away from her face. Deep down, where it counted the most, Dahlia knew he was exactly what he seemed to be. And it wasn't as if she lied to him. She did live her entire life in the sanitarium, at least the part that mattered most. And she did work for the government recovering information. And she wasn't altogether certain in the beginning that they hadn't sent a hit squad after her. She didn't trust the NCIS any more than she trusted anyone else. She honestly didn't know the truth of it, and she still didn't.

If one of the NCIS agents from Jesse's office hadn't betrayed them, how would anyone know about her? She was a ghost, slipping in and out, able to block the security systems. Dahlia never left a trace of her existence. She wasn't caught on film accidentally; it wouldn't happen. She disrupted the cameras all the while she was inside. So who knew about her, and how did they know?

Nicolas appeared in the doorway. "Come away from the window." There was no urgency in his voice, but it was an order. He was in hunter mode, and she recognized it instantly. Dahlia didn't ask questions, she simply took a rolling dive across the bed and hit the other side of the floor. Behind her, the glass shattered, spewing shards in all directions. A bullet whined over her head and buried itself in the wall. Dahlia kept rolling until she was at the door. She crawled out on her stomach. "How'd you know?"

"I just know." He reached down and pulled her around the corner of the doorframe. "We've got to get out of here. You need clothes, shoes, whatever. You have thirty seconds."

"Gee thanks. I appreciate it." She could see he was already in full gear, pack and everything. "Did you throw my things in your pack? My crystal spheres?" Sitting on the floor in the upstairs hall, she dragged on a pair of socks and hastily pulled on the boots he'd brought up from the kitchen.

"I've got them. Hurry up, we have to go to the roof."

"Are you certain?" She didn't bother to ask how he knew. He was a GhostWalker, and they each had their talents. Nicolas *knew* things. The right things.

"I'm certain." He gave her a hand up, and indicated the window overlooking the courtyard. "We go out that way."

"I'm right behind you."

CHAPTER

EIGHT

Dahlia pulled on the dark sweatshirt Nicolas tossed to her as she followed him to the window. He opened it silently and swung out, sliding his hands up the wall to find finger-holds. Dahlia couldn't help but admire how smooth, efficient, and silent he was, like a spider going up the side of the building. She followed him, every bit as quiet. This was her specialty, adhering to the side of buildings and moving in secrecy. It was one of the things she felt most comfortable doing. Evidently, Nicolas did as well. His level of energy was so low, she would have sworn he had ice in his veins. They might have been going for a casual stroll. She was very grateful that she couldn't detect any tension from the energy surrounding him.

Dahlia was very small and it enabled her to fit closely against the wall, to become part of the shadows she spent most of her time in. She was also able to blur her image enough to help blend into her surroundings. Nicolas was a big man and carried a heavy pack. He should have been more easily seen, but she could see why he'd earned the title of GhostWalker. Even knowing where he was right above her, she couldn't hear him as he moved, not even the whisper of clothing. She closed her mind to thoughts of him and climbed as if she were alone.

Her fingertips found cracks and her toes found places to dig in as she moved up the building to the roof. She slipped over the side, taking great care to stay low, to keep from being seen. She crawled on her stomach, like a lizard, across the roof, pulling herself along with elbows and hands and knees. She gained the street side and stopped beside Nicolas, staying quiet, waiting for him to signal they could go over the side and head for the street.

He put his hand on her arm, a brief touch, raised his hand, and flattened his palm. She shook her head briefly. She was *not* willing to wait up on the roof while he took all the risks. If he were going into the streets, she would go with him.

Don't argue with me. I've got rank on you. The words pushed into her mind. She was startled for a moment. She'd forgotten he was a strong telepath.

No one has rank on me. We'll go together.

We can't afford you to be anywhere near violence. Even up here, you'll catch the backwash of it. It makes sense for me to do what I do best.

Dahlia closed her eyes. Why had she ever named him killer? *Nicolas.* She didn't mean for her heart to be in her voice. In his mind. An intimate connection between them. *I'm sorry. Maybe I should have told you everything, after all, your life is just as much at risk as mine is.*

He turned his head, his black eyes boring into hers. Arctic cold. And then, without any warning, his gaze smoldered. Went midnight black. Burned with such intensity she gasped. His mouth settled over hers. His lips were soft but firm, pressing into hers, so that her mouth opened for him. So that the taste and texture of him invaded her body and mind, poured into her with the force of concentrated silken heat and hot promises. His mouth moved over hers, his teeth nibbling at her bottom lip, at her chin before sliding away from her. They stared at one another for the beat of eternity while the clouds spun overhead and danger prowled in the street below them.

Stay here.

Dahlia took a deep breath and nodded. She made herself breathe again as he slipped over the edge of the roof. He left his pack and rifle and went in silence. She strained to keep him in sight, following his progress as he climbed down two stories, his darker shadow blending in with the night. He moved fast, a smooth descent that made her think of a night creature. She watched as he gained the small patch of shrubbery close to one of the three men stealthily waiting outside the windows and doors on the street side of the house. He was much taller than the bushes, yet he seemed to blend, his body nearly indistinguishable from the leafy branches.

She loved watching him move. He came up behind the man nearest him, standing directly behind him, close enough to breathe on him. She caught the glint of metal in his hand and closed her eyes, bracing herself for the violence of the act to swallow her. Her stomach lurched. She detested the act of taking life. She had developed her own philosophy based on the books that had appealed to her. She did believe everything in the universe was connected and that each life had a purpose. While she certainly believed in defending her own life, she had firsthand knowledge of the severe repercussions. Violence, once committed, lingered behind and subtly worked on those sensitive to its ugliness.

She lay still. The waiting was much more difficult than she'd anticipated. She could feel the gathering of energy from the men below, surrounding the house and cutting off escape. They were in various stages of adrenaline high and nervous anxiety. She was no telepath and couldn't read their thoughts, but she was certain Nicolas could.

Dahlia? I think these men are from the Naval Criminal Investigative Service, or at least were sent by them. Let's hang back and watch them. If they came to assassinate you, we can still slip away. I don't know why they'd fire a shot through the window, that doesn't make sense, but it doesn't feel right to me. They're too cautious. This feels exploratory, not a hit. We don't want to make any mistakes and kill an innocent.

I don't want to kill anyone, innocent or not. She let her breath out, opened her eyes and blinked. Nicolas was nowhere in sight. She would never find him now, even with her awareness of him. He was a chameleon, blending into his surroundings.

We prefer GhostWalkers. There was a tinge of amusement in his voice. *The night belongs to the ghosts.*

She rolled her eyes. He actually sounded arrogant. Men were strange, there was no doubt about it. *Do you want me to carry your pack and rifle off the roof? It isn't going to be safe up here, no matter who they are.*

His hand slipped lightly over her mouth and Dahlia was rolled over to lie on her back staring up at him. He was on his belly beside her, grinning as her eyes widened in shock.

You're lucky I don't kick you off the roof. She took refuge in false annoyance. She couldn't help drinking in the sight of him, nor ignore the relief that swept through her. Which, she decided, was annoying in itself. She loved being independent. It was the best part of who and what she was. He seemed to be destroying her solitary nature.

Nicolas shrugged into his pack and retrieved his rifle. *Follow me.*

Dahlia bit down on her lip to keep from muttering curses. She lacked social graces, no doubt about it. Following him gave her a great view of his backside so she wasn't going to complain . . . *this* time. The man certainly enjoyed snapping out orders at every opportunity. Her heart was still pounding from him sneaking up on her. No one had ever managed to get close to her without her knowledge, because the energy always reached her first. It was something she'd always taken for granted. She was beginning to realize she couldn't take anything for granted around Nicolas.

She did her best rendition of a lizard, scooting across the roof to the far side. Nicolas waited by the edge, drawing a rope from his pack. She touched his arm and shook her head, pointing to an inch-thick cable running between the two buildings. *Jesse has those placed around any safe houses or buildings we might use.*

His eyebrow shot up. *You think I'm going to use that to cross over?*

Baby. Dahlia took the lead, stepping with confidence onto the thin cable. She wished she weren't wearing boots. Light-soled shoes worked best for cable-walking, but there was little wind to push her around as she made her way across.

The cable stretched between the buildings, two stories off the ground. Nicolas watched, his heart in his throat, as her slight figure covered the distance. This was no slow, arms out for balance, circus walker. She moved with complete poise and assurance. He dared not touch her thoughts, afraid of distracting her, yet he desperately wanted to know what was happening in her brain to allow her such complete control. There was no way he was walking across that thin little cable. His stomach was in knots by the time she reached the other side.

Nicolas took a breath and let it out, relieving the terrible tension that had built up in him. Nothing either of his two grandfathers had taught him had prepared him for meeting Dahlia. He was grateful for the discipline and control of both mind and body. It had, at times, been rigorous, but it was his background and his military training that allowed him to be with Dahlia.

He slung his rifle around his neck, checked to make certain he could move freely without being seen, and slipped off the edge of the roof, going hand over hand to the other side. It was a long way. He was halfway when he felt the first stirring of an awareness of danger. Immediately he stopped moving and scanned the surrounding area. His visual of the street was somewhat impaired by two tall trees. He shifted slightly, moving with more caution.

Do you feel it? Dahlia's voice was a mere whisper in his head. The bridge between them was shaky. He felt more of a push of energy than anything else, almost as if she'd sent it his way to share the feeling of danger within it.

Drop back where you're safe from attack. The second the words left his mind he wished them back. She was not a woman to be idle when there was danger. She'd spent far too much time on her own, and she'd relied heavily on her own judgment. He had to find a way to curb his over-whelming protective instincts.

Dahlia clenched her teeth and didn't respond. In her life, very few people ever tried to give her orders. Even Whitney had given up after a few harrowing accidents. It wasn't just other people's emotions, it was her own she feared most. She had a fiery temper and all the Zen meditation in the world didn't seem to help her when someone tried to boss her around.

She watched as Nicolas made his way hand over hand across the distance, breathing a sigh of relief when he swung silently onto the roof. She dropped back to give him more room. He crawled over to her.

Something is different. The energy is very violent. It feels the same as when we were in the bayou.

Dahlia didn't look at him when she gave him the information, and he took that as a bad sign. She was definitely not happy with him assuming command. *I feel it too. My best guess is this: the team entering the house now has a military background and they're looking for you and Jesse. I believe they're NCIS. The team coming up behind them are the ones from the swamp and are most likely here to kill you. Do you agree?*

Dahlia watched him crawl to the side of the roof where the gutter ran the two stories to the ground. *Yes. And I think the second team is aware of the NCIS men and intends to kill them.*

I'd have to agree. Nicolas took a small metal object from his pack and began tapping a rhythm on the gutter. He repeated the rhythm over and over. Long and short, dots and dashes. A warning to the men sent out by the NCIS that they were in for a firefight. Morse code wasn't used much anymore, but many of those in the Navy had learned it. As he tapped out the warning, he sent a subtle "push" for the men to readily hear and recognize the age-old warning.

It was Dahlia who first felt the rising tension from within the house. *They know. They got your warning.* She didn't know if it was the level of malevolent energy finding her or the continual use of telepathy, but her body was beginning to react. She tried to hide it from Nicolas. He was slithering into position, sliding his weapon forward, fitting the butt of the rifle snugly into his shoulder, and putting his eye to the lens.

Listen to me. Don't get upset until you hear me out. His voice whispered in her mind. Touched her insides with danger all around them. She wanted to reach out and hang onto him to keep the energy at bay, but he needed complete concentration. *I want you to leave now. We can set up a rendezvous point. I'm going to have to kill someone. I can't leave the men in the house defenseless. Those stalking the NCIS team have mortars, and we know they aren't afraid to use them. Your people don't have that kind of firepower. There are civilians in the area. This could turn ugly very fast. If you go, I have only myself to worry about. I know you can make your way through their lines. If you stay, Dahlia, you're going to be too sick to walk out on your own.*

He was right, and she hated that he was right. *I'll go, but we can't go too far. We can backtrack these people or better yet, follow them back to Jesse. If you do have to kill them, don't kill all of them.* She tried to sound grown-up and calm about it. In her line of work, no one died. She went in under cover of darkness and played the same games she played as a child. No one was around to see what she did and no one ever got hurt. In the last few hours she'd seen more death and violence than she ever wished to see in a lifetime.

Nicolas wanted her clear, but not so far away from him that they might get separated. *Go to the church in Jackson Square. You can get to the roof. I'll meet you there. If something goes wrong, get to the NCIS. Don't try to find Jesse by yourself.*

Dahlia didn't reply. She sensed the movement of the men in the darkness and began to crawl backward, away from Nicolas. The farther she got from him, the more the energy began to mass around her. She felt the familiar signs. The hair on her body standing up. The churning in the pit of her stomach. The pounding in her temples. The last thing he needed was for her to pass out, or worse, have a seizure.

Silently reciting a calming mantra, Dahlia made her way to the other side of the building and slipped over the side. She knew they would never spot her, not unless it was entirely accidental. There were advantages to being small. She lay flat against the side of the wall as she climbed down, using finger and toeholds she found in the cracks. She was always patient, making the descent in silence and without haste. Movement caught the eyes, so most stealth was done with care and in slow motion.

She felt for the ground with her toe, connected and jumped, landing softly in the dirt beside the house. She remained there, crouched down, orienting herself to her position and the light patterns cast from the streetlights and windows of the surrounding buildings. She could no longer see any of the men near the "safe" house. Jesse had been wrong. Someone knew about it. He worked for the NCIS, and yet someone who shouldn't have had found the safe house. Who could have tipped them off? Someone from Jesse's office, or had they tortured the information out of him? The idea made her sick. She couldn't imagine Jesse telling anyone anything. He was always confident to the point of arrogance. And he was dedicated to his job and country. The idea of someone breaking Jesse's code of honor was abhorrent to her.

She slipped into the shadow of the building and edged around the corner, feeling for the energy that would tip her off to the fact that she wasn't alone. Energy was a double-edged sword. As it collected around her, she lost the ability to "feel" precisely where it was coming from. Energy poured from the house, masses of nerves and fear and the determination to live. The NCIS team inside the house had expected to find her alone and had gone in "soft," not looking for trouble. They knew now that they were surrounded and in for a firefight from an unknown enemy.

Nicolas was determined to even the odds. He lay on the roof, his sites steady on his first target. If they were going to wipe out the NCIS team, he was going to make certain they paid for it. For the first time, he was slightly distracted, part of him wanting to touch Dahlia and know she was safe. He was certain he would know if she ran into trouble. He steadied his finger and kept his eye firmly against the scope, hoping she was far enough away when he pulled the trigger.

DAHLIA went to her knees as the wave of violence swamped her. She clutched her stomach, fighting off dizziness. White spots danced in front of her eyes. She could feel her airway begin to close. She pushed herself up and staggered through the narrow pathway of bushes and garbage cans, holding on to branches as she gasped for breath. She tried to control the sound of her breathing. Sound traveled in the night, and even with the music that seemed to pour from various establishments a street or two over, she knew the kind of men hunting for her would be tuned to the slightest noise.

She had to cross an open street. There was no one in sight, and the violent energy was so strong it was impossible to tell if anyone was close to her. She had to chance crossing. It was imperative to get as far from the battleground as possible. She glanced around, one last cautious look, and started across the street, moving as quickly as she was able to on rubbery legs. Her vision blurred. The streets were uneven, cracked and pitted in places. She stumbled and hoped if anyone saw her they would assume she'd been drinking. She was three quarters to the other side when a man stepped out of the shadows and off the sidewalk. He was carrying a gun, and it was pointed right at her.

Dahlia felt the waves of malevolence pouring off of him but she kept walking, her gait stumbling and uneven, muttering to herself as if she didn't notice him. She doubted if anyone knew what she looked like. The French Quarter was packed most of the time, even in the early morning hours before dawn, and tourists drank all the time. She glanced up when she was only a few feet from him, feigned surprise, hoping she looked like a regular on her way home.

"Are you coming home from a costume party? Nice getup." She slurred her words and swayed drunkenly, inching closer to him, trying to get within striking distance.

Confusion hit her, a wall of it, as he tried to assess if she was a danger to him. She wore a black sweatshirt and boots, but her hair was flowing to her waist and she obviously was without a weapon. She was too small to be a physical threat. The man visibly relaxed. "What the hell are you looking at?"

She muttered something wordless, hoping to continue her impression of a drunk.

He reached out and caught her arm, pushing her toward the wall. "What are you doing out this late?" Holding her there, his hand gripped her breast hard through the material of her sweatshirt.

Dahlia calculated the odds of fighting him off while maintaining her drunken charade. He was hurting her with his squeezing. He suddenly laughed. She realized he believed all the fighting was taking place around the corner. He was bored and a little angry that he didn't get to participate, instead regulated to standing guard. He was tired of watching the action and had made up his mind to have a little of his own.

She waited until he lifted his head and exposed his throat. The moment he did, she hit him with the edge of her hand, putting her body weight behind it, at the same time trying to slide sideways, using the wall to help her get away from him. He was enormously strong, grunting and choking at the blow, but doggedly moved sideways with her, keeping her body pinned between his and the wall. He hit her hard in her stomach with his clenched fist, stepping back, still gagging, as she doubled over. He raised his gun, the butt end toward her face.

Dahlia knew immediately he was dead. Her mind and body went nearly numb. Inside of her head, right before the white-hot pain exploded through her body, she heard her own scream. The force of the bullet drove the man backward away from her, so that he crumbled like a rag doll and settled onto the sidewalk in a lifeless heap. His gun clattered to the walkway beside him. It seemed to happen in slow motion, her vision narrowing to the grim image of death.

Immediately she was swamped in the aftermath of the violence, her body taking the brunt of the destructive energy as it raced to claim her. She fought back, trying to stay conscious, trying to find a way out from the raw, swirling force threatening to take her over. The air crackled with electricity. She saw white arcs of it zigzagging above her head. It was only then that she realized she was on the ground, inches from the downed man.

Dahlia began to crawl, a grueling effort when her body felt like lead and pain roared through her at her movement. She inched her way along the walkway. The smell of urine and blood was overwhelming and added to the misery of her churning stomach. She was sick several times as she clawed her way down the block.

Nicolas came out of nowhere, his hands running over her body, probing for injuries. She knew it was him by the way he touched her, by the way the energy retreated to give her breathing room. She couldn't see through the dancing white spots and strange webbing that shrouded her vision, but she touched him to reassure him she was fine.

"Relax, honey," he ordered. "I'm taking you out of here."

She wasn't going to object. She just wanted to sleep for a long, long time.

Nicolas swung her over his shoulder, needing both hands free. Her stomach was tender, and she was definitely moving in and out of consciousness. He anchored her with one hand and took off away from the area. He'd warned the men inside and he'd taken out a couple of the enemy for them, before spotting Dahlia in trouble. She was his first priority, his only priority now. He had a few bolt-holes of his own. And damn it, his heart was still pounding with fear for her. He had one shot, one chance to save her, and she'd been so close to her assailant.

He moved into the shadows, sliding through the night. When he encountered a late-night crowd, or the street cleaners, he went up and over the building. Before he left on this mission, Gator had shoved maps into his pocket to houses in the bayou Gator's family owned, but rarely used. He used his powers unashamedly to keep people looking the other way as he took Dahlia out of the town.

He blamed himself for her pale, almost translucent face and the terrible toll the violence had taken on her body. He'd viewed the tapes from her childhood and teenage years. He knew what violence did to her, yet she seemed so self-assured, so confident, even "normal" as they moved through the Quarter to get to the condo, he'd managed to make himself believe she could take the continual assault of energy flowing around her.

Dahlia stirred, her fist clenching in the back of his shirt. "Put me down before I get sick down your back." Her insides hurt, more from the punch than vomiting, but she wasn't taking any chances with humiliating herself further.

Nicolas halted immediately and lowered her to the ground. They were near the river and the ground was uneven. He used it as an excuse to hold her when she was swaying slightly. "I'm sorry, Dahlia, I didn't have a choice."

"I know you didn't. I could have handled him if I hadn't been so sick. I just can't be around anyone, Nicolas." It had to be said. She didn't have to like it. For a while she'd held out hope she could find a way to live with people, maybe somewhere near Lily where she could visit occasionally and have a friend to share things with. She hadn't dared think of keeping Nicolas in her life. She couldn't be around him and not have fantasies.

Dahlia clung to him, his shirt bunched in her fingers. "I need to sit down. No one is chasing us, are they?" She didn't feel anyone hunting them, but she was on overload and just couldn't tell if they were in immediate danger.

Nicolas helped her walk to a bench. She sank down gratefully, putting her head between her knees to combat the dizziness and dragging in great gulps of air. "We have to go back." She looked up at him. "We do, Nicolas. This may be the only chance we have to track them back to where they're holding Jesse." She raised her gaze to his. "We have to get him out. Those men are killers. I don't want to think what he's been going through all this time."

Nicolas shook his head. "You aren't in any shape to go rescue anyone, Dahlia. For all we know, he could be dead."

"I have to know one way or the other. Please, Nicolas. I have to do this, and I don't think I can do it alone."

"Can you walk on your own?"

She listened for frustration. For impatience. She waited for the negative energy of his true feelings to swamp her, but he seemed as rock steady and as calm as ever. "Yes. I'm a little shaky, but I've been worse." She forced a wan smile. "It always helps to pass out."

"Let's get moving then. We don't have a lot of time to pick up their trail. It isn't like I can carry a rifle through the streets of the French Quarter either. We're both going to have to be fully alert."

She watched as he broke down the gun with quick and efficient movements. She knew he was giving her a few more minutes to rest. When he was finished and the gun was safely stored in his pack, he handed her the canteen.

"You're like a walking miracle. Prepared for anything, aren't you?"

"It takes skill and dedication. What about you?" He watched her repeatedly rinse her mouth and spit out the contents. Finally ridding herself of the bad taste she took a long drink, and he found himself mesmerized by the way her throat worked as she swallowed.

Dahlia handed him back the canteen and wiped her mouth with the back of her hand. "I'm a seat-of-the-pants kind of person."

"I don't think I entirely believe that," he said with a small smile. He reached down and pulled her to her feet, retaining possession of her hand. "We're just strolling through the Quarter, Dahlia. We have to avoid the condo if at all possible. With the firefight and a few men down, the police are going to be swarming around that area."

"And the NCIS. They'll send their people, and just about everyone else. My guess is they'll put out an OPREP-5 Navy Blue. That's an operational report, a high alert, to include

outside agencies such as the FBI that there's trouble."
Dahlia added. "Did everyone get out alive?"

He shrugged. "I have no idea. I did what I could and
then came after you."

Dahlia looked away from him. Everything had gone
wrong, and people were dying. She didn't engage in fire-
fights or assassinations. "I think I'm in the wrong business," she admitted as she walked beside him.

Nicolas set the pace, a casual stroll. He knew the importance of blending in, of becoming what people expected to
see. In the early morning hours just before dawn, street
cleaners, deliverymen, and police officers would be out.
With the shoot-out between military and unknown as-
sailants, the Quarter would be buzzing with more activity
and curious people than usual at such an hour. The French
Quarter was a small place, and word of the firefight would
spread fast. There would be so many rumors, no one would
be able to sort them out for weeks.

Dahlia concentrated on breathing in and out. She shut
out the fact that at any moment the police might stop them
and ask questions, or that a member of her own NCIS team
or the killers might spot them. She tried to look like a
woman out for a very early stroll with her lover. The idea
of Nicolas being her lover was almost more than she could
handle. He made her feel ultrafeminine, and no one in her
life had ever managed to make her feel that way. She didn't
think much about being a woman. What was the point,
when her body temperature was either too hot or too cold?
And what would happen if they did try to have sex? Just
kissing nearly caused the eruption of a volcano.

Soft laughter played down her spine, made her shiver
with awareness. Nicolas brought her knuckles briefly to the
warmth of his mouth. "You're thinking things best left alone."

"I know." She was unrepentant. "But if all I have in my
life is just thoughts, then I'm not going to waste the opportunity." She was still fighting to breathe, to shake off the trembling and feeling of sickness. She didn't want to talk, except
maybe to hear the sound of his voice. She wanted to walk the

streets of the French Quarter and just for that short time pretend she was normal. She wanted to have her dreams of the man walking beside her and not think about death and spies and men selling out their country for money. Mostly she didn't want to think about energy and the effects on her body. She needed a nice peaceful place to hibernate in for a while.

Nicolas glanced down at the top of Dahlia's bent head. He tightened his fingers around hers. She was withdrawing from her surroundings. He could feel the way she mentally pulled back, the way she went inside herself, behind the protective walls in her mind she'd built for herself.

Lily had been working with the GhostWalkers for some time to teach them ways to build barriers in their minds against the continual assault from everyday life. Until Lily had worked with the men Whitney had experimented on, they were all in various stages of dysfunction. Dahlia had managed to find a much more flimsy version of a barrier, but she'd done it on her own.

Nicolas never minded silences. At times he needed silence nearly as much as he needed solitude and to be outdoors surrounded by nature. Finding that Dahlia was very similar made him surprisingly happy and at peace, even in the midst of their situation. As they crossed the street, he could see the police cars up and down the block where the condo was. He leaned down. "Your enemies have someone watching all this. We need to spot him before he spots us."

He halted abruptly, almost as the words came out of his mouth, pressing her back into a small alcove, shielding her with his larger, heavier frame. Nicolas allowed his pack to rest on the ground, just out of sight of the street. He placed one palm against the wall, effectively caging her in, his body language blatant, possessive, deliberately easy to read. He bent down toward her, looking every inch her lover. "He's on the roof across the street, watching the cops. I don't see any military personnel, but I *feel* them. Someone is nosing around trying to figure out what happened. We could find them, identify ourselves, and get you somewhere safe."

Her face was pale. Small beads dampened her face around her hair. Her skin was hot to the touch. "I'd have to allow them to lock me up. I'm classified, and can't just blurt this out to anyone. I have to get Jesse out before I turn myself in."

"The NCIS have no idea what happened, Dahlia. They could very well be suspicious that you're somehow involved. You have the brains to be behind something like this, and you're different. Anything or anyone different is an easy target."

"You sound worried that they're going to try to kill me." His fingertips were moving over her face, just brushing back and forth as if he enjoyed the texture of her skin. Dahlia felt the touch all the way to her toes. Deep inside where heat collected and pooled in her most feminine core, she felt her body clench strongly in reaction.

"I just want to know if you want out now, Dahlia. I can go after Calhoun myself."

"While I'm nice and safe." She was looking out from under his arm, searching for the man on the roof. "I don't think so. This is my mess and I intend to clean it up. Don't be fooled just because I get a little sick around people and violence. I'm perfectly capable of taking care of myself."

He didn't point out that he shot a man to keep her alive. "Can you see him? The blond on the roof?"

"Yes, he's glanced this way a couple of times. He has a pair of binoculars."

"Then we'd better give him something to look at." He stepped closer, his body nearly touching hers, but not quite.

Dahlia instantly felt the temperature around them rise. "This is risky."

"Kissing you?" He cupped her chin firmly, captured her gaze with his.

"You can't kiss me, Nicolas." Her heart pounded so hard she was afraid it might burst. His face was so perfect to her, etched in granite, the hard lines and planes that of a man, not a boy.

He bent his head slowly toward hers, holding her gaze.

He stopped when his lips were a mere breath away. When she could taste him. When her heart went from pounding to fluttering and her body began sizzling with electricity. "I think kissing you is a very good idea."

She felt his words vibrate through her entire body. He didn't actually need to kiss her for her mind to go into meltdown. It happened just thinking about kissing him. "You have such a great mouth, Nicolas. Tempting, you know? But lightning happens when we kiss. We don't want to draw attention to ourselves do we?"

"Is that a trick question? If I say no, does that mean I don't get to kiss you? Because right now, kissing you seems the most important thing in the world."

She loved the way his magic voice roughened and his eyes went from ice to a blaze when he looked at her. "Well, then, who am I to tell you to have good sense?" The words came out in a whisper. She could barely breathe with him so close to her. How was it possible to form a rational thought?

He smiled. Right before he kissed her, he gave an arrogant, self-satisfied male smirk. And then she couldn't think anymore, not even to reprimand him. She was lost in the hot urgency of his mouth. They merged, fused together, burned up in each other's arms. And the strange thing was, only their mouths were touching. His body remained so close she felt the heat of it arcing through her, around her, but he was careful to keep their bodies apart. And it was the only thing that saved her from melting into a puddle at his feet.

She went weak in the knees and light in the head. The earth shifted and moved. Colors danced behind her eyes, and a strange purring was in her mind. She wanted to climb inside of him and take refuge, take shelter in the cool pools she saw in his mind. How he could be so cool inside and heat up her world so rapidly, she didn't know. And she didn't care. Only his mouth and the magic it made mattered.

CHAPTER

NINE

Nicolas lifted his head with more reluctance than self-control. He should never have initiated a kiss with her on the street. His body reacted immediately with urgent demands. Worse, his head seemed to be spinning along with his surroundings. He dropped a brief, hard kiss on her upturned mouth and turned his head slightly to get a view of the watcher on the rooftop across the street from them.

"I think my vision's blurred," he murmured.

She responded with a hesitant laugh. "If that's all that happened, you're a heck of a better kisser than I am. I can't stand up."

"I'm afraid to touch you. We might both go up in flames."

She sighed. "The story of my life. What's our friend doing?"

"He's climbing off the roof. People will be all over the streets soon. He can't afford to get caught up there. He would have done better to be on a balcony watching like everyone else is."

"If you ever decide to get out of the business, you might want to write a manual." She couldn't take her gaze from his face, not even to look at the man they needed to follow. She felt mesmerized by Nicolas. The pad of his thumb was caressing her chin, stroking back and forth in a small rhythmic movement that both fascinated her and sent a shiver down her spine. "Have you ever been anyone's obsession?"

The faintest trace of a grin softened his mouth. "Only those who want to kill me."

"Are there many?"

"Not alive." He shifted and scooped up his pack. "I don't like people trying to kill me, obsessed or not. I have a rule about that. Come on." He took her arm. "He's on the move. Just walk with me, flirt a bit and hold my hand. We'll catch an early cup of coffee."

"You want me to blend." She sighed and tossed back her abundance of hair. "I've never been much of a blender. I prefer the dark corners myself."

"I don't want him to get a look at you."

"They don't know me. I was trained under another name. Even if they manage to find that information, it won't do them any good."

He glanced down at her. "The name you trained under was Novelty White. Which of course translates to Dahlia Le Blanc. Not very clever."

She shrugged. "It wasn't my idea. How would you like to be called Novelty?" She wrinkled her nose in disgust. "I was a teenager, for heaven's sake."

"You have a point. I would have thought you would strenuously object."

"At the time, I gave very little input. I was going through my silent stage." She glanced at him with a small smile. "You know the 'I'm the superior teen and you're just lint' stage. Mostly I wanted to defy and irritate Whitney. I took great pleasure in making him angry. Did he really get rid of everyone but Lily? Because if Lily is real, so are the others."

"Do you remember them? The other girls?"

"Some of them. Most are vague, but there are a couple of the others like Lily I remember. Flame. She had another name, but I'm not certain I remember it."

"Iris," he supplied. "Whitney really hated anyone calling her Flame."

"Whitney hated us all, period. We didn't do what he wanted, when he wanted. He needed robots, not children."

"Well, if it's any consolation, Dahlia, he didn't do much better when he recruited us. We were a failure to him as well. All military trained. Good backgrounds. Strong and disciplined, yet we didn't fare much better than all of the little girls he gave away."

"Poor Lily. It must have been such a blow to her finding out the truth about him. I remember her as being gentle and kind. She was smart, really smart. I remember sitting up with her at night talking about planets and the Earth's rotation, but it may just have been a dream, after all, we couldn't have been more than four or five. If I ever snuck out of my room and Whitney caught me, I was punished."

"How?" Nicolas was intrigued with the conversation, but his attention remained on the man they were shadowing along the street. "How did he punish you?"

Dahlia looked up at his face. She had told him more about herself in the small space of time they'd known one another than she'd ever told anyone. She wondered if he really had cast a spell. How else could she explain the way she felt and acted around him?

He tilted his head and raised an inquiring eyebrow.

There was no point in fighting it. She was going to tell him. "I had this old ratty blanket. I used to pretend my mother made it for me and that she sent it with me when she gave me up. More than likely he bought it along with purchasing me, but still, it was a fantasy that helped me keep calm on the days I thought I'd go mad and my head would explode."

"You kept it, didn't you?"

Her gaze shifted from his. "Sure. It was one of the few things I had of my past. It's not like I had grandparents and uncles and aunts. I treasured the small things." She pushed her free hand through her hair. "I try not to think about them too much—Milly or Bernadette or my home, or my things. If I do, this terrible sorrow and rage wells up and mixes together until I know I'm dangerous." She glanced at him. "It's probably a good thing I met you. I'd be accidentally starting fires all over the place."

"I saved the blanket for you." He wanted to gather her into his arms when she talked about her past. Hold her against him where he knew he could keep her safe and shelter her from the pain of not having the most simple of necessities . . . a family. What had Whitney been thinking, sending the little girls into the world with no one to protect them? He'd given them money and thought that would be enough.

She looked up at him from under long lashes. "You're angry."

"I'm sorry. Are you feeling it?" She was pressing her hand to her stomach. It was the third time she'd done it, almost without thought.

"No, your energy level is very low. I'm getting to know you better. You do this thing with your eyebrows."

"I do not. I worked at learning how to keep my face perfectly without expression."

"It is," she assured, "all except the eyebrow."

His hand tightened around hers, and he drew her fingers to his hip, holding her hand there as they boarded the ferry to take them across the river to Algiers. Nicolas kept her a good distance from their quarry, keeping the early morning crowd between them for a screen and making his body language shout possession and jealousy. Few men were going to approach them when he was keeping Dahlia so close to him.

"Thanks for saving the blanket. It means a lot to me." She felt absolutely silly admitting it. A raggedy blanket from her childhood. Her only memento of her fantasy mother. It was a pathetic thing to have to admit to him . . . to herself.

His fingers brushed her face in a gentle caress. "I managed to snag a few of your books and a sweater as well. I wish I could have gotten more for you."

"I didn't have all that much that mattered, Nicolas. Better that you got out alive." She peeked under his arm. The wind was cool coming off the water in the early morning hours. Dahlia lifted her face to feel the breeze. "He's coming this way."

"Is he looking at us?" Nicolas sounded calm, almost bored. He shifted his body slightly to better protect her.

"No, at the water. But he's coming right toward us."

Nicolas concentrated on connecting with the man as he approached the railing of the ferry. He wanted to get a feel for him, to "read" him in the way of the GhostWalkers. Sometimes it was easy to read thoughts if they carried a strong enough emotion, but oftentimes, it was very difficult to find the right path for one person in a crowd. Most of the time he caught a jumble of impressions, rather than clear thoughts, when there were many people around.

Nicolas caught Dahlia's arm and forcibly turned her around to look out over the river, shifting his body from her left side to her right. *Stay calm, Dahlia. The man we're looking for is on your right side, just a few feet from us.*

What do you mean? He'd set her heart pounding again. She was getting tired of pounding hearts. She was really getting tired of being in the vicinity of so many people. Even with Nicolas touching her, she was on the receiving end of strong energy.

The man in the blue shirt must have been hired to watch the building, probably for a woman somewhere in the crowd. He's reporting to the man in the dark shirt.

Dahlia didn't turn her head, but continued to stare out over the water. Small whitecaps foamed on the river. A barge slid past them. Her stomach lurched and her fingers dug into Nicolas's arm. "He's going to kill him." She said the words so softly it was impossible to hear, yet she knew immediately that Nicolas was aware of it as well.

Dahlia was already on overload from the earlier violence.

Another wave of it might bring on a seizure. Nicolas forced a laugh and swept her up in his arms. Two tourists having fun on their vacation. She settled her arms around his neck and buried her face against his throat as he swung her around and carried her to the other side of the ferry. "You are *not* going to get sick, Dahlia." He made it a command.

There was a small silence, and he felt her lashes flutter against his skin. "I'm not? Why is that?"

In spite of the gathering force already battering at her defenses, there was the smallest note of amusement in her voice. He could feel the way her skin heated as if she were burning from the inside out. A fierce need to protect her welled up in him. It was so strong it shook him. "Hang in there, Dahlia, we'll get you through this. And you're not going to get sick because I told you not to."

He felt the brush of her lips against his throat. His insides did some sort of curious melting thing that annoyed the hell out of him. Why was it she turned him inside out? He lived his life able to walk away from anything or anyone, yet he knew his life was tangled up with hers and he'd never be able to extract himself. At the touch of her mouth on his bare skin, his groin tightened. It would have been so much easier if it was just the explosive chemistry between them, but he knew it was far more. He wanted to carry her off, just keep going. He could take her into his beloved mountains and no one would ever find them. Not even the other GhostWalkers. He could keep her safe there and away from the things that were so hard on her body and mind.

Dahlia leaned into him, pulled his head down to press her mouth against his ear. "Your energy level is coming up, and it isn't sexual. You're allowing yourself to be upset over me. This is who and what I am, Nicolas. If you're going to spend any time at all with me, you have to accept it." She pulled back to look up at him, her dark eyes very serious. "I want you to really know what it's like being with me. I'm never going to be the type of woman you go out to dinner with or sit in a theatre with. I don't have that kind of control. Think about what life would really be like with me, not some fantasy that is so far from reality it would never last more than a day or two."

"My fantasy is to have you to myself, not in a restaurant or a movie theatre. I'd like you to myself. I'm not someone who needs a lot of people around me, Dahlia."

She felt the burst of violence blossoming over her, through her. She took a tighter grip on Nicolas, pressing herself into him, the only sanctuary left to her against the aftermath of a killing. The breath left her lungs in a rush. She closed her eyes, knowing the body was in the water and no one had seen it go in. The man in the blue shirt had been stabbed and shoved overboard, but he wasn't dead as the water slipped over his head and took him below where no one could see his last struggles for life. But she could *feel* it. And she could feel his last energy rising up to scream for acknowledgment and justice.

Her throat swelled, closed, so that she was gasping for air. The violent energy slammed into her body hard, driving her to her knees in spite of Nicolas's grip on her. She couldn't see, couldn't think, the pressure building in her head, in her brain.

Nicolas pulled her to his chest, and she was helpless to stop him. Helpless to warn him that she had to get rid of the energy or the seizures would start, Dahlia stared at the water in desperation. Too many emotions churned in her stomach, adding to the terrible washing of energy over her.

"Look at me, Dahlia."

"No!" She hissed the word at him, clenching her teeth, fighting off the need to claw and scream. Her body was on fire, burning from the inside out.

Nicolas's fingers bit into her arms. He gave her a small shake. "Share it with me. He's a pro, Dahlia. He killed with everyone around and no one saw it," Nicolas said grimly. "If fireballs start hitting the deck or you start vomiting, he's going to notice."

She swore, doubling over with the pain. Sweat broke

out. She *detested* Nicolas in that moment. Seeing her so vulnerable, always at her worst. Damn the man for insisting on coming with her, and damn him for witnessing her breakdown. If she seized in front of him she would never be able to look at him again. Desperately she tilted her head, not an easy thing to do when every movement sent knives stabbing through her skull. Her eyes met his.

Nicolas bent his dark head until his mouth was inches from hers. "Share with me, Dahlia. Let it out."

He terrified her with his courage. He had no idea what could happen and neither did she. She opened her mouth to protest, to warn him, but it was too late. His lips met hers. An arc of electricity sizzled between them, zapped through her body to his. Heat poured through her to him. She gasped, her fingers digging into his chest. The temperature soared between them. Dahlia made a small sound of protest, of fear, but his hand skimmed over her breast and circled her throat. She heard him groan, the sound husky and very male. The energy immediately became charged with sexual tension, heightening her every awareness, her every sense.

Nicolas pressed his body against hers, his arms, steel bands. His hands lifted her, pressed his raging erection tightly against her feminine mound. "Wrap your legs around my waist, damn it," he ordered desperately. He wanted to tear the thin cotton pants from her body and the jeans from his. He needed them to be skin to skin. He wanted the satisfaction of driving into her hard and deep, pounding flesh against flesh. . . .

"Stop!" Dahlia pressed her hand to his mouth. "Nicolas, stop."

He heard the sob in her voice. It shook him enough to push past the red haze of sexual need. Nicolas fought down the terrible hunger tearing at his gut, pounding in his head, and roaring through his body. The force of the energy shook him as it enveloped him with the same greed it used on Dahlia. Slowly he allowed her legs to drop to the ferry. He took a deep calming breath, rested his forehead against hers, and breathed with her. His body was as hard as a rock, so painful, he was certain his skin might split open. And the heat was unlike anything he'd ever experienced. The most frightening thing of all was the desire to throw her to the deck and tear the clothes from her body. For a single heart-beat, everything in him, mind, body, and soul, urged him to do just that. He shook with the need to possess her.

"It's the energy," she whispered. Dahlia was fully aware of the danger she was in. She could read Nicolas's eyes, blazing with heat and hunger. He was half-mad with it.

"I know that," he snapped. Immediately he regretted his reaction. The idea was to ease the energy level for her, not make it worse. She didn't react to sexual energy in the same way as she did to violence, but he hadn't counted on the two energies mixing until he had to fight himself just to maintain control. "Are you feeling any better?"

Dahlia nodded. "Yes, I'm not so sick. I'm sorry, Nico-las." She wanted to get away from him. Away from herself. It was one of the worst moments she had ever endured. Nicolas Trevane was a man of honor, yet she had shown him a monstrous part of himself no man should ever have to face.

Nicolas allowed the energy to slowly disperse, as its natural form required. He breathed it away, willed it away, accepted the wash of heat and let it go. Cautiously he looked around. They were in a secluded corner, but anyone close couldn't have failed to feel the heightened sexual en-ergy flowing around them. "Dahlia, maybe this isn't such a good idea. He isn't going to be easy to follow." He had no idea what to say to her, how to apologize. He shoved at his hair with an unsteady hand.

"You mean with me along."

"He knows the territory and we don't."

"I know most everywhere around here. I don't sleep much at night so I wander around. It's safer than in the daytime. I can avoid the heavily populated areas but still feel as if I'm part of the human race." Why was she telling him these things? Dahlia couldn't believe she was telling him every little detail of her life. She sounded pathetic, even to her own ears. Worse, each time she revealed a piece of information, she felt his inner struggle not to react to it. "I can guide us sufficiently and maybe even take a reasonable guess at his destination."

"I'm tall and you're short. He'll have noticed everyone on this ferry. I've tried using a 'push' on him to look the other way, but he isn't susceptible. He wouldn't have missed our fireworks just now. We can't be seen following him."

"I'm very good at not being seen." Dahlia wanted to drift into unconsciousness, to slip away from the battering she had taken from the violent swirl of energy. It was a normal reaction, much like after having a seizure. Her body and brain needed to shut down for a while. She blinked rapidly to keep from closing her eyes and fought to stay on her feet. Her insides hurt from the punch she'd taken. Her internal organs felt swollen and bruised, and her mind felt battered by the continual assault of energy coming from being in close proximity with so many people along with the violence of murder.

"It may be the best thing if I dropped you at a hotel," he persisted.

She hung onto her temper by a thread. This was her problem, not his. "You can go to a hotel," she counteroffered. She felt humiliated and frustrated, and more than anything she wanted to be alone, but she wasn't going to have him take over her job. And there was that secret fear of him now. Fear of his enormous strength and what he could do to her if he lost control. She hated herself for that.

Nicolas sensed her rising temper. The aftermath of the energy was preying on both of them. "I need to call Lily and see if she has any information for us," he said mildly. "The cell phone doesn't like this area much, but a little ways out and I might be able to get her."

Dahlia gripped his shirt with both fists. As long as she maintained the physical contact with him, the energy didn't overwhelm her completely. It was another source of irritation to her. She didn't want to have to hang on to him like a clinging vine. "Cell phones have a way of disliking the bayou and the river. It must be a water thing."

"But what about when you weren't in the bayou? Surely Calhoun gave you a cell phone to keep in touch when you were in town."

"I melted two of them. He decided it wasn't worth it."

He looked down at her to see if she was teasing him. Her gaze was all too serious. "You melted them?"

She nodded. "I melt things. Accidentally."

Nicolas wasn't touching that. Considering all the melting going on inside of him any time he was close to her he could believe she'd melted a couple of phones. After all, they were much smaller than he was. His breath chuffed out and he took her hand, deciding to try to defuse the situation. "Try not to melt any body parts."

They lagged behind the crowd as people began to disembark. Nicolas kept his eye on his quarry. "Look how he moves, Dahlia. He's probably ex-military, most likely a mercenary. I'll bet he's good in a fight. Watch his eyes. Nothing gets by him, he sees everything. He just murdered a man, yet he's not even in a hurry."

Nicolas didn't want to draw attention by lingering too long away from the group, yet it was important to keep Dahlia protected from prolonged exposure to so many people. He timed their exit by watching the man in the dark shirt step to one side and light a cigarette. Clearly he was waiting for the crowd to get in front of him. Nicolas kept Dahlia to the far side, shielding her with his body as they sauntered past.

His energy is very malevolent.

Don't get sick or I'll start asking you if the baby is all right in front of him.

Dahlia nearly choked. She kept her head down and one hand pressed tightly against her stomach where she'd taken the punch. Every step hurt. Longingly she glanced at the water. She would love to be back on her little island, surrounded by her books.

Nicolas tightened his fingers around Dahlia and pulled her closer to the shelter of his body. He walked past their quarry without even glancing at him, leaning down to murmur some nonsense into Dahlia's ear to make it appear they were completely absorbed in one another as well as to further shield her body from sight.

And he wished they were really completely absorbed in one another. He'd never had anything or anyone shake his calm, rational world the way Dahlia did. He'd built his entire life on the principals his grandfathers had taught him. He thought he was prepared for everything. He *had* been prepared for everything—until Dahlia. He could barely keep his mind on saving their lives or tracking his quarry. As they walked in the general direction of the popular restaurant located on the bluff overlooking the river, he struggled to make sense of the havoc Dahlia wrought on him.

Dahlia was a firestorm to his ice. Where he was cool and calm, she was fiery and seemed out of control, battered by the very energy of every living thing. Where did she fit into the universe? How did someone like Dahlia survive in a place so hostile to her nature? And why was it so damned necessary to him that she survive in a place *with* him?

He could accept the physical attraction, even though the intensity might be disastrous. He could even accept his deep need to protect her. He was always the one that looked out for his men, and he took the role seriously. That was part of his character and he was well aware of it. But to find himself obsessed—and that was a good word for it— was uncomfortable. He was trying to keep them both alive, and all he could think about was Dahlia. The sound of her voice. The way her smile flashed at him unexpectedly. It was unnerving how much he thought about her.

"Don't think about it too much, Nicolas," Dahlia advised in a low voice.

"About what?" He kept his voice even with an effort. She said she wasn't telepathic on her own and didn't read minds. He didn't want her reading his confusion. Until he knew the answers, he wasn't willing to share the questions.

"Whatever it is you're thinking about. It isn't worth getting more upset over."

"People have upsetting thoughts, Dahlia."

"I know. Believe it or not, I'm a person, and I actually do think about things. I even have regular emotions. I once saw a man kick a dog, and I got so upset three houses behind him caught fire. I was nine years old." She glanced up at him, checking to see how he took it. Telling him something important. Something they both had to know. "Can you imagine if I ever got into an argument with my husband? He's silly enough to disagree with me over the amount of milk that goes into tea or some other inconsequential thing. Poof. He goes up in smoke."

When he looked down at her, she was already looking beyond him to the river. "What happens when you feel pain?"

"From the overload?"

"No, just regular pain. You stub your toe. You get a cold. You get punched by some man in the street because I'm too slow on the trigger." There was a hiss of anger in his voice. It came out of nowhere, that slow smoldering burn that seared his belly and flared with a dark heat that threatened to consume him. His palm slipped over her stomach and lay there gently. The touch was meant to be impersonal, to soothe her. To take away the pain. It turned into something altogether different. Not sexual, but intimate. And her skin burned through the thick material of the dark sweatshirt. Or maybe it was his skin. He shouldn't have been able to feel her, yet he did.

She closed her eyes against the emotions swamping her. Or maybe it was energy, she honestly couldn't tell anymore. She wanted to run away from him. Away from everyone. Her head pounded and her skin itched and felt too tight for her body.

"Don't try to run out on me, Dahlia," Nicolas cautioned, reading her easily. His voice roughened, sounded edgy. "You're so busy trying to keep an emotional distance you're forgetting what we're doing here." He pulled her from in front of the window where her face could be reflected and drew her around the side of the building, pushing her back into the heavy shrubbery.

Her black eyes blazed at him. "Of the two of us, you're far more afraid of emotional commitment than I am. I may have limits, but at least I put myself out there. You're so busy taking care that nothing disturbs your perfect tranquility that you've forgotten to live your life."

The air fairly crackled with electricity. Nicolas could feel the rising energy beginning to surround them. It fueled the raw emotion building inside of him. He also glimpsed their quarry walking along the street toward a small blue Ford that was parked a block up from them. The man seemed to be in no particular hurry, almost sauntering as if he hadn't a care in the world.

He glanced around, saw a taxi parked close to a restaurant. Certain the cab was waiting for customers, Nicolas had a twenty-dollar bill in his hand when he signaled. He kept a firm grip on the nape of Dahlia's neck, keeping them connected. He told himself it was because he needed to stay close to her to keep the energy at bay, but the truth refused to stay in the back of his mind. *He* was the one that needed the connection. They were at odds, and he needed the reassurance of physical contact.

"You're dragging me." Dahlia pointed it out with a little bite in her voice.

Nicolas actually snapped his teeth together, inwardly swearing. It was insane the way he was always so off balance around her. Insane, and damned uncomfortable. The worst of it was, she could walk away from him. She might not like it, and she might even fantasize over him now and then, but she could do it. And she was the emotional, fiery one. He couldn't walk away. He had no idea how it happened, how she had managed to crawl inside of his lungs until he couldn't breathe properly without her.

"Get in the cab." He made it an order knowing she hated orders.

He didn't know how it happened. He had been perfectly

fine without her for years. He'd never given much thought to finding a woman to share his life. He lived a life of solitude, going where he wanted, not tied to anything emotionally or physically, and it was his preference. Until he found himself in Louisiana with a woman who could shake him up with one look.

Dahlia slid onto the backseat of the cab. The pressure welling up in her chest was amazing. Anger was hot and furious. Just like the intensity of the passion she shared with Nicolas. She dragged air into her lungs. They fed off each other. There was no other explanation. When she touched Nicolas, he cleared outside energy away from her. When they formed the arc of energy between them, they built the strength and passion of it together, one feeding the other's intensity.

She cleared her throat as Nicolas folded his much larger frame into the backseat beside her. She waited until he gave the driver instructions before sliding her hand into his. She waited to see if he'd pull away from her. The waves of anger were still rolling off of him, but his fingers tightened around hers.

"We're amplifying each other's emotions." She said it in a low voice. Starkly, without embellishment, staring out the window while she did so.

Nicolas closed his eyes briefly. She was right, and he'd known it all along. The knowledge that he'd been aware of it on some level, yet allowed his emotions to be amplified anyway bothered him almost as much as his need to be with her. What did he really know about her, after all? He looked down at her. She was everything he'd ever wanted, he just hadn't known it. What the hell was he going to do about it? He rubbed his thumb along her fingers in a small gesture meant to soothe.

Breathe with me. He needed her to draw him back from the edge of some precipice he didn't fully understand. Whatever anger had swirled in him so stark and raw and ugly had turned just as fast to a fierce, driving need to merge with her. To drag her as close to him as he was to her.

He wanted her to need him on the same stark elemental level. It was difficult for him to have to admit he wasn't as in control of his thoughts and feelings or even his world as he had always believed.

Dahlia felt the change in the energy as they both began meditative breathing. Rhythmic, controlled, deep. She felt the dark anger evaporate, released with the air moving in and out of her lungs. Out of his lungs. A flash of excitement sent a fresh wave of energy spilling around them. She tried to breathe through that as well.

What is it?

You felt that? Dahlia watched him nod. *We're getting more in tune with one another. I feel the slightest change in your mood and now you're able to do the same with me. You never felt energy like that before, did you?*

Nicolas took his time thinking it over. He could catch thoughts at times. He could definitely sense emotions. If he had ever "felt" energy, it was prior to a physical attack on him. Perhaps black anger in a very aggressive person. Was he gaining strengths? He didn't know if he wanted the same curse as Dahlia had been gifted with.

It's just that we actually controlled the energy together, Nicolas. The excitement radiated out of her. *Maybe our first try wasn't that successful, but this really worked. I've never really controlled it. I've managed it. Kept it under wraps until I could find a place to get rid of it, but we actually breathed together and I found the tranquil little lake in your mind and the energy just floated away.* Dahlia couldn't begin to tell him what a breakthrough it was. She'd tried for years to do meditation and chanting practices and nothing had ever worked. The meditation had helped to ease the burden, but she had never managed to just allow the energy to dissipate. With Nicolas, she had finally accomplished it. It seemed a miracle to her.

I've noticed your ability to use telepathy has grown stronger. I don't need to hold the bridge entirely by myself. You're meeting me halfway.

Dahlia blinked. *I am? That doesn't make sense. I have no*

telepathic ability. I never have. I can send my thoughts if the other person is a strong telepath and they do all the work.

I'm not doing all the work. Nicolas put his arm around her. She'd gone from angry to happy to alarmed in the space of a few minutes.

What does that mean? Dahlia didn't want to be telepathic. She had enough to handle with the "gifts" she had.

"Pull over," Nicolas said suddenly, startling her. "Right here, let us out."

Dahlia looked out the window and saw they were well out of town, just over a bridge near the water. The cabbie parked under a small grove of trees. Nicolas handed him several bills before getting out of the car. He was careful to retain possession of her hand and to keep the taxi between them and any observers. Almost immediately he drew her into the sanctuary of the grove of trees. They watched the cab drive off.

"Where is he?" Dahlia hadn't seen either the blue Ford or its driver.

"On the other side of the bridge. He pulled onto a dirt road and got out of the car. He was walking up the road."

"That's not good. There's no cover."

"I didn't expect them to make it easy. They'd want an out-of-the-way place they could use to get information out of anyone they bring there, and one easily defended. With no ground cover along the road they can see anyone approaching."

Dahlia sank down gratefully onto the ground and drew off the sweatshirt. It was already hot, and the tank top she'd worn beneath was clinging to her skin. "I guess we wait here all day?" She braided her hair and tied it into an intricate knot to get it off of her neck. Her body desperately needed sleep, and it would allow her not to dwell on what had flared between them on the ferry.

"I'm going to scout the area closer to the road and make sure I'm right, but yes, we can rest here." He lowered his pack to the ground beside her. "At least you're outside and away from people."

Dahlia bunched up the sweatshirt and curled up on the ground, her head pillowed on the thick material. "I'm going to sleep while you go do whatever it is you do. I'm exhausted."

She looked vulnerable lying on the ground. His stomach tightened into a knot. Nicolas hunkered down beside her, handing her the canteen. "I won't be long, Dahlia." He pushed stray tendrils of hair from her face.

She gave him a faint smile. "Take all the time you need. I intend to sleep. I require a lot of sleep in highly traumatic situations. This would be one."

He continued rubbing strands of her hair through his fingertips. "I thought you had a difficult time sleeping."

"I said I require sleep. It isn't exactly the same thing."

"Are you going to worry about me?"

"Absolutely not. You're a grown man."

He laughed. "You have a little mean streak in you."

She looked smug. "It's what makes me so appealing."

He started to rise. Dahlia caught his arm. "Did you bring that raggedy blanket with you?"

Nicolas could feel the sudden tension rising between them. She did her best to look nonchalant, as if it didn't matter in the least, but he swore he could hear her heart pounding. Her gaze shifted away from his and her hand dropped away.

"I've got it." His voice was gruffer than he intended. He found the piece of cloth with its tattered edges pushed down inside his pack. He extended the scrap of material.

Dahlia half sat to take the blanket from him. She reached for it slowly, her fingers curling around it almost reverently. He watched the way she stroked it, like a child might, almost as if she didn't know what she was doing, or as if the gesture were automatic. Her fingertips brushed the edges, a small caress. She smiled up at him. A genuine smile, but there were tears in her eyes. "Thank you, Nicolas." Her voice sounded strangled.

Everything in him wanted to gather her into his arms. "You're welcome Dahlia." He turned away from her because he had to. Because his feelings overwhelmed them both. Because she would think it was pity, and she'd hate him for it. Because she was eating him up inside. Watching her take comfort in a silly piece of cloth, as if the damned thing represented her family, her past. . . . And it did. He cursed Peter Whitney as he walked away from her.

Nicolas wanted to be her comforter, not some scrap of material that should have been tossed out years earlier. Not once in his life had he ever thought he was in over his head. Not as a boy in mountains when his grandfather had vanished, leaving him to find his way home. Not in the dojo during training when he was "attacked" by several grown men with much higher rank, not during his Special Forces training or the first time he was dropped into a jungle alone on a mission. But he did now. He had no idea how to bind Dahlia to him.

As a child he'd grown up without a mother or even a grandmother. He had never really explored emotional relationships or marriage. He'd never been given advice on the matter. The closest he'd really come to seeing a relationship was watching Ryland Miller pursue Lily. The man had lost his mind. Nicolas had a feeling he'd joined the ranks of men losing their minds over women.

Nicolas shook his head as he moved along the edge of the river, keeping to heavy brush. He needed a good position to study the terrain they'd be crossing that evening. He also wanted to get some numbers on the force they'd be facing. It was possible Calhoun was already dead and they were putting their lives in jeopardy for nothing. He was on a reconnaissance mission, and it was familiar to him. He could lose himself in the work and not think about the violence of his emotions when he dragged Dahlia's body to his. Not think about the heat and the need and the aching hunger. He groaned and closed his eyes, shaking his head, drawing on his inner strength to push her out of his mind. He achieved a measure of calm, but had to acknowledge she was with him, somewhere twisted around his heart and entwined deep inside him where he never was going to get her out.

Nicolas cut branches from a plant that grew in abundance along the river. He fashioned a covering for himself, taking his time, weaving it into a fair replica of the bushes he would be moving through. He had all day, and he was a patient man. He simply became the plant, moving in slow motion across the reed-choked bank so sluggishly it was impossible to detect him. He lay right out in the open, on his belly, stretched out among the plants and bushes, crawling his way up the river until he had the old dilapidated house in sight.

Nicolas found a perfect spot, lying in mud on the edge of the river, water lapping at his stomach, reeds and bushes climbing around him, and a good view of his quarry. Throughout the day there was little activity at the house. He counted three guards. One was sleepy in the sun, uncomfortable in the heat and humidity, identifying himself as no native of Louisiana. Another paced continually, repetitiously choosing the exact same route as he chain-smoked. The third man took his job seriously. He ignored all exchanges between the other two guards and studiously lifted his glasses to his eyes, sweeping the river, the road, and all surrounding areas of the house with meticulous care. None of the three were the same man who had been on the ferry. That meant at least four were guarding Calhoun, if he were in the house.

CHAPTER

TEN

Nicolas returned to Dahlia well after the sun went down. She sat beneath the trees, looking like a beautiful porcelain doll. Her skin was flawless, so perfect she seemed to glow. There were a few twigs and leaves in her hair, but instead of detracting from the beautiful picture she made, her disheveled hair made him think of wild nights and hot sex. A white sheet with small lilacs strewn across it was spread on the ground. Two paper plates held cold fried chicken and beans and rice. "You're sunburned," she greeted, smiling up at him.

"You've been busy," he observed. He wasn't certain he liked the idea that she'd been out shopping while the enemy was in the same area, but he kept his opinions to himself.

"I thought you'd be hungry and thirsty after lying in the sun all day."

He was already drinking. The water cooled his throat as it went down. He was parched. He'd left the canteen with Dahlia and, although the river kept him reasonably cool, he was dehydrated. "You were right." He felt hot and muddy and a mess.

"If you want to wash up, I discovered a little potting shed just on the other side of the grove, and it actually has a sink and running water." Dahlia jumped up. "Come on, I'll show you."

"I'll find it." Looking at her hurt. He could clearly see he was beyond all help when it came to Dahlia Le Blanc. He caught up his pack and took off in the direction she'd pointed. Even his lungs didn't work right around her. Somewhere along the line they seemed to have reversed roles. He'd always been the calm, in control of his feelings type, and Dahlia had been the opposite. Now, he swore she'd done something to change all that. He'd gone off into the field and everything had worked exactly as it was supposed to, but then he'd come back, taken one look at her, and everything went berserk in him. It wasn't a comfortable feeling looking at her and not knowing what to do. It was her eyes that haunted him.

Deep in the depths of her eyes, when he met her gaze, he caught a glimpse of scars, terrible wounds that had never quite healed, but were still raw and painful and hidden from the rest of the world. But he saw those wounds when no one else could, and he knew he was born for her. He was born to heal her. He had been told, assured over and over, that he had the talent buried within him, yet when he looked at her, when he touched her, there was no lessening of her pain from her past. If anything, he seemed to add to that silent burden.

Nicolas found the small shed behind another, larger workshop. He stripped off his filthy shirt but didn't bother changing his trousers. He and Dahlia would be in the water part of the time and he didn't want all of his clothes wet. He washed up carefully, even rinsing his hair. For the first time it mattered to him what he looked like to someone.

She wore the same determined smile as before when he returned. "Come and eat, Nicolas. You can't go after Jesse until it's dark so you may as well take a short nap."

Dahlia waited for him to settle onto the sheet she'd "borrowed" from a clothesline. He looked so good she was afraid she might blurt out something all too revealing, so she kept quiet and just watched him as he devoured the chicken and rice and beans she'd acquired from a small deli a few miles up the road. It had been a hike, and she'd had to be in a small crowd while she sorted out what Nicolas might want to eat, but it was well worth it when he was so obviously enjoying the meal. She felt proud of herself and maybe even a little bit wifely, which was really silly and annoyed the hell out of her. But she couldn't stop smiling like a goofball. The sleep had done her good, and she felt much better and able to cope once again. She was ashamed of her anger earlier and hoped her gesture made up for it.

"I didn't see any sign of Calhoun," Nicolas admitted as he mopped the last of the beans off the plate. "But they had the place heavily guarded, and they wouldn't need to do that if he were dead or if they were holding him somewhere else. I think we have a good chance of finding him alive, Dahlia."

"Do you think any of those men are like us? Ghost-Walkers?" She used his definition deliberately to try it on. To see if it fit her. To be part of something when she had nothing. "Because Jesse is telepathic. I can't reach him, but maybe you can."

Nicolas had thought of attempting to reach out many times during the long hours of lying in the sun trying to see into the house. He was wary of a trap. He was certain Jesse Calhoun's kidnappers had wanted Dahlia to follow them. It had just been too easy. They were expecting her to try to rescue her handler. Nicolas couldn't imagine the man taking the kind of abuse and torture he'd witnessed just to set the stage. He doubted if Calhoun was in on whatever was going on, but the men were too well trained and too heavily armed not to be part of something very well funded and dirty.

"I don't know. I can reach a specific person if I have established a link with them, but unfortunately, Calhoun and

I didn't have time to do that. If anyone in the house was telepathic, they might pick up on the communication. I don't want to risk tipping them off. They might kill Calhoun before we have a chance to get him out of there."

"I can slip past them, Nicolas."

His head went up alertly, black eyes going ice-cold. "I'm sure you can, Dahlia, but that isn't how we're going to handle this one."

Dahlia tried not to bristle at the hard authority in his voice. "Don't get military on me. This is my mess, remember? I'm thinking I can slip inside and make certain he's there before you come in. Why risk it, if Jesse isn't even there? It would be silly."

His fingers itched to shake her. She sat across from him looking cool and calm and determined. No, stubborn. She looked stubborn. There was no other word for it. "You look stubborn, Dahlia, not reasonable. Cut it out. This isn't a democracy."

"Exactly. I'm so glad you agree with me. You can hang back and do what you do. Put your eye to the scope and protect me, and I'll just slip in under cover of dark and take a look around. They can't have a crack security system in so short a time, and in any case, I've dealt with hundreds of security systems."

"I'll bet you have. So you think I should let you walk in there all alone with at least four men trained in military tactics." He held up his hand before she could reply. "Because it doesn't make a bit of sense to me to send you in there when we expect to find Calhoun tortured and in pain. We both know he was shot. What kind of energy is he putting out, do you think? What kinds of energy do those four men combined put out? I'd have to say it would be poor planning to send in a woman of your size, incapable of hauling him out, with your kinds of problems. I'd find you on the floor having seizures, and I'd have to haul both of you out."

He hurt her. He saw it in her eyes before her lashes came down. A glimpse was enough to cause his gut to tie itself into knots. "Damn it, Dahlia, I'm telling you the truth, and you know it. It would be suicide sending you in there alone. Don't look at me like that, you know I'm right."

She steepled her fingers, pressed them tightly together. "It could happen. I'm not going to deny that it could happen. On the other hand, I've refused to live my life being afraid. What else are we going to do? I can blur my image and slip into small places. Believe me, they won't see me. The other choice is . . ." She trailed off, looking up at him, spreading her hands out in front of her.

"I'll go in. I'm a GhostWalker, Dahlia. I do have a few talents of my own."

"But you can protect me with a weapon. I'm not certain I can do the same for you. I've been taught to fire a gun and I can hit a target, but I doubt if I could actually hit a human being. I'd try, Nicolas, but the repercussions would be so bad I'd get hit with the energy of just the intention of trying to kill someone. You've seen how bad it is."

"I've felt it as well," he agreed grimly. He never wanted to experience it again.

"Back at the house, I wanted to help Jesse, to keep someone from hurting him. I didn't mean to set anyone on fire, just scare everyone, when they were taking Jesse. I don't have any control when the energy is severe like that. I could burn down the house with you and Jesse in it."

Dahlia tried to keep her voice even. She had never felt so worthless in her life. Nicolas had managed to reduce her to a burden. She looked away from him into the trees, breathing deeply to keep her rising emotions under control. She needed to be away from everyone, to return to the sanctuary of the bayou. It was the only place she knew. The only one she called home.

"Dahlia." Nicolas reached out and brushed tears from her face. "I can't change who I am, not even for you."

She jerked her head away from the caress of his fingers. "I don't understand what you mean."

"It means I always go in first. It means I have to take the

hot mission. I live by a strict code, and it's a matter of honor with me."

She sat in silence for few minutes before scooting back toward the broad trunk of the nearest tree, giving him plenty of room to lie down. "It doesn't negate what you said. I would be a burden to you if I went in. To both of you."

Nicolas sighed as he stretched out on the sheet, lying with his head in her lap. She didn't protest, and her hand immediately nestled in his hair. She began rubbing strands of his hair between her thumb and finger. "I didn't say burden, Dahlia. You could never be a burden. I have to do this my way. The way I was trained. You have something you're very good at doing. This is what I do."

She leaned back against the tree trunk. "What am I supposed to be doing while you're in the house alone?"

"Waiting. We're going to need to get him out fast if he's alive. He'll need medical care immediately. We'll have to contact your people and get him to a hospital."

His voice was drowsy. Dahlia looked down at his perfectly sculpted face. Her fingertips traced his strong jaw. "I don't have any people. I do work for them, but I'm not one of them. It isn't the same thing. Jesse's NCIS; I'm nobody."

He tried to analyze her voice. Was the ache of loneliness in her words or her tone? Or maybe it struck a cord in him. Even in training he had felt apart, until he had made an attempt to learn to utilize the healing skills both grandfathers said were strong in him. He had volunteered to be enhanced, mainly in the hopes of opening his mind to the healing arts. He had gained many psychic talents, and for the first time he had felt a part of something bigger, yet he still, to his shame, could not tap into the strong resource his grandfathers had been so certain was within him.

He reached up and took her hand, settling his fingers around hers. "You aren't nobody, Dahlia, you're a Ghost-Walker. They hired you because you're exceptional at what you do. We don't do too bad together for a couple of people that are used to being alone, do we?"

A faint smile curved her mouth. "At least I've learned not to singe fingers."

A night breeze came up off the river, helping to ease the heat of the day. "I enjoy being with you Dahlia. Singed fingers or not."

Dahlia looked down at Nicolas. His eyes were closed, his voice sleepy, drifting into no more than a murmur. There was a quality about him that she found restful. She had worked at finding peace in her life, a sanctuary, but it had always been alone, her home, the bayou, never with a person. She had been unable to spend more than half an hour at a time with Milly or Bernadette or Jesse. Yet she was with Nicolas almost continually, and the more physical contact she had with him, the easier it seemed to be.

She remained quiet, willing him to sleep. He never seemed tired, yet she could see the lines of strain on his face. She smoothed the lines gently with her fingertips, went back to combing his hair with her fingers. She needed to touch him. She *wanted* to touch him. He slept lightly. She was very aware on some level he would know the liberties she took, but it didn't matter. Let him sleep and dream of her.

Dahlia's fingers slid over his chest, beautiful fingers with more strength than he expected. More magic. Her fingertips played a sultry rhythm on his skin, tightening every muscle, heightening his pleasure. She seemed small and fragile to him, but there was purpose in her touch. Demand even. The night breeze fanned his skin, cooling the rising heat and adding to his sensitivity.

Nicolas knew he was between sleep and awake, somewhere in the twilight in between the two stages. He might have been dream-walking. He was capable. It didn't matter to him, and he refused to analyze it. He wanted her touch more than he wanted to know what was reality.

He heard her whisper, as soft as any breeze, the warmth of her breath sliding over his face. A brush of her lips against his. Soft, teasing—little feathery kisses tantalizing him. Her teeth nibbled at his lower lip. Her tongue traced the outline of his mouth. His heart thudded in his chest, the echo in his head like thunder.

He shaped the back of her head with the palm of his hand, crushing her silky hair in his fingers, and held her to him so she couldn't escape. Why did he always feel as if she were on the verge of slipping away from him? He was dreaming. It was his dream, and he wanted to kiss her. His mouth took possession of hers. He was lost there in the silken heat. He gave up all pretense of sleeping, wanting it to be reality, losing himself in her taste and texture. "Dahlia," he whispered her name against her skin. Inhaling her scent, taking her deep into his lungs. "What are you doing?"

"Losing my mind," she whispered back, her mouth on fire, pouring molten lava into his bloodstream. "Just this once I wanted to feel like a real woman. You were lying there so beautiful, so peaceful, and the night is so perfect, I almost forgot what I am." She lifted her head, resisting his firm grip, her black eyes liquid with sorrow. "It's time to wake up."

Nicolas caught her face in his hands, held her there. He knew what she meant, but he wasn't willing to let his dream go. "We've been awake. All this time, we've both been awake, Dahlia." He kissed her eyelids gently. The tip of her nose. The corners of her mouth. "You're a Ghost-Walker, and there's nothing wrong with that."

She pulled away from him and settled back against the tree. "For a man who is very grounded most of the time, when it comes to me, you're not very realistic. You took a terrible chance on the ferry. What if instead of the violence being diluted by the sexual energy, you'd been burned when it flashed? Did it occur to you that could have happened just as easily?" She pressed her hand to her mouth. "It occurred to me."

"Of course I thought of it, Dahlia. What was the alternative? I could have thrown you in the river I suppose, or let you have a seizure right in front of everyone." *Right in front of me. I can read your thoughts, remember? I knew if it happened you'd never want to look at me again.*

Her head snapped up, her eyes beginning to smolder with temper. "So you risked your life rather than allowing me a little humiliation? Damn it, Nicolas, that doesn't even make sense. I don't need a white knight." If anyone needed a white knight it was definitely Dahlia. And worse, the thought of the risk he'd taken for her nearly curled her toes. She rubbed her pounding temples. "Did it occur to you that you could have raped me right there in front of all those people?" She said it deliberately harshly, needing him to snap out of his dream world so that she would too.

Nicolas sat up, a wry smile touching the corners of his mouth. "Well, no, it didn't enter my mind. That came as a shock. Now we know what can happen when the two energies meet. What were you feeling?"

Her face flamed bright red. "I think that's beside the point. We shouldn't have tried something without knowing what would happen." She *detested* her prim voice. "Isn't it about time you get going?"

He glanced at his watch. "I want them to be tired and sloppy. Besides, the conversation was just getting interesting."

"You're going to make me answer, aren't you? I thought you were a gentleman."

"Only when it serves my purpose," he answered without hesitation.

Dahlia rolled her eyes. "If you must know, I was feeling the same way. Aggressive and out of control."

"So you wanted to tear my clothes off."

"It isn't funny, Nicolas. It could have turned ugly."

"But it didn't Dahlia." He leaned into her, his larger body moulding against hers. His lips skimmed her cheek, teeth teasing her lower lip until her body relaxed beneath his. "It didn't because we controlled it. We may have been shaky, but it worked. We didn't tear the clothes off each other, and you didn't have a seizure. We now know we can dilute the violent energy by mixing it with another kind. Next time, I'll just tell outrageous jokes."

Her hands slid over his. "You take too many chances, Nicolas. I was so afraid for you."

There was a small catch in her voice that tugged at his insides. "You were the one in danger, Dahlia. I'm a hell of a lot stronger than you, and you weren't exactly resisting."

"And you would never have forgiven yourself, Nicolas. I've lived with this. I've done terrible things. They were all accidents, but in the end, it was my responsibility because I couldn't control my own emotions or handle the sheer volume of energy building up in me. You've built your entire life around discipline. I'm the ultimate in chaos, don't you see that? I work hard at establishing order, but I disrupt the natural flow of energy. I can't stop it from happening, so I've done my best to find ways to disperse it. If I didn't, the pain would have driven me completely insane. I *had* to learn how to bring order, it was the only time I wasn't being battered by the effects of gathering energy. It isn't going to change. If there had been a way to change it, I would have found it already."

"Dahlia, I'm going into that house, and I'm bringing Calhoun out. You damned well better be here when I get back. I'd find you, and believe me, you'd see that I'm not always in control, so get it out of your head that you're sneaking off to save me from myself." He caught her shoulders and gave her a small shake. "I'm a grown man. I make my own decisions. I'm not having you 'protect' me any more than you want my protection. Got that?"

Dahlia sighed, wanting to be upset that he knew what was in her mind, but inexplicably pleased that he was insisting she wait for him. "I've got it. Just don't go getting yourself killed. That would make me mad, and God knows, I'd probably burn down half of Louisiana."

He pulled out his cell phone. "*Don't* melt this. We need it."

"Then why are you giving it to me?" She dropped the small cell onto the sheet.

"You may need it. Lily's number is programmed in."

Dahlia looked with interest at the cell. Lily was just on

the other end of the phone. Real-life Lily, not a figment of her imagination. Not the one in her dreams. The temptation to pick up the phone was nearly as strong as her sudden fear. Her mouth was dry. "Be careful, Nicolas. Don't get over-confident. You have a tendency to be that way."

"I'm never over-confident," he denied. Nicolas caught Dahlia's chin and brushed his mouth gently over hers. "You listen to me this one time, Dahlia. If something goes wrong, anything at all, you haul butt out of here fast. You have the cell phone and the number. Call Lily. The Ghost-Walkers will be here as soon as possible."

She caught at him before he could turn away. "You listen to me this one time, Nicolas. If anything goes wrong, don't be a hero. Haul your butt out of there and in one piece. We'll call Lily, and she can send the others."

He looked down at her for what seemed an eternity, a moment stretched out in time. His hard features softened. Tenderness crept into the black obsidian of his eyes. "I hear you. I'll come back."

Nicolas felt her fingertips cling just for a moment and then slide from his arm. He went with the minimum amount of equipment, wanting to get in and out as quietly and as fast as possible. He slipped into the water, a dark shape moving upriver, toward the house. He made no noise, not even a light splash to give away his position. The current was strong but he stayed close to the bank, maneuvering in the reeds and brush and rock. He allowed only his head to surface, his gaze wide open and watching the guard facing the river. With the boulders behind him and the bushes screening him, he knew he was in a good position to remain hidden.

Tension rose in him. A bad sign, one he'd come to recognize as a warning signal. The guard stared at the black surface of the water for some time before turning away. From watching earlier in the day, Nicolas knew the guard would blind himself temporarily by striking a match and lighting a cigarette. He waited for the inevitable moment, and as soon as the match flared, Nicolas slid from the water onto the embankment, yards from the house. There was no cover whatsoever. He laid on the ground, in the open, a part of the rocky terrain, moving a scant inch at a time.

He had already crawled the path he would take in his mind throughout the day while lying in the river, and he knew precisely where he would go and what he would encounter. There was no dog to sense his presence and the guard was bored and irritated with his assignment, but Nicolas didn't rush. There had been one man on the alert, watching diligently and occasionally reprimanding the other two guards.

He worked his way to the parameter of the house and discovered a thin wire stretched low to the ground between two trees. He'd caught a flash of light from the area twice and suspected something had been strung up as a hasty security measure. It was lower to the ground than he would have liked. He couldn't simply ease his body beneath the wire as he would have preferred. He had to go over it, and that meant rising without so much as a blade of grass to give him cover.

Nicolas waited in the darkness, breathing lightly, his senses flaring out to "feel" movement in the night. Something crunched in the rocks by the corner of the house. Footsteps coming his way. The one guard who paid attention to his duties was making his rounds with his usual thoroughness. Nicolas eased his hand down his leg until he felt the familiar grip of his knife. Careful to make no noise, he drew the weapon from the sheath strapped to his calf. Using psychic pressure was always a dicey proposition. He willed the man to look the other way, careful to keep the suggestion a light one. If he met with heavy resistance, he would have to stop instantly. Some people had very light resistance and agreed readily with every suggestion, no matter how subtle. Others had stronger barriers and often resisted and even became suspicious, or uncomfortable, looking around, shaking their heads, obviously fighting the "push" to act out of character.

The sound of a scream burst from the house. Instantly

the night insects went silent. The guard on the porch tossed his cigarette aside and leaned down to call to the one circling the house. "He's not going to tell Gregson anything. Why doesn't Gregson just kill him and be done with it?"

"Shut up, Murphy and get back to your watch."

Murphy cursed and spun away from the railing. "With all the screaming going on, Paulie, don't you think the neighbors are going to call the police soon?"

"By the time anyone hears him way out here, Gregson will kill him, and we'll be long gone." Paulie stopped walking and backed up until he could clearly see all of Murphy. His boots were no more than five feet from Nicolas's head. "And you'd better stop yelling, the woman might show up."

Murphy turned back to the railing, a snarl on his face. He glared down at Paulie. "I think all the screams coming from the house are going to tip her off that we're here."

Paulie shifted his rifle. It was the smallest of gestures, but a clear signal. "You've always been too squeamish, Murphy. Just do your job."

Murphy spit over the railing and walked away, his boots making an angry sound on the wood.

Paulie stood for a moment staring up at the house before turning away to once more make his way around the parameter, just inside of the thin wire. He passed within inches of Nicolas. The guard wasn't looking down at the ground, but out into the darkness.

Nicolas remained still until Paulie had turned the corner of the house. He eased himself up and over the wire. Almost immediately Murphy, up on the porch, returned. Nicolas froze, "pushing" him to look the other way. The cries in the house had died down, but Murphy was clearly uncomfortable with what was going on. He lit another cigarette, staring out over the river blindly. Only when he began to pace restlessly away from the railing did Nicolas gain the path to the house.

The windows along the side were locked. It didn't present much of a problem. He could work uncomplicated locks. These were classic sliders. With all the practice Lily had made the GhostWalkers do, such a minor thing didn't even cause headaches anymore.

Get the hell out of here, Dahlia. It's a damned trap. The male voice was weak and edged with pain, but carried the unmistakable command of a man used to obedience.

Jesse Calhoun must have felt the surge of power when Nicolas manipulated the locks. *I'm not Dahlia. Are any of the guards telepathic?*

Nicolas felt Calhoun's shock and instant withdrawal. *Come on, man. I don't have a lot of time before the guard comes around to this side of the house. Dahlia's waiting close by.*

You're the shooter. In the sanitarium. Their plan went all to hell because of you.

How many inside?

Four. I don't know how many outside, but they've got the house covered. And they have sensors in the rooms. I'm dying anyway. You can't save my life, I've lost too much blood and my legs are hamburger. Just get Dahlia out of here.

I'm coming in now.

Calhoun cried out in pain, a long scream that tore at Nicolas's gut. He had no idea if Gregson was still in the room torturing Jesse, or if the scream was meant to cover any sound. Regardless, Nicolas took the opportunity to slide the window open and slip into the house. Using his enhanced abilities, Nicolas tripped the sensors throughout the house as he went up the wall to the ceiling, knowing they would come for him. They wouldn't know which room he was in, and they would have to search each one. To do that would divide their numbers.

He clung to the walls like a spider, pressing with his hands and digging with his toes, moving up in the corner until he loomed over the door. He didn't have long to wait. The door burst open, and the shadowy figure in the hall let loose with his weapon. Bullets chewed up the walls and floor, knocked out the pane of glass.

The man stepped into the room, sweeping the area with

his flashlight. Nicolas sprung onto the floor behind him, landing lightly on the balls of his feet, transferring his knife from his teeth to his hands as he did so. Others were pouring bullets into various other rooms. He loomed up behind the guard, a silent, lethal shadow and was gone just as quickly, rolling down the hall, away from the thud of boots toward the darkened alcove. Just above the window seat was a wide built-in cabinet. Nicolas went up and over the cabinet to lay in the darkness, fitting the familiar grip of the Beretta into his palm.

"It's her, damn it," someone snarled. "Get in the room with Calhoun. Put a knife to his throat. If she gets that far, threaten to kill him. She'll cave."

The house was eerily silent after the command was issued. Nicolas listened for the heavy tread of boots leading to Calhoun's room. Two men were coming toward Nicolas, answering Gregson's order.

He's coming to put a knife to your throat. Don't react. I'll take him out. Nicolas warned Calhoun of the intent.

I'm telling you it isn't worth it. Get the hell out while you have the chance. Calhoun's voice was shaky, even in Nicolas's mind.

Can you take out the one coming for you?

Too weak. Can't even lift my arms.

Nicolas made out the men moving like shadowy wraiths down the narrow hall. It was a bad position for them and they knew it, moving into the doorways for cover, but wary of the rooms once they found their fallen comrade.

You're a GhostWalker, Calhoun, same as I am, the same as Dahlia. Turn him away from you. Buy me some time. Nicolas made it a command. Calhoun was a Navy SEAL. No matter who he worked for, once a SEAL, always a SEAL. He knew what an order was, and he would obey it with his last breath.

It was significant to Nicolas that Calhoun didn't question what a GhostWalker was. He'd heard the term before, and that was a piece of information worth remembering. Only a select few with high-security clearance were familiar with the term. Jesse Calhoun hadn't been among those trained with Nicolas. Where had he come from?

The lights flickered on. Immediately it was a disadvantage for him. Ghosts walked in the dark. Nicolas concentrated on the circuit breaker, on blowing the circuits. It wasn't easy. He didn't have the gift as some of the other GhostWalkers did. Almost immediately lightbulbs throughout the house began to pop. Sparks and glass rained down. Wires melted, plunging the house once again into darkness. Flames licked up the walls and spread across the ceiling, casting orange shadows everywhere. Nicolas couldn't generate that kind of heat. Dahlia was helping him, focusing energy and aiming it. As always with Dahlia, the results were far more than she'd hoped.

Nicolas waited until two men went past him before sliding silently to the floor, replacing the Beretta with this knife. He made his way along the hall, keeping behind the two men leading the way for him, his footfalls exactly matching theirs. The lead man shoved open a door on the left and instantly Nicolas smelled blood. The scent was overpowering, sickly sweet. Worse was the smell of infection. Like the ghost he was, he moved up directly behind the man closest to him and caught him around the neck with a thick arm, the knife slicing deep.

Nicolas felt the surge of power as Jesse Calhoun tried to keep the first guard's attention as he came toward the bed. Nicolas lowered the body to the floor and stalked after the lead guard. The man already had his knife out as he approached the wounded NCIS agent. Nicolas was on him before he could reach Jesse, dropping him to the floor without caring too much about the noise.

"Nicolas Trevane," he greeted, watching Calhoun closely for signs of awareness. The GhostWalker program had been small.

"I know who you are," Calhoun responded. His voice was a thread of sound. The very act of speaking seemed too much for him. "Get Dahlia clear. They can't get their hands on her."

Nicolas waved him to silence. He could feel Dahlia's presence, although he'd told her to stay as far from the house as she could so that any violence taking place would be dispersed naturally before he ever called her in. He waited in the darkness, afraid for her, wondering if she was ill, while only a few feet from him Jesse Calhoun lay dying. He heard Gregson call out to his men just as a hail of bullets cut through the wall. He threw himself onto the floor and reached up to drag Calhoun off the bed.

The NCIS agent was a dead weight, already unconscious when he hit the floor. Nicolas pulled the mattress down to provide a little more cover for the wounded man as the bullets tore great gouges out of the wall behind him. He retreated to the window. The glass had been broken out by bullets, leaving behind jagged shards hanging in the frame. He broke the remaining glass out with the butt of his gun and slipped out to gain the roof. He found himself directly over Murphy's head. The guard was leaning down, trying to get a sight into the house.

Nicolas stilled, aware of the seconds ticking by. Seconds Jesse Calhoun didn't have. He leapt out of the darkness, giving Murphy no time to fire off his weapon, his knife finding the target, and slipping away, back into the shadows to stalk Paulie.

The bullet came out of the night, clipping his shoulder, removing material, skin, and hair as it slid past, burning as it kissed him. He was spun around, but went with the momentum, allowing it to carry him over the roof to the deck below. He landed on his feet in a crouch and rolled across the expanse of flooring to gain the series of planters and the relative cover they provided.

"We've got her cornered, Paulie," Gregson shouted. "She's on the deck."

Nicolas crawled backward until his boots touched the railing. GhostWalkers preferred high ground, but he'd take low if it was all that was available to him.

"It isn't the woman, Gregson," Paulie informed his boss. "Too big. I think I winged him though. Give me a minute to get into position and we'll end it."

Nicolas slid over the railing, coming to ground just below the deck. He traveled the same path the guard had walked, moving around the exterior of the house until he had gained a position close to where Gregson's voice had come. He waited, counting the seconds, sending a subtle push toward the man to speak again.

It was in Gregson's nature to control a situation, and the push found contact. "Drive him toward me, Paulie."

It was all Nicolas needed, that single sentence to give him the exact location. He drew and fired in one smooth motion, going for the kill. He immediately moved, hurrying along the path to the corner.

"I knew he'd open his big mouth," Paulie's voice came from a few feet away and down low as if he were lying on the ground. "And I knew you'd nail him."

Nicolas froze, trying to discern the guard's precise location. Heat flared all around him, the temperature rising fast. Orange-red fireballs streaked through the sky, arcing along the river and dropping to the earth to blast into the ground. Nicolas threw himself flat, rolling to fire off three shots in Paulie's direction. The ground shook with the force of the fireballs as they slammed into earth. He heard Paulie grunt, the sound a good distance from where he'd been.

Nicolas closed his eyes and sent his mind seeking until he found the target. Paulie was crawling toward him, wincing away from the fire raining down from the sky. Nicolas tracked him, first with his mind, then with his gun. He took aim and squeezed the trigger.

CHAPTER

ELEVEN

"He's dying, Nicolas." Dahlia staggered toward the man lying unmoving on the floor. "Jesse." Tears glittered in her eyes. "I can't lose you too. Don't do this." Crouching beside him, she caught his hand, held it tightly, and looked up at Nicolas. "Do something." Dahlia had never seen anything resembling the raw flesh that passed for the lower half of both of Jesse's legs. She could see bones and muscles and there was so much blood. Too much blood. He had burn marks on his chest and several cuts, but it was the horror of his mangled legs that made her terrified for him.

"I've called for an ambulance, Dahlia, and the NCIS has agents coming as well. Lily's contacted them, and they'll be here in a few minutes." Nicolas couldn't look at her. She was as white as a sheet, her eyes too large for her face. Her body trembled under the strain of the aftermath of so many deaths. She'd already been sick once, and he could see her fighting for breath. She was soaking wet and streaked with mud from traveling along the river's edge. He had no idea how she managed to get to him, lugging his pack along with her. The pack weighed as she much as she did, but she was there, her eyes filling with tears and tearing out his heart. There wasn't a damned thing he could do about it either. "We can't be here when they come."

"You can save him, Nicolas," Dahlia said. "I know you can. I feel the power in the room with us. You have to try. He won't last until the ambulance gets here. You know he won't. You told me your grandfather felt it in you a long time ago. He could heal, so can you."

"I told you I couldn't heal anyone, Dahlia. I've never been able to." Failing her left him feeling worse than he had felt at any other time in his life. "I'm sorry, I wish I could save him for you, but I can't." It wasn't as if he couldn't feel the power moving through his body. It was there, a tight coil he could never unfurl. He had tried so hard in his youth to learn the secret, spent time in the mountains on vision quests, had meditated, all to no avail. He couldn't bring the power out of his body and into another's no matter how grave the injury or how important the need.

"There's all this energy bombarding me, surrounding us. It's violent and ugly, but we've mixed it before, we can do it again, this time use it for something good. You have my crystals in your pack. I can aim and focus the energy through the crystals. You kept us joined while you were here alone, you can keep us joined so you can use the energy. I've never been able to release energy through crystals but I think you can."

"I don't know the first thing about crystals, Dahlia." He didn't. His people used herbs and smoke and spirits, not rock and mineral.

"I know about crystals." The energy was flowing to her from every part of the house, rushing to overtake her like a great tsunami. She rocked back and forth, pressing her teeth together, fighting to stay conscious. "We have to do it now, Nicolas."

He dropped to his knees beside her. "We can't stay here, Dahlia. It's too dangerous, and the cops are going to be trigger-happy when they find the dead bodies outside. I'll try, but we have no more than a few minutes. Then we go." He was already pulling her crystal spheres from the pack. "Which ones?"

"The amethyst to focus. The rose quartz for healing." She reached for the familiar balls, her fingertips gliding over the surfaces. At once the calming affect relieved some of the terrible pressure building throughout her body.

Nicolas put his hands over Jesse Calhoun's chest. His hands felt icy cold. He felt the power moving inside him, but there was a barrier he couldn't begin to bridge. For Dahlia's sake, he began the age-old healing chant his Lakota grandfather had taught him.

Dahlia reached out, the crystals tight in her fists, and laid her hands, palm down, over Nicolas's. At once he felt a jolt through his body, a sizzling whip of electricity, and the hot flow of energy pushing through Dahlia to him and back again. The heat emanating from the spheres seared his skin as he passed his hands over Jesse's body. His discipline stood him in good stead, not allowing anything into his mind but the healing of the NCIS agent's torn and mangled body. The steady beating of the heart. The flow of blood through the arteries and veins.

Nicolas felt the burn of the energy swelling in volume, flowing around him and through him, a turbulent mass increasing in strength as Dahlia focused and aimed it through the crystal spheres. She pressed the amethyst into his hands. For a moment time seemed to stand still. A strange purplish-pink light glowed beneath Nicolas's palms and radiated out over Jesse's body. Nicolas blinked, and it was gone, perhaps only a figment of his imagination, but the heat was all too real. Power shifted inside his body, the tight coil slowly began to unfurl, to spread and grow.

He no longer felt himself, but a part of something vastly larger, atoms stretching through the universe, flowing around him, gathering inside of him. Dahlia put the rose quartz in his hands and at once he felt the flow of energy. It moved through his body, sizzled in his veins and arteries, even his brain, drawing always toward his hands, toward the crystals there. Toward the mangled body of Jesse Calhoun. The light glowed brightly beneath his palms, radiated around Jesse and seemed to sear over the wounds, almost cauterizing them as the power flowed from him to the man lying so still on the floor.

Red lights flashed along the walls, breaking the spell. Nicolas let his breath out slowly and pulled back into himself, feeling strangely drained. He slumped over Calhoun, staggering for a moment. Dahlia reached out to steady him. He looked down at her small hands on his arm and then at Jesse Calhoun. The man's eyes were open, and he was staring at him with a kind of awe.

"What did you do?"

"The police are coming. An ambulance. I've got people standing by to intercept and keep you safe, Calhoun. We've got to go, but you're going to live."

Calhoun's gaze shifted to Dahlia. "Someone wants her dead." His eyes closed and he seemed to slip back into an unconscious state.

Nicolas answered him anyway, just in case he could still hear. "She'll be safe with me." At once Nicolas tossed the spheres into his pack, noting almost absently that they were still warm. "We've got to go now, Dahlia."

She stared down at Jesse's body. He was breathing easier, and the blood no longer seeped from the wounds on his calves. The bones were obviously shattered, but his color seemed better and the bluish tinge was gone from around his mouth.

"I think it helped, Nicolas. I really do." Dahlia took the agent's pulse. "His heart is stronger."

"We've got to get out of here now, Dahlia." Nicolas caught her arm in a firm grip, tugging at her to get her away from Calhoun's side. "Can't you hear the sirens? The police are going to be swarming around this building soon, and we can't be here."

"I'm staying with Jesse," Dahlia said quietly. "I'm not leaving him like this."

"You're coming with me," Nicolas stated, his bronzed features settling into harsh, implacable lines. "Calhoun is either going to live or he's going to die, but staying here and sacrificing your life isn't going to change his fate. Get on your feet Dahlia, or I'm carrying you out of here."

She had never heard Nicolas use that particular tone before. She could hear the sirens getting closer and closer. "I can take going to jail," she said.

"You won't go to jail, Dahlia, you'll die," Nicolas said. He took several steps toward the door, simply dragging her smaller body with him. "Think with your brain, not your heart. Someone took a shot through the window at you in the safe house. Who knew about the safe house? It was a member of the NCIS, it had to be. The people you work for. Are you going to believe that was an accident? They weren't sent there to kill you, I read that in the team leader's mind. They were supposed to go in soft, going in to see what had gone wrong. They should have been checking to see who was in the house, get you out safely, and protect you until they caught whoever was responsible, yet someone got trigger-happy." He shifted his pack to his other hand and kept moving. Dahlia was coming with him, slower than he would have liked, but listening rather than fighting him. "Who knew about the sanitarium? The others couldn't have followed you there. They arrived *before* you. Someone had to have tipped them off."

"What about Jesse? If what you're implying is true, he could be in danger as well." But she was picking up the pace, knowing what he said made sense. Too much sense. Someone had betrayed Jesse Calhoun and sent the wolves after Dahlia. It was why everything about the mission had gone wrong. Someone Jesse trusted had tipped off the enemy. Nicolas couldn't fight off the police any more than she could, and Calhoun would die if they took him with them.

"Lily's sending the GhostWalkers in to protect him. I laid it out for her when I called her. She knows he needs protection, and she has the military contacts to make certain he'll get it. No one's going to kill him in front of the cops. They'll be planning to make their try at the hospital, but they won't have the chance. Lily's got a helicopter standing by for him. He'll get the best care possible. Either what we did will work and he'll hold until they get to him, or it won't, but we gave him a chance. That's all we can do for him." He caught her shirt and tugged her away from the entrance. "Not that way. Go through the window on the river side. We're going to have to go into the river. They'll put a spotter in the air so we'll have to get completely out of this area."

She switched directions immediately, hesitating only a moment when she had to step over a body before going to the window. The glass was shattered and she went through the opening, uncaring of the few remaining shards. As many times as Nicolas had viewed the tapes of Dahlia, he still found her physical abilities astounding. She somersaulted through the narrow opening, landed on her feet, and hit the ground running, heading for the river. She was small enough that it was nearly impossible to see her in the darker shadows once she gained the river's edge.

Pandemonium broke out in the driveway as police cars and an ambulance screamed to a halt. In the distance, Nicolas could hear the helicopter. He moved as fast as he dared across the open space until he gained the river. The police would search the water. It wasn't a refuge. Dahlia hadn't waited for him, but was already making her escape, not wanting the new rush of energy to overtake her as the police, pumped with adrenaline, searched the area.

The current was strong and fast moving and Nicolas worried about Dahlia's smaller body being carried away from him. He caught up with her, reaching out to snag her shirt as the current took them downstream. She kept her legs tucked and floated in silence without looking at him, but he could feel the way her body trembled and shuddered continually.

Nicolas couldn't help the surge of triumph invading his mind. He was certain they had managed to save Jesse Calhoun's life. There was no real way of knowing until Lily had a chance to inform him of Calhoun's condition, but he'd felt the power moving through him into Calhoun. Even if it only happened that one time, it was worth everything to him. His fist tightened in Dahlia's shirt. She'd made it happen. It had been Dahlia who opened the floodgates to allow him to utilize the healing power he'd been born with. Dahlia had handed him his lifelong dream and didn't seem to realize the significance of what she'd done. She took psychic energy for granted because she'd known no other way of life. He'd struggled from his boyhood vision through an adult nightmare, and she had just made all of it worthwhile.

Dahlia.

I'm cold.

Everything in him stilled. It was the first complaint Nicolas heard her make. There was no whining in her tone, just a simple statement of fact, but it alarmed him.

We'll be out of this soon. I've got us a place to spend the night. It even has hot water.

He stayed very close to her as they floated part of the way, allowing the river to carry them downstream faster. When the current began to increase in strength, Nicolas caught at Dahlia and dragged her smaller body to the edge of the river, staying in among the reeds and rocks. She didn't resist him or try to pull away from him. That was nearly as alarming as her complaint.

Dahlia lay on the riverbank listening to the distant sounds of the chaos reigning at the house they'd just left. There were clouds in the sky and clouds in her mind. She had nothing left. Not her home or her family or even her possessions. Now, she wasn't even certain her job at NCIS was left. Did they think she was the traitor? That she'd sold out for money? That she'd been a party to Jesse's torture and her family's murder? Someone in the home office of the NCIS had traded information on her for a great deal of money. She hoped it was worth it to them, because it left her with nothing.

"Are you all right, Dahlia?" Waves of sorrow poured off

her. While he was feeling his most triumphant, almost a euphoric feeling, she was grieving. Nicolas swept back the cloud of wet hair from her face. "What are you thinking about?"

"Home. Family. Betrayal." She turned her head to look at him. "You're right, of course. Someone had to have sold me out. No one else knew about me other than a few I took my orders from. I was classified, their secret weapon. Someone at NCIS sold Jesse and me out for whatever those poor professors discovered."

"The stealth torpedo."

"I hate that thing." Dahlia shivered. "We need a boat. Stealing is my specialty. Give me a few minutes and I'll have transportation. At night, in the bayou, the canals all look the same on the waterway," she added as a precaution.

"I'll get us there, Dahlia," Nicolas promised. He considered protesting as she slipped away to find a boat for them, but decided against it. He had respect for her skills. She knew what she was doing. Maybe that was what worried him the most. If she wanted to slip away from him . . . this was her territory. She knew the bayou, and she knew the islands. He could find her, but it would take time.

He thought about her tone. *Home. Family. Betrayal.* He had experienced the loss of his grandfathers and his world had turned upside down. Dahlia was grieving in the midst of running for her life. She had spent most of her life being betrayed on some level, and he was asking her to trust a complete stranger. Not only to trust him with her life, but with her heart.

"Are you going to go to sleep or come with me?" Dahlia's voice called to him from the water. Few people could sneak up on him without his knowledge, and the fact that she had reinforced his belief that she was a true Ghost-Walker.

He sat up and searched the river. There was no boat that he could see, but he followed the sound of her voice, walking through the reeds around a narrow bend. The boat lay low on the surface, Dahlia barely a dark shadow sitting in one end. Nicolas lowered the pack into the boat, regarding it with a prejudiced eye. "Are you certain that will hold me? Is it a child's toy? A raft?"

Her answering laugh was soft and fleeting, but it was there. "Big baby. Get in. It doesn't make much noise and it's sturdy. Of course once in a while alligators think they can crawl aboard and share the space. I'm letting you do the navigation, and if you get us lost, I won't let you live it down."

The small teasing note in her voice surprised them both. Dahlia rubbed at the mud on her face as she watched him climb gingerly aboard. The shallow boat rocked but didn't submerge as he settled next to the tiny engine. "You look good with mud all over you," he observed.

"It's just as well," she replied. "I seem to spend a lot more time with mud on me than with makeup." She turned her head toward the middle of the river. "Get us out of here, Nicolas. I need to be away from everyone and everything."

In profile, even in the night, he could see the sadness on her face. He reached out and touched her, ran his finger down her cheek. "It will be all right, Dahlia."

She didn't answer but settled into the boat and kept her face averted from him. He indicated his pack. "If you're cold, there's a jacket in there."

That earned him a faint smile. "The magic pack." She opened it and drew out the amethyst spheres. "I think you saved Jesse. Thank you."

He nodded solemnly. "I think *we* may have managed it. I never felt that kind of power before. I've felt it gathering inside of me, but I was never able to focus it or use it. You did that for me."

"Did I?" Dahlia spun the set of balls beneath her fingertips, concentrating, her tone vague as if she weren't paying him much attention.

"You know you did."

"I know I should be very sick from everything that happened, but I'm not. We used up the energy together. It wasn't just me. Violent energy is the worst kind. It's like handling unstable nitroglycerin." She kept the spheres spinning beneath her palm, staring at them intently rather than at Nicolas. "I'm shaky, but I'm not overloaded. Whatever we did together helped."

"Energy naturally wants to disperse," Nicolas said.

"Yes, it's a law of nature, yet I disrupt it. I draw energy to me like a magnet. I haven't really figured out precisely how. And I can't change it or lessen the drawing."

Her voice was matter-of-fact, thoughtful even, but some small note alarmed him. She was in a pensive mood, and he felt his hold on her was fragile, tentative at best. He could almost feel her slipping through his fingers. He waited to answer her, choosing his response carefully, wanting to coax her to stay with him of her own free will.

He could sense that she wanted to leave. He touched her thoughts, an invasion of privacy, but the thought of her disappearing made him feel desperate. She was close to tears, somber, feeling both melancholy and edgy at the same time.

"It's a good thing, what we did together tonight, Dahlia." He appealed to the scientist in her. "I wonder if we could find a way to utilize and disperse all the energy flowing toward you if we practice together more. I feel it more and more, not the way you do, but I can tell it's there now. If we work together we might find a use for it. I doubt Calhoun would have made it until the ambulance arrived if we hadn't harnessed the energy, not to mention it was a great feeling to use something so ugly for something good."

That caught her attention. She nodded in agreement. "I didn't think of it like that. I suppose we could try again to mix different types of energy. I can focus fairly well if I'm not too overloaded, and for some reason, you lessen the impact when I'm physically touching you." She looked out across the river at the city lights. "It's so strange to be so close to people, yet so far away from them at the same time."

"Have you ever worried that this superconductor business

you do to help relieve the buildup of energy might be harmful to you?"

She glanced at him, then away, her shrug small. "Of course I have. What are the long-term health risks with energy overload versus spinning molecules in my body? There haven't been a whole lot of studies done on that yet."

"Consulting Lily might be good idea." The more he brought Lily into the conversations with Dahlia, the more Dahlia seemed to accept the idea of her position with the GhostWalkers.

"I'll discuss it with her if it comes up. I don't want her to think I'm just meeting her so I can use her. We've all been used just a little too much."

Nicolas was silent, trying to think of something to say to comfort her. Words eluded him so instead he drew out the map Gator had given him. "My friend grew up here and owns several pieces of property, most out of the way. You have a choice of a small cabin with running water out in the bayou or a fairly large house sitting on a prime lot at the end of a road just off the river in Algiers. Both have generators so we'll have hot water."

"Take me to the bayou. I want to go home."

The sorrow in her voice was almost more than he could take. He wanted to gather her into his arms and shelter her against his heart—and it was the dumbest thing he'd ever thought, but it didn't matter. The need persisted. He shook his head to clear it. She twisted him up inside, something he'd never experienced, but he decided being with Dahlia was well worth every unfamiliar emotion.

"The most unexpected thing is the intensity." He murmured it out loud.

Dahlia looked startled, but she didn't lose control of the spinning balls. They moved beneath her palm in a pattern directed by her fingers, yet she never touched the spheres. "What are you talking about? Did I miss something?"

"You bring out very intense emotions in me," he admitted with studied casualness. He wanted to wipe the grief from her face and replace it with anything else. If that took talking about his feelings, so be it.

She stared at the balls for so long he was afraid she might not respond. "I don't think we should talk about it."

Unexpectedly, he threw back his head and laughed. "Do you have any idea how pathetic I sound, Dahlia? This is classic role reversal. *Women* beg men to talk about relationships. *Men never* want to talk relationships. You're supposed to want this conversation."

She raised an eyebrow but didn't look up. "No."

Nicolas groaned. "If the guys ever hear of this I'll never live it down."

She turned her palm over and gathered the spinning balls into her hand, her fingers closing over them as if holding a great treasure. "Guys? The other GhostWalkers?"

He nodded, thankful he'd found a way to capture her attention. "Yes, they give each other a bad time, but they're all very close."

She settled into the bottom of the boat opposite him, stretching out her legs as if she were sore. "I can hear the distance in your voice, Nicolas. What's wrong with them?"

Inwardly he winced. Trust Dahlia to catch the slightest discordant note in the inadvertent way he'd worded his comment. It didn't matter though, he'd caught her interest and had turned her thoughts away from bailing on him. "You're getting to know me too well. There's nothing wrong with any of them. I think of them as family. I just can't be too close to anyone."

"Why?"

He shrugged. "I don't know. I just never learned. I think it's an art. I spent a lot of my childhood away from people, and I guess I'm just more comfortable on my own. I feel a great deal of affection for all of the GhostWalkers. Even Lily."

"Why would you say it like that? Even Lily? The Lily I remember was always sweet and careful of other people's feelings. She always gave up what she wanted for everyone else." There was a hint of belligerence in her voice.

Of course she would pounce on that. He nearly groaned aloud. *Lily*. The one person Dahlia remembered fondly from her childhood. "I love Lily. I do. It's just that she's a woman."

"*She's* a *woman*?" Dahlia kicked at his boot. "What does that mean? I happen to be a woman. What's wrong with women?"

He grinned at her, a flash of his white teeth in the darkness. "Now I'm the one who'd like to change the subject. Lily's a courageous woman, Dahlia, and she's married to a man I consider my best friend. Without her, I might not be alive. She saved all of us with her courage. Believe me, I not only feel a great deal of respect for her, but also affection. She's just so damned hard to talk to."

"And that's because?" she prompted.

His grin widened into a smile. "Because she's a woman, obviously."

That earned him a small laugh. Dahlia wiped at more of the mud. "I'm almost afraid to meet her," she admitted. "She was the one person I built up as larger than life. I needed her to be real, and because I was a child, so young, the memories wanted to fade, so I made up things about her."

"If you're worried the real woman won't live up to the one you created, she will. Lily's a very special woman. She opened her home up to all of us, provided medical help for Jeff, who'd suffered a seizure and a stroke. She's worked tirelessly to help us build enough barriers to go into the world without an anchor for short periods of time. The hope is eventually we'll all get strong enough to have families and live in the world like normal people."

"I've thought about that term so much over the years. *Normal*. It's such a little word, yet it means everything."

"It means nothing at all," he contradicted. "There is no normal. Define normal for me, Dahlia. We're all normal and yet abnormal."

Now that the action was over and the night had closed in, Nicolas was becoming all too aware of her. He directed the boat off the river and up a canal heading toward the very heart of the bayou. All the while, his gaze kept straying back to her. She was tired and needed rest desperately. She was soaking wet and streaked with mud. It didn't matter. His discipline was beginning to fray around the edges. His self-control was losing the battle with the demands of his body.

She glanced at him, a quick, under the lashes look that said volumes. The harder he tried to keep his thoughts from turning sexual, the more he fantasized. He knew he wasn't containing his sexual energy very well, but there was something about the way the boat rode over the water and the night enclosed them.

Dahlia sighed loudly and tapped her fingers on the bottom of the boat. "You have three distinct thought patterns. Violence, food, and sex. Not necessarily in that order. And why your sexual energy would be a million times greater than violent energy, only a therapist could tell you."

There was more than a little humor in her voice, allowing some of the tension to ease out of him. "Don't you think that's a good thing?"

"I think you're seriously disturbed. Don't you ever just want to curl up in bed and go to sleep?"

"I thought you were action oriented," he teased.

"I thought you were sane."

But she was looking at him. He could feel her gaze moving over his body, a silken sweep that left him as hard as a rock. The boat chugged lazily through the canals, carrying them through a grove of trees. The branches swept the surface, long dangling arms of green to brush across his shoulders. Moonlight spilled onto the water, a silver ball shimmering in the depths.

"I love it out here. Does that make me sane?"

"Yes." There was pleasure in her voice. Warmth. She yawned. "I wish I had more clothes. I'm tired of being wet and muddy."

"I was trying to get you to the point you didn't think clothes were strictly necessary."

She laughed softly and drew her knees up to her chin. "Really? And how long have you been planning on getting me naked?"

"Since I caught a glimpse of your bare bottom. The image is there, Dahlia, forever in my mind, and weak man that I am, it isn't going away. You didn't help matters when you unbuttoned your blouse either."

"How very reassuring. Are you about to start fixating on my breasts again?"

He closed his eyes and savored the memory of the sun shining through her wet shirt. "You're incredibly beautiful, Dahlia."

She was silent, watching him closely. *Feeling* for his emotions. Checking to see if he was sincere. "Thank you. That's a nice thing for you to say." She rubbed her chin on top of her knees. "Mostly I've been told I look like a witch. Too-big eyes, too much hair. Too small, too everything. No one ever used the word *beautiful* before."

"*Incredibly* beautiful," he qualified. "Get it right Dahlia." He consulted his map again and turned without hesitation into another branch of the waterway. "We're almost there. And I love your eyes." He was particularly smitten with the small expanse of skin around her midriff and her intriguing belly button.

Dahlia wasn't about to tell him what she found attractive about him. He was already far too arrogant and sure of himself. He didn't need to be told she could barely contain her own sexual energy. She loved the way he felt around her. She'd never had anyone want her the way he did. She could feel the energy pouring off of him, reaching out to swamp her, to raise her own temperature several degrees.

She rubbed her chin back and forth across her knees, her body feeling too full and heavy and tight in her skin. It shocked her how sensitive her breasts were, rubbing against the material of her shirt and aching with need.

"You feel it too, don't you?" he asked.

"I feel what you're fantasizing," she admitted.

"Other men must have had sexual fantasies when they

were around you. What about Calhoun? Come on, Dahlia, is this really a first?"

"Yes. And I don't like it. It makes me moody and uncomfortable and edgy. I feel like scratching your eyes out for making me feel this way. And that sets up violent energy and that sets up heat and eventually something—or someone—gets burned."

She did sound edgy. He shouldn't have been pleased, but he was. He could make her feel all those things when no one else had. "Well, at least life with me isn't boring."

She smiled just like he knew she would. She didn't want to, and she hid it against her knees, but he caught the brief flash of her teeth and the curve of her mouth. "I should have told you I love your mouth. Every time I look at your mouth I want to kiss you."

Dahlia wasn't touching that. She watched the outline of an island take shape. "Is this the place?"

"If Gator drew the map correctly. What's that noise?"

"Alligators calling to one another. They're in love."

They rounded a bend, and a small dock came into sight. The cabin was just back from the pier. Grass covered the ground surrounding the house. To his dismay, an alligator rested on the wooden dock and another in the yard. "Do you think they moved in while Gator was gone?"

"It's very common on these small islands to have alligators share your yard."

"Well get your flamethrower ready, we may need it."

Dahlia burst out laughing. "You don't give off enough energy to stoke the fires, Nicolas."

He turned his head and looked fully into her eyes, causing her heart to jump wildly. "Little liar."

Nicolas's tone was so silky smooth, such a promise of passion and pleasure Dahlia shivered, her entire body aching in reaction. How in the world could he make her so aware of him not only as a person, but also as a male? It was silly. It was too dangerous. Someone had to think with brains instead of other portions of the anatomy. She sighed and stepped out of the boat, carefully avoiding the alligator as she tied the boat to the dock. "We're just visiting," she assured the creature.

"Don't you dare pet it, Dahlia," Nicolas warned, his heart in his throat. He wouldn't put it past her. "You give me gray hair with the way you seem to have no fear." He pushed a hand through his hair in agitation. "I think I've been more afraid since I've been around you than at any other time in my life. And it's damned uncomfortable."

She watched him shrug into his pack. "I've been taking care of myself for a very long time, Nicolas."

He didn't answer but went past her to the cabin. A member of Gator's family checked on it weekly, keeping the bayou creatures from invading, so the cabin was neat and tidy and the propane gas tank was full, allowing them to have hot water. Nicolas lit a few of the gas lamps rather than working on the generator. They were both tired and needed a hot shower and sleep.

In spite of the slight wound to Nicolas's shoulder, he insisted Dahlia take the first shower. She was grateful for the warmth of the water as it washed the mud and grime from her body. There were gobs of mud in her hair, something she hated, and she shampooed it several times to make certain it was clean. Her arms ached when she lifted them to rinse the heavy mass of hair, she was that tired, and yet with the water pouring over her sensitive skin, she could imagine Nicolas's hands and mouth following the trail of the small droplets. She closed her eyes and turned her face up to the spray, hoping to wash the thought of Nicolas away. *Needing* to wash him away.

The door opened and she whirled around. The curtain was steamy but still transparent. Nicolas grinned at her, holding his hands up, a clean shirt in his fist. The smile faded from his face as he stood there looking at her. He cleared his throat. "I'm just getting the dirty clothes. I thought I'd wash everything and hang it up to dry. At least you'd have clean clothes. I brought you another shirt." The entire time his hot gaze burned over her body, touched her in places so deep she thought she might melt.

"Go away, Nicolas. Right now." She didn't try to hide from his gaze. She didn't want to. She *wanted* him looking at her, devouring her with his eyes. She was in dangerous territory, they both were, but when he looked at her like that, she couldn't help but want him. Her voice was nearly an invitation.

"I'm going, Dahlia, but only because you're so tired I can feel it. I'll wash the clothes tonight. You crawl into bed, but leave room for me." He didn't want to turn away from her. It was hell having the ability to feel her emotions, to read how tired she was and how much her body needed to sleep.

"Do you think sharing a bed is a good idea?"

"It's the only idea. If I can't at least lie down beside you, I'm going to go out of my mind."

"Have you considered that if we really made love, Nicolas, we could set the bed on fire?" Her fingers slipped over her breasts with the bar of soap. The water cascaded down to rinse the bubbles away.

Nicolas sucked in his breath. "You're deliberately torturing me."

"Probably," she agreed.

He stood for a moment in silence, looking at her with far too much hunger, then he abruptly gathered up her soaked clothing and went out.

Dahlia slumped against the shower stall wall, staring after him, her body overheated and throbbing. She had no willpower when it came to Nicolas Trevane. She shouldn't sleep in the same bed with him, dressed only in his thin shirt and nothing else, but she knew she would.

CHAPTER

TWELVE

Dahlia woke to heat. To fire consuming her. The light fabric of her shirt almost hurt her ultrasensitive skin. Hands stroked her thighs, soft hair brushed along her skin. She felt the lick of heat as a tongue slid up her leg. If she were dreaming, her body thought it was real and was responding with a buildup of pressure she couldn't begin to ignore. She turned her head and met Nicolas's dark stare. Her heart jumped at the concentrated hunger in the depths of his gaze.

"How long have you been awake?" Her mouth had gone dry and her pulse was racing. He was turned on his side, propped up on one elbow, watching her intently.

"Hours. I don't know." He reached out and touched her lower lip with the pad of his finger. "I dreamt of you taking a shower with me. And then I dreamt of you swimming naked with me. And then I dreamt of waking up and finding you next to me just like this."

She couldn't stop the slow smile. "You were dreaming very specific details, because I felt you touching me."

"Where was I touching you?" There was a raw ache in his voice.

"I felt your hand on my thigh."

He shifted position, a small movement, but it brought him close to her. His head dipped lower toward her stomach as his hand slid slowly up her thigh as if savoring every moment. "Like this?" His voice was a sinful temptation, nothing less.

She closed her eyes briefly and shifted her legs until his heavy erection was pressed against her skin. Until she could feel the drop of moisture bearing witness to his urgent need. "More. It was more, and your hair brushed over my skin and felt erotic." She touched his hair. He wore it long, and it was falling free around his face. He was a beautiful man with a darkly sensual body made to bring women long nights of passion. Her fingers slid over his face, the angles and planes, memorizing his handsome features.

His hands pushed her thighs apart, moved up to find the buttons of her shirt, slowly slipping each button free. "Do we need this?"

"We might. We might need a bucket or two of water, Nicolas." Her breath caught in her throat when his knuckles brushed her breasts. "This is so dangerous. Are you sure you want to take the chance? We have no idea what could happen."

"Aren't we scientists?" He pushed aside the edges of her shirt and bent his head to press a kiss on her tantalizing midriff. "I thought we were scientists. Experiments are our life's blood." His silken hair caressed her skin, sent shock waves rippling through her body. His lips traveled lower, found her belly button so his tongue could take a leisurely dip.

Every cell in her body came alive, sang, burned. The air crackled around them. Dahlia stiffened and pushed at his head. "Did you hear that?" She turned her head to look around them. The heat enveloping them was fierce, the sexual energy rising to engulf them. Tiny sparks glittered in the air like sparklers.

He kissed her stomach, blazed a trail of dancing flames from her belly button to the triangle of inviting curls at the junction of her legs. "Fireworks. Naturally there will be fireworks. Stay with me, Dahlia, don't think of anything beyond me."

Her fingers fisted in his hair. "I don't want anything to happen to you." His hands whispered over her thighs, added to the heat building in the room, building in her body. Dahlia heard her own soft moan and moved restlessly, needing more. Aching in places she didn't know she had.

Nicolas rested his forehead on her stomach for just a moment, trying to catch his breath. His hands trembled as he caressed her skin. He wanted to go slow, to make this time perfect for Dahlia, but the pressure inside of him was building in direct proportion to the heat surrounding them. It felt as if a volcano lived and breathed inside of him. He wanted to ravage her, drag her into his arms and devour her hungrily, but he forced a slow assault, using his years of discipline to savor the softness of her skin. To hear her small gasps as he kissed his way along the curve of her hip and the nip of her waist. His tongue teased each rib and found the underside of her breast.

Dahlia nearly came off the bed. "Nicolas, it's too much." She had two handfuls of his hair, her hips moving restlessly in invitation, but her eyes wide with fear. "I don't know if I can stay in control."

He nibbled his way around her small breast. "The beauty of sex is that you aren't supposed to stay in control. You get to let go." His breath was hot against her nipple, teasing it into a tight peak.

"What if I start a fire?"

"What if you don't? What if we have our own fire, right here, burning between us, using up all that wonderful energy? I'm willing to try." He closed his mouth around the tantalizing invitation of her breast. "I'm more than willing to try."

She cried out, wrapping her arms around his head to cradle him to her as lightning forked through her body. If fires started around her, she wasn't certain she'd know; she was burning from the inside out, a conflagration she couldn't hope to put out. There was only Nicolas with his sinful mouth and his commanding hands and the sheer pleasure coursing through her body. The energy building heightened her senses, drove the heat through her until she felt liquid and needy.

His hands were everywhere, but never fast, moving with leisurely slowness, as if they had all the time in the world. Dahlia didn't know if she could stand the slow assault on her body. His mouth moved over her breast, nuzzled her nipple and flicked it with his tongue. Each time he pulled at her breast a fresh trickle of warm welcoming liquid glistened invitingly between her legs.

His hand glided up her thigh, cupped her entrance. Dahlia gasped as his finger slipped into her.

"You're so tight, honey, and so hot, and I don't know if I can wait."

"I don't think you should."

"You have to be ready for me. I don't want you to be uncomfortable. There's no reason for it. It just takes a little bit of patience." He rested his head on her stomach while his finger pushed deeper into her. His tongue traced the edge of her triangle. "I can be patient." He prayed for patience.

"I don't think I can." Dahlia looked up to see sparklers in the air. Her hair crackled with the building electricity. "We have to do something right now."

Nicolas took her gasping plea as an invitation. He lowered his head between her thighs, one arm, an iron band, thrown across her to hold her down for his assault.

Dahlia's wits scattered in all directions, a sob escaping, her body rising up off the bed, writhing against the sheets. "I can't breathe." She was going to shatter into a million pieces. The entire room was going to go up in flames. The sparklers were bursting into colors overhead and raining down. She heard her own cry, a raw shout of pure passion she couldn't suppress as tremors shook her, and the lightning now seemed to sizzle through every vein, ever cell and nerve ending.

Nicolas slid over her, his wide shoulders blocking out everything in the room as he pushed her thighs wider to accommodate him. She pushed forward desperate to feel him inside her. Every single part of her body was throbbing for him.

"I'll be careful, Dahlia. I'll do my best to stay in control and make sure there's little chance you'll get pregnant."

"You don't have to worry about getting me pregnant," Dahlia said, her hands bunched in his hair. She wanted him deep inside her more than she wanted anything. He just stayed there, pressing part way into her and driving her wild. "I'm on birth control."

His head reared back, his black eyes moving over her face. Edgy. Almost angry. "Why the hell would you be on birth control if you aren't sleeping with anyone? Who, Dahlia? Calhoun?"

She stared back at him for a long moment. "Are you insane? You're going to get jealous because I'm on birth control when it's obvious I've never been with a man?"

Nicolas groaned. His entire body was on fire, was as hard as it could be, and he was arguing with her over something utterly ridiculous. Of course she hadn't been with anyone, and what difference would it make if she had? He hardly recognized his own primitive reactions. The sexual energy surrounding them had to be stimulating every reaction and heightening his senses and emotions. "Yes, I am insane," he admitted. "I want you so much I don't even know what the hell I'm saying anymore."

"Then shut up and kiss me. And for God's sake, Nicolas, get inside of me before this entire island goes up in flames."

He leaned down as she strained upward to find his mouth with hers. He kissed her with every fiber of his being, a hot blend of passion and possession. Their mouths clung together until she fell back, her hips rising to meet the slow thrust of his. He was stretching her, pushing through her hot, slick folds, burying his body deep to join them together. He felt thick and hard and too big for her body. The burning increased as he thrust deeper.

"Nicolas." She didn't know if it was a protest or a plea. Lights were dancing behind her eyelids and flames licked at her skin like tiny tongues. Real or imaginary, was beyond her determination. She wanted to lift her hips, to drive herself onto him, yet at the same time, she wanted to run from the waves of sensations she couldn't stop. The world as she'd always known it seemed to come crashing down around her in splashes of color and sparks and waves of intense pleasure that rocked her body.

She clung to him, digging her fingers into his arms to anchor herself in some reality. The sexual energy crackled and danced around them, through them, building the pleasure almost to the point of pain. He moved. She cried out. He caught her hands and pulled them over her head, gripping her tightly while he surged in and out of her.

Nicolas knew he was losing control, that the energy invading them was beginning to consume them both, but they were so caught up in the throes of making love, so completely lost in each other's body, it didn't matter. He let himself go with it, burying himself deep in the haven of her body, allowing the hot, tight slickness of her to carry him away.

He felt her body tightening around his, the small muscles gripping and clamping as he increased the pace, adding to the friction and the wealth of heat and fire. He didn't want it to end. He never wanted it to end, but her body was already rippling with life, a strong orgasm that rushed over her like a tidal wave and carried him with her.

Nicolas heard his own voice, a harsh, hoarse cry torn from his throat. His fingers tightened around hers as he emptied himself into her, thrusting hard, wanting to be as deep inside her as he could get. He lay over her, not wanting to move, wanting to feel her body pinned beneath his. He bent his head to capture her breast in his mouth, feeling the exquisite clamping of her muscles around him in another explosive shock wave.

Strangely, he didn't feel completely sated. His body was, for the moment, although he was still semihard. He wanted to eat her up. He felt on the edge of violence, a primitive possessive darkness that welled up out of nowhere and took hold of him. He lifted his head and looked warily around the small cabin, as if seeking someone, or something, that might try to take her from him. The sheer intensity of his feelings shocked him. It was as if he was driven to possess her. To leave his mark on her skin, on her breast, inside her body. His tongue stroked caresses over her, lapping at the valley between her breasts. "I don't want to stop."

It was a small admission, and it didn't tell her of the terrible driving need he couldn't seem to get back under control, but she felt it. Felt his tension rising instead of dissipating. The energy was relentless, demanding every ounce of force it could get from their union.

Dahlia had to tug her hands loose to frame his face. She forced her body to relax beneath his, accepting the way his hands immediately began to stroke her, to claim her body for his own. He was everywhere, touching her, kissing her, scattering her thoughts in all directions while he explored her body with a voracious appetite. He didn't leave a single spot untouched, bringing every nerve ending to life, tasting and caressing. His touch was so tender she felt close to tears, and then he was almost rough. To her astonishment and pleasure, her body responded to his with rushes of hot liquid. She felt as if she could never get enough of his body, of his touch or his kisses, always wanting more.

He took her a second time, riding her hard, needing everything she could give him so he could find peace in the midst of the whirling energy. It seemed elusive, impossible, as the pressure built inside of him, even stronger than the first explosion had been. Flames danced on the windowsill, and he wasn't certain which of them was generating the fire this time, but he couldn't seem to get enough of her. He couldn't touch her enough, or kiss her enough. He wanted his mark on every inch of her body. It was imperative to know she was there under his body, accepting his possession of her, *needing* it in the same way he needed to bury himself inside of her.

He built the heat fast and hot, reveled in her urgent moans, kept her hungry for him, wanting him long into the night. He took her the third time with tenderness, so gently, so reverently, she climaxed almost immediately, bringing him finally to some sense of peace, as if they had finally used up all the energy engulfing them from sheer exhaustion. Nicolas pulled her body into the shelter of his and held her tightly. The air around them was blessedly still and a tranquil sense of harmony settled over him. He kissed the top of her head, rubbed her rich hair with his chin. "Are you all right?"

Dahlia looked around the room to see if they'd done any major damage. The windowsill looked a little singed, but there were no fires. She closed her eyes. "We didn't burn anything down. I'd say that was a major plus."

"Did I hurt you?" He nuzzled her neck. "I couldn't seem to get enough of you no matter what I did." He could see the marks on her breasts, her throat, even on her hip, strawberries that proclaimed she belonged to him.

She laughed softly, but didn't open her eyes, drifting on a wave of pleasure. "I noticed. Is it supposed to be like that?"

He tunneled his fingers into her hair. "I may have gotten carried away."

"I was always told a man couldn't, you know, go more than once."

"Me too. Guess we proved that myth wrong. Or maybe it was the energy pouring through the room. It can be quite useful." The drowsy note in her voice tugged at his heartstrings. She seemed perfectly content, not questioning his darker reaction.

Nicolas stroked a finger down her cheek. She was so fragile and vulnerable lying beside him, yet he knew there was tremendous power in her small form. "Do you know how different my life is, how much you've changed everything in just a few short days? I never dreamt I'd be lying beside a woman and know that's where I was supposed to be."

Her fingers tangled with his. "It's because I'm so restful."

The faint twinge of humor in her voice was every bit as potent as her sultry tone. "I'm sure that's it," he agreed. "Go to sleep, Dahlia. I doubt if I'll be able to wait very much longer to have you again."

"Well restrain yourself. I'm very tired. Too tired to find my own space." She yawned and burrowed closer to his body. "I never thought I could ever sleep like this, with someone wrapped around me. I read about it in books, and now I know why they do it. They're so worn out they *can't* move. It isn't an option."

Dahlia drifted to sleep with his soft laughter in her ear. She dreamed of him. Dreamed of a life with him. The sound of children laughing mingled with his laughter. She felt his arms around her, the warmth of his body close to hers, and she knew she loved him. That she would always love him. That without him, she would never feel alive again. Dahlia woke choking, her heart pounding, a cry torn from her throat.

Nicolas flung himself over her, his gun tracking around the room. "What is it, Dahlia?" He could feel her heart, wild and frenzied. His hand found hers and he pulled it to his own heart in a vain attempt to calm her. "There's nothing here. We're safe."

She tried to withdraw, to tug away her hand, to roll into a ball out from under him. Nicolas was too heavy and there was too much of him. He seemed to surround her, his arms and legs everywhere.

The gun slid back beneath the pillow and he shifted to blanket her body, his hands stroking silken strands of midnight black hair from her face. "It was a bad dream, Dahlia, nothing more. We're perfectly safe here." Her eyes were wide with terror and he glimpsed the wounds there, raw, never healed, the wounds of a child without love or family. One that had suffered far too much. Lights flickered and shadows moved. He glanced toward the source, a window a few feet from the bed. Tiny flames danced around the wood.

He framed her face with his hands. "Calm down. Look at me, Dahlia. Tell me what's wrong or I can't help."

"You! Us! What was I thinking? Let me up. I have to get up." She pushed at his chest frantically, but without any real strength. It was more of a gesture of despair.

"Dahlia." He said her name sharply, waited until she focused on him. "You have to tell me what's wrong." He bent his head to brush kisses across her eyelids, the tip of her nose. To feather coaxing little kisses along the corners of her mouth and chin. All the while he ignored the crackling of the flames along the windowsill. Dahlia had to calm her mind or the fire would spread.

"Don't do that. Don't make me care about you." She pushed at him with frantic hands, her dark eyes very black and liquid with sorrow. "I can't care about you and survive."

"Breathe with me. Calm down so we can just sort this out together." He kept a tight rein on his emotions, the burst of fear that he might lose her. Dahlia. Slipping through his fingers like water once again.

She calmed beneath his touch and the soothing tone, lying there looking up at him with utter terror on her face. "I can't need anyone, Nicolas."

"Of course not," he replied. "We're the same. We don't *need* anyone. We're *choosing* to share our time together. There's a difference."

Dahlia dragged air into her lungs, heard the crackle of flames and swore softly. "I have to put that out. I'm going to end up burning this cabin down yet."

"Let it go. It will go out if you stay calm. You had a bad dream, that's all."

She shook her head. "I had a good dream. It scared me more than all the bad dreams in the world ever could."

He brushed back her hair, his fingers lingering against her skin. "Do you think this is usual for me? I've never spent the entire night in a woman's bed. I never wanted to. I didn't like sharing my space with anyone until I met you. I'm not using you, Dahlia. I'm not going to say I don't love your body, because I do. I could spend a lifetime making

love to you and I'd never get enough." Before she could answer him he bent to take possession of her mouth. Her
beautiful, perfect mouth. He'd had a few dreams himself
and they all had revolved around her sultry lips. His hand
buried deep in her hair anchored her head so he could ex-
plore the rich taste of her. For a moment the room spun as
if she were so enticing she made him dizzy.

He lifted his head. "Better?"

Dahlia touched her lips with her fingertips. "I honestly
don't know." She glanced at the windowsill. The tiny
flames were gone, leaving behind only black scorch marks.
"How do you put out fire with fire?"

"One consumes the other?"

"Maybe, but why didn't I ever discover that? I've tried a
hundred ways, maybe a thousand ways, to neutralize the
energy, but it never occurred to me that I might mix it with
another kind of energy. I thought it would just grow in
strength."

Nicolas fell back against the pillow laughing. Dahlia sat
up and glared at him. "What's so funny?"

"You. You're so funny. We just shared hot sex, awesome
sex, the kind of sex a man can only dream about, and you're
analyzing it all like a scientist. So much for my manly
male ego." He wrapped his arms around her and pulled her
down onto his chest. "I think you're good for me."

She found herself raining kisses over his face, teasing
the corners of his mouth and sliding her tongue along the
seam of his lips just to watch desire flare in his eyes. There
was a lot of power in being a woman, she decided as her
hands caressed his chest and slid a little lower just so
she could feel him catch his breath. Immediately she felt
the hard, rigid length of him growing along her thigh
where she wrapped her leg over his. It was happening all
over again. She started out in control and then she was
melting inside, wanting to please him, wanting to watch his
eyes grow from icy cold to fiery inferno.

Gasping, she pulled back, sitting up, her thigh still over
his. Her hair was wild, spilling around her shoulders and

tumbling down her back. "I don't want to feel this way about you."

"What way?" He reached out and cupped the weight of her breasts in his palms, his thumbs brushing her nipples gently. "I want you to want me."

"If it was just that . . ." she trailed off with a small gasp of pleasure as he dropped one hand to the enticing triangles of curls, his fingers burrowing into intriguing crevices and hollows. She shifted, her bare bottom rubbing over him deliberately so that he responded with a soft groan.

"You're doing that woman thing, Dahlia. The thing you didn't want to do." Nicolas felt more relaxed than ever, leaning back, his head on the pillow, his body coming to life and Dahlia sitting so close to his groin he could feel the damp heat beckoning to him. She looked beautiful sitting there with her hair all over the place and her skin gleaming at him, looking soft enough to eat. He stroked her breast and ran his finger along her ribs to the indentation of her waist. "While you're sitting there, maybe you could just reposition yourself a little to the left."

"What woman thing?" she demanded, tossing her head, sending the curtain of silky hair swinging along with the tantalizing sway of her breasts. Her fist curled around his erection, tightened, loosened, fingers dancing and teasing, robbing him of his ability to think for a moment.

He watched her through half-closed eyes as she lifted her hips and with painstaking slowness, lowered her body over his. He didn't move, allowing her to be in control while she mounted him, while she took him into her body. He could feel the way he pushed through her tight folds, the way her body was tight and slick and hot, welcoming his. He lay there, wondering why he had found her after all this time, why she connected to him, and how she was capable of sending such sensations of pleasure forking through his body when she began a slow, sexy ride.

He ran his hands over her skin. Her unbelievably soft skin. He traced the curve of her breast, the tuck of her waist, and the small curve of her hip and leg. When it wasn't enough to watch her, to see her body sliding up and down his, he caught her small hips and took over, relentlessly driving them both to the brink and then slowing down to allow them to catch their breath. She was flushed, her eyes bright, her head thrown back. Dahlia loving sex with him. The sight of her like that sent an explosion welling up from somewhere deep inside him, gathering with a great force and pushing through his body like a wall of fire. She cried out as her muscles gripped and squeezed, and rippled with shock from her own release.

Dahlia bent over his chest to lay her head on him. He wrapped her in his arms and held her while their hearts raced and their lungs burned for air. Nicolas wanted her to stay there, right on top of him, her body still a part of his while he held her close. There was something comforting in having her so close to him, skin to skin. An intimate connection.

"I want you to take notice, Nicolas," she pointed out, not bothering to lift her face from the warmth of his neck, "I refrained from whatever woman discussion thing you were accusing me of. You can't throw it in my face."

"Yes I can," he objected, capturing her hand as it smoothed over his skin. He nibbled on her fingers. "You were definitely headed toward a relationship discussion. See? As a woman you couldn't help yourself."

"Is it in the manual?"

"Yes, page ninety-two I think. Right there in bold print, it warns men about the relationship discussion *all* women," he bit on the end of her finger for emphasis, "that would be you, must have with their poor unsuspecting man."

"I see. This relationship manual certainly has a lot of information in it."

"It's thick," he agreed.

"I'll bet it took you a long time to read it and commit it to memory."

Her tone was mild, but he sensed a trap. He looked at her carefully, but she had her eyes closed and was nearly purring while she laid on top of him, her hair spilling around them like a silken waterfall. "I knew it would come in handy one day." He couldn't help the smile in his voice or his mind.

Outside the bedroom window, an alligator began to bellow with love, calling loudly for a mate. The sound reverberated through the room, making Nicolas nearly jump out of bed. As it was he brought up his gun and swept Dahlia onto the side of the bed with one arm. She collapsed into a small heap, laughing at him. "You're saving me from an alligator."

"If you don't stop laughing, I may feed you to the thing. What the hell is that racket?" He glared toward the window as he sheepishly slipped the gun back beneath the pillow.

"It's an alligator lovefest. Go to sleep. They're just beginning a sweet serenade. I hear it all the time out here."

He rolled over to come up on his elbow. He propped up his chin so he could stare down at her. "Tell me something about yourself. Something you don't share with others."

The smile faded from her lips. "Nicolas, I don't share anything with anyone. Jesse was my closest friend, and I only saw him when he needed me to go out on a mission. When he came to give my orders we played chess once in a while, that was pretty much the extent of our time together. Milly and Bernadette took care of me, in fact, Milly's always been with me, as far back as I can remember, but I didn't share my innermost thoughts even with them. I didn't dare."

"Why not?"

"They didn't encourage that sort of thing, and I knew they reported to someone. I didn't want that, so I was careful. Even as a child I was careful." She sat up, the long fall of hair cloaking her in mystery. In the dark, her eyes took on a haunted look. "I'm still careful. I don't know how this all happened with you. I try not to think about it too much or I want to run."

He glanced toward the door where the alligator nearest the bedroom seemed to have a caller waiting. "I wouldn't suggest it at the moment. I think we're surrounded."

She paced across the floor on bare feet, snagging the

shirt that had been discarded many hours earlier and shrugging into it. "Were you ever lonely when you were in the jungle, or did it seem like home to you, Nicolas?"

"It seemed like home. I knew the rules and relied on myself. I liked the sounds and smells and it was all familiar to me."

"That's the way I feel about the bayou. It feels safe to me. It's the only place that does. I understand the rules here, and I wasn't lonely." She turned her head to look at him over her shoulder. "I might be now that I've met you and got a taste of how other people live." Her smile was sad. "I should have thought about it before I let myself get in too deep with you."

"What's too deep, Dahlia?" She was doing it again. She was so elusive he felt nearly driven to desperation. Nicolas took a deep breath, centered himself, and forced down the unfamiliar panic. "Come here, honey. Don't get so far away from me." There were a thousand secrets in her eyes, a thousand wounds. A lifetime of distrust and betrayal. Isolation. How did one overcome such things? Nicolas padded after her and drew her gently into his body.

Where before, the potent combination of Dahlia and sexual energy had sent him into a frenzy of need, of desire, now he felt tenderness, a need to comfort her. His kisses were gentle, coaxing, completely undemanding. "We don't have to think about this too much, Dahlia. We both know we're in untried territory. We have no idea what's going to happen between us in the future. I know I want to be with you, and I know myself. I'll find a way for us."

Her hands came up to cover his. She was trembling. He knew she was afraid to face what must lie ahead for them. She'd taken steps out of the safe world that had been created for her. There was safety in not caring too much, not being involved too deeply. Dahlia had strict limits she set for herself and she stayed within those limits. He was dragging her further and further out into the open.

He brought both of her hands to his mouth and kissed her fingers. Kissed her palm. He wanted to make it better for her, take away the sting of not knowing love for all those years. He wanted her to recognize the real thing. He didn't dare speak of it, he knew she'd bolt. He was getting to know her now, the sudden spurts of terror that woke her in the middle of the night. "Where were you going?"

There was a small silence. "The roof. I always feel better when I go up to the roof."

Why did he hate the thought of her spending so much time in the middle of the night sitting out on a roof? He hugged her closer to him, scattered kisses through her hair. "Stay with me, Dahlia. Just lie in my arms and let me hold you. I'd say we'd leave the door open, but our friendly alligator is getting more and more passionate out there. I don't want him to visit us." Nicolas drew her back toward the bed. There was some resistance, but not much. She went with him, one slow step at a time, almost as if she were testing herself.

Dahlia went with Nicolas because she couldn't resist him. He seemed to have a very negative effect on her self-control. She wanted to spend every moment with him because someday soon, she would be alone again. It was already too late to protect herself. It had never occurred to her she would find herself falling for him. The very thought of it made her slightly ill. She had learned to enjoy her solitary life. There were hundreds of benefits. She just couldn't think of them when she was wrapped so tightly in his arms. When he was touching her with such tenderness she ached inside.

Dahlia allowed him to tug her into the bed beside him. She fit her body into the curve of his and instantly felt contentment. It shouldn't have been that way, she should have felt just the opposite. She never allowed anyone to touch her, and she spent only short periods of time with people, yet she wanted, even needed to be with Nicolas. And that was terrifying.

His arms crept around her, his fingers tangling with hers. "Stop shaking."

"Are you as afraid as I am?" Maybe it was admitting too much, but she had to ask. She had to know.

"Of course I am. This is new territory for both of us, Dahlia. I'm as vulnerable as you. I honestly don't know how you got in, but I need you with me."

"I'm not very lovable, Nicolas. I know that. I accepted it a long time ago." When there was only Whitney standing in the dark telling her she was uncooperative and she wouldn't ever get to have the things the others got. Even then, even as a child, she rebelled against that hard, absolute authority. She taught herself things didn't matter. People didn't matter.

Nicolas buried his face in the silken tangle of her hair and inhaled their mingled scents. "That's not true, Dahlia. There was nothing wrong with you as a child, and there isn't anything wrong with you now. Why do you think your nurse stayed all those years? Loyalty to Whitney? A paycheck? She was as isolated out in the bayou as you were, maybe more. She *chose* to stay with you, even if it meant deceiving you and living a limited life. She had no other children. I saw the earlier tapes, when you were a child. She was there, much younger, but she stood up to Whitney for you. And she was frightened by what he'd done."

She rubbed her chin on his forearm. "You mean by the monster he created."

"Not a monster, Dahlia. A GhostWalker. There are more of us than you know, and we are a family of sorts. You aren't alone."

She closed her eyes. She wasn't alone at the moment and that was enough for her. Nicolas wanted to believe in fairy tales. She'd read her share, hoping for miracles, but in the end, there was no hundred-acre wood to play in with little stuffed animals. There was pain and crushing disappointment and betrayal. Tears burned behind her eyelids, but she refused to shed them, holding Nicolas close to her and allowing the rocking of his body to soothe her to sleep.

CHAPTER

THIRTEEN

"Someone's outside," Nicolas whispered, leaning across her to get his gun. How he managed to be on the wrong side of the bed again was beyond him. He felt the familiar butt of the Beretta in his hand just as the front door opened. He shifted to put his body between Dahlia and the open door of the bedroom. They had slept far too late for it to be morning. Sunlight poured through the window along with the heat.

"I know you're holding a gun on me, Nico," Gator's voice called from the front room. "Put it away. It's not very nice when I've been so hospitable." Suddenly Gator was framed in the doorway, grinning at them, his black, unruly hair tumbling into his face and his piercing blue eyes bright with laughter. "Oh, I see you are most friendly with each other. And Lily was so worried." He turned his head. "Ian, Tucker, come look at this. Our man has found himself a little kitty cat."

"Shut up, Gator, or I'm going to shoot you." Nicolas put the gun away and looked down at Dahlia. She had the covers pulled up to her chin. Her eyes were enormous and getting bigger by the moment as more GhostWalkers crowded into the doorway to gape at the sight of Nicolas, the loner, in bed with Dahlia.

"And you said he didn't know what to do with a woman," Tucker Addison accused the tallest of the group, Ian McGillicuddy.

"I stand corrected." Ian gave Nicolas a small salute.

Dahlia made a small distressed squeak. Nicolas picked up the gun. "I'm going to start shooting if the lot of you don't get out and close the door."

"What a poor sport," Gator groused. "And it's my house." He reached for the doorknob, winking at Nicolas as he closed it firmly.

There was a small silence. Dahlia groaned and pulled the cover over her head. "I'm never getting up again. Go away, Nicolas and take that motley crew with you. There is no way I'm going to face all those men."

"There weren't that many," he coaxed, tugging at the cover. "At least they didn't walk in, in the middle of one of our firestorms."

"Nicolas, I don't have any clothes." She sucked in her breath, her eyes going wide. "You don't think Lily is with them, do you?"

"No, I'm sure she stayed behind with Ryland." Throwing off the covers he stretched, then turned back to her, gathering her into his arms. She was stiff, resisting him. Nicolas blew warm air against her skin. She shivered in response. He lowered his mouth to her neck and kissed his way up to her ear.

"That's not fair," she pushed at him. She was utterly annoyed that she sounded breathless. That she *was* breathless. "You can't be doing that."

"You're getting upset, and that means energy is going to come storming into our bedroom. It's all in the line of duty." He found her mouth, taking full advantage when she opened it to protest.

She wrapped her arms around his neck and pressed her body close to his, her tongue sliding along his teeth, teasing his tongue, drugging his senses with her potent response. He thought himself so controlled, but she shattered his discipline every time. His fist bunched in her hair and his mouth fused with hers as he held her to him. There was instant, urgent need, a tidal wave of heat pouring over both of them. He felt her breasts push against his chest. One leg wrapped around his thigh. He could feel her hot and wet and inviting. The need was beyond his ability to stop. He knew part of it was the fierce energy surrounding them and their sexual desires feeding one another, building too fast, too out of control, but it didn't matter. Only Dahlia mattered with her petal soft skin and incredible heat.

He caught her leg, guided it around his waist to align their bodies. She made a soft kitten noise, very close to a purr that nearly made him crazy. His head roared with thunder. Lightning seemed to strike behind his eyelids, lashed through his blood. He caught her hips with both hands to hold her still while he entered her. The breath left his lungs in a sudden rush, the now familiar sparks lit up the air around them. Electricity crackled and snapped around them, barely registering in his mind. She was tight and hot and gripping him with a fierce need and hunger every bit as urgent as his own. She practically melted into him, riding him as hard as he was thrusting into her. The only thing in his mind was to bury himself deeper and harder with each stroke. He wanted to crawl inside of her, to feel her hot, slick sheath wrapped so tightly around him.

Dahlia wanted to lose herself in him, in the fire and heat and passion of Nicolas Trevane. He kept her from thinking too much, kept her from facing things and people she didn't want to face. He did things to her body that burned up the energy, even the sexual energy surrounding them, every bit as efficiently as when she raced over rooftops in the city and through the swamps in the bayou. She could feel the pressure building too fast, too soon, a flashfire between them that ignited instantaneously and just as quickly was used up. She clung to him, digging her fingers into the hard muscle of his shoulder, attempting to take back some of the control to ride slower, wanting to curb the gathering force. It was too late. He was filling her, the friction turning her insides to an inferno, pushing them both over the edge into a wild orgasm. She lay in his arms while her body rocked and rippled. For a moment she was certain the earth moved.

Nicolas held her close to him, his face buried in the mass of silken hair, just breathing her into his lungs. "I wish we had more time, Dahlia."

"Me too," she agreed, turning her face up to his throat. She pressed her lips against his chin. "I wish we could go some place where no one would find us and it wouldn't matter if I didn't have any clothes." She sighed. Not so much for her lack of clothes as the inevitable task of facing his friends.

"I'll find you something to wear, Dahlia," Nicolas said. "Stop worrying over silly things." He lifted her chin to kiss her one more time before padding across the floor to look in his pack.

"I don't think clothes are silly when there are men in the other room," she pointed out. "Unless you want me to go parading around in front of them like this."

"That wouldn't be safe for anyone," he said and turned to glare at her. His quick flash of primitive possessiveness died a quiet death as he looked at her. Dahlia sat in the middle of the bed without a stitch on looking incredibly sexy with her hair tousled and tumbling down her back. He swallowed a sudden lump. "You have perfect breasts."

She laughed, just the way he knew she would, the worry in her eyes gone. "You definitely have a fixation."

He loved the sound of her laughter. For all of her childhood nightmares and the terrible reality of her life, Dahlia found ways to laugh, to genuinely enjoy her world. Her laughter was contagious and all the more treasured because it was rare. "I love to make you laugh."

"That's good, because you always manage to say something outrageous. Are my jeans dry?"

He went into the bathroom where they had hung all their newly washed clothes to dry. "Your jeans are still wet,

Dahlia, all the clothes are. I don't have anything small enough for you. I thinking we're going to have to do a little clothes shopping."

"I'll wear them wet. Better to have clothes than not with your friends waiting outside." She tried desperately to push down the apprehension flooding her. It was natural, but for her dangerous. She should have been embarrassed about making love to Nicolas separated only by a wall from a roomful of other people, but she wished she could stay lost in the heat and safety of their union.

She sighed. She really was becoming one of those women who wanted to cling all the time. As long as Nicolas had his arms around her, she felt very protected. Now, having to dress and face a roomful of strangers, she felt more vulnerable than she'd ever felt. Dahlia tried to analyze why. She had long ago trained herself to care nothing for others' opinions of her. The hurtful remarks had taken their toll, and her temper had spiraled out into a wave of retaliation each time. It was dangerous to care what others said or thought about her. And it was horribly humiliating to have anyone witness her breakdown of control.

Dahlia took the shirt Nicolas handed to her. "How's your shoulder feeling this morning?"

"It's fine. A scratch. The bullet just kissed me thanks to you. Your fireworks distracted him long enough to save my life. He should have just shot me instead of talking about it."

She leaned over to brush a light kiss over his shoulder. "Well, I'm very glad he didn't. Give me a few minutes to pull myself together and I'll be right out."

"Don't disappear into the bathroom and leave me without my jeans."

She looked him up and down, a slow smile curving her mouth. "I don't know, I rather like you like that."

"That's because I'm astonishing."

"Oh, is that the reason?" How had she become comfortable with him? How come every time she looked at him she wanted to trace the weathered lines in his bronzed face and smooth back the tumble of dark hair? What made her melt inside when nothing and no one had ever done so? The intensity of her emotions shook her, frightened her. Just as before when she'd awakened with her heart pounding in the middle of the night, her pulse went wild and tiny flames licked at the windowsill.

Nicolas glanced at the dancing flames and back at her. A slow smile softened the hard angles and planes of his face. "You just can't get enough of me, can you? I see your call sign, wanting me to come back to bed."

She flung the pillow at him, laughing because she couldn't help herself. "A sane man would run from a room where a woman sets the windowsills on fire." The tiny flames were already dying down into embers. "He wouldn't come running."

"But the wise man knows the real fire is in the woman in the bed, and he rushes to her side to put it out." He spoke in his best "wise man" voice.

She flung the second pillow at him. "How much damage did I do to your poor friend's house?"

Nicolas looked at the scorch marks around the window. Most were from the night before. "It adds charm to the place. The resale value is bound to skyrocket."

Dahlia shook her head at his outrageous comment and reluctantly abandoned the relative safety of the bed. "I'll come out in a few minutes, just give me a little time to prepare myself."

"If you aren't out in a few minutes," he warned, "I'm coming in to haul you out."

She rolled her eyes, not impressed with his threat. She could see how Nicolas could be intimidating to most people, but she knew him fairly well now. He would never do anything on purpose to hurt her. "I said a few minutes."

She took her time over her hair. She had no makeup and rarely wore more than mascara and lipstick, but still, it would have made her feel less vulnerable had she had makeup. Her jeans were uncomfortable and a little wetter than she would have liked, but the shirt was a deep blue and hid the fact that she hadn't bothered with her wet underwear. Her skin was getting chafed from constantly wearing soaked clothing.

Dahlia took a deep breath and pushed open the door. She knew they were all GhostWalkers with heightened awareness, and she knew they would know the moment she walked into the room, but she still wasn't prepared for the sudden silence or the way all eyes turned on her. She felt as if she were caught in the glare of a bright spotlight. Her hand slipped into her pocket to caress the amethyst spheres that always seemed to impart comfort to her. She expected waves of energy to hit her, but the impact was minimal. Nicolas and at least one other in the room helped to ease the bombardment from natural thoughts and emotions.

"Dahlia." Nicolas crossed the room to slip his arm around her, knowing the contact would help provide a further barrier. "Come in and meet everyone." At the sight of her looking small and fragile and apprehensive, every protective instinct he had welled up. "I know it's a bit overwhelming to meet us all en mass, but at least you'll get it over with quickly."

"Kaden Bishop, ma'am." A tall man with intense eyes and a hard edge to his mouth greeted her first. Dahlia knew immediately he was an anchor. He had the same calming effect on her that Jesse Calhoun and Nicolas had.

"Sam Johnson, ma'am." A handsome man with coffee-colored skin, stocky and powerfully built with heavy muscles, he seemed to take up a lot of space.

"Ian McGillicuddy, ma'am," the tallest of the group proclaimed. He had a shock of chestnut, reddish hair that any woman would have wanted and laughter in his brilliant brown eyes. His skin was fair, and to Dahlia he looked like a giant.

Dahlia nodded to the three men and turned her attention to the other side of the room. Her mouth was inexplicably dry. Nicolas seemed to sense her rising tension because his hand tightened on her arm as if afraid she might run. The urge was there, welling up, robbing her of any semblance of calm.

"I'm Raoul Fontenot, ma'am, but everyone just calls me Gator." The owner of the cabin had a rich Cajun accent and the bad boy look that could melt hearts at twenty paces. Dahlia felt the cabin was growing smaller with each introduction. Each man stood tall with wide shoulders and bulky muscles. She felt ridiculous standing near them.

Nicolas exerted pressure on her, and she realized she had taken a step toward the front door. She made herself stop, forced a smile when her lips were frozen.

"Tucker Addison," the last man said. It was impossible to adequately describe his skin. A rich dark bronze stretched over rippling muscles. His hair was closely cropped in military style, but she could see tiny spirals springing up ruthlessly in spite of his efforts to tame it.

"Nicolas has talked about all of you." It was the only thing she could think to say.

Gator grinned at her. "Now, ma'am, don't be believing anything that heathen says." He dropped the ends of most of his words, using *don* instead of *don't*, but she recognized the rhythm in the way he spoke. It was familiar, a drawling warm molasses that spread over a listener slowly. It was something to hang onto in the midst of such a large gathering.

Dahlia curled up in the chair nearest the door, thankful it was open and she could hear the noise of the swamp. It helped to steady her. "It was nice of you to lend us your cabin."

He shrugged. "It's all in the family, *ma cher*." He looked at Nicolas. "Jeff Hollister would have been here, but he's still recovering. Lily works that poor man on his therapy every day. He says she's a nag, but she's got him walking with a cane now instead of the walker, so he's improving."

"Lily won't let him do anything else," Sam said with satisfaction.

Dahlia could feel the affection the men had for their injured comrade. Some of the affection was mixed with anger. The energy was moving through the room to her, gathering together to surround and pour into her own terrible mix of emotions. "Who is Jeff Hollister, and what happened to him?"

"He's a GhostWalker, the same as we are *cher*," Gator provided. "He had a stroke and a few complications, but he's going to be all right."

She felt the instant flash of anger welling up in the men. On the heels of that strong emotion came the thought of betrayal by one of their own. The anger increased tenfold and hit Dahlia hard. She fought back the rise in the temperature, the churning in her stomach. Helplessly she looked at Nicolas.

Before he could touch her to lessen the impact, Ian McGillicuddy swore, his fist clenched tightly. "Damned traitor looking to sell us all out for money tried to murder him. And Jeff wasn't the first. We lost two good men, Dwayne Gibson and Ron Shaver. Both murdered on the job and dissected like a couple of insects."

The wave of energy combined from the rising emotions in the men contained within such a small area hit her so hard she cried out, a sharp denial as the pressure built beyond her capability to control it. She was too confined, had not even allowed herself the amethyst spheres to relieve the tension. She lunged out from under Nicolas's hand and away from the men toward the door, doing her best to direct the blast away from the house. The door and most of the doorjamb vanished as a fireball slammed through the opening out into the yard. Flames raced up the wall to the ceiling and spread across the yard to the very edge of the water.

Nicolas caught her before she could race through the open door. "You'll get burned, honey, stay back until we get this out." His voice was very calm. "I need all of you to work at putting out at the fire, but while you do, breathe slowly and evenly and meditate. We need calm."

He folded Dahlia into his arms, tight against his body, rocking her gently back and forth. "It's no big deal. We weren't prepared for the way we would all feel over Jeff. He's the kind of guy you can't help but like, and I guess we all have the same buried anger. Someone tried to murder him and it's left him fighting his way back. Our anger just came out unexpectedly."

"Do you need another anchor?" Kaden asked.

Nicolas hesitated. He didn't want Dahlia to need another anchor, but if they wanted the energy to quit feeding the fire, Kaden could help draw it from Dahlia. "Just put your hands on her shoulders."

The others quickly doused the flames in the house and worked to extinguish the ones outside. Dahlia stood between the two men, her body trembling and her head throbbing with pain. Anger could produce fire faster than anything else. She had to keep working at not being angry with herself. Why hadn't she been prepared for such a thing? The moment she was calm enough she pulled away from them. "I have to go outside right now."

Nicolas watched her go. "She's heading for the roof, but she'll believe she can never be with people after this." He shook his head. "I know what she's feeling right now, and it's not good. I should have briefed you all on the severity of the repercussions of her talents."

"Let me see if I can talk to her, Nico," Kaden suggested. "I'm an anchor, and if I can convince her she can have a fairly decent conversation with me, she might try again."

Nicolas fought down the completely humiliating and ridiculous jealousy he couldn't quite suppress. It annoyed him more than any other trait. It was something he thought petty and unworthy of a man. Kaden was a trusted friend, and he was honestly trying to help. In any case, Nicolas would stay out of sight, but near enough if Dahlia needed him.

"Talk about Lily, Kaden," Nicolas advised. His voice sounded a little too tense for his liking, but he forced a quick, grateful smile. "I'll be close in case she decides to take off."

Kaden nodded and went up the side of the house, moving quickly across the roof. Dahlia sat on the highest pitch, pale lavender balls spinning through her fingers as she looked out over the water while the wind tugged at her hair. She looked very alone.

She didn't look up when he moved up beside her and sat down. "In case there were too many of us introducing ourselves, I'm Kaden." He smiled, in what he hoped was a friendly fashion.

She rubbed her chin on her knees and breathed deep to keep the tension inside of her from exploding out. Berating herself for her lack of control hadn't helped get rid of all the energy. "You're what Nicolas refers to as an anchor, aren't you," she confirmed, pressing her lips together.

She was moving spheres through her fingers fast. Kaden found it almost hypnotic. "Yes, I can draw strong emotions away from the others so they can better function on a mission, but the emotions don't amplify my own the way the energy does you. We must seem a bit overwhelming to you. When men go into combat together they develop a certain camaraderie and often joke with one another to ease the tension." He watched her closely, feeling her emotions, knowing she was on the edge of flight. "Lily wanted to come with us, but we convinced her you would prefer she looked after your friend. Ryland is with her, and no one will get past him if he's on guard."

Dahlia made herself answer him when her heart was pounding and conflicting emotions swirled hotly inside of her. "That's good." Being with the men only brought her to the realization that she couldn't ever have the life she dreamed of. There would be no house in Lily's neighborhood. No barbecues in the backyard with her friends. Her emotions were too close to the surface. She wasn't like Nicolas—no matter how hard she tried, she didn't have his discipline, his self-control.

Why she felt so threatened, so afraid, she had no idea. Maybe she didn't really want Lily to be a living, breathing person. Dahlia couldn't bear to be disappointed. To find Lily different than the illusion she'd built up. Or maybe it was more than that. Dahlia rubbed her chin harder on her knees. Maybe the thought of Lily alive and well and happy in the world while Dahlia had to be alone was too much to bear. Dahlia hoped she wasn't that petty, but suspected she was. "Did anyone say if Jesse was going to live?" she asked, determined to try to appear normal.

Kaden shook his head. "He's in intensive care. They operated on his legs and gave him massive amounts of blood. The doctors couldn't believe he was still alive, but he's hanging in there. I think he has a good chance."

"And Ryland was warned not to trust any of the agents from the NCIS, right?"

"He's been alerted. How in the world did the Naval Criminal Investigative Service manage to recruit you? You weren't twenty-one when you began working for them nor did you have a bachelor's degree, which I believe is essential to fulfill the requirements."

"That's true, but I'd been in training since I was a child and I was tutored, so yes, in spite of not having attended college, I could pass anything they threw at me. And the bottom line was, I could provide a service no one else could." Her fingers slid over and around the set of spheres, moving them continually, not noticing when they took to the air above her fingertips.

Kaden tried not to stare at the spinning balls levitating just above her hand. She was in a great emotional turmoil, and he had the feeling she might bolt at any moment. "What do you do for the NCIS?"

Her dark gaze moved over his face. "All of you have security clearance. Didn't Lily find that out when she was researching me?"

"Not exactly. We knew Calhoun worked as an agent for them so the natural progression was that you did as well. Your identity is buried a whole lot deeper than Calhoun's."

"That's good to know." But it meant she was right. No one had discovered her identity; they'd found her because someone in the NCIS had betrayed her as well as Jesse. Jesse had suffered for it and could very well die. She sighed and kept the balls spinning in the air above her fingertips, concentrating on them so that the energy rising from her confused emotions could be used as fast as she produced it. "I do recovery work mostly. I retrieve things that belong to the government. If we can't get them back any other way, or secrecy is imperative, I'm their woman."

Her heart hurt. Actually hurt. She had to keep from pressing her hand against her chest. She could barely breathe. It took all of her concentration to appear normal to the GhostWalker when the energy pouring into her and around her was building to explosive levels a second time. She remembered sitting so many hours on the roof of her home, wondering why she wasn't like everyone else. She remembered moving through the streets at night and stopping to listen to mothers crooning to babies. One woman in particular had caught her attention. She rocked her baby on the front porch and sang softly to the child. Dahlia had gone home and wrapped her small raggedy blanket around her and sang the song to herself, rocking to try to feel whole just once. She detested pity parties, and she was in a full-blown one, unable to rise above it.

"Lily's very anxious to meet you. She sent you a letter."

Dahlia looked up quickly. "A letter from Lily?"

"Yes." He fished inside his shirt pocket and pulled out a small scented envelope.

Dahlia stared at it, inhaling sharply. The writing was small and neat and very feminine. Her heart lurched inside of her and a pain began somewhere in the region of her stomach. Her emotions were already unstable, and just the idea of a letter from Lily terrified her. Shaking her head, she stood up and backed away from Kaden, heedless of the danger on the steeply pitched roof.

"Dahlia." Kaden stood up as well. "I didn't mean to upset you." His gaze shifted to a spot behind her, the only warning she had.

Nicolas's hard body pressed tightly up against hers, his arms sliding around her as he reached for the envelope. "I'll take it. You didn't upset her, Kaden. It's the energy buildup. We need to give her a break."

"Dahlia, you should have told me," Kaden said immediately. "I'll leave you two to do whatever works to make you more comfortable."

Nicolas held her to him, caging her like he might a wild bird. "Don't do this, Dahlia," he whispered against her neck when Kaden made his way off the roof. "Stay with me. I know it isn't easy, but we can find a way."

"How?" She wanted to be angry, but all she could feel was despair. "Damn it, Nicolas, I *hate* to whine and feel self-pity. It's useless. But I can't do this. I can't be with all these people and not overload. How in the world do you think there's going to be a happily ever after? You'll have to go your way, and I can't go with you. And there's Lily." Her voice broke off and she leaned into him. "I don't want to read her letter or see her. I don't. I can't. She'll be everything I ever wanted in a sister. Everything I ever remembered, and I won't be able to have her. I should never have started anything with you. Never."

Nicolas moved his mouth over her bare neck, kissed his way along her shoulder. "You're afraid, Dahlia. That's natural, but it isn't like you to run from a problem."

"I can't do this, Nicolas. You know what could happen. I'm so close to losing my mind it's unbelievable. I can't control my thoughts or my emotions. It's a dangerous state for me to be in, especially around so many people. They can't go without feeling anything. It isn't possible."

"I know it isn't, Dahlia, I'm not minimizing the risk, but the risk is worth it. I'm not willing to walk away and pretend we didn't meet. You're a GhostWalker—you belong with us. That means we find a way to make it happen. You're not alone anymore. We've got good minds, and you know Lily is brilliant. We'll find a way to ease this. Nobody was hurt and no one is upset. We have accidents happening all the time. They might not be fires, but they can be just as dangerous. We've all had to find ways to cope. Did you see any of them staring at you as if you were different? You're the same as we are. We all have these things happen to us." He repeated it for emphasis, wanting her to believe. *Willing* her to believe.

His mouth was melting her with heat. The energy pounding at her, swarming around her, pouring into her began to subtly change. She could feel the change. Her heightened sexual awareness. Her body coming alive and every nerve ending waiting in anticipation. She closed her eyes against the tidal wave of passion. "Do you think we can spend the rest of our lives making love when we have company?"

"I wouldn't mind it, although I doubt if it's very practical. But sitting on the roof isn't exactly practical either."

"It works."

"So apparently does sex," he pointed out with satisfaction.

Unexpectedly she laughed, relaxing into him. "You sound so smugly male. Honestly Nicolas, you have such a thing about sex."

"Only with you. I'm not willing to give up, Dahlia. You're not a quitter. You've fought for a life since you were a child, finding your own way to deal with the energy when you had no help. You'd never be able to live with yourself if you quit now."

She turned in his arms, tilted her head to look up at him. "If I didn't find a way, I knew I'd cease to exist. I knew the energy would win. This is different. I had dreams, Nicolas. Everyone has to be able to dream. If I can't have reality, I have to be able to have dreams, and if I can't maintain with all those people," she waved her hand to indicate the GhostWalkers, "then I have nothing left, not even my dreams."

"You'll have me, Dahlia. We've spent days and nights together and we've both survived. I'm not going anywhere." His hands gripped her upper arms. "I've looked for you all of my life. I never thought I'd ever have a woman of my own, but I've found you. You given me more than you'll ever understand. If our visits to Lily have to be short in the beginning while we learn to handle the energy, she'll understand. We'll keep working until we get it right."

She closed her eyes and buried her face against his chest. Everything he said made such sense to her. The frightening knowledge was blossoming inside of her. She was falling in love with Nicolas Trevane. She couldn't bear the thought of losing both Nicolas and Lily. He might think they could conquer the massive amounts of energy, but he'd never seen houses on fire. "I don't have your emotional control, and before you quote me all the Zen masters, I've studied their teachings. I've meditated in so many different positions I turned myself into a pretzel. It didn't do me any good. My feelings are so amplified by the energy I myself produce with my emotions. I'm frightened right now, and upset. Can't you feel the energy massing around us?"

His hands slid up her back to the nape of her neck. "Yes. Can you feel that when you're touching me, the energy lessens in intensity? I can teach you the things my grandfathers taught me. Ways to stay above the emotion and let it dissipate naturally."

"*You* do that. You're an anchor. It isn't your training."

"How do you think I manage to have such low levels of energy even when I'm in a life-or-death situation? It's training. You have the discipline, Dahlia. You're already using it when you rotate the spheres and allow the energy to disperse through physical activity. Come on. We don't have rooftops to leap over, or cables to run across, but we can wrestle a few alligators."

She allowed herself a second brief spurt of amusement. "*You* can wrestle the alligators, Nicolas, it sounds too muddy for my liking. I really don't like mud in my hair."

"You're such a girlie girl."

Dahlia did laugh then, a genuine laugh. The sound carried out over the bayou, taking with it some of the terrible pressure in her body. "Are you trying to challenge me? Goad me into some kind of he-man competition? That is such a juvenile male thing. *Women, real* women do not have to prove anything to men. We already know we're the superior gender." She stepped away from him and moved across the roof with her easy, sure steps.

As always, Nicolas marveled at her balance. She turned her head and smiled, a particularly mischievous smile that turned his entire body rock hard and his insides to mush.

He would never get used to the effect she had on him, but it was growing on him. He could live with it. In fact, as long as he didn't have to admit it, he liked it.

She somersaulted off the edge of the roof and landed like a cat on her feet, already running through the lush vegetation. She was small and light, barely skimming the ground as she ran, fitting onto a narrow path that would be difficult for his much larger and heavier frame.

"That's taking unfair advantage!" he called after her, leaping from the slope of the roof to the ground.

He followed her through the swamp, pacing himself, careful not to catch up, but close enough to keep her in sight. He loved the effortless way she ran. The smooth fluid motion and the lightness of her feet. Within minutes he was watching the sway of her bottom, the way the material of her jeans stretched tight across her buttocks, cuddled and framed her flesh. He'd never forget that first glimpse of her naked butt, just the briefest sight, but it had been enough to bring on a million fantasies.

Nicolas ran behind her and thought about the curve of her hip. Her smooth, flawless skin beneath the jeans. He closed his hands into tight fists, imagining sinking his fingers into her, kneading her bottom, pulling her tightly against him. It was becoming much more difficult to run as with each step his body seemed to harden into one long ache, but his mind refused to give up the erotic images. Every fallen log he ran by he visualized draping her over and driving into her over and over again. The sunlight would gleam over her skin, and he'd watch the way they joined so perfectly together.

He groaned aloud as his erection grew heavier, pushing tightly against the material of his jeans and rubbing uncomfortably. He felt the merest brush over his skin, as if a butterfly had slipped into his jeans and landed on his penis. The wings seemed to flutter over the sensitive head, skimmed the long root, and then warm breath engulfed him, warm, moist heat and a tongue lapping.

He staggered, halting instantly, grabbing the nearest

tree for support. Laughter floated back to him. Dahlia turned, standing in the sunlight, rays scattering all around her, lighting her face, her smile, her tongue, as she wet her lips and threw her head back in a sultry invitation. Her black eyes laughed at him. Challenged him.

"Come here." He couldn't go to her. He couldn't walk.

"I don't think so," she answered and turned and ran, leaving him swearing and aching and more in need than ever.

He took a step. Her tongue dipped and stroked. He *felt* it. It was impossible to walk with his body nearly bursting through his jeans. The zipper hissed down and relief was instantaneous. He wrapped his fist around his painful erection and stood waiting for her next move. He felt her teeth nibbling. His body jumped under his hand. Two could play at mind games. And he was fairly certain he was an expert at fantasies.

He pictured her spread out in front of him, her body open to him, little moans escaping from her throat. His mouth was already busy at her breast, hot and strong and moist, laving her nipple and taking tiny bites until she shifted helplessly and her moans increased.

"That's not fair!" She stood a few feet from him, her hair tumbling down in a silken cascade. She was breathing heavily and both hands cupped her aching breasts.

"Open your shirt."

"I'm not opening my shirt. It will only encourage your little breast fetish."

His eyes were on her hands. She moved her palms over her nipples, trying to relieve the ache. He looked up at her face. She was intent on following the stroke of his hand, wrapped around his erection. Her tongue darted out and moistened her lower lip. His body took on a life of its own, nearly jumping out of his hand. "Come here, Dahlia," he said again. "I need you."

CHAPTER FOURTEEN

Nicolas was pure temptation, a devil standing there with his sinful smile and his dark, mesmerizing eyes. How could she possibly resist him? His reaction to their little game was enormous. And enticing. She took a step toward him, drawn in spite of herself.

"Unbutton your shirt. I want to look at you."

His voice was so husky, so raw with hunger, a shiver went down her spine. He wasn't in a playful mood anymore, and it showed in the lines of passion etched so clearly into his face.

Dahlia slipped each button free and allowed the shirt to gape open so the sun could caress her breasts. She cupped the weight of them in her hand, feeling achy and tight and swollen. But her gaze remained on his enormous erection and the drop of moisture glistening in anticipation of her compliance. She took another step toward him.

"Take off your jeans."

She swallowed a sudden spiraling fear, but slowly did as he ordered. She pushed the jeans from her hips and down her legs, stepping out of them. She wore nothing underneath. She watched his breath quicken. Saw his hand tighten, glide smoothly up and down once, twice, in an effort to get relief. Dahlia reached down with one hand and snagged her jeans as she walked to him. "What exactly do you want?"

She walked close enough that her hair slid over the sensitive head of his erection as she dropped the jeans at his feet.

"Take off your shirt. I want to see you."

Without a word she allowed the shirt to slip to the ground. Her hands covered his, slid lower to cup and squeeze his tight sac gently. She allowed her palms to slide over his hips and thighs as she knelt on the jeans in front of him.

Nicolas felt his breath slam out of his lungs, leaving him burning for air. Her mouth slid over him, hot and moist and as tight as a fist. Her tongue danced along his ultrasensitive rim, sending shivers of excitement down his spine and flames burning through his bloodstream. She had taken his fantasy right out of his head, all his thoughts as he'd run behind her, and now she was putting them into action. Her mouth was a miracle of heat. He flung out a hand to find an anchor but could only bury his fingers deep in her hair, urging her on while his hips began to follow the rhythm she set.

His teeth clenched and every muscle tightened. His blood sang and his heart pounded. The bayou came alive around him, dancing with sparklers, tiny stars of brilliant colors, and the electricity zigzagged in an arc as the sexual energy gathered to them, amplifying their every sensation. His fingers skimmed the sides of her breasts, went back to her hair as she performed an amazing dance with her tongue and then suckled as if he were an addicting confection.

Nicolas had never felt such a combination of savagery and love at the same time. A part of him was aware the energy influenced him, but very little of his brain seemed to function. He could only feel—and need. He knew he was being rough when he dragged her closer to him, wanting her to take him deeper, but he couldn't seem to stop. She tantalized and tormented him and the more she did, the more the terrible pressure built until he was certain every part of him would detonate.

He could hear animal sounds, a growling deep in his throat. He wanted the heat of her surrounding him. She was driving him over the edge and wasn't nearly finished with him. He tugged at her hair, a small painful pull, exerting pressure on the roots. Even the silken strands in his fists felt erotic. She looked up at him, licked her lips, as he pulled her easily to her feet. His hands slid over her body. He enjoyed the fact that he was so much bigger, that his palms could cover larger sections of skin. He kneaded her breasts, bent his head to find her mouth, taking possession, not giving her a chance to catch up to his hunger. He nibbled at her mouth, a craving for her taste nearly driving him out of his mind. The pressure in his body, driving upward from his toes to his skull was enormous. He opened her thighs, using his legs so his hand could slide over her flat stomach to the mass of tiny curls. He found them moist with heat.

She was steamy for him. Waiting for him. He knew how she would feel when he entered her. He craved the hot, slick wetness. His fingers pushed into her channel. She cried out his name, her breath coming in gasps. He pushed deeper, forcing her to ride, wanting her to be at the same fever pitch as he was.

Only when she was gasping, her body rocking and tightening, wave after wave, did he look around to spot the nearest fallen log. Fortunately it was only a foot away. He half carried her, throwing her shirt over the log and bending her over it so the curve of her bottom was thrust upward for him. The sun lit up her skin. He stared down at her, kneading her flesh, rubbing his erection along the seam of her perfect cheeks. Her channel was hot and slick and he nuzzled it lovingly. She pushed back, trying to get him to enter her, but he held on, prolonging the moment, enjoying the friction and the sight of the moisture on her skin. He felt a primitive lust building and building and just as wild was the need to know she was his. He had no idea if it was a by-product of the energy or his ancestors, or his bloodline, but there was nothing sweet or gentle in his hunger for her, his addiction to her body or his need to know she belonged to him heart and soul.

He wanted that first moment of entry, as he thrust hard, as he took her with his hands on her hips and her hair spilling around her and her breasts jutting toward the ground, to last forever. Her sheath swallowed him, so tight he grit his teeth. He could bury himself deeper this way, thrust harder, driving into her over and over with long, fast strokes while she bucked and cried out and her muscles clenched and grasped at him. The energy poured over them both until every nerve ending and every cell was alive and wired into erotic passion.

Once he looked up and thought he saw a lightning bolt arcing in the clouds overhead, but nothing mattered but her hot silken sheath squeezing and rubbing with a velvet friction so tight he knew he would never last as long as he needed to be sated. He pulled her back toward him with each stroke, riding her hard and furiously, wanting to crawl inside her body and join them together forever. If there truly was ecstasy in the world, Nicolas knew he'd found it. He pounded into her soft body, and she shoved back just as hard, crying out with pleasure, completely uninhibited with him. She wanted him with the same fierce intensity and she never tried to hide it.

Caught up in the maelstrom of sexual energy, they were wild and frantic. Taking Dahlia was as necessary to Nicolas as breathing. He couldn't begin to think or function until he sated the terrible hunger, the *emptiness* he felt. He took a deep breath, the gathering before a storm, as he felt her body tighten around his. He felt the muscles of her body surrounding him tightly grasp him, greedy for every drop of his passion. Greedy for every sensation he could give her. He was burning out of control, everything in him concentrated in his groin. Thunder was in his head, pounding in his ears. And then he was pouring his seed into her, hot and strong and deep. His hips thrust hard over and over into hers, driving deeper, wanting to be forever a part of her.

Gasping for air, Nicolas bent over her, resting his head on her back while their hearts pounded with the same ferocity with which they'd made love. He didn't want to leave the sanctuary, the paradise of her body. As many times as he'd taken her—and it was many now—each time seemed better than the perfection of the time before. He pressed a kiss to the base of her spine as he eased his body from hers. "I love the way you play mind games, Dahlia. Feel free to indulge any time."

He was the only thing holding her up. Dahlia was almost euphoric, yet her body well used, deliciously sore. She could feel his prints on her skin, his mark deep inside her body. She doubted if she would ever be whole without him. She rested against the fallen tree while his hands massaged her bottom and sent more ripples through her deepest core. After such a firestorm of frenzied lovemaking, she felt she needed the easier deep contractions to come down from wherever she was floating.

Slowly she turned and leaned back against the log. "Why is it I never seem to have my clothes on around you?"

Nicolas bent his dark head to hers. "Because I love to look at you." He framed her face with his hands and held her still for his kiss. He made it loving and tender, a direct contrast to the wildness of his lovemaking. "Not only do I love to look at you, Dahlia, but I love to hear the sound of your voice. And I love your expressions. I have the feeling I've already fallen in love with you, that I'm in way over my head."

Dahlia stared up at him, blinking rapidly, feeling as if her heart stopped in midbeat. She was naked and vulnerable and he was declaring his love to her. "Don't love me, Nicolas. Don't do that."

"I think it's too late, honey. I think I fell like the proverbial tree."

She shook her head. Her breasts swayed, drawing his immediate attention. At once he brought his hands up to cup the slight weight in his palms. His thumbs feathered back and forth gently over the peaks, sending streaks of lightning through her body. Her womb tightened again. He was going to give her another orgasm by just touching her. She shivered beneath his caressing hands while her body rocked with pleasure.

"I could get used to you." She could barely manage to get the words out.

"That's what I've been trying to tell you. Just don't break my heart, Dahlia. I've never handed it over to anyone before."

She placed both hands over his. "I've never had *any-one's* heart. I don't know the first thing about keeping hearts. You're taking a terrible risk."

"That's what I do best." He took the shirt from the fallen log and shook it out, held it for her so she could slip her arms into the sleeves. "Are you feeling relaxed now?" He pulled the edges of the shirt together and buttoned it up.

"I was until you started throwing around the L-word. That's enough to scare anyone." His knuckles brushing her breasts were enough to send her body throbbing all over again. And maybe she was far more relaxed than she thought because her legs were rubbery and threatening to give out on her.

Nicolas zipped up his jeans and retrieved hers, carefully shaking them out, slapping at the material to remove the dirt. "This role reversal has to stop. I'm the man and you're the woman. Women love to hear the L-word. It's been that way for centuries. Don't muck up the proper order of things."

"Is there some sort of guidebook for relationships?" she asked curiously. "I've never seen an actual relationship. Jesse never mentioned a girlfriend, and Milly and Bernadette *never* talked about men. I think they thought if they did it would upset me."

"Why would that be?" Nicolas watched her shimmy

into her jeans. There was something very feminine about the way she put on her clothes. He could watch her dress and undress forever.

"Because I'd never have a boyfriend, of course."

"I've always thought that was such a stupid word. *Boy*friend. Aren't we adults? And that sounds so insipid. I'm much more than your boyfriend."

"You are?"

He caught her hand and dragged her close to him. "You know damn well I am." He caught the glint of humor in her eyes and laughed with her. It felt good. The last of the energy dispersed, lifting the weight from Dahlia's shoulders.

"Just how far do you plan to take this whole relationship thing, Nicolas? Because if you're thinking of going much further, I definitely need a manual of some kind."

"I'm taking it all the way. You won't need a manual, because I can supply all the answers." He grinned at her as he started back along the path to the cabin.

Dahlia sent him a quick smile and concentrated on the sensations of what they'd just shared together. She knew how draining it was living every day with the surging energy. It could come at the most unexpected and unwanted times, simply by a brief spurt of anger or melancholy as she was feeling now. When she was with Nicolas, reality seemed to slip away, and for a few brief moments she could believe that they would be together, that she could live a seminormal life. The moment the real world intruded, truth hit her hard. Already apprehension at facing all of the men was growing with each step she took toward the cabin. She knew Nicolas thought her undisciplined, but to marshal one's thoughts and emotions every waking minute was nearly impossible.

"How do you keep your emotions so under control, Nicolas? Even when you're doing things that have to bother you?" She glanced up at him to make certain her question hadn't upset him.

"I don't do anything unless I believe it is necessary. If it's necessary then there's no reason for me to be bothered by it. The universe has a natural order. I do my best to flow with it and not try to control things outside of myself. The truth is, control is a myth. You can't control another person or even an event. You can only control yourself. So that's what I do. If it becomes necessary to go out on a mission and a job has to be done, I do it. There's no reason to complicate it with unnecessary emotion."

"And you can do that?" Some of what he said made sense, but she had to admit some of it bothered her. "If you'd been sent here to kill me would you have done it?"

"I wouldn't have come unless someone gave me a damned good reason, Dahlia. You've never done anything to warrant a death sentence."

She rubbed at her forehead where the aftermath of her headache still lingered. "I'm glad I don't have to make those decisions. I suppose there's a sort of safety in having the psychic abilities I have. I can't deliberately cause harm to someone without severe, immediate retribution. I know they wanted to train me as a weapon, but I couldn't do all of the things necessary. For all the problems mine might cause, I guess it saved me from having to make decisions I might not want to make."

"Did you enjoy learning martial arts?"

"Yes." Dahlia could hear the sound of hammers and saws ringing through the bayou as they got closer to the cabin. Her stomach tightened. She drew a deep, steadying breath and continued walking with him as if she didn't hear a thing.

"Good. I have a beautiful dojo in my home. You'll enjoy it."

"For some reason, I had the impression all of you stayed with Lily at her house."

"We do temporarily. She was generous enough to open her home. Whitney added special walls to help keep out sound and better protect Lily. We train there, conducting exercises to strengthen the barriers in order to permit us to stay out in the world without anchors for longer periods of time. We all have our own homes. Mine is in California up in the

mountains. I have several acres, and the gardens are beautiful. I have a crew maintaining the property while I'm gone."

She heard the pride in his voice. He cared about his
home. "Tell me about the house."

"It's a mixture of East and West. The Japanese design is
very open and gives it a sense of tranquility. I feel peace
when I'm there. I enjoy working with plants, and fortunately, the weather is mild enough that the gardens stay
green nearly year round. You can hear the sound of water
running in the creek, and we incorporated a small natural
waterfall and pool into the gardens. I have beds of herbs
and healing plants as well." He sent her a quick grin. "I was
optimistic I'd learn to heal."

They were close enough to the cabin that Dahlia could
hear the sounds of the men's voices as they good-naturedly
ribbed one another back and forth. She stopped on the
worn trail to look up at Nicolas. The sun cast streaks of
light through the midnight black hair and kissed his skin
with bronze so that he seemed almost glowing to her. "I
can picture you working in your garden. Funny that I never
even considered it before. You told me about both of your
grandfathers, but I think I was only seeing parts of you, not
putting you together as a whole." She slipped her arms
around his waist and tilted her head up to his. "I want you
to kiss me again so I'm thinking about that when we see
the others instead of the humiliation of setting Gator's
house on fire."

Nicolas didn't hesitate. He caught the back of her head
in the palm of his hand and lowered his mouth to hers.
Each time he kissed her the way she tasted, the melting of
their bodies, always moved him so unexpectedly. He
doubted if he would ever get used to the feel and taste of
her. She had crawled inside of him and there was no way to
get her out. He started out kissing her gently, tenderly, but
in the end he was a starving man, craving more, kissing her
over and over.

"Hey!" Gator's voice drew them apart. "Nico, you get
your hands off *cha d'bebe* and mind your manners."

Dahlia drew away, her face coloring in spite of her resolve not to let them embarrass her further. She was definitely *not* Gator's sweet baby. The man could curl a woman's toes just with his smooth voice. And he knew it too.

"I think your *bebe* made the first move," Sam called from the corner of the house. He had a saw in his hands and was grinning at them.

Gator's hand went to his heart. "Say it's not true, *ma cher cherie*. You have not allowed this corrupter of women to tempt you, have you?"

Dahlia raised her eyebrow and looked up at Nicolas. Nothing seemed to affect him, not being caught kissing her and certainly not their teasing. He looked as inscrutable and as composed as ever. "Do you corrupt women?"

"That's Gator's department. The ladies always go for him. He has that bad boy look and the Cajun accent, and he speaks French and they all go wild."

Dahlia leaned back against Nicolas, accepting the protection his body offered, not because she needed it, but because she sensed *he* did. Nicolas had no more experience in relationships than she did, and he was uncomfortable with the easy camaraderie the other GhostWalkers were attempting to establish with her. She realized he wasn't nearly as sure of himself and of her as he let on. "I can see that about Gator. He's smooth when he dishes out the bull, you know what I mean?" She winked up at Nicolas.

Nicolas felt his heart do a curious somersault. Dahlia created an intimacy with him, a bond, and he knew she did it for him, not for her. He thought there was something remarkable about small, unexpected things when someone did them for him. He had been young when he lost his Lakota grandfather, and his Japanese grandfather had rarely been demonstrative, but Nicolas remembered the impact when he would do some small thing to show affection.

He cleared his throat. "I know exactly what you mean."

Gator threw back his head and laughed. "She's a good one, that woman. You hang onto her, Nico."

"I intend to," Nicolas answered.

"Gator," Dahlia gestured toward the cabin. "I'm sorry I set your house on fire. Things like that happen a lot around me."

"A little fire is nothing to worry about, *'tite soeur*. We fixed it right up." His grin turned mischievous. "I saw sparks in the air over by the old pond. I was most worried the two of you were having a bit of fight, but now I think it was something altogether different."

Dahlia couldn't help but laugh. It wasn't just his outrageous behavior, but his easygoing attitude and charming accent. And he had referred to her as *little sister.* Part of her wanted to bask in that.

Nicolas was obviously reading her thoughts. *Gator is anything but easygoing in a fight, Dahlia. He's one of the best we have. All of them are. Never underestimate him.*

I wasn't worried. I just think he's . . . she hesitated, substituted, *cute.*

Cute? You think he's cute? What's cute about him?

She loved the teasing note in his voice. Nicolas was so much more relaxed around her now. They were actually reaching a point where they seemed to fit with one another. He could tease her about another man and the earlier jealousy didn't flare up. *Well, yes. He's got that smile, that really bad boy smile, and a great backside.*

On page eighty of the relationship manual, it clearly states you cannot look at another man's backside, especially if you think it's great.

Her laughter floated out over the bayou. Great tall herons flapped their wings and continued walking on their stilt-like legs through the reeds. Several frogs croaked, and both Kaden and Ian stuck their heads around the corner.

Kaden gave her a little salute. "I'm glad to see you're feeling much better."

"Much, thank you, although I'm a bit embarrassed that I set Gator's house on fire."

"I told you there was no need to be upset, *ma cher*," Gator said. "We wouldn't want the men to be getting bored. I put them to work."

"Still, I hate the loss of control," Dahlia said, determined to try to fit in with the GhostWalkers. If she was the same as they were, and they could understand the complications facing her and maybe find a way to make her life better, she was going to give it her all. "I've worked very hard for as long as I can remember and yet I'm still making childish mistakes. Part of it is my own temper."

Nicolas ruffled her hair, wishing he could find the right words to say to comfort her. "You're too hard on yourself. We're all learning about this. Did you ever think one of the other missing girls might be out there somewhere alone, not knowing what happened to her? Maybe thinking she's insane? The more we find out what you can and can't do, the better it is for all of us. Experiments are risky and there are mistakes made, but they're necessary. You have to think of being around the GhostWalkers as an experiment. None of us would ever condemn a mistake."

The men gaped at Nicolas. "That's the most I've heard him say in three years," Sam said. He turned to the others. "You ever hear him talk that much?"

"I wasn't sure he could talk," Tucker Addison replied straight-faced.

"He talks," Dahlia said defensively.

"Beggin your pardon, ma'am, but he's just plain antisocial," Sam pointed out. "Always has been, always will be."

Dahlia lifted her face to the breeze, inhaling deeply. "Why is it so much easier? Is it because I'm outdoors? What are you all doing differently?"

"We're capable of keeping our own emotions in check, Dahlia," Kaden said. "We talked it over and decided that was the best course of action for your comfort when you're around us."

Unexpectedly she felt tears burn behind her eyes and she slipped her hand into her pocket to feel the familiar comfort of the amethyst spheres. "Thank you. It's amazing that all of you can keep a barrier up around your emotions. None of you are going to suffer any ill effects are you? I'm well aware the use of talent can sometimes be painful."

"No, it just requires a little discipline," Gator said. "Some of us have it naturally, but Tucker there, he's working on it."

The men grinned at Tucker. *Tucker's one of the most patient and calm on the GhostWalker team. Nothing riles him. He used to work on the antiterrorist team before he came to us and he's as steady as a rock,* Nicolas supplied via their mental connection.

"Can you teach me the same thing?"

"Sure." Kaden spoke again. "Lily has us all do mental exercises every day, just like weight lifters. It's stopped most of the side effects, although the first few weeks were difficult. Now we just do them automatically. It keeps us sharp for the work we do."

Dahlia walked with Nicolas around the cabin to the front entrance where a new door and frame were already in place. "Do all of you have different psychic abilities?" It was much easier dealing with the men now that they were doing their best to barricade all emotions, sparing her another bombardment of energy.

"We share various talents," Sam said, "although each of us has several and some unique only to us. For instance, Gator comes in right handy when guard dogs come running at us. He can get wild animals to turn into pets."

Dahlia turned her head to look at Gator, who was draped against the wall looking sexy in his open shirt with his white teeth flashing and his dark hair spilling across his forehead.

Gator grinned at her. "I'm reading your thoughts, *ma cher cherie.*"

Nicolas pulled a knife out of his boot and studied the long blade. "She isn't your anything, swamp man." His voice was as cold as ice, but Dahlia dealt in energy and to her relief, Nicolas was definitely amused.

"That be the jealousy talking," Gator said, in no way perturbed. "I can't help the way the women love me. I was born with the gift."

The men hooted and made rude noises. "You were born

with a gift of bullshitting," Sam pointed out, "but that's about it." He looked at Dahlia. "Pardon me, ma'am, but it's the truth."

"I rather thought it was," she agreed.

Another roar of laughter went up. Gator clasped both hands over his heart. *"Tu m'a casser le coeur, j'va jamais."*

Dahlia smirked. "I didn't break your heart, Gator, and if I did, I'm certain you'll recover from the blow."

He grinned. "But French has a music all it's own. *D'accord?"*

Gator could definitely melt hearts with that grin. *"D'accord,"* she conceded.

"Quit flirting, Gator," Tucker said. "You're riling up Nico. You mess with the wrong end of the crocodile and you're going to get teeth."

"He doesn't look too riled to me," Gator answered. "He looks like he's fallen into a deep dark well and there's no bottom in sight."

Another roar of laughter went up. Dahlia found she was actually enjoying herself. It was a momentous moment, one she'd always remember. She was in the midst of several people for the first time in her life, laughing and conversing, and the energy hadn't swamped her. If it never happened again, she would always be grateful to the GhostWalkers for giving her this time. "It's such an amazing gift you've all given me," she said. "I've never done this before. Just had a conversation with a group of people."

"Better you picked us than anyone else," Gator teased. "We're all good-looking, 'cept old stone-faced Nico there. Why trouble yourself with anybody else?"

"I don't suppose you cook?" Tucker inquired hopefully.

"Did you think because she can start fires she'd be great with a grill?" Gator asked.

Dahlia tried not to let the color sweep up into her face, wanting to enjoy the camaraderie they were offering her. They teased and razzed one another and now extended it to her. She couldn't object over the subject matter, as sensitive as she felt over it. She'd have to get over it around them.

"The thought occurred to me," Tucker admitted. "I'm starving. Gator, didn't you stash us some genuine food?"

"That wasn't my job. I'm not the supply person," Gator denied. "I found shelter for us, isn't that enough?"

Dahlia glanced up at Nicolas. He reached out and took her hand. "Don't mind them, they'll find something to eat. Besides, Gator never goes anywhere without food."

"If he didn't this time, Gator's going to be alligator hunting," Sam said. "I've heard they're good to eat."

Dahlia shook her head. "I'm not eating an alligator. I was raised with them. It would be like eating the family dog."

"They are the family dogs," Gator said, glaring at Sam. "You keep your hands off my gators. They've been in the family for years. If you're all that hungry, go pick a few shrubs. There's edible weeds on this island, you're just too lazy to find them."

"Can you talk to the alligators?" Dahlia asked. It suddenly occurred to her how astonishing that would be.

"I don't exactly talk to them," Gator explained. "It's more like directing them. It's easier with dogs or cats, but I've tried it with reptiles. Alligators are fairly difficult, but I've gotten them to move away from an area they wanted to stay in. I don't think it's useful because it would take me too long to get them to obey me. If we were in a firefight, we'd be moving too fast."

"A lot of what we can do is easier and faster if we're all together," Kaden explained. "We all have talents, but we seem to become stronger when we're together, which is why, when we go on a mission, we generally go in small units."

"I've always worked alone. If I had a partner and he or she became frightened, or excited or was injured, I wouldn't be able to function properly," Dahlia said and looked up at Nicolas to make certain he understood what she was saying.

He frowned at her. "You're functioning with no problems right now," he pointed out.

"True, *I* am," Dahlia said, "but some of you are having trouble keeping emotions and thoughts in check. It isn't natural to do it for long periods of time."

"We do just fine together," Nicolas said.

Dahlia rolled her eyes. *This is exactly why I don't have a partner. I'm the one who has to guard my emotions when people act idiotic. I can't take it, Nicolas. It's just plain silly to get all chest pounding on me.*

I was stating a fact.

No, you weren't, you were giving me one of your mini lectures.

"I don't give lectures," Nicolas said aloud.

"What about Jesse Calhoun," Kaden interrupted quietly. "Did you do much work with him? Did he ever go out with you on a mission?"

It seemed a casual enough question, but Dahlia instantly felt the shift. Tension went up just a notch, and everyone was suddenly paying close attention, waiting for her answer. "We worked together. He was always the handler, sending me in. I only had contact with him when it came to my missions, but he never accompanied me, it didn't work that way." She chose her words carefully, searching the energy for a sign of where the sudden change of subject was heading.

"Nicolas mentioned that Jesse Calhoun is a Ghost-Walker. Is that true?"

Dahlia nodded her head slowly. "He's definitely an anchor and a strong telepath. He's an ex SEAL and a very good agent. He can track almost anything."

"How does this whole thing work with you and the NCIS? Do you do investigative work for them?" Kaden continued.

Dahlia's fingers curled around the amethyst spheres in her pocket. "No, I'm strictly recovery. Jesse does investigations."

"Who else?"

She shrugged. "Todd Aikens. He's a SEAL as well. He and Jesse are very close. Martin Howard, he works with both Todd and Jesse sometimes, and there's Neil Campbell. They're all friends. I've not met them, just heard Jesse talk about them. I've heard him mention a couple of other names as well."

"How many others? Are they like Jesse?"

"I told you, I don't know. I just know of them. I've never worked with them." She was beginning to feel as if she were being interrogated.

"Would any of them know you were going into recover the data?" Kaden asked.

"Only Jesse as far as I know. Well, his boss would know, and maybe Louise, the secretary. I mean she'd guess. If Jesse's called in and asked to do an investigation and then I'm called in it would be obvious they're using me for something to do with the investigation, I'd think. And I only do recovery."

"By boss, you're referring to Frank Henderson?" Respect crept into Kaden's voice. Henderson was a legend in the military.

"Yes, he heads up the NCIS. Nothing happens without his knowledge. He's very hands-on with the investigations and he wants up-to-the-minute reports. He runs a tight ship."

"How do you pass the data to Calhoun?" Kaden persisted.

"I recover, drop it in a safe zone, and tell him in person where it is. He goes and gets it and takes it back to the NCIS."

"Have you checked in to the office at all?"

She shook her head. "I figure someone there has to be selling information. I walked into a trap. And they knew where I lived. And they knew about the safe house in the Quarter. That could only have come from the NCIS office. The computers are regularly gone over by the techs, so I doubt if someone could have found me through all the security that way."

"And someone took a shot at her," Nicolas added.

"Call them now," Kaden advised. "Talk only to Henderson. Tell him you think there's a rat and that's why Calhoun was taken to a safe location and is under guard. Tell him you want to bring the data in, but you don't trust anyone. He'll set up a meeting to do the exchange, and we'll be there to protect you."

She shook her head. "It's too risky. He could get killed."

"You don't think he's the traitor?"

"Not for a minute. I don't have a single doubt about him. Have you ever met him?" Dahlia's voice was fierce. "He loves his country. He's served it all his life. He would never, under any circumstances betray it or his men. He has a code of honor he lives by and he's as solid as they come."

"You like him."

"I've grown to respect him." She glanced apologetically at Nicolas. "He talked me into working for the NCIS when I was just a kid. I'm not going to use him as bait to bring out the traitor. Besides, he'll expect the data, and I don't have it yet."

"What did you just say?" Nicolas's voice was very quiet and sent a shiver of alarm down her spine.

CHAPTER

FIFTEEN

Dahlia shrugged her shoulders, striving to appear nonchalant. "That data still has to be recovered."

There was a small silence. The GhostWalkers exchanged long looks. "I thought you'd already recovered the research," Nicolas said. "Why would these people be coming after you if they still had it?"

"Well, they don't have it. Halfway into the mission, I realized it was a setup. I knew they were dangling bait, false bait—I'd read the original data the professors had before they were murdered. A few days earlier, when I was scouting the building, I thought I recognized one of the men on the same floor where I'd been told the data was. It nagged at me that I'd seen him before somewhere, but I couldn't place him. I'd already broken in and had accessed the computer and I skimmed the report and realized it was a fake. That triggered my memory of the man. He'd been a student at the university, just walking by in the hall outside of one of the professor's offices. He had glanced inside the door, and that attracted my attention. He didn't turn his head in any obvious way, but I knew he was looking in. People just don't do that ordinarily, so he stuck in my mind."

Gator rubbed his head. "I'm confused, Dahlia. You spotted this same man in the building where you were scouting to break in?"

She nodded. "But I didn't place him. It's been a year since I was at the university taking a look at the documents."

Sam laughed. "Don't apologize. Most people wouldn't have noticed him, let alone recognized him a year later."

"Well, it would have been a lot safer had I recognized him immediately. Instead, it took me skimming the document and realizing it was a false one as well. For a minute I thought maybe the company had been sold false data, but then I remembered where I'd seen him, and I realized the data was flagged and I'd be having company any minute."

She glanced at Nicolas. Waves of dark energy swarmed around her. "You're getting upset. I'm alive and safe, and it wasn't all that difficult to get out of there. The biggest problem was the research data. I didn't want them to be able to move it. I was fairly certain they didn't have much warning so they couldn't have buried it all that deep. Most people think in terms of protecting a computer, but a really good hacker can get through most computers given the time. I figured they didn't put anything on the computers just because of that. And if I was right, that meant there was only the one copy. And if there was only one copy, they had it locked up tight."

"A lot of assumptions in a short period of time, especially when people are coming after you," Kaden pointed out. "You should have gotten the hell out of there."

"I was fairly certain I could stay hidden. And I also knew I could provide a few diversions. I was more worried about the security system where they had the data. I assumed they'd beef it up and maybe provided a human guard or two. I wish I had your ability to coax someone to look the other way."

Nicolas folded his arms across his chest, his bronzed

features an implacable mask. "So you stayed even though you knew it was a trap and you had no backup. Calhoun couldn't have even gotten to you if they'd found you. You saw what they did to him. They would have killed you. You must have known that, Dahlia. They had to be putting out some malicious energy."

She could feel his level of anger rising, a very unusual emotion for Nicolas. If the others hadn't been there, she would have reached out to soothe him, but she felt inhibited by their presence. Inwardly she sighed. She had no idea how to act around other people. What kind of relationship did Nicolas and she really have? They'd slept together. Lots of couples slept together and it didn't mean anything at all.

"Yes it does." Nicolas said the words aloud deliberately, said them between his bared teeth. He said them aloud to show her he was seriously staking his claim. He didn't care how primitive she might think him. She wasn't going to have sex with him and throw him out, damn it. They belonged together. There was law and order in the universe. She wasn't going to turn him inside out and upside down and then toss him out like garbage.

"Stop it!" Dahlia backed away from him to the doorway. "You're acting like an idiot."

The other GhostWalkers exchanged raised eyebrows, clearly not feeling the hostile energy pouring off of Nicolas the way she did. Dahlia didn't understand how they could be so protected.

"Well, now, ma'am," Sam said, scratching his head. "This is the first time I've ever heard anyone call Nico an idiot." He quickly held up his hand for peace when she turned to include him in her glare. "I'd be obliged if you let us in on what's going on. To be honest, no one dares to call him much of anything."

"Why not?" Dahlia flicked a quick look at Nicolas, who leaned one hip against the wall and managed to look lethal just standing there.

"He's a dangerous-looking fellow," Sam pointed out.

"And he's handy with guns and knives and all sorts of other nasty weapons a pretty little thing like you wouldn't want to know about."

Dahlia knew immediately Sam was diffusing the situation, and she was grateful for the instant reduction of energy. She had the impression of a smile in her mind, but Nicolas's expressionless features didn't reflect one.

"Please go on, Dahlia," Kaden prompted with a small warning glance at Nicolas. "What did you do?"

Nicolas's black gaze iced over, but he refrained from speaking.

"I went into my invisible mode and made myself quite small. I can't blur my clothes, so I always note the walls of the places I'm going and try to wear clothes that blend. I can manipulate the surface of my skin, which helps to blur my image somewhat. It allows me to slip past the guards. I hid in a vent while they searched the building. I purposely chose the smallest one I could find so they would overlook it, thinking I couldn't possibly have used it to hide. It was a very uncomfortable couple of hours."

Kaden nodded his head. "Your 'invisible mode' is really more of a chameleon mode, right?"

"Exactly. I've practiced until I can blend into most backgrounds."

Tucker inhaled sharply. "I saw that on the tape during your training. It must come in handy. Wish I could do it."

"Why didn't you just get the hell out of there?" Sam asked curiously.

"I figured they'd move the real data. I was fairly certain they'd check to make certain I hadn't found it and they'd lead me right to it. I wouldn't have to check every box in the vault, and I'd be able to get it and get out fast."

Nicolas paced away from the small group. Dahlia's tales of her adventures were holding the GhostWalkers spellbound, but they made him ill. Nothing and no one had ever affected him as she did. He felt her inside of him. Inside his head, his body, even his heart. It was crippling to a man like him. He had to have a clear head and his body couldn't be tied up in knots, especially around Dahlia. Just the thought of her in such a dangerous situation sickened him.

He took a deep breath, made every effort to clear his mind.

"Nico," Kaden called him back to the group. "If we're going to help Dahlia plan going back in to recover the data, we'll need you on board. You're carrying most of the load, moving the energy away from all of us."

Nicolas glanced at his friend and then back into the murky waters of the bayou. Kaden was carrying a good bit of the load as well. He was every bit as strong an anchor as Nicolas was, and he guarded the other men carefully. He sighed. As much as he liked Kaden, he didn't want his friend to be the one drawing the energy away from Dahlia, or worse, diffusing it with whatever emotion was the most flammable.

He nodded at Kaden. "Don't worry, I'm on board."

Dahlia walked over to him and put her hand on his arm. It was a small gesture, but he knew the cost to her. She wasn't a woman who touched others, and certainly not publicly. His thumb feathered over her wrist. "What did you do?"

"I waited in the vent until I heard them call off the search and then I followed the primary suspect, a man by the name of Trevor Billings. He heads up one of the many departments at Lombard Inc." She named a primary company the defense department often used for building prototypes and weapons. The company was reputed to be heavily guarded and under the tightest of security. "Billings has been a suspect for some time. The NCIS believed he was selling weapons to terrorists and other governments, basically anyone who can pay for them, but they can't prove it. The word is, he has a small army of his own and a couple of senators in his pocket to insure he gets the contracts he wants. Jesse believed someone inside the NCIS was tipping him off when anyone came up with new ideas for weapons and Billings was stealing the data before the contracts were given out. That way, he didn't have to pay off his senators and he didn't have to share with anyone. He just creates a couple of accidents for the professor, or whoever happens to think up the idea, and then he claims it belongs to his company and sells it to the government, or whoever is the highest bidder. It's a win-win situation for him."

"It's not a bad idea. If he uses accidents and covers all of the United States, not hitting in the same place too often, he could really have something and no one would be the wiser. People get government grants all the time to think things up. From one end of the country to the other, teachers and students and private corporations seek grants," Kaden mused aloud. "I can see how it would be much more profitable to him to get the data and suddenly come up with the idea himself and then market it."

"Jesse wanted it stopped," Dahlia said. "He wanted proof that Billings had those professors killed, and he wanted the data back."

"Well we certainly wouldn't want to disappoint Jesse, not with your life at stake," Nicolas said. There was a small note in his voice that sent alarms skittering down her spine. There was ice in his eyes and in his veins and his mouth was a merciless slash.

"I take a great deal of pride in what I do. I'd never failed before, and I wasn't about to do so this time." Dahlia wanted to sound calm, but to her horror, she actually sounded as if she were appeasing him and that brought her own temper flaring. Snatching her hand back, she glared at him and paced away from the suddenly smothering group. "I don't have to explain myself to you or anyone else. I stayed to get the job done, that's all." *Why* did she feel she owed him any explanation at all? No wonder there was a need for a relationship manual. Men were idiots. *Supreme* idiots, and women were just as bad trying to soothe men's egos.

Nicolas followed her, feeling a fool. He knew part of the problem was the close proximity of so many men to

Dahlia. He was still fighting off the feeling of watching her slip through his fingers. Combined with his fear for her safety, he was reacting to the amplification of his own emotions by the very energy he was drawing away from his men and from Dahlia. He sighed. So much for self-discipline and control.

I'm sorry, Dahlia. I really am.

She wanted to stay angry with him. There was a form of protection in staying angry, but the aching sincerity in his voice was her downfall. She took the hand he held out to her. He drew her close to him, so close she could feel the heat of his body through the thin material of their clothing.

"I'm good at what I do, Nicolas. If there's danger, I'm careful to keep it to a minimum. And my size is an advantage. I work at night when most people are already gone. Most of the time, I'm in and out and no one is ever the wiser."

"Dahlia," Kaden said, "you must have to travel. Do you fly? How do you get around the traveling aspect of your job?"

"Private plane. I always use the same pilot. He's ex-military as well and works for the NCIS. He was a Green Beret. Most of the men I've met from the NCIS division were in some kind of Special Forces training." She looked at Kaden. "That's not normal, is it?"

"Are they GhostWalkers, Dahlia?" Kaden asked.

"I have no idea." She shrugged lightly and then pushed a hand through her hair. "Maybe. Maybe that's the connection between them. They all seem to know one another and are close. Max is the pilot, and when I'm with him, I never seem to have problems. We don't talk much, so I didn't give it a lot of thought. He's very quiet."

"Max who?" Kaden signaled to Tucker to bring out the satellite phone to call Lily. The more information they had the better.

"Logan Maxwell. Everyone calls him Max." She watched as Tucker talked into the phone, relaying the information. It amazed her that Lily was on the other end. For so long she didn't know if Lily was a figment of her imagination or if she were real. Now, she was almost afraid to believe in her.

Tucker looked at them, his expression grave. "Someone's been trying to track us. They're using sophisticated equipment to do it. This place might not be safe anymore."

Dahlia felt her heart thud. None of the men looked particularly concerned. They were used to the violence in their world. She took a deep breath and tried to look unafraid. It wasn't so much the terror of having mortar rounds fired at her, so much as the onslaught of the violent energy seeking her out in the aftermath. It seemed such a weakness in the face of the strength the other GhostWalkers possessed.

Nicolas slipped his arm around her shoulders. "How do you contact Maxwell for a ride when you're heading out for a mission?"

"Jesse usually arranges transport, but I also call Henderson's secretary and she arranges it for me. She gives me the location of a small field and a time. Max is always there well ahead of me and ready to take off."

"So let's do that. Call the secretary, what's her name?" Kaden asked.

"Louise Charter. I've never met her face-to-face, but I've spoken numerous times with her on the phone. She's a nice woman."

The men exchanged a long look. Dahlia's eyebrow shot up. "What? You aren't going to tell me that Louise is behind all this. She's close to sixty. She's the widow of an FBI agent."

"We'll see," Kaden said. "Let's arrange for transport to the DC and Maryland area so we can pay a little visit to the agents. I think it would be most helpful to get to know them."

"And dangerous," Tucker pointed out. "If they're Ghost-Walkers."

"And if they are, where did they come from? Why haven't we heard of them?"

"Calhoun knew about us," Nicolas said quietly. "He

recognized my name, and he didn't bat an eye over my talking telepathically to him. He knew."

Dahlia immediately felt the impact of the weight of their combined gazes. "Don't be looking at me. I'd never heard of you. If Jesse knew, he didn't say a word to me."

"Where is the data now, Dahlia?" Nicolas asked point-blank.

"In the vault. I just moved it from one box to another. They have a very secure vault, each of their researchers has access using codes and prints and keys to sensitive materials. I didn't have time to get it out of the building. I was afraid I'd be caught, and I wanted to safeguard it. I thought it was better to let them think I smuggled it out and go back later and get it. So I moved it."

"How'd you get past the security?" Kaden asked.

She shrugged. "I followed them in. It wasn't that difficult. They weren't looking for me and I jammed the cameras. I'd been doing it on and off for days so they thought they had a glitch. No one thought to look in the shadows to see if I was following them. It was more difficult getting out than getting in."

"So now you need to break back into the building and bring the data out before they discover they still have it," Kaden concluded.

"That's about it," she agreed.

"Call the secretary and set up transport, Dahlia," Nicolas said. "We'll go along and make certain things run smoothly. And if we're lucky, we'll flush out the traitor while we're at it."

Dahlia shook her head. "I work alone. I can't work with anyone else. You know that, Nicolas. It's too dangerous."

Kaden laughed lightly. "You obviously haven't worked with the GhostWalkers, Dahlia. The recovery is your job. We're just going to go along to smooth the way. Don't worry, we work well as a unit."

Dahlia hesitated, wondering if they were railroading her. She needed time to think things through before committing herself any deeper into the company of so many others. But somehow, in spite of her misgivings, the phone was in her hand.

"I'm going to have a lot of explaining to do," she pointed out.

"Exactly," Nicolas said.

The men watched Tucker as she talked to Louise Charter. He was carefully looking at the screen of his laptop. "Oh, yeah. We're being traced, people. I've thrown up a couple of smoke screens, just enough to keep them thinking we aren't on to them, but they'll find us. We already know they have a team in the area."

"Or what's left of it," Nicolas said.

"Keep talking, Dahlia, let them get a good fix on us," Kaden advised.

Dahlia scowled at him. She was unused to taking orders and especially not used to allowing enemies to pinpoint her exact location. She was a woman of the shadows, and being in a spotlight was extraordinarily uncomfortable. She looked up at Nicolas. His wide shoulders blotted out the sunlight, so that for a moment, she saw only him. He seemed invincible, a man who would never give up, never stop. She kept chatting with Louise, talking about nothing important, yet counting every second until Tucker signaled to her.

"Henderson wasn't available, which means he was out of the office, or he would have insisted on talking to me. Louise wanted to forward my call to him, but I declined," she explained. "So now what?"

"Now we know someone in that office is hunting you," Kaden said.

"I knew that already. How does that narrow it down?"

"I don't think it's all that easy to bug the NCIS secretary's office and trace a call," Kaden answered. "I'd have to say we need to look very closely at the secretary."

For some reason, the idea that Louise could be the traitor made Dahlia feel sick. She liked Louise. Maybe she didn't know her all that well, but she liked her, and she had contact with very few people. She was beginning to believe most of the world was made up of deceivers. Part of her wanted to remain forever in the shadows. It seemed so much safer there. Out in the open, she was so much more vulnerable. She forced a small smile. "I need a little space. While you all eat, I think I'll take a little time for myself." She didn't look at Nicolas when she said it. She needed space from him as well.

Dahlia went for the roof, the safest place she could think of while she sorted things out. They had little time. Either the NCIS had traced the call to ascertain her whereabouts, or someone else had done so, someone who wanted her dead. Either way, it was more than likely they would have company very quickly. She pressed her hands to her face, forcing the air through her lungs. Her life had been turned upside down in a few short days. She'd had no real time to think, or plan. She just kept moving to stay alive. She hadn't even been able to grieve properly for Milly or Bernadette.

She felt for the familiar comfort of the amethyst spheres in her pocket. She had to focus on the mission. Before anything else, she needed clothing. Everything she owned was gone, blown up along with her home. She'd need to use the money Jesse had stashed in the safe house for clothes. She knew the importance of blending into her surroundings.

Dahlia lifted her face to the slight breeze coming in off the water and listened to the comforting sounds of the bayou. All the while she knew a part of her was waiting for Nicolas to come to her, and that frightened her more than the coming trouble. Music drifted up to her, cheery, upbeat strains of reggae. Gator began to sing. She watched as he pulled out a grill and began to prepare for a barbecue. It was strange to sit up on a roof and think that she might actually be part of something like a backyard barbecue.

Dahlia watched the men gather around Gator as he drew the outline of the small island in the dirt beside the grill with a long stick. Gator drew in the shoreline and trees. Nicolas stepped up to study it. Dahlia strained to hear them over the music. None of them seemed to care whether she heard or not as they planned what appeared to be a defense against an invasion.

"We'll want to know where they're going to come in. Gator, you know the island best, as well as the terrain. Let's choose our spot and direct them to an appropriate landing area," Nicolas instructed. He glanced up at Dahlia and winked.

Somehow, under the circumstances, she didn't find it all that reassuring.

"Away from the cabin," Gator said. "We'll have to block off a couple of the landing areas using natural barriers as roadblocks so they don't get suspicious. I've got a few signs that will scare them off anyplace we want to protect."

"We'll want to draw them into a natural ambush area. Set up a few claymore mines with trip wires," Nicolas said.

"I'll cook," Sam offered. "Ian knows his way around the claymore mines. Besides, he likes all those bugs in the swamp."

Nicolas ignored him. "We'll need trip flares set up anywhere there's a possible landing site where they can sneak up on us. Tucker, you want to take care of that? I'll need the rest of you to help with barriers once Gator gives us a location for the ambush. I want this tight, no mistakes. Let's limit where they can come onto the island as best we can. We want them all in the same spot before we spring the trap."

Gator's stick continued to draw lines. "This is the canal. I'm thinking we set up shop here, Nico. It's not too marshy, and they'll be more apt to choose to walk through it then some of the other spots. They'll think the bushes will be to their advantage as well, but they'll be in a box. Half a mile up is a rock face and we can close in on either side and behind them."

Nicolas studied the map drawn into the dirt from every angle. "It's a go then. We have to take out the dock, Gator, otherwise, they may try a frontal attack using a mortar to take out the cabin."

Gator shrugged carelessly. "We all have to sacrifice.

Let's get to work. Sam, don't you ruin those ribs. I marinated them with my special secret sauce."

"They're safe with me," Sam said. "I'll tear down the dock while the ribs are cooking. Watch for leeches, boys," he added cheerfully, waving at them.

The men split up, jogging toward the areas directed. There were three main docking areas and one that could be used if necessary. Tucker set up the trip flares while Gator posted warning signs of sinkholes near the shore. He'd used the signs years earlier to keep the police from searching the island for his wayward brother. To make the intended landing spot more enticing, they drove a couple of old posts deep into the mud for a boat tie off and stamped vegetation into the ground to make the path appear used.

Dahlia stood on the roof and watched them work. The men shed their shirts and spent time dragging brush and placing objects in various locations. She could see a film of dirt rising in the air, but she couldn't really tell what they were doing. All the while the music blasted a happy beat, and the smell of barbecued ribs provided a rich aroma.

Dahlia climbed off the roof to stand on the shoreline as Sam pulled apart the rickety dock. He carefully carried each plank out of sight. "What are you maniacs up to now?" she asked, her hands on her hips. If they were planning violence, she wasn't catching a hint of fear or anticipation. They all seemed to be working readily with a happy smile. If anything she caught hints of hunger as the aroma spread across the small island.

"We're just working up an appetite," Sam assured. "Turn those ribs over, will you? If I burned them, the others would feed me to the alligators."

"Speaking of which, one or two have joined us," she pointed out.

Sam glared at the creature closest to him, sunning itself on the bank not more than a few feet from where he was waist-deep in the water. "Ugly things, aren't they? Damn thing looks like it's just waiting for me to turn my back on it."

Dahlia sauntered over to the grill and frowned down at the ribs. "I'd offer to keep an eye on the alligators for you, but I'm thinking you're holding something back from me. You and your little band of island boys busily working up an appetite just doesn't work for me, you know?" She glanced past Sam deliberately. "Oh, look, a little friend for alligator to play with."

Sam whirled around hastily, staring out over the water. "Where?" He twisted back in an attempt to keep an eye on the alligator sunning itself on the bank. "Where is it?" He yanked a plank loose and held it up as a weapon.

Dahlia carefully turned each rib over, secretly thrilled with the new experience. "I may have been mistaken."

"That's not nice. That's just not nice at all," Sam said, glaring at her.

"Well, it *could* have been an alligator, but more likely it was just bubbles or a floating stick or something like that. You aren't nervous standing in the water like that, are you? I read a book on alligators, and I think they like to come up from the deep to strike, but maybe that's sharks."

Sam swore and hurried out of the water, dragging the plank with him and keeping it between him and the alligator on the shore. The creature didn't move or give ground, but it did emit a low warning growl.

Dahlia burst out laughing. "You're afraid of that little bitty alligator, aren't you? It's not even full grown."

"That's just wrong, girl," Sam said. "I hope Nicolas knows what you're really like. I'll bet he's never seen the mean side of your mouth."

"Of course not." Dahlia admitted blithely. "Are you going to tell me what your little merry band is up to?"

"Merry band?"

"I read Robin Hood, didn't you?"

Sam wiped the sweat from his face as the others came back to camp. "Thank God, you're back, don't leave me with her again. She's worse than the alligator."

* * *

"I'M getting the feeling we should move," Ian said. "I've got that itch crawling down my back." He shoved the plate of rib bones away from him with evident satisfaction. "You sure know how to put on the grub, Gator."

"Hey! I did the cooking." Sam glared at Dahlia. "And it wasn't easy."

"I'm going to be seriously pissed if someone blows up my cabin," Gator said. He winked at Dahlia. "I've got a few little surprises of my own if they set foot on my property."

"It isn't going to help much if they use mortar rounds," Nicolas pointed out. "Let's get out of here before we find ourselves in a trap."

Dahlia watched as the men silently shouldered their packs. She had no idea why they'd calmly waited for the enemy, going so far as to tear into the food with gusto, seemingly without a care in the world. She could feel the tension rising in her with each passing minute, yet none of them exhibited the least amount of anxiety.

She set out with them in the boats. Nicolas was with her and Kaden was with Tucker and Sam in a second boat while Ian and Gator took the third. They moved without haste along the channel toward another small inlet only yards from Gator's cabin.

Dahlia cleared her throat as they began to pull the boats through the reed-choked marsh. "Exactly why aren't we headed for the airstrip?"

"Don't worry, Dahlia," Sam called cheerfully.

Too cheerfully, she decided. She looked at Nicolas suspiciously. "What exactly are you doing?"

"I'm going to stash you somewhere safe, and we're going to do a little recon."

"And you didn't think it necessary to tell me about it?"

"I should have," he admitted, "but to be honest, I just presumed you'd know we'd bait the trap and draw them in. We don't like unfinished business, Dahlia. These people are here for one purpose only. That's to get you. I'm not leaving until there's no threat to you from anyone here."

His merciless tone sent a shiver down her spine. She looked away from him, back toward the river. Whatever code Nicolas lived by, hunted by, believed in, was intertwined inexorably with the man he was. The man she was beginning to fear she was falling in love with. She should have known he would never leave a threat to her. He was incapable of such a thing. There was no point in protesting the danger, or pointing out they could make a run for it. Running wasn't in his character unless it suited his purpose—unless it suited his hunt.

She looked at him and saw the warrior in him, a throwback to a people of integrity and honor. To a people valiant and courageous. He would take the fight wherever he needed to go, and he would be relentless in his pursuit. Dahlia sighed softly. "I can just bet what your recon is going to be."

Nicolas turned to signal the others to get rid of the boats. He took her arm. "Let's get you out of the line of fire. How far do you have to be to keep the energy from finding you?"

"I've never actually measured the distance." She didn't know whether to be angry or grateful. That was the trouble with relationships, she decided, a woman was always torn between feeling protected by a man like Nicolas and wondering if she should just kick him for his overbearing behavior.

He brought her hand to his mouth and nibbled on her fingers, his black gaze studying her face even as they picked their way through the brush. "You aren't worried, are you?"

"Why should I be worried? It's just another day in the neighborhood. You know—bombs, fires, people shooting at you. Why would I be worried? Especially since we could be clothes shopping or boarding a plane. I'm not in the least worried."

"Hmmm," he mused aloud. "I read about this in the relationship manual. It's called *womanly sarcasm* and usually means a man is in deep trouble." He found a cool spot hidden near the center of the island. "You stay here until I come and get you."

"What exactly do you think you're accomplishing by this?"

"I'm keeping the enemy off our backs while we hunt the traitor and recover the data," Nicolas replied. He bent his head to kiss her. "Be here when I get back."

He made himself walk away from her, telling himself she'd be there waiting for him when he returned, knowing her decision could go either way. As he approached the others, he signaled and they immediately went into combat readiness, taking out their weapons and shouldering their packs, scattering into the thick reeds to lie in wait for the enemy to arrive.

The sound of oars splashing in the water was enough to send several birds into the air and to silence the hum of insects for a few moments. And it was enough to warn the GhostWalkers. Gator signaled he'd spotted the boat as it cautiously circled the island, looking for a suitable landing spot. Gator used the sounds of the bayou, a perfect imitation of an aroused alligator to give them a number. Five occupants. Nicolas spread his fingers, gestured to the others.

The moment they knew the incoming boat was docking exactly where they'd planned, the occupants tying up to the two posts standing upright in invitation, the GhostWalkers slipped into the water, using reeds as breathing tubes as they sank beneath the surface to make their way across the canal to box in the enemy. Once in position, they waited beneath the murky water for the signal from their point man to proceed.

Nicolas felt the tap on his arm and sent the gesture through the line to his men. They raised slowly, blackened water creatures armed with M-4s and knives, their choice weapons of war. As still as statues, they remained in the water, camouflaged by the reeds and plants with only their heads and shoulders above the surface, rifles trained on the enemy.

The five killers spread out, moving onto the island in

silence, two using the path that had been made for them, the other three a good distance away. Nicolas and the GhostWalkers rose up out of the depths of the waters without a sound, slithering onto shore, bellies to the ground, rifles ready. They were a solid unit, had worked many missions, and knew exact positions without ever having to look. They pushed their way through the dense shrubbery following the five assassins, staying low to the ground, unseen, unheard.

A frog set up a chorus of sound. An alligator bellowed. A large bird rose into the air with the flapping of great wings, and the wind moaned through the brush. Gator lay flat, concentrating on the beehive clinging to the branches of a tree just ahead of the five men. At once the bees became agitated, buzzing angrily, emerging from the hive in a black swarm. Snakes plopped into the water, the sound carrying loudly through the waterway. Lizards and insects skittered in large masses across the ground.

The five men began slapping at the bugs and bees swarming around them. They ran in an effort to get away from the stinging bees. One ran into the first claymore mine and tripped the wire. The explosion was loud, and the others immediately went to ground, blasting away with weapons at empty air.

Nicolas took the higher ground, maneuvering into position to pick them off one at a time. Kaden flanked him, choosing a target as well. They fired almost simultaneously. The two remaining turned their weapons toward the sound of the rifle fire. Sam signaled he had the shot and took it, Tucker following suit.

Almost at once they heard the explosion behind them, coming from the other island. A fireball whooshed through the air and landed in the water, sizzling as it disappeared in the midst of black smoke. Nicolas swore. "Clean up here," he snapped and ran to the water to cross the canal.

Dahlia was in the middle of a seizure when he found her, the violent energy burning through her veins, convulsing her body again and again. He knelt beside her, took her hand, hoping to draw the energy away from her.

"How bad?" Kaden came up behind him.

Knowing it couldn't be helped, but that Dahlia would hate anyone seeing her so vulnerable, Nicolas indicated for Kaden to take her other hand. Between the two anchors they were able to draw the last of the violent energy away from her body until she lay still.

She turned her head away from them and was sick repeatedly. Nicolas handed her a wipe from his pack. She took it with shaky hands. Her head was pounding, a ferocious pain that refused to let up. "I don't think we judged the distance very well." It was a poor attempt at humor, but the best she could do under the circumstances.

Nicolas's stomach knotted at her words. He lifted her, ignoring her protests, and took her to the boats. "We'll find a place to shower and change clothes. You can rest while I go shopping for you." It was all he could think to do. Even holding her, she was hunching away from him, avoiding his gaze, keeping her face averted from Kaden.

"The transport will be waiting," Kaden reminded.

"Let it wait," Nicolas said grimly.

CHAPTER

SIXTEEN

Logan Maxwell was stocky with wide shoulders and bulging muscles on his arms. His ice-cold blue eyes assessed the group of men as they approached him in tight formation, weapons drawn, facing outward, tracking the area around the airfield.

"Expecting trouble?" he greeted.

"Yes," Nicolas answered, nodding toward the gun in the pilot's hand. "Aren't you?"

"I was expecting Dahlia, not an army."

"We're escorting her. We're her bodyguards." Nicolas kept eye contact, two males staring one another down.

Max kept the stare going but raised his voice. "Dahlia? You all right?"

In spite of having cleaned up and dressed in the clothes Nicolas brought her, Dahlia was still pale and wan from the seizure. Her headache was a killer. She just wanted to lie down and sleep as she always did after such an event. The men had her cut off from the pilot, separated by their bodies and guns. She forced a casual shrug. "I'm fine, Max.

They're all just a little overprotective after what happened to Jesse," Dahlia answered. "They insist on coming along."

Max refused to break eye contact with Nicolas. "Not if you don't want them to come. Say the word."

"You think you can take us all?" Sam asked, amusement in his voice.

"You never know," Max answered.

Dahlia sighed. "I can't take it when you all act like this. It's embarrassing. I'm tired, my head aches, and I'm sick of all of this. I'm getting on the plane."

"Not yet," Nicolas said and signaled Tucker and Sam to enter first. "Stay close to me, Dahlia." He didn't look at her when he gave the order, didn't take his eyes from the pilot, but he was very aware of her. How fragile she seemed. How far away from him, although they were close enough he felt the brush of her skin against his.

"There's no one on the plane," Max said. "She always flies alone with just me."

"Not anymore she doesn't," Nicolas answered, his obsidian eyes as hard and as unflinching as rock. "Not since someone in the NCIS sold her out."

Max stood very still, and then he slowly holstered his gun. "Dahlia, have you spoken with the director, told him about this?"

"No, but he has to be thinking the same thing. It wasn't all that hard to figure it out. Someone killed my family and burned down my home, Max. No one knew about me other than a few people at NCIS."

"Including me," Max said quietly.

Dahlia shrugged, hating to voice the suspicion out loud. She had very few friends, if one could call them that. They were acquaintances really, but she didn't have enough to throw them away. And she'd always liked Max.

"Her last mission was a setup," Nicolas supplied, his black gaze unswerving.

A muscle jumped in Max's jaw. He swore under his breath. "Jesse Calhoun is my friend, Dahlia. I've always felt responsible for you. You should have called for backup. Once

I fly you somewhere, my orders are to stand by to fly you back, which is exactly what I did. You never said a word."

"I was late." She said it softly. "Two hours late."

Max swore again.

"Get in the plane, Dahlia. I don't like how exposed you are out here," Nicolas ordered. "We can sort it out in the air." Although he was grateful she obeyed him quickly, it was unlike her to do so without a comment on his arrogance, and that bothered him. Dahlia beaten down was too much for his heart to take. He stayed very close to her, almost pushing her with his body in an attempt to get a response from her, but she kept her head down.

The men moved in the same tight formation, Dahlia locked in the center while they escorted her to the waiting plane. Max followed her into the small compartment. "You should have said something, Dahlia. You should have at least reported it to the director. Henderson would have had me bring you in to protect you."

"No one was supposed to know about me, Max," Dahlia pointed out. She sounded weary, sad. Already moving away from them all. "What does that tell you? And how did they know where I lived?"

"You can't think someone at the NCIS is involved."

"When they sent a team in to find me at the safe house in the Quarter, someone took a shot at me. They knew right where to find my home in the bayou, Max. It isn't that easy to find." She didn't look at him but kept her face averted.

Nicolas put his arm around her and drew her close, the grief in her voice twisting at his guts. "You can see why we're not taking any chances." He had already done his best to probe Logan Maxwell's mind, but the man had strong barriers up. The same kind of barriers Lily Whitney had taught the GhostWalkers through mental exercises. He recognized the mark of Special Forces, a warrior trained and honed by battle. Maxwell wasn't the type of man to back down easily, and Nicolas doubted if he could be bought.

They settled in the plane with Max behind the controls. "Jesse know about these men, Dahlia?"

"Nicolas is the one who pulled him out of the fire, Max," Dahlia said quietly. "And if Jesse lives, it was Nicolas who saved him."

Max glanced at Nicolas, noting the proprietary way he held Dahlia, the protective body language. "Then I owe you. Jesse's a good friend of mine. You all better strap yourselves in for takeoff. I'm not hanging around just in case. I heard Jesse was in bad shape. The admiral went to see him, but wouldn't disclose where he was, not even to us. And he wouldn't say what happened to him or what kind of shape he's in."

"And that should tell you something," Nicolas pointed out.

Dahlia looked from one man to the other. Nicolas could be terribly intimidating when he chose, and right now, he had his stone face on. His eyes were hard obsidian and his mouth was a merciless slash. He pinned Maxwell with his icy cold gaze and refused to let up.

"I suppose it does," Max agreed with a heavy sigh. "I don't want to believe it, but I'm afraid the evidence points that way." The engine was already on and the plane began to vibrate as he went through his checklist automatically before taxiing down the runway.

Nicolas waited until they were in the air. "Jesse Calhoun is a GhostWalker, psychically enhanced. I'm guessing you are as well. How did Whitney get ahold of you? And do any of you have the physical and mental repercussions associated with the experiment?"

Max's cool gaze swept over both Dahlia and Nicolas. "You know I can't talk about that."

"But you know Dahlia's a GhostWalker." Nicolas made it a statement. "It's why they used both you and Calhoun. You're anchors. She could travel with you without too many repercussions." Just the mere fact that Maxwell knew the term *GhostWalker* spoke volumes.

"I'm not at liberty to discuss the matter," Max intoned, staring straight ahead.

"You don't have to. Calhoun recognized my name, and

he knew what I was. He's a strong telepath and there's no way he was born that way. We also are aware Dr. Peter Whitney enhanced several men using his own private laboratory when complications began to arise from his military experiment. He didn't want all his eggs in one basket, so to speak, and if we were all murdered, he had a few for backup, just in case."

Dahlia made a soft sound of distress and turned her head away, reluctant to allow them to see her expression. Whitney had been the monster of her childhood, but as a child, she'd believed his experiments had been done only to her. She'd even been told the other girls were a figment of her imagination and at times believed it. "What was wrong with him?" she murmured aloud. "How could he experiment on human beings? He knew what was happening to us when we were children, but he repeated the experiment, not once, but twice. It's horrifying." She didn't realize her fingers had curled into tight fists until Nicolas put his hand gently over hers. She looked at Max. "I trusted you. Both you and Jesse. You knew I felt isolated and alone, yet neither of you said anything or even mentioned you knew Whitney. Damn you both for that."

"Dahlia, I take orders just the same as you," Max pointed out. "You had to have known about Jesse. He was too strong of a telepath for you not to have known."

She turned her head to look at him, her gaze bleak and flat. "I was supposed to guess that Whitney had destroyed more lives? That you and Jesse would conceal it from me?" She pulled her hand away from Nicolas, suddenly unable to bear his touch. Any touch. Her chest ached and her throat burned. "I don't buy the excuse, Max. I have a high-security clearance, and I certainly could know about others like me."

Dahlia pulled her knees up to her chest and wrapped her arms around her legs, rocking back and forth for comfort. She made herself smaller, wanting to disappear, wishing for the sanctuary of the bayou. Why was she doing all of this? She'd never done anything she didn't want to do, and she damned well didn't want to be sitting in a plane with Maxwell, surrounded by the GhostWalkers. She knew if she looked at them, she would see pity in their eyes, on their faces. She'd never accepted pity, not even from herself. She owed Rear Admiral Henderson nothing after this. She'd always done good work, always made the recovery no matter the circumstances. Damn them all, and Jesse and Max most of all.

Nicolas wanted to smash something—or someone, preferably Logan Maxwell. How could he blame Dahlia for wanting to withdraw when it seemed that everyone she came into contact with betrayed her on some level? What could he say to prove his own feelings for her were real? How could she believe anything was real when the very people she worked with, worked for, had helped to keep her isolated? They had to have known her life was hell, yet they hadn't reached out to her, hadn't made any effort to let her know she wasn't alone. He could feel her slipping through his fingers once again, and this time, he couldn't blame her. How did one instill trust when all she'd ever known was betrayal?

He studied her profile. Her eyes were liquid, but she didn't shed tears. He almost wished she would. Instead, she was gathering up her grief over the loss of Milly, Bernadette, and her home and belongings and the betrayal of Jesse and Max, cementing them deep inside. She was building the necessary barriers to protect herself and others. He could feel the energy gathering around her, swarming to her as her emotions deepened. The temperature in the cabin rose. He wondered if Max knew just how close she was to losing her control and just how dangerous it would be if she did. "Dahlia." He said her name softly to bring her complete attention to him.

Dahlia swallowed the hard lump burning in her throat and shifted her gaze to Nicolas. He was holding out his hand to her. She stared down at it. "Are you worried about me blowing up the plane with all your men on board?"

Nicolas felt, more than saw, Max stiffen at the controls.

Dahlia had spoken softly, but even over the noise of the engine he heard. Had she meant him to? Was it a threat? Nicolas doubted it. Dahlia was upset and she had a temper, but she would never risk the lives of the other GhostWalkers because she felt betrayed. It wasn't in her character.

"I thought if you held my hand, it would be more comfortable for you," Nicolas answered truthfully. "I've reached the point where I can feel the energy as it is drawn to you. It's massing fairly quickly in such a confined space."

"I appreciate that you and Kaden are working so hard to allow me to be in such close proximity to others." Dahlia slipped her hand into his.

Nicolas tightened his fingers around hers and held on. She sounded like a little girl politely thanking him for a Christmas present. Not at all like Dahlia. He felt almost desperate to get her alone. She had slept for a half hour while he had shopped for clothes for her, but even after a shower and clean clothes, he could see she wasn't back to herself. She was withdrawing more and more into a place where he couldn't follow her.

"Is Jesse safe?" Max asked.

"Yes," Nicolas answered. "They have him stashed in a good hospital with the best surgeons and he's well guarded."

"How can I help find the traitor? You must be going after him if you're heading to DC. I can help."

"It's good to hear you say that, Maxwell," Nicolas said complacently. "We were hoping you'd be cooperative."

Max cast him a suspicious glance. "I know the agents in our office in DC. I can't imagine any of them betraying their country. Or Jesse for that matter. Who are your suspects?"

"Everybody is a suspect until we find otherwise," Nicolas said. He watched Dahlia closely as he carried on the conversation with the pilot. All the while his thumb brushed back and forth across her inner wrist and he willed her to snap out of her depression. Had they been alone, he was certain he could find a way to make her laugh again, to shake off the melancholy, or maybe it was the seizure. He didn't know a lot about seizures. That was Lily's department. He knew seizures were dangerous and that Dahlia was humiliated that they had found her having convulsions. She hadn't spoken to him all the way back to the Quarter, or even later, in the hotel after her shower when he'd drawn the sheet over her and promised he'd be back with clothes. She'd been so unlike herself, no snappy comebacks, no sassy remarks.

Dahlia, don't go so far away from me. Nicolas made his tone as intimate as possible. *I know you're tired and upset, and you have every reason to be. If you want to toss your job with the NCIS, I'm behind you all the way. Just don't put me in with the rest of them.*

Dahlia leaned her head back against the seat. His words slipped into her mind almost seductively. His voice was tender, gentle, whispered over her skin and found its way into her heart. Tears burned close, and that was unacceptable to her, not in front of all these people. Not in front of Max. *Don't be nice to me right now, Nicolas. I need you to wait until we're alone.*

His heart nearly stopped. She was telling him things she didn't even realize herself, but he knew. Deep down, where it counted, he knew. Dahlia wasn't turning away from *him*. She didn't want kindness, she was too vulnerable. She was waiting until they were alone. He tightened his fingers around hers and held her hand for the rest of the flight. He didn't talk to the pilot again until they were circling above the small, private landing strip.

"Don't put down yet. Circle low so we can take a look at what we're up against." Nicolas bent forward, peering out the window. Kaden and Gator did the same, using high-powered glasses to check the terrain.

Max complied and set the plane down when Nicolas gave the order. He had almost brought the plane to a stop at the end of the runway when Nicolas reached over and removed his gun. "Wouldn't want you to get any ideas. We'd like you to be our guest for a while."

"This isn't necessary. I'd never harm Dahlia, and Jesse's my friend."

"Then you won't mind coming with us for a little while. We won't be long. The investigation should only take a day and then we'll need you to fly us out of here."

"Dahlia," Max brought the plane to a complete halt and turned off the engine. "You don't believe I'd hurt you, do you?"

She looked him straight in the eye. "You already have." She took the hand Nicolas held out to her and swept past the pilot, leaving him to the waiting GhostWalkers.

Nicolas walked her to one of the waiting cars Lily had provided for them. Dahlia hesitated when he opened the passenger door for her. "Where are we going?"

"To a condo. Lily has a couple of places available for us. I asked her to give us one of our own. The others will be close by."

Dahlia slid in and waited until he was in the driver's seat. "What about Max? I'm disappointed in him, but I don't want anything to happen to him."

"We'll hold him until we've gone in and checked the residences of the agents for anything that might tip us off to who's behind all this. By now, Lily's talked to the admiral, and he'll know what we're doing."

She averted her face and stared out into the gathering darkness. She didn't want to talk about Henderson. He had to have known of the GhostWalker program. He certainly knew Whitney, and he knew about her. If both Jesse and Max had been psychically enhanced, Henderson would have known. And he'd let her believe she was teetering on the brink of insanity, not confirming nor denying Lily and the other girls' existence. What had been the point? What would it have hurt to tell her the truth?

"Why didn't he tell me, Nicolas?" Did she want to know? She could feel her insides knotting, tensing, churning with a kind of fear she didn't want to identify. Was she finally overloading?

He reached over and put his hand over hers. "Dahlia, whatever these people do, they think they're doing it for their country. It's never personal with them. Henderson has spent his life in service. He may have thought he was protecting everyone. You're an unknown to them. If they watched your childhood unfold on those tapes, if they followed your training, they'd see one side of you only. All the times you couldn't control the energy and accidents occurred are caught on tape. That's what they'd see. Not the Dahlia who practices with amethyst spheres until she can use the energy up. Or the Dahlia who works at becoming a human superconductor and races up the walls."

"Floats," she corrected.

"What?"

"Technically I float, not race," she explained.

Nicolas smiled. "And they don't see the scientist in you. They've missed all that about you because they see one side. When people don't understand what's happening, they're afraid. Whitney never figured out what was wrong. He didn't factor in that you would draw energy in complete opposition to the laws of the universe. Because Whitney didn't know about the energy and couldn't explain what was wrong, Henderson and his people didn't know."

"You always seem to say the right thing to make me feel better."

Nicolas didn't think so. She wasn't feeling any better, but she was making an attempt to make him feel better. He remained quiet until he found the condo and got her inside. Lily had promised there would be clothes for Dahlia and sure enough, the closet in the bedroom had several pairs of jeans, shirts, and a dress or two and the dresser had underwear. Dahlia stared down at it then looked at him inquiringly.

"Lily. Don't ask me how. We give her a shopping list, tell her where we want the stuff, and she delivers. Anything from weapons to ladies' underwear."

"She's very involved in what you all do, isn't she?" She worked to keep the wistful note from her voice.

"Yes. She's a tremendous asset to us. Whitney set up trust funds for all of us, but when we're out on a mission or we're working for the Whitney Trust, Lily uses the power and money behind her name."

"Does that bother you?"

"No." He shrugged. "Whatever works and smoothes the way." He lifted the pair of silky pajamas from the drawer. "These are beautiful, but I'm fond of you in my shirt."

Dahlia took the pajamas out of his hands. "You've never seen me in anything else. You might change your mind." The pajamas were a soft pale blue. The top was a little sexier than she'd ever worn, but Nicolas had seen her without clothes so she didn't mind trying it. "I'm going to take a shower. Would you mind trying to find something for my headache? It just refuses to go away."

"I've got something in my pack." He retrieved the pack from the entryway where he'd left it when he'd gone through the condo on a quick check for exits and fast escapes. The water was already running and the bathroom steamy when he stepped inside the tiled room. Dahlia was in a large square Jacuzzi, her body covered with churning bubbles and her head pillowed by a small rolled towel on the back of the tub. He could see her breasts floating enticingly, peeking through the curtain of bubbles. Steam drifted around her, giving her a mysterious, elusive appearance. Her mane of black hair was slicked back from her face and her incredible skin gleamed at him. Nicolas felt the sexual jolt all the way through his body. How could he look at her body, her incredible skin, and not feel the urgent demand of every cell in his own body? She opened her eyes to catch him staring at her.

"Are you coming in?"

His breath caught in his throat. "Is it a good idea?" There were lines of weariness on her face and he couldn't tell if the droplets of water on her face were from the steam or from tears. "Baby, you're so tired, and I don't know if I've got the willpower it would take to keep my hands to myself."

"I want you to come in with me. The water's hot and relaxing. We both need it, and it was such a nice surprise."

Nicolas didn't wait for a second invitation. He

stripped quickly, loving the fact that she never took her eyes from him. She didn't wince or look away from the stark demands of his body. He watched her take a deep breath and let it out, focusing on him completely in the way she had.

He stepped to the side of the Jacuzzi. "It is a nice surprise." He stepped into the hot churning water. At once the bubbles licked at his thighs. Before he could sink down into the water, Dahlia cupped his sac, her hands hot and moist. The temperature in the room increased along with his pulse.

"Has anyone ever told you what a really extraordinary person you are, Nicolas?"

He felt her breath on him, the flick of her tongue. He closed his eyes for a moment, briefly savoring her touch. "Dahlia." He caught her shoulders and held her away from him. "This isn't about me. I want you, honey, you have no idea how much, but when we stop, it's all going to be there between us, and I don't want that."

Dahlia leaned back again, her expression impossible to read. "So what do you want, Nicolas? Everyone wants something."

"Of course I want something. Don't you? Don't you want something for yourself? Doesn't a relationship matter to you? Isn't that wanting something? Hell, yes, I want something from you, and it isn't just your body."

"Is that what you think I was offering you?"

"Wasn't it?"

Dahlia was always as honest as she could be with herself and she didn't like the answer. "Okay, maybe I was. Maybe I wanted that to be what you wanted from me."

"I love you, Dahlia." He sank down into the churning water and pulled her into his arms. "I love all of you."

She turned her face into his throat and wished she could cry like a normal person. She felt she was screaming inside, clawing at her own heart, yet she couldn't tell him. Couldn't share it with him. This one person who had shown her kindness. Who proclaimed to love her for who she was, monster or not. She kissed his throat and pushed away from him.

"Did you bring the aspirin?"

"I left the tablets on the sink." Nicolas leaned back as she climbed out of the Jacuzzi. "This is one of those moments when the relationship manual would come in handy, don't you think?"

A fleeting smile curved her mouth and was gone. "I don't think the manual covers this, Nicolas. I don't think anything does."

She took the tablets and dried off, leaving him to the hot water as she paced through the house in her silken pajamas. Dahlia wandered through each of the rooms on bare feet wondering what it would be like to be a normal woman with a family, to have a house like this one and fill it with laughter and happiness. Her hair was damp from the Jacuzzi and made a wide wet column down her back. Even the water bubbling around her, as hot as she could stand it, could not take away the ferocious headache jabbing through her skull. She paused by the window and stared out into the night, feeling restless and moody. She wanted to walk away into the night and disappear. Had she been in the bayou, she might have done so.

Nicolas came up behind her and leaned over her, putting a hand on either side of the windowsill caging her in. "Come to bed, Dahlia. You need to sleep."

She didn't turn around but pressed back against his body. "It's strange knowing someone wants me dead," she mused aloud. "All of my life, I've known I was different and maybe in some way a monster, dangerous to others. I even knew I wasn't lovable, but I never once thought they would want me dead."

He rubbed his face against the nape of her neck. "No one is going to kill you, Dahlia, not if I have anything to say about. And you're very lovable. I don't love anyone else. I haven't since I was a boy."

She ignored his confession because she had to. She couldn't think about Nicolas and what it would mean if he were like the others. "I thought they were my friends, Nicolas. Max and Jesse. I thought they cared about me the way friends care about one another." How could she say she wanted to doubt him? That she was afraid if he was deceiving her in some way she would never recover? How could she admit she was a coward, wanting to run from him even more than the others.

"Calhoun was tortured, Dahlia," Nicolas reminded. "He refused to give them any information about you." He straightened up, turned her around to face him, catching her chin so she was forced to meet his black gaze.

"That's so," she conceded, "but then if his orders were to never say a word about me, wouldn't he follow them, the same way Max followed them?"

It was the first time he heard a trace of bitterness in her voice.

"Don't do that, Dahlia, don't let them change you. Don't let anything change who you are. You made your own world with your own code, and you did it yourself. It defines who you are."

Dahlia looked up at his sculpted face and the dark intensity of his eyes. "You believe that, don't you? You think I'm worth so very much."

"To me, everything," Nicolas admitted.

"Why? Why am I important to you, yet someone else would want me dead? Why would my mother give me up to an orphanage rather than keep me? She just threw me away, and the orphanage people followed her example. I don't even know the first thing about my culture, about my people. I don't even know who my people are."

"The GhostWalkers are your people. Does it matter so much where we came from? It's who we are now that counts." Nicolas led her toward the bed. There was too much pain and sorrow in her eyes. "You need to sleep, Dahlia, nothing is so important that you should put off sleeping. It will help your headache."

She just stood there looking helpless, very unlike his Dahlia. Nicolas lifted her easily into his arms, holding her tightly to his chest. He feathered kisses from her temple to the corner of her mouth. "You just need to sleep, honey. Let it all go away."

Dahlia allowed him to put her on the bed, and when he lay down beside her, she turned to him, familiar now with the heat and comfort of his body. She didn't want to need him, but she found she did. She didn't have any fight left in her and she needed his strength.

Nicolas glanced at his watch. His team was moving at three, to see what they could find in a soft probe of the NCIS agents' homes. He had plenty of time, it was barely dark. He gathered Dahlia close and rocked her gently. "All the gifts you have, Dahlia, are incredible. Yes, there are drawbacks to using them, but we saved Calhoun's life together. He wouldn't have made it without us working at healing him."

"Healing is your gift, Nicolas, not mine." Her voice was drowsy, her long lashes feathering down toward her cheeks.

He kissed the top of her head. "I think you're wrong. I may have the power inside of me, but it's locked away. Without you, I have no key. That's what you are, you can focus the power and aim it exactly where it needs to go. I simply release it. We work well together."

"I'm tired, Nicolas. Really, really tired."

The sheer weariness in her voice was heartbreaking to him. Nicolas held her closer to him, wanting to find a way to comfort her. He kept rocking her, as gently as he could, brushing kisses in her hair until she fell asleep in his arms.

Nicolas lay awake just watching over her. He'd found himself in many tight corners in his life, but none had ever felt like this one. He looked down at her face and wondered how she had become so important to him, so *necessary* to him. She looked like a porcelain doll with her petal-soft skin and her exotic eyes. He smoothed back the tumble of hair when she curled up tighter into the fetal position.

She made a soft sound of distress, then a low keening noise. Nicolas felt his heart shatter when she sobbed in her sleep. Her fists clenched and her body trembled, and the sounds were wrenched from her as if she couldn't contain the overwhelming grief one more moment.

"Baby, don't do this." He whispered the words. Why had he thought if she cried she'd feel better? It was too much, too much sorrow for her. He pulled her beneath him, lying over her, somehow trying with his body to protect her from the grief.

She came awake, her eyes wide, black. Swimming with tears. "Nicolas? What is it?" She touched his face, the lines of worry there.

"You're crying, honey. I thought it would be good for you to cry, but not like this, not in your sleep where I can't share it with you."

"I can't be crying." Dahlia wiped at the tears on her face with a kind of horror. "I never cry."

"You are crying."

"I can't stop." She looked desperate. "Make me stop, Nicolas. Make it stop."

Nicolas found her mouth with his, kissing her deeply, taking the cries from her throat and swallowing them, making them his own. He took her breath into his body and swept his tongue over her tears, tasting them. Keeping them. He deepened the kiss, urgency mingling with tenderness, taking her away from a place he couldn't follow her to, bringing her back into his world. Their world.

The silk of her pajamas rubbed over his skin, her skin, feeding the growing need rising in a slow smoldering heat between them. He ran his hands over her body, cupping her breasts, feeling the tuck of her waist through the thin layer of silk, shaping every curve even as his mouth stayed welded, kiss for kiss, to hers. "It's all right, *kiciciyapi mitawa*," he whispered. "Everything will be all right." He kissed her eyes, his tongue capturing more tears before they could fall, going back again and again to her soft lips. "You're with me. You'll always have me."

He kissed her with long drugging kisses, making her almost senseless, unable to think anymore, taking every sorrow and replacing it with erotic pleasure. All the while his hands stroked and explored, slowly pushed the silken pajamas aside until he had bare skin. Until she lay beneath him completely naked, her eyes wild for him, pleading with him, and her hips rising to try to meet his.

Nicolas shook his head, his expression tender. "Not this time. I want you to know I love you, Dahlia. I want you to feel it. I'm going to make love to you, a long slow assault on your senses. I want you to know you're mine, that you really belong with me." He bent his head to her throat, lapped at the valley between her breasts. "You're so beautiful." He murmured the words against her breasts, took her nipple into her mouth, heard her soft cry and took his time, paying attention to both breasts and her narrow rib cage before taking a small foray across her stomach to her belly button.

"Nicolas," Dahlia caught two fistfuls of hair. "I can't stand it. I want you."

"Yes you can. You can stand me loving you." He traced the path lower, spreading her thighs with gentle hands and dipping his head to taste her.

Dahlia's hips lifted for him, giving him the opportunity to cup her bottom and bring her to him. He took his time, enjoying her frantic little cries, a stark contrast to her earlier sobs. She tried to pull him over her, to wrap her legs around him, which only opened her more to his exploration. She came with a wild bucking of her hips. He entered her, felt the continuing ripples as her muscles gripped him tightly and spiraled out of control. He moved then, long deep strokes, robbing her of breath until her eyes began to glaze and he felt her nails dig into his back, and he laughed softly with satisfaction as she came again.

Breathless, Dahlia could only lie beneath him as Nicolas began to ride her in earnest, his body surging with strength into hers, bringing her to another fever pitch when she thought it impossible. She clung to him, watching his face, the stern, almost harsh angles and planes that were so beautiful to her. She could see his pleasure growing with each thrust of his hips. His hands bit into her hips and dragged her to him with each stroke so that they came together hard, so that the pleasure was so much it bordered on pain. She could feel him moving in her, deep in her tight folds, her heat surrounding him, drawing him to her very core. The pressure built and built and the air sparkled and sizzled and the flames flickered everywhere, and deep inside when the volcano thundered and spread fire through her body, through his, she felt utter contentment and total peace.

Dahlia lay still, so spent she couldn't move. He should have been too heavy but she wanted him draped over her, tangled with her, arms and legs everywhere so she couldn't tell where he started and she ended. "What does *kiciciyapi mitawa* mean?"

He kept his head on her breasts. "What?"

"You called me *kiciciyapi mitawa*. It sounded so beautiful. It wasn't Japanese. What was it?"

"It's the voice of Lakota. It would sound silly in English." He cupped her breast, his fingers moving lightly over her skin. His breath warm on her heart.

"I want to know. It didn't sound silly when you said it. It sounded . . . beautiful. It made me feel beautiful. And loved."

He kissed her breast. "I called you my heart. And you are."

CHAPTER
SEVENTEEN

The street, in the upscale neighborhood, was empty at three in the morning. The wind blew gently through the flower beds and across recently mowed lawns. A dog lifted its head as the breeze carried an unfamiliar scent. He got stiffly to his feet and faced the west, a growl rumbling deep in his throat. Dark shadows darted through the street, moving fast, a blur as they scattered to surround the large, two-story house at the end of the quiet cul-de-sac.

The dog barked a warning, but stopped abruptly when one of the shadows turned back and stared at it. The dog retreated slowly, the hair settling on its back as it once again lay down on the porch, eyes brightly watching the intruders moving around the house into position.

The light from the streetlamp didn't quite reach to the house itself, set back as it was from the road. Trees darkened the surrounding yard even more. Shadows flitted around the yard, and swarmed up the sides of the house in complete silence like dark wraiths.

Nicolas went up the side of the house, a spider crawling

up to the second story. He studied the window for some time before proceeding to the roof. Crouching on the slope he spoke into his radio. "We've got ourselves a real operator," he whispered. "I found a string across the window. Use extreme caution."

"One on the front door," Kaden confirmed.

"And back," Sam intoned.

"So they're either expecting trouble or want to know if someone is nosing around. How many good citizens go to that much trouble?" Kaden asked.

"Soft probe," Nicolas reminded. "We're going in soft, information hunt only. We want to get in and out without being detected. If they have silent alarms on the outside, I'd say we're going to have a little trouble inside. Be ready."

"We're always ready," Gator's soft drawling voice replied.

Nicolas silently lowered his body to the edge of the windowsill. The smartest and easiest of all alarms was a tiny bell hooked in place to tinkle a warning. If the NCIS agents had been Special Forces, they wouldn't look to easily bypassed security systems for protection. Already, Ian was circumventing the system. It wasn't hard with their particular psychic skills.

The house was used when three of the agents were in town. The intelligence Lily had given them was that the three agents, Neil Campbell, Martin Howard, and Todd Aikens, were all out of town. The house should be empty, but if not, and they awakened at an inconvenient time, well, Nicolas was remembering Dahlia's sobs in her sleep, and he wasn't feeling particularly generous or gentle.

"Two cars in the garage." Ian's voice was a soft whisper in his ear. "Security system is down. There was a backup, but it didn't last long."

The team had decided to use radios instead of telepathic communication just in case anyone in the house was like Logan Maxwell or Jesse Calhoun. They might feel the subtle flow of power or even hear what was said. The team was used to working mind to mind, but their first training had been the miniscule radios so they were accustomed to them.

"We've got at least one, possibly two or three inside," Nicolas reported to the others. "Proceed with extreme caution." Lily always supplied them with state-of-the-art equipment and the latest was an air-cooled, sealed CO_2 mini laser glass cutter. It had a circular suction cup pivot and cut completely silently. The laser cutter was microcomputer controlled, with the computer built into the case of the laser assembly. A computer was necessary to prevent the laser from cutting completely through the glass and passing into the room and burning things in its path. It cut almost through, leaving the suction cup with its levered handle to pull the glass out. Lily would be happy to get the report that it worked silently and efficiently, allowing him to remove the glass without triggering the alarm set on the inside sill. He set the glass aside carefully in preparation to enter the room.

"Strobe, damn it, strobe," Gator reported.

Nicolas bit back a particularly ugly curse. Gator shouldn't have made such a mistake. A tiny strobe light was often used. If the switch were tripped at the window, the light would flash brightly. The light was tiny, but the strobe would awaken anyone trained to sleep lightly.

"Fall back," Nicolas ordered. His gut was churning. He was taking his men into the line of fire armed only with nonlethal ammunition. They didn't want to take a chance on harming a civilian, and being GhostWalkers, they were certain they could get in and out of the house unseen. But the house wasn't empty, and the men inside were combat trained.

"Negative, sir, the room's empty."

"Fall the hell back now, soldier," Nicolas hissed, his voice implacable. "He's in there waiting for you. Secure that position and let's contain him."

"Yes sir," Gator responded. "Securing position."

Nicolas felt carefully along the inside of the windowsill

for the trip wire to a bell or the switch for a strobe he was certain would be there. The others would be more alert now that they knew there were alarms inside.

"In," Kaden announced. "Downstairs, dining room. Don't like the feel, Nico. There's power here, and someone's using it. Shotgun strapped to the tabletop. Ninja stars in the silverware drawer. Dining room's clear."

"Intercept," Nicolas ordered immediately. Kaden was a strong telepath. He could hunt down another without breaking a sweat.

Nicolas held the bell still with his mind while he made his entry. "In. Left bedroom. I feel a surge here as well. They've been warned. Be ready."

He felt the first assault to his brain, a jab, much like a punch coming at him, but mental rather than physical. He blocked it before it could incapacitate him. The Ghost-Walkers had practiced such attacks as well as fending them off, but they had never used them or had to defend against them, and Nicolas found he was slower at it than he would have liked. "Game seven. They're using our game seven to attack," he announced. Each of the mental attacks had been choreographed much like a chess game. Whitney had done the choreographing. He sent his own move crashing back before they could follow up, a blaring punch much like shards of glass jabbed into the skull. He wanted them to know they weren't the only GhostWalkers in town.

He felt the instant withdrawal. The shock. Much like the shock Jesse Calhoun had exhibited when they'd first touched mental paths.

"In," Ian's whisper was in his ear. "Through garage into kitchen. Two booby traps, one fairly lethal. Found interesting food in the freezer. A Beretta. Isn't that your weapon of choice? Kitchen's clear."

"Their communication path is shut down," Kaden said with evident satisfaction.

"In office, ground floor," Ian said. "Checking for IDs and any incriminating evidence. Keep them the hell off my back."

"Kaden, stay on Ian," Nicolas ordered.

"Naughty, naughty, handgun taped under desk," Ian added.

Nicolas stayed to the shadows of the room, checking the ceiling, the closet, and the corners for an occupant. There was no sound. No breathing. But someone was close. He could feel him. Smell him. Knew him by his finely honed instincts. He waited in silence—a heartbeat, a second. Survival instincts took over, and he upended the bed, rapid firing his weapon, the rubber bullets spraying in a tight arc across the floor where the bed had been. In the small confines of the room, the shots were thunderous, hurting his ears. He saw the flash of fire as the agent snapped off live rounds simultaneously. Upending the bed knocked the aim off and the bullets thunked into the wall somewhere behind him. Nicolas heard the impact as the rubber bullets struck flesh. Something metal clattered to the floor. He rushed forward, kicked the gun away from the downed agent and hastily checked him, knowing the agent felt as if he'd been hit in the chest with a sledgehammer.

He was alive, but he was fighting mad, yet unable to move from the powerful kick of the rubber bullets knocking him against the wall. Nicolas searched him for weapons, found two knives and a clip. He taped the man's hands, feet, and mouth and left him to search for the second agent.

"They have live rounds," he reminded his men.

"I've got one trapped in the bedroom, right side, corner," Gator said. "He's armed."

"Stay out of the line of fire, but keep him contained," Nicolas ordered. "Tucker, you in?"

"I'm tearing apart the bedroom. Lots of weapons in the closet. C-4 and plastic. A couple of detonator caps. I think my boy likes to play with bombs. Bedroom clear on ground floor."

"Anything fancy? We're not looking at money here," Nicolas said.

"Nothing down here," Ian said. "Looks clean, damn it."

"Dart board with a nice set of throwing knives," Nicolas reported as he reentered the bedroom where the downed agent was tied up. "My friend looks a little pissed, but I can't say as I blame him." He tossed the room hastily, searching quickly for anything that might identify a traitor. Too much money. Too many luxuries. A book of matches or a pen with the name of the company Dahlia had been sent in to recover the data from. Even a university sweater or jacket from the campus where the three professors had been murdered. He went to the man, crouched down beside him. "You okay?"

The man watched him through wary, ice-cold eyes. He nodded his head.

"I'm looking for a traitor. Someone who would sell your friend Jesse Calhoun down the river. You have any ideas?"

The agent frowned, shook his head. Nicolas felt the push at his brain, but his barriers were strong and impenetrable. Just to stay in practice, he pushed back until the agent glared at him and subsided. Nicolas reached out and ripped the tape from the man's mouth. The agent swore like a sailor.

"You have something to say worth hearing?"

"I don't know anything about a traitor," the agent said, "but if you know something about Jesse, I want to hear it. You owe me that much."

"You shot at me."

"You broke into my house."

"You've got some illegal weapons here," Nicolas pointed out mildly.

"Is he alive? What the hell's going on? Jesse Calhoun is a friend of mine. No one will tell us anything other than he's in a hospital, somewhere we're not allowed to know about."

"And so you protected yourselves here, didn't you?" Nicolas said thoughtfully. "You decided whoever went after your friend, could very well come after you."

"It's logical."

"What's your name?"

"Neil Campbell."

"Tell the agent in the other room to walk out with his hands in the air and no weapons on him. We'll talk," Nicolas offered. He knew the others were hastily going through the house, but his gut told him the two agents they'd cornered were innocents.

Neil hesitated and then shook his head. "I can't get through to him."

"I'll tell my man to allow you to speak to him. You don't want him dead, and we've got him boxed in. I don't want any of my men dead." *Kaden, monitor them if you can.*

I'm on it. As always Kaden was relaxed. *He's telling his buddy to come out without a weapon. That we're Ghost-Walkers looking for a traitor in the NCIS. He says he believes us.*

"There are three of you who use this house. Where's the third?"

"You have intel on us."

"That would be affirmative. I can tell you every bone you've ever broken in your body. I even know about your training with Whitney."

Neil's face shut down immediately. He stared blankly at Nicolas. Before he could protest, Nicolas shook his head. "Don't bother. I've already gotten the 'I'm not at liberty to discuss that' speech. I don't need confirmation. You, Maxwell, Calhoun, your buddy," he jerked a thumb toward the other bedroom.

"Norton, Jack Norton," Gator said into his radio. "He's very cooperative." The molasses in his voice was dripping, which meant his prisoner was combative.

Nicolas froze for a moment when he heard the name. It was legendary in the world of snipers. *Kaden, did you get that? Tell the men to spread out, look for another sniper hidden somewhere. High ground, he'll go up. Jack has a twin.*

In spite of his tension, Nicolas kept his expression tranquil and continued with his conversation as if he hadn't recognized the name. "And your buddy Norton all volunteered for a classified experiment Dr. Peter Whitney talked you into. He enhanced your psychic abilities and you were trained as a unit to work missions using your new talents. Unfortunately, there are severe repercussions to using them. All of you suffer continual headaches and other much more debilitating effects. When you've all had enough and want to learn how to function in the world without having to have the protection of your anchors at all times, put out the call to Lily Whitney, the doctor's daughter, and she'll help you."

Ian's voice whispered in Nicolas's ear. "Lot's of security on the computer. Far more than normal."

"Bringing him in," Gator reported.

Nicolas stepped to the side of the door and waited for Jack Norton to be brought into the room. He was a stocky man with beefy arms and chest, the defined muscles of a man who worked out daily and kept in shape. He looked a fighter, and his eyes were flat and cold and immediately jumped to Neil and then back at Nicolas with the promise of retaliation.

"Kneel down, Norton," Nicolas ordered. "Keep your fingers locked behind your neck. You search him, Gator?"

"Knife the size of a sword on him," Gator commented. "And just to be special, he had several throwing knives on him too." He winked at Nicolas. "Thought I might miss those while I was staring in awe at that he-man knife."

Norton flicked him a look, cold as ice. Gator smiled at him.

"You okay, Neil?" Norton asked.

"I'm okay. My chest hurts like hell."

"I know you," Nicolas said. "We crossed paths a couple of times in a couple of countries. What else do you have on you?"

"Couple of small knives and a couple of guns."

"That's not possible." The smile vanished from Gator's face.

"This is Jack Norton, and you should have recognized the name," Nicolas told the Cajun, then turned his attention back to the agent. "The house is one big booby trap. My men are finding weapons all over the place. You think someone's after you?"

"We heard someone took out Jesse Calhoun," Norton answered easily. "Mind if I put my hands down?"

"Yes I mind. We're all safer this way. Take it as a compliment. You have a certain well-deserved reputation. Where's your brother?"

"Probably looking down a scope at you right this minute," Norton said complacently.

"He's carrying live rounds, Jack," Nicolas said. "Tell him to stand down. I don't want any of my men getting hurt and this turning into a useless bloodbath. We're on an information hunt."

"Ken will just hang back, making sure no one does anything stupid," Norton replied. "You're not going to find the traitor in this house."

"He has information on Jesse," Neil said.

"He's in bad shape," Nicolas told them. "We've got him stashed in the best hospital and he's guarded around the clock by a couple of ours. Henderson went to see him. They're not letting anyone else close."

"You bring him out?" Jack asked.

Nicolas nodded.

"Then I owe you."

"Just keep that brother of yours from shooting any of my men. I'd hate to have to kill someone I like." Nicolas spoke into his radio. "We aren't going to find anything here. Break off and let me know when you're clear."

"Is our computer intact?" Neil asked.

"You won't know he touched it," Nicolas answered. "Make sure you get a doc to take a look at your chest. You're going to carry a few bruises. Later gentlemen." He kept his gun steady, dead center on Norton's chest as he backed toward the window. "I'll just go out this way and keep an eye on the two of you while my men get clear." He spoke conversationally, even nonchalantly, but his skin crawled with the idea of the legendary Jack Norton and his twin brother Ken, lying in wait for him. There were few men as good as him in the jungle, but Jack Norton was one of them. And he was just as good at the end of a rifle, maybe better.

No one had mentioned the Norton twins in the intel he had on the house, or even on the NCIS. He couldn't imagine Lily missing something like that, which meant Norton had either come in on his own because he'd heard about Jesse Calhoun and Calhoun was a friend, or he'd been brought in by the director to investigate his office because the admiral had come to the same conclusion as Dahlia. Someone in the department was a traitor.

He kept his gun trained on Norton until each of his men gave him the all clear. He did a small salute and vanished, sliding into the night as quickly as he could, feeling the itch between his shoulder blades as if he were being tracked with a bullet.

Once away, he breathed a sigh of relief. The Norton twins. Who would have ever guessed they'd come out unscathed in a confrontation with them? He was very lucky to get his men out unharmed. He knew Jack Norton was thinking the same about tangling with him. He let his breath out slowly wishing they were finished for the night. But they weren't.

"I'm picking up Dahlia. Will meet you all at the target."

Nicolas was thankful to be alone in the car for a few minutes. The responsibility of protecting his men was no small thing. He took it seriously, and he'd known it might all go to hell. They had one day to search the house, and that wasn't nearly enough time to canvass the place and find a time to break in when no one was at home. They'd been lucky coming out unscathed when the notorious Norton twins had been in residence. He couldn't blame Gator. No one alive that he knew could handle Jack Norton and come out on top. The only reason Gator wasn't dead was because Jack was a patient, steady man and didn't make mistakes. He was sizing up the situation, feeling his way before making a kill. They'd been lucky. Very lucky.

Dahlia ran lightly across the lawn, dressed in a black jumpsuit, her hair pulled tightly into a thick, intricate braid. She tossed the small bag filled with the new clothes into the backseat and slid into the car beside him. "How'd it go?"

"They're clean," he answered.

She took a long look at him. "Is everyone okay?"

"Yes, but we don't have a lot of time with this, Dahlia, we want you out of there before it gets too light, or before anyone has a chance to figure out where we're hitting next. You'll have to get in and out quickly. We want Maxwell to fly us out of here before anyone has a chance to come looking for us."

"Is he at the airfield?"

"Kaden's making peace with him, bringing him food and filling him in so he'll be cooperative. The plane will be ready when we get there. The others are setting up to protect you if necessary."

"It won't be."

"This isn't the same as a recovery, Dahlia. You're interrogating her while we search the house. We don't want her to know we're there. She could panic and try to phone the police."

"She won't." There was confidence in Dahlia's voice.

Nicolas felt the tension ease out of his muscles at her tone. He hadn't realized how worried he'd been about her. She'd been so broken earlier, but she looked rested and relaxed and completely poised.

Dahlia studied his face. "You look tired, Nicolas. You haven't had any sleep."

"I'll sleep on the plane. Our intel wasn't all it could have been. It was a little dicey, but we got out of there intact. Have you ever heard Calhoun talk about a man named Jack Norton?"

His voice as always was easygoing, soft, almost sensual, but she knew him now on a much deeper level and she felt a sudden chill down her spine. "Jesse mentioned someone named Jack packed him out of a firefight once when he was wounded. He never mentioned a last name."

"Did he mention a twin?"

She nodded. "A brother, yes. I don't remember his name."

"Ken. Ken Norton."

"Why? Who are they?"

"Hopefully not the enemy. Jack's the kind of man you never want after you. He never stops. He just keeps coming. He was there, in the house."

Dahlia frowned. "This is getting so messy. All because a group of professors had an idea."

"An idea that could change the balance of firepower on the sea," he reminded.

"It's an idea. An unproven idea," she said. "Money is just so ugly."

"It makes people ugly," he qualified.

"Would this Jack sell out for money?"

"Not in a million years. If he's looking for the same person or persons we're looking for, I'd have to say, they may as well shoot themselves now because they're already dead. He didn't know what happened to Jesse. Neither did Neil. No one's talking yet, so that's a good thing. We know he's safe enough while we're figuring this all out." He parked the car in front of a modest home in a nice neighborhood. The porch and swing looked inviting. The car was a midsized Toyota Camry. "Nothing extravagant."

Dahlia started to open the car door, but he caught her hand, preventing movement. "You're wired, right? Did you test it already?"

She rolled her eyes. "We tested it twice. Ian is recording everything and you'll be able to hear."

"Be careful." He didn't know if it was the near fight with Jack Norton, but he was reluctant to let her out of his sight.

Dahlia leaned into him, pressed her lips against the corner of his mouth. "I do this all the time, Nicolas. Stop worrying."

She slipped from the car and ran across the lawn. He

saw her get out of the car, knew the direction she was running, knew what she was wearing, but she seemed to fade into the landscape. It was the strangest thing. It wasn't as if she could blur her clothing. Nicolas rubbed his eyes and looked again. He heard her soft laughter in his ear. "Put your glasses on."

"You're doing more than blurring your face." He loved the sound of her laughter. His insides performed a strange melting that left him unreasonably happy.

"Well, a girl should be somewhat mysterious. Wouldn't want your life to be boring."

He strained to catch a glimpse of her. Brush moved along the far flower bed. He saw her spring from a low fence onto the steeply slanted roof and run along the edge as if she had some kind of suction cups on her feet. His heart in his throat, he directed his men to surround the house and follow her in while she engaged the occupant in conversation.

"Stop worrying," Dahlia whispered. She could feel his energy no matter how much he tried to spare her. Nicolas wasn't the type of man to happily send his woman off on a mission he considered dangerous. And that was just one more thing separating them. She needed the stimulation and the continual physical and mental activity her job provided for her. She had no idea how she'd cope without the outlet.

She ran lightly along the roof, her slight weight allowing her to be very silent as she approached the entry point she'd chosen. A window was slightly open, raised a couple of inches invitingly. The screen was of little consequence. Hanging upside down, she extracted it easily and placed it carefully on the roof where it couldn't slide off.

"No real security system other than the alarm Ian interrupted," she murmured softly, feeling a little foolish talking to the team. She wasn't a team player, and she felt a bit self-conscious knowing they were all watching and monitoring everything she said and did.

She lowered her body until she could reach the edge of the window and tugged to bring it up. As she did so, she whispered softly. She wasn't a strong telepath, she couldn't read others that easily, but she could mesmerize with her voice, especially if the person was sleepy, drunk, or very susceptible. She kept her voice beguiling as she slid down the wall and rolled through the window, landing silently in a crouch, her gaze scanning the room as she continued to give the order to sleep. She was in the bedroom of Director Henderson's secretary, Louise Charter, who lay sleeping peacefully. One hand was flung out just touching the end table where her alarm clock sat.

"I'm in," she announced softly. "She's alone, but I haven't checked the house." It was usually the first thing she did to insure her safety, but Nicolas had been adamant that she only deal with the secretary. She moved through the room first, searching it carefully, going through the drawers and the closet. She noted each item of interest. "She's definitely seeing someone."

Next to the phone was a framed photograph of Louise Charter and a young man of undetermined age, perhaps thirty or forty. He had his arm around her and was smiling down at her upturned face.

Dahlia sat at the end of the bed. "Louise." She said the name softly, gently. Put persuasion in her voice.

Louise opened her eyes and gasped, half-sat, and pushed at the fall of tumbling blond hair threaded with gray. "Dahlia. I recognize your voice. What are you doing here? Are you in trouble?" She sat up all the way and reached for her robe in a no-nonsense fashion. "I can call the director and have help here immediately for you. He's been out of the office and unavailable, but I can reach him in an emergency."

Dahlia smiled at her, amazed that Louise would be so complacent to find her sitting on the bed. She was certain Louise was sixty, although she certainly looked younger. "Thank you, I'm fine. I just need information, and I didn't want to use the phone. I was afraid it might be dangerous."

Louise nodded her understanding. "I think the director has been afraid of that as well. He's very secretive at the moment, even with me, and I've been his private secretary for twenty years."

"So you don't know where he is?"

Louise shook her head. "Not at the moment, but he's always in touch. Have you spoken with him since all this happened?"

"Briefly," Dahlia lied. "He's gone to see Jesse."

At once Louise looked distressed. "How would you know where the director is?" The thought was clearly upsetting.

"He told me when I asked him about Jesse."

Louise nodded, still frowning. "Please don't repeat that to anyone, Dahlia. You shouldn't have even told me." She sighed. "Poor Jesse. I'm told he'll never walk again."

Something inside Dahlia went very still. Her heart began to pound. She felt the swarm of energy. Louise's distress, her own rising anger. With an effort, Dahlia pushed down her temper. "Who told you he would never walk again?"

Louise frowned. "I'm sorry, Dahlia. I didn't mean to upset you. I should have thought before I spoke. Jesse's condition is very serious. His legs are damaged beyond repair. It's no secret. I thought you knew."

"Have you seen him?" Dahlia's fingernails bit deeply into her palm. She wanted to reach out and shake the woman. The energy poured into her so that her stomach churned and pressure built in her chest. Electricity crackled in the air.

Louise looked around her, frowning at the static electricity in the air.

"Have you seen Jesse? I'm so worried about him." Dahlia thrust her hand into her pocket and found the amethyst spheres, palming them for added control. Wisps of Louise's hair were standing at attention, drawn by the static building in the air. Dahlia feared if she didn't control it, lightning would arc.

"No, dear," Louise sighed. "I wish I could have. Martin told me about him. Martin Howard." She gestured toward the picture. "We're good friends, and he knew I was worried, so when he found out, he told me."

"How would he have found out?" Dahlia frowned and clenched her fingers tighter around the spheres. "I even asked the director, and he didn't give out any information."

"Dahlia, why would anyone keep Jesse's condition a secret from all of us? There's a lot of classified information, but an injured friend isn't one of them." Louise spoke very gently, reminiscent of her calm, pleasing voice on the phone.

Dahlia bit down hard on her impatience. "It does seem rather ridiculous, unless someone is out to kill him."

Louise opened her mouth and then snapped it shut again. She studied Dahlia's face for a long time. "Out to kill him? Deliberately? Dahlia, you'd better tell me what's going on."

"Someone destroyed my home and killed my family, Louise. And they tried to kill Jesse. It was a setup from the very first. I walked into trouble. They didn't follow me home, they were there ahead of me. I don't exist to anyone except the NCIS. And even there, only a few people know about me."

Louise shook her. "That can't be. Only a handful of people know about you, Dahlia, even at the office."

"So my guess is, the director is protecting Jesse even from the other agents until we find out who is behind this."

Louise's faded blue eyes met Dahlia's squarely. "That's why you're here. You think maybe I had something to do with it." There was great dignity in her voice and a wealth of pride. "I've served as Frank Henderson's secretary for over twenty years, and long before that I served in positions of trust. I've never divulged a secret in my life. And you can't count Jesse's condition, as nothing has crossed my desk calling it classified information."

"I'm just trying to keep from getting killed, Louise," Dahlia said. It was hard not to believe the woman. The energy coming from her was not that of pretense or subterfuge.

"Does Frank think I've betrayed him?" When she asked the question her voice wavered and cracked, but her expression was one of pride and dignity. "Do you?"

"I honestly don't know what to think, Louise. I was hoping you might have a few ideas. The person has to be NCIS. There's no one else."

Louise was quiet for a few minutes, obviously giving it some thought. "I can't imagine anyone in our office being a traitor, Dahlia. The agents are close, but they're very professional. Most have served in the military, all of them are intelligent and dedicated." She rubbed her forehead, looking dismayed.

"Maybe someone slipped up and told a girlfriend or wife."

Louise shook her head. "They wouldn't do that, Dahlia. Their lives are at risk. They know that." Her head went up. "You mean me. You have the mistaken idea that I'm an old lady with a young boyfriend. You believe I would trade information for a chance to have him in my bed? Martin Howard is totally dedicated to his job. He's a decorated officer and a wonderful man, and he certainly isn't my lover. He would never betray his country, and I certainly wouldn't do so either."

"I never said that, Louise."

"You were thinking it." She put a hand to her throat. "Is that what everyone is thinking of me?"

Dahlia forced herself to touch the other woman. She laid her hand on Louise's wrist, wanting to calm her. Needing the gathering energy to give her a respite. The more Louise became upset, the more the heat rose and the pressure in Dahlia's chest increased. Outside, an owl hooted— once, twice. Dahlia breathed a sigh of relief. "Louise, I don't think the director would ever believe for one minute you would betray him. He's protecting Jesse. Are the NCIS offices routinely swept for bugs?"

"You'd have to ask the director."

It was a standard Louise answer and one Dahlia had heard more than once over the years. "We'll find whoever

is doing this. I know there are all kinds of very sophisticated ways to bug an office or listen to conversations. I'm
going now. One last question. Did Martin ever tell you who
told him the news about Jesse?"

"No. I didn't ask. I just presumed that all the agents had
been told. In fact, I was a little hurt that the director hadn't
informed me as well."

"I wouldn't mention it again, Louise, not to anyone."
Dahlia patted the secretary's hand and stood up. She was
desperate to get out in the open, away from the woman
who was feeling a mixture of confused emotions.

"I won't."

Dahlia went out of the house the same way she'd entered, swinging through the window onto the roof and running fast to the corner of the house where she somersaulted
onto the ground. She hurried to the waiting car. Nicolas
pulled away from the curb the moment she was safely inside and headed for the airfield.

"Did you find anything?" Dahlia asked, breathing slow,
drawing the spheres from her pocket so she could begin to
dissipate the energy. "I don't think she has anything to do
with it."

"Dahlia, she's the only one who knew about Jesse's
legs," Nicolas pointed out gently. He reached across the
seat to wrap his fingers around her thigh, to help draw the
energy from her.

"That's not exactly true," she said thoughtfully. "Martin
Howard told her."

"If she was telling the truth."

"I don't think she was lying," Dahlia replied stubbornly.
"It isn't her."

EIGHTEEN

Dahlia sat cross-legged in the middle of the floor, several rose quartz spheres spinning beneath her fingertips. She ignored the men gathered around her, particularly Max, who was staring in shock as she levitated the balls beneath her palm.

"Look at that. Can any of you do that?" he asked.

Kaden shrugged. "Haven't tried it yet, but we're going to," he admitted.

Dahlia glanced up at his face and burst out laughing. There was something to camaraderie, something she'd been missing all of her life. "I want to watch when you do," she said.

"Well you can want, but it isn't happening," Sam protested. "You'd be laughing at us, and we can't be having that."

"Men are such babies." Dahlia looked over to Nicolas. He'd been on the phone with Lily and Ryland for some time and he had his stone face on. His eyes were flat and cold and she knew he was still upset over the position he'd put the

men in, entering the agent's house without the proper intelligence, not realizing the Norton twins were there.

Max had insisted he be let in on whatever they were doing, and no one objected all that much. He didn't seem to
be much of a prisoner, moving freely about the condo Lily
had arranged for them to stay in. He was definitely trying
to hear what was said, hovering near Nicolas, and occasionally pacing restlessly.

Nicolas put down the phone and turned to the others. At
once all conversation ceased. "Calhoun is in a bad way. It
doesn't look good for his legs. They've operated and will a
second time, but there's a lot of damage, especially below
the knees." He rubbed his hand over his face. "Louise
Charter had correct information. They don't think he's going to ever walk again. At least not on his own two legs."

Max turned away and stared out the window. Dahlia sat
very still, absorbing the sudden flare of energy while the
men tried to suppress their emotions. She couldn't suppress her own. She pressed her fingertips to her eyes. "It
doesn't seem possible."

Nicolas crossed to her immediately, standing behind her
as he put his hand on her shoulder in an attempt to offer
comfort and take some of the energy from her. "We knew
he was in bad shape, Dahlia. At least he's alive."

She didn't trust herself to speak. She'd been hoping for
a miracle, and in reality they'd been given one—Jesse was
still alive. On some level she'd known when she saw the
damage to his legs that it would probably be impossible to
fix it, but she had held out hope anyway.

Nicolas crouched down beside her. *Lily will see to it that
he has the best doctors, the best care. She'll make certain
he's guarded around the clock. And she'll try to do even
more because she knows he means so much to you.* Kiciciyapi mitawa, *look at me. I'm speaking the truth. She
won't let him go.*

Dahlia blinked back tears that seemed all too close. Was
it because she found herself leaning on Nicolas's strength?
She didn't know. Didn't care. She looked into his eyes. Into

his heart—and saw herself there. She smiled at him. *I'm beginning to believe in her. In the GhostWalkers.*

Nicolas ruffled her hair and went back to the desk. "We brought some photographs out of Louise Charter's home early this morning." He held them up. "Has everyone gone through them?"

"Not me." Dahlia put out her hand.

Kaden passed her the glossy snapshots. "There are a lot of pictures of Martin Howard."

"Did Lily have any information on him?" Dahlia asked.

"Martin's a good friend of mine," Max interrupted. "He's a decorated officer in the Green Berets and someone I've always been able to count on. He's a good man, and has served his country since he was eighteen years old." There was a hard edge to his voice.

Nicolas pinned him with a cold, flat gaze. "No one wants to look at friends, Maxwell. If you can't do this, we'll understand." His voice held no inflection, but Dahlia winced at the clear reprimand. Max bit back a curse and paced across the room to the window.

"Lily found a few interesting things," Nicolas continued. "Martin Howard isn't the name he was born with, and Louise Charter isn't having an affair with him. Apparently, Martin was born into a small-time Mafia family right here in Detroit. His name is actually Stefan Martinelli, and Louise is his mother's cousin. When his parents were killed in an automobile accident Louise and her husband took in him and his four brothers and helped raise them."

"Which explains why he's always around her house and in so many photos," Max said, folding his arms across his chest.

"Yeah," Nicolas agreed. "To make a long story short, Martin changed his, and his four brothers', last name in an effort to keep them away from the kinds of activities his parents had been involved in. They lived in Maryland near Louise and Geoffrey Charter until they all graduated from college. There were some minor incidents with the law, but Geoffrey got them through it."

Max leaned against the wall. "So he was born into an

Italian family with ties to the Mafia, but apparently he did everything possible to keep himself and his brothers out of that kind of life."

Kaden flicked Max a quick glance. "It does sound that way, doesn't it? What else did Lily find, Nico?"

"All the brothers went into the service. Martin led the way, and the rest followed. Most of them went to college and then joined. Martin joined and went to school while he served. He provided for the others along with the Charters." Nicolas looked up at Max.

"I know he's been in a couple of fights," Max said. "Haven't we all?"

"Did you know his brother Roman has been in and out of the brig a dozen times and has been busted several times down from his rank as an officer? He's been a trouble-maker both in and out of the service."

"We all have relatives," Max said.

"Not all," Dahlia objected.

"Ma cher." Gator pressed his hand to his heart. "There you go again. Denying our relationship."

Dahlia smiled and blew him a kiss.

Nicolas's black gaze settled on Gator's face. Gator just winked at him, flashing his bad boy grin.

"Quit baiting the tiger," Kaden advised.

"Alligators eat tigers for breakfast," Gator bragged, his white teeth bared as he leaned his hip lazily against the wall near the door.

The knife came out of nowhere, flying so fast it was a blur through the air, driving into the wall and taking the ends of Gator's shiny black hair with it.

Laughter erupted while Dahlia stared in horror at the blade buried nearly to the hilt in the wall. She hadn't felt the slightest surge of energy, violent or otherwise. Nicolas looked innocently at her. Gator shrugged his wide shoulders, the grin still in place as if someone throwing a knife at him was commonplace.

"You all are nuts," she declared. "That wasn't funny."

"Actually, *'tite soeur,* it was," Gator said and pulled the knife free. He sauntered over to Nicolas and handed him the weapon, handle first. "I'd fight over you anytime, little sister, and if your man wouldn't, he's not much of a man."

Dahlia frowned at them. "It's a wonder any of you are still alive." She began flipping through the photos. "By the way, just for the record, when I go into the building tonight, I don't want anyone around. You all worry too much about me, especially Nicolas, and I can't afford a backlash of energy. All of you will have to just stay put."

Nicolas raised his eyebrow, his tough features completely expressionless.

"That's a big negative," Sam said.

"I don't think so," Kaden objected simultaneously.

Gator just laughed. "Oh, *ma cher,* your sense of humor is growing being around us all." The smile widened. "Or are you just trying to give Nico heart failure?"

She ignored him and looked at Max. "They seemed to forget I've managed all these years without them."

"What exactly are you planning on doing, Dahlia?" Max asked.

There was a sudden silence. They all looked at her. "Well, gee, Max, I don't know. Something to do with my job. You know, that highly classified job we both share."

"I don't see Jesse here giving you orders."

"No you don't, do you, because he's laid up in a hospital somewhere and I'm going to find out who put him there." Dahlia's black eyes flashed, glittering like hard gems. "They killed Milly and Bernadette, Max. And I'm finishing my job."

"Did you talk to the admiral?"

"I don't have to talk to the admiral to finish my job."

Max shook his head and looked over at Nicolas. "And you're fine with this?"

Before Nicolas could reply, Dahlia glared daggers at Max. "*He* has nothing to do with it. He doesn't work for the NCIS, I do. He isn't my boss. Just back off trying to be intimidating, because it irritates the hell out of me." And it did. Her temper was rising in direct proportion to the testosterone levels in the room.

Nicolas was happy to see the real Dahlia back in fighting form. She didn't lie down for anyone. Not that she was going anywhere as dangerous as Lombard Inc. without the Ghost-Walkers to protect her, but what was the use in arguing with her? He wasn't going to change, and neither was she. It was good practice for the men to have to guard their emotions carefully in the field. He met Maxwell's eyes. The man subsided immediately with a small nod of understanding.

"See anything in the photos?" Tucker asked. "I looked through them, but I was mainly looking for places, more than people. I know you think Charter's not involved, Dahlia, but I did find this." He passed a pen deliberately to Max to give her.

Max sucked in his breath, reading the advertisement for Lombard Inc. Without a word, he handed it to Dahlia.

She took it reluctantly, turning it in circles. "Anyone could have given this to her. They're everywhere. It's a big company."

"It's a tie to her," Nicolas said. "And to Martin."

"What other information do you have on him?" Max asked.

"Lily's thorough. We have everything from his grades to his classified missions, but what interests me the most is his relationship with his family. He's an extremely loyal man. Not only to his siblings, but also to Louise Charter. I think it's genuine. I think he'd exhibit the same loyalty to his country and to the NCIS and his friends," Nicolas mused aloud.

Kaden nodded. "I see where you're going with this."

"I don't," Dahlia said. "Are you eliminating our only suspects?"

"Who else has access to the Charter home, Dahlia?" Nicolas asked. "Who else would come and go?"

Her fingers curled around the photos. "But how would they get classified information? Louise knows me, knows my clearance, and the only thing she really told me in the entire conversation was Jesse's condition and that's because no directive came down saying it was to be treated as classified. She'd never sit down to dinner, even with someone she considered a son, and reveal government secrets." Dahlia shook her head. "I don't know Martin Howard, but if he's as solid as you all say, I can't imagine he would be that chatty either."

"Trust me, he would never say a word, accidentally or not," Max affirmed.

"No, but his brothers would have access to both the Charter home and her office. She would allow them to come see her at work, even meet her to have lunch, that kind of thing. The same with Martin. Why would they ever suspect a family member of planting bugs? Techs go over the computers, but considering there's so much security in the rest of the buildings, how often do you think the offices are swept? Even if a bug was found on the secretary's phone or her computer was attacked, would anyone suspect a member of her family?" Kaden explained it carefully. "I think it would work over time, drop in, have lunch, pass the time, no one would give him a thought. He could collect a lot of information."

"Which brother?" Max asked.

"My bet is on the troublemaker, Roman. He tried to follow in his big brother's footsteps but wasn't successful. He tried for the Green Beret and wasn't accepted. He tried for the psychic experiment program and his troublemaking record blew it for him. Without Martin's interference, he very well might have gotten a dishonorable discharge. He's out of the service now and claims to be a student, and self-employed, but Lily's investigator couldn't figure out what he does."

"A student where?" Dahlia asked.

"Rutgers," Nicolas said in his quiet voice.

Dahlia spun around and stared at Nicolas. "It has to be him. How could it be such a coincidence?"

"What does Rutgers have to do with it?" Max asked. "I know that Jesse was poking around there."

"Rutgers lost a few professors with grants to develop a new weapon for the defense department," Dahlia explained.

"So there's definitely a tie-in between Jesse's investigation and where Roman Howard goes to college," Kaden said.

Dahlia began to rotate the spheres again as the energy in the room began to build. The men were working at keeping their reactions very low-key, but they were human. "If it's Roman, and he doesn't work for the NCIS, how would he have been able to go out with the NCIS team to the safe house to take a potshot at me?"

"More likely, he followed them and waited on top of a building for them to point the way. Once he knew where you were, he took his shot and got the hell out of there," Kaden said. "That's what I would have done."

She sent him a faint smile. "How very reassuring. I think all of you need some lessons in passive behavior." She turned her wrist over as she levitated the spinning balls in her hand. "It's getting late, gentlemen, and I've got work to do."

She stood up, stretched, and pushed the small spheres into her pocket. She glanced down at the handful of photographs. The top picture seemed to be of a woman sitting on a wrought iron bench overlooking a river. Dahlia went very still. The woman had her back to the camera, but she looked familiar. And the river was all too familiar as well. She looked up at Nicolas, sorrow in her eyes.

Tekihila, *my love, what is it? You look as if you could shatter at any moment.*

Dahlia immediately straightened her shoulders. "If you'll excuse me, gentlemen, I have to change." Clutching the photographs, she hurried to the room she was using as her private refuge. She knew, without looking, that Nicolas was right behind her.

He waited until she closed the door before he took the photograph from her hand. "Who is it?"

"Look at the picture. Look at the knitting basket. That's Bernadette. She's sitting on the bench overlooking the river right there by the Café du Monde." Her voice sounded hoarse.

"Roman was following her."

"How?" She turned to look at him, her face so pale her skin looked translucent. "You tell me, how could he know about Bernadette?"

She was so agitated he could feel the heat in the room. Sparks touched the curtains, licked at the edges of the walls. Nicolas took the pictures from her hand and tossed them on the bed, enfolded her into his arms and locked her against his body. She was trembling. He bent low, his mouth against her ear. "We can do this together, Dahlia. You're not alone, and whatever we find we can handle together."

"Do you think she betrayed me, and they killed her after they used the information?" She was angry. So angry she *wanted* to fling fireballs in every direction. How could Bernadette do such a thing to her? To Milly? For what? Dahlia had all the money they needed. The women never wanted for anything. If they bought it, the trust fund paid for it, no questions asked.

"You aren't thinking clearly," Nicolas kept an eye on the flames lengthening, spreading up the walls. In another minute, he would be forced to take action. He wanted her to control herself before the fire got out of hand. "If they found you at the NCIS, they must have found Bernadette and Milly. You would have been impossible to stalk, your movements were too unpredictable, but the two older women would have had a routine. They had to follow them to find the sanitarium and ultimately, you."

She heard the crackle of the flames and took a deep, calming breath. "I'm sorry, I know better than to get so upset. You're right, of course. I should have thought of it." She turned her face up to his. "If we're going to stop the fire, you'd better kiss me."

He caught her chin firmly and lowered his mouth to hers. "What a chore." He brushed her lips gently, enticingly. Teasing her. Nibbling at her lower lip to distract her. To feel her shiver in his arms. Wanting the thrust of her breasts against his skin and melting softness of her body as she went pliant. It wasn't about stopping a fire, it was about redirecting the fire. He wanted the flames in her. In him. Sharing their skin.

His teeth tugged at her lower lip until she opened her mouth for him, allowing his tongue to sweep inside, to claim her. To lick away the flames on the walls and put them where they belonged, in her mouth, in his. His arms tightened around her, his hands restless, skimming down her back, cupping and squeezing her bottom, dragging her up and into his groin. The energy took them, as it always did, a storm flaring into an instant wildfire. He loved the way the energy was eaten up by the flames, by the way their mouths clung and melded, hot and wet and needy.

Dahlia felt right in his arms. Each time. Every time. Sometimes when he sat away from her, he felt the ice-cold blood running in his veins and knew he had mastered his emotions. Maybe too much. And then she'd look at him. One smoldering look and he'd heat up, feel everything. Every emotion a human being was meant to feel.

He slid his hands back up her body, cupped her head while he kissed her, again and again. Long, slow kisses and fierce, hot ones. She pulled away first, lifting her mouth inches from his. "Do you kiss me like that because of the energy? Or because you want to kiss me like that?"

"I *have* to kiss you. I *need* to kiss you. I'll never get enough of kissing you. If the energy needs us to find ways to use it up, I consider it an added bonus in our relationship." His fingers slipped into her hair. It was always so impossibly shiny. He loved the sight and scent of it, the feel of it. "I'm very much like you, Dahlia, I rarely do anything I don't want to do."

She stepped away from him reluctantly. "Well, you kept the house from burning down. Lily will be happy if she's the one who rented it for us. I want to look at the rest of the photographs. Maybe I'll see something else familiar."

He handed them to her.

"Nicolas? Thank you for saying what you did about Bernadette. I don't know why I jumped to the wrong conclusion like that. I think I'm more upset over Max than I want to admit. Why wouldn't Jesse and Max tell me they knew Dr. Whitney? Why didn't they say he performed the same experiment on them?"

"You didn't exchange much information with them," he pointed out carefully. "You're all taught to keep secrets.

That's the name of this game, Dahlia. Maxwell and Calhoun are agents for the NCIS and before that SEALS. They aren't going to talk out of turn. You can't blame them for that."

Her black eyes met his. For the first time he thought she looked like the mysterious witch some called her. There was something haunted and magical in her gaze. "Yes, I can." The way she said it had him believing in voodoo and witchcraft. A slow, Cajun drawl, every bit as soft and sexy as Gator's but with a soft hiss of a promise of revenge. It actually sent a chill down his spine.

Dahlia dropped her gaze to the pictures she held in her hand. She didn't want to think about betrayal. She'd start another fire for certain and that would lead to kissing Nicolas, and he drove every sane thought from her head. She was recovering the data tonight so she couldn't afford to get distracted. She forced herself to look at the photos. Several were of the Quarter. Obviously the photographer planned to show he'd been vacationing. Many were at the French market where Milly and Bernadette often bought produce. There was even a picture of the narrow alley and the small yarn shop where the women purchased their knitting supplies.

Dahlia sat on the end of the bed and spread out the pictures. There was one taken of a storefront and the reflection of the photographer was clearly in the window. She picked it up and studied it carefully. "I've seen this man."

"How could you know? The camera hides his face." But Nicolas was watching her. Dahlia was methodical and very controlled when she wanted to be. She was being very thorough, meticulously studying the photograph. If she said she'd seen the man before, he was certain she had.

"This is the man I saw at Rutgers just outside Dr. Ellington's office. And then I saw him again when I was scouting the Lombard building. This is definitely the same man. I know it's him. It's the way he holds his head, just a little tilted to the side and down, but he's watching everything. He was stalking Bernadette." She pointed to the shadowy outline of a woman reflected in the glass. "That is Bernadette. She's wearing her sunhat." A sad smile flitted across her face. "She always called it a bonnet. She made them because she loved to sew, to create things." Dahlia forced herself to stop rambling. Her throat felt raw.

Nicolas pressed his lips to her temple. "You're closing in on him, Dahlia. I hope he feels your breath on the back of his neck."

She turned into his arms almost blindly, instinctively. She wanted to be held and comforted. At that moment she didn't care how much she was relying on him. She was just grateful she had him.

Nicolas simply held her, rocking her gently back and forth. He knew she was hurting. She'd lost everything and this one, elusive man had everything to do with it. Nicolas just needed the name. Needed it confirmed. Then he would go hunting.

"You can't, you know," she said softly.

"Can't what?" His fingers tangled in her hair, rubbed the silky strands to relieve his spurt of anger, of suppressed rage that someone would so carefully destroy Dahlia's life.

"I know what you're thinking. You become very calm, very centered, and your energy level drops more than ever. I've figured it out. Your anger is ice cold, not fiery hot, and you contain it. You let it build and you use it when you work. This man isn't your target. He isn't your job."

He bent down to brush the top of her head with a kiss. "I'm going to be there tonight, Dahlia. I'm not letting you go to the Lombard building alone. You won't see us, or hear us, but if you get in trouble, we'll be there to pull you out."

She pulled away from him, her expression stubborn. "I didn't go with you on your job. It will only break my concentration knowing you're there."

"You can be angry with me over this," he said, "and I'll understand, but it won't change my mind. I'm being honest with you. It's impossible for me to do anything else."

"So what does that mean? Every time I go out on a job, you're going to be following me because you think I'm not capable of handling it?"

"No, because I'm not capable of handling it. There's a

difference. Can you live with that? With me being who I am?" He caught her arm when she turned away from him. "I'm asking you to understand what I'm really like. I have my own drawbacks, Dahlia. I'm going to be damned difficult to live with sometimes."

Her eyes widened in shock. In terror. "I didn't *ever* agree to live with you."

"No," he admitted, "but you're going to agree."

"You're so arrogant, Nicolas. Sometimes it sets my teeth on edge."

He tried not to smile. "I know it does." At least she didn't say she wouldn't agree to living with him, so maybe when he mentioned marriage, she wouldn't just faint on him. Or put on her running shoes.

She tossed the pictures on the bed and rummaged through her clothes to find something to wear. Lily had been thoughtful enough to replace everything on the list Nicolas had given her for Dahlia, including her work clothes and tools. Because it was Lily she sent along as many other items she could get quickly and thought would be useful. Dahlia was pleased with the assortment and the tightly woven clothes with a myriad of zippered compartments to store necessary items and keep her hands free.

She slicked her hair back and braided it a second time as tightly as possible. As she slipped her hands into the thin gloves she glanced at Nicolas. "Well? If you're coming, you'd better get ready."

"We've been ready. Our gear is already in the cars. Do you want a radio?"

She shook her head. "Too distracting. I have to rely on myself, Nicolas. I can't change how I do things at this late date. When I go in, I have to believe in myself, not think if something happens you can rescue me. I don't need rescuing. If I'm in trouble, I'll get myself out." She pinned him with her black gaze. "Is that understood?"

"Perfectly clear." He caught up her equipment bag and carried it out of the room.

Dahlia started after him and then went back to look at

the photographs scattered across the bed. She picked up one and stared down at it, at the man who had orchestrated the murder of her family. It took a few moments before she realized the temperature in the room was climbing fast and her fingers were burning black holes in the evidence she would need to show the director. She tossed the picture away from her, but sat down on the bed to look at the others. Nearly all of them were taken in the French Quarter in New Orleans. Why did Louise have the pictures?

"Dahlia?" Max stood in the doorway, his piercing blue eyes watching her.

She lifted her chin, drawing in air to calm herself. It was sheer hell being around so many people and trying to guard her emotions. She couldn't imagine how difficult it was for them to be around her. "What is it, Max?"

"I wanted to say I was sorry. I've been thinking a lot about what it must have been like for you and you're right, I should have told you I knew Dr. Whitney. You know all the problems with the experiment, everything that we suffer using the abilities we have and how difficult it is to block out the people around us. You probably know more than we do." He tapped his finger on the door. "The thing is, we were warned someone was trying to kill us all. That someone knew about us and had already been killing others like us." He jerked his chin toward the outer room where the laughter and easy camaraderie of the GhostWalkers could be heard. "Someone definitely killed members of their team, and we didn't want to be next. We all went deep undercover and buried the information on us through as many layers of red flags as we could. Admiral Henderson helped us out."

"And you didn't think that I was in danger?"

"We should have, Dahlia. We should have taken steps to protect you as well."

She knew she shouldn't ask. She already knew the answer, but she couldn't stop herself. "Why didn't you?"

Max looked down at his hands, closed them into two tight fists before looking her straight in the eye. "We trained together and trusted one another. You were an unknown.

You have powers and complications none of us had, and we didn't know if we could trust you not to turn on us."

"You still don't know that, Max." It was a knife, she decided. He'd taken a knife and just plunged it through her heart. She wished she could be cold and distant and not feel anything. Hurt was just as dangerous as anger. Getting near people was hazardous and perhaps even perilous for someone like her.

"I do know, Dahlia, and I should have known it months ago. Jesse should have known it. We were wrong. I know that doesn't help with the way you're feeling, but I wanted to say it. To at least let you know how I felt."

She didn't know whether to thank him or spit in his face. She could only stand there helplessly wondering if it was possible to have a silent meltdown.

"I hope that confession made you feel better, Maxwell," Nicolas said. His tone was low and mean and sent a shiver down Dahlia's spine. "No, you didn't call her a freak or different, but you damn well made her feel that way, didn't you? And all for what? This little speech was all about making you feel better, not Dahlia. Now you can go home and tell yourself you apologized, and that should make it all right."

Dahlia turned away from the two men. The air crackled with electricity, the energy suddenly alive and breathing like a monster while the two men faced each other with ice-cold eyes and anger fed by the violence of the gathering storm both inside the house and out.

She pushed past both men, afraid of the flames dancing behind her eyes. Afraid of the anger she felt at Max and Jesse and the admiral. She had spent most of her life learning control, but when surrounded by so many people with such strong emotions, it seemed an impossible task. She nearly ran into Kaden. He caught her shoulders to steady her, and at once, some of the pressure eased.

"Just breathe, Dahlia. Stand outside if you have to. That's what we do when the overload hits us. You have every right to remove yourself from the situation. Just because you're in a house with people doesn't mean you can't have privacy."

He walked with her to the door and opened it, allowing the night air inside. "Lily is an incredible woman. She was raised with every luxury and she knows which fork to use at a dinner party and who's who in the world of high finance. She can mingle with the president and not bat an eyelash. In fact, she has, but she walks out when she needs to walk out. It's one of the first rules she taught us about being in a crowd or a social situation. You just look mysterious and intriguing."

Dahlia laughed. "I'd really look mysterious and intriguing if I started the White House on fire. Somehow I don't think I'll be doing much mingling in that direction."

He grinned at her. "Can you imagine the Secret Service hunting for the firestarter, and you're sitting at the table with the president, looking innocent?"

"Thanks, Kaden." She looked into the night. The clouds boiled and churned, darkening the sky even more. The wind whistled between the buildings and bent the trees and bushes nearly double. "Look at this. When did this storm front move in? I checked the weather earlier and they said *possibility* of a storm. I don't think the weather people ever get it right. Do you think anything else can go wrong tonight?"

Kaden turned to look at Nicolas coming up behind her and nodded. "Yes, ma'am. I'd say all kinds of things could go wrong."

Dahlia knew Nicolas was there by the strange reaction of her body, the way it came to life. The way the energy dissipated. By the stillness in Kaden. She refused to turn around, staring out into the night instead. "You didn't do anything stupid, did you?"

"No, but I wanted to," he replied honestly. "I'm sorry, I didn't help the situation any by getting angry, did I?"

"No, but part of me was glad you said it."

Nicolas wrapped his arm around her shoulders. "The weather is looking a little grim. Maybe we should postpone this until the storm passes."

"No, the storm might help. I want this over with."

"All right, we'll set up then. You ready?"

"As I'll ever be."

NINETEEN

Dahlia inhaled the night. She always felt safe in the cover of darkness. Her body was already humming, the adrenaline pumping through her veins, and her brain was on overdrive. This was what she loved, utilizing the unusual talents she had. It was what always saved her, what always kept pain and heartache at bay. She could walk through the empty streets and look at the homes and imagine she was part of a community. She could walk along the sidewalks and stare into store windows and pretend she was shopping with friends. She could almost be normal in the dark of night.

High above the streets, she shot out a cable to hook on the rooftop of the Lombard building. She tested the line to make certain the hook was secure and then anchored it. All the while she watched the building and moved from angle to angle to get a feel for the rhythm and movement taking place in the offices on each floor and on the roof.

A guard with a dog walked the ground-floor corridors. The building was dark above the third floor. It looked empty and inviting, but her senses told her it wasn't so. The vault was in the center of the building. Not the basement as one would think, but where all the researchers could have easy access. The building was built like a hive, with the vault as the center hub of activity. It was an enormous room with security cameras and panels for retinal scans, fingerprints, and access codes. She had watched two of the men insert keys into the locks and turn them simultaneously to gain entrance into the vault. Everything from data to prototypes was locked up in the vault when the researchers went home. It was the perfect place to hide stolen data. Who would ever know the difference?

Lombard Inc. had a good thing going. They stole ideas, hid them in a vault where no one would look, and after a few weeks or months, pulled the ideas back out of storage, modified them slightly, and put them into production under their own label. It was an amazingly effective, lucrative scheme. And now they'd decided to line their pockets even further by developing classified weapons and selling them to any government or terrorist group willing to pay an exorbitant price.

Dahlia turned her attention back to the problem of getting to the rooftop without being detected. The wind was particularly vicious, one of the greatest hazards of using a cable to cross between high buildings. She studied the angles of the roof with an expert eye. When cable running, she started out firmly on the cord, but most of the time, she did levitate just above it, and it took tremendous concentration on her part to generate forward momentum while levitating. It was actually faster to run, but not quite as safe. The steady drizzle wouldn't help, making the cable slick, so she decided to do a combination of both.

Dahlia leapt out onto the cable, and began to run, nearly levitating as she raced across the long stretch between the two buildings. The wind blew in fierce gusts, almost as if it were taking deliberate aim and blowing straight at her to knock her off the cable. It caught her sideways a couple of times, nearly taking her off the thin line strung between the two rooftops. She never looked down, never took her eyes or her mind off her destination. She could control the sag in the cable and even the sway to some extent, but it was impossible to control the wind. A particularly strong gust caught her from the side, slamming into her hard enough to throw her off the cable.

Startled, she fell, flinging out her gloved hand to catch the braided steel as she toppled. Her fist closed around it, nearly yanking her arm out of her socket. She could hear Nicolas's gasp of horror echo in her mind, but he shut off his thoughts to allow her complete concentration. She caught the cable with both hands and dangled several stories above ground waiting for the wind to die down. With few structures to impede it, the wind could be ferocious.

Using her gymnastic and high-wire skills, Dahlia swung her legs up and over the cable until she was hanging by her knees. Drops of rain splashed over her neck and ran down her face. Dahlia reached through her legs and pulled herself into a sitting position. Below her, the streetlights looked a hazy yellow through the dreary mist. She stared down at the strange-colored halo of light to orient herself when she saw the shadow move out of the alcove of a doorway. Recognition was immediate.

There had always seemed a furtiveness about the way he had moved. Roman Howard, Martin's brother, had been the man at Rutgers University, just outside Dr. Ellington's office. He had walked by casually, just like any other student, but she had noticed him because he caused every instinct to flare into self-preservation mode. He had been hunting that day, already staking out the professor and marking him for the kill. Dahlia had been just another student herself, and he hadn't noticed her blending in as she always was able to do, a chameleon when necessary.

High above him, with the wind and rain in her face, she watched him cross the street to the Lombard building and stand in front of the entrance, looking around him guardedly, as if he suspected someone was watching him. This was the man who had killed her family, destroyed her home, and nearly killed Jesse Calhoun. He betrayed his country and his own family, using his relationship with the woman who raised him as her own son and his brother, to further his own ends.

Dahlia watched as Roman Howard walked back down the sidewalk, using the building's reflective glass to try to search for hidden eyes. He was clearly uneasy, but he eventually went back to the entrance and punched in a code. How would he have one, and why? He was supposed to be a student, self-employed. Lily's investigator had found no evidence of him working for Lombard. They were a large firm and often received government contracts. Many of their research and development teams had security clearance. There had been no mention of Roman Howard having such a clearance.

It was only when Dahlia felt the precarious sway of the cable and heard the sizzle of the rain that she realized the temperature around her was going up in direct proportion to the anger building inside of her. She took a deep breath and let it out. She had to keep things cool and under control. The recovery of the data on the stealth torpedo was of utmost importance. It had to come first, before anything else. She didn't dare release more energy to the atmosphere when she was up on a cable.

She put first one, then a second foot on the thin cord and went into a crouch. Her mind immediately countered every problem the way it would in a chess match, finding points of balance in the gusting wind, finding the best angle for her body to prevent another incident. It was a fight with the distraction of wind and rain, but she kept the cable taut, using her mind. She was more cautious this time, feeling the way with her mind as she began to move forward. The wind kept the line swaying continually, so Dahlia had to counteract with her own brand of persuasion, using her psychic ability to hold the braided cord still. She picked up speed, but not enough impetus to propel her onward as she levitated. She had to actually push off the cable with her foot to keep forward momentum going.

It should have been nerve-wracking, and probably was to the GhostWalkers, but Dahlia reveled in the difficulties. Her mind and the extraordinary amounts of energy gathering in her body needed the constant challenges. She made it to the roof of the Lombard building and stood for a moment, regulating her pounding heart and controlling her breathing as the adrenaline flooded her body. She was used to that as well, the aftermath of the incredible feats she performed and the rush she got when she realized she was still alive.

Before stepping off the cable, she searched with both mind and body for cameras, motion detectors, and any other security devices. Her body was a reliable tuning fork, something, she was certain, to do with high frequencies. She could jam them, but she didn't want to alert anyone to her possible presence, especially with Roman in the building.

I want you to abort now. It was a clear order. *Roman Howard entered the building and he was clearly agitated and suspicious. I don't like the entire smell of this. Abort. We'll try another day.*

I saw him go in. He doesn't make a difference. We can't risk it, Nicolas. I've allowed too much time to go by as it is. The data could easily be discovered by one of the researchers. I moved it, but I didn't hide it.

Dahlia felt the full force of his frustration, the edge of his anger at her for not listening to him. But it wasn't Nicolas's responsibility if an enemy got their hands on the research for a weapon as potentially destructive as a stealth torpedo would be. She steeled herself to oppose him.

Don't distract me. If you can't lay back, wait for me at the house.

There was the same force of frustration, but he held back his anger. He simply was silent. They both knew he'd never leave.

Dahlia dismissed him from her mind and concentrated on finding any new security precautions. She'd scouted the rooftop numerous times, but not since she'd paid Lombard

Inc. a visit. She was certain they would have beefed up their defenses.

The rain stopped, although the wind persisted, rising almost to a howl so that she had to crouch low, taking shelter beside one of the series of pagodas that housed the heat exhaust vents. She remained very still while she studied every detail of the roof, trying to orient herself to the earlier layout and what detail might have changed.

There was a small dark spot up near the top of the casing housing the wide cooling coils. The roof was as artfully done as the building itself, which gave Dahlia room to move between the pagodas and stay out of the camera's vision. The camera itself was set on a sweep of the roof. She timed it twice to make certain she had enough time to fully disappear down the vent before it would pick up her entry.

She waited until the camera swept past the pagoda and immediately sank down into the shaft. It was easy enough to slip down, using her hands and feet to guide her until she reached the turn. It was a closer squeeze, but her small body fit nicely. She had memorized the layout of the building and followed the narrow vent that took her to the elevator shaft. She had used it before and was familiar with the way the vent opened into the shaft. She had to be careful with the screen, holding it even as she pushed so that it wouldn't fly down the shaft to the basement level. She maneuvered it carefully aside and peeked into the shaft.

The shaft was the fastest way to get to the hub of the building where the enormous vault room was. The elevator bypassed the floor unless one of the elevator's occupants had a special key and the correct access codes. Dahlia didn't bother with elevators; she simply climbed down the shaft, using safety grips when possible, or cracks for fingers and toeholds when there was nothing else. The vent she needed was in an awkward position above her. She hooked a line to a safety grip, metal sliding against metal. The grating noise was overly loud and seemed to reverberate up the shaft.

Dahlia waited a moment or two until she was certain it was safe to proceed. She swung like a pendulum, back and forth, pushing off with her feet until she was able to swing high enough to hook her heel over the edge and hold her body there while she tied off the rope for a fast getaway. It was a simple enough matter to pull her body into the tube, but she did it in slow motion, inch by cautious inch, fully aware of the motion detectors scattered through the vent. It took a tremendous amount of concentration to keep them still as she crawled carefully through the narrow tube.

A strange buzzing began to grow louder and louder in her head. It was annoying, developing into a pressure, making her temples throb. Keeping her mind centered on the motion detectors was difficult with the buzzing interference. Her stomach began to churn. Dahlia stopped moving and lay completely still, recognizing a psychic attack. It had never happened to her before, but she knew it was an outside source. Tiny beads of sweat broke out on her forehead. She forced air through her lungs as the pressure in her head increased until it felt as if a vise gripped her skull.

She tried to be small and far away, thinking of the bayou and the sound of the frogs and alligators, the continual lapping of the water, anything to take her mind off the increasing pressure. She pictured it in her head, the island that had been her home with the myriad of flowers and bushes and trees scattered everywhere and the wildlife she spent a great deal of time watching from the roof of her house.

Slowly, she felt the pressure ease. Whatever was coming after her, hadn't succeeded, but she felt sick and dizzy so she lay still waiting for her mind to clear before she proceeded. Was Roman Howard capable of such an attack? He hadn't undergone the psychic experiment. Martin had. Martin had been taught such attacks.

Dahlia kept her head down, resting on her hands as she tried to piece it all together. She didn't dare move until she was controlling the motion sensors, and adrenaline was still racing through her body. Everyone who had undergone the experiment had some psychic ability prior to allowing Whitney to enhance what was already there.

Dahlia, you're scaring the hell out of me. Did he hurt you? Just his voice calmed her. She felt the air move through her lungs and her nerves steadied.

Did you feel that? she asked.

All of us did.

Can he hear you? Can he feel the surge around him when we communicate like this? She didn't want another attack until she was out of the narrow confines of the tube.

No, I've worked at sending only to one person. Martin Howard is concealed just outside the building entrance. It looks as if he followed his brother here and is waiting for him.

Was it Martin who attacked me?

It was impossible to tell who generated the attack or if it was specifically meant for one person. Our best guess is, whoever initiated the attack did so because he feels our presence and is uneasy. He was trying to draw us out.

Dahlia frowned. It made sense, but if he knew she was in the building and was hunting her, it made it all the more dangerous, especially if he were feeling strong emotions and he got close to her.

Are you going to abort?

Nicolas kept his voice neutral this time, and she was grateful to him. She had to think it through before she made a mistake. She took another breath, let it out slowly. *I'm so close, if I leave now, I'll have to do this again. I'm going to see if I can get in and out without trouble before I turn away on this one.*

She felt more than heard the echo of Nicolas's disappointment, the sheer frustration of not being able to command her the way he could his men. Was she being stubborn? It was one of her worst traits, but she didn't think so. It wasn't stubbornness, it was fear. She didn't want to be responsible for the research falling into the wrong hands and she never wanted to come back to the Lombard building.

When this is over, I want to see where you live, Nicolas.

I promise, Dahlia. Just don't let anything happen to you.

She took another breath and concentrated on the sensors. When she was certain she controlled them, she scooted forward until she was against the screen in the tunnel leading to the vault room. There were six access tunnels, all with the same camera setup and heavy doors. The security was tight, requiring retinal scans and codes. And that was after coming off the secure elevator that required the proper set of keys and a different access code.

She pulled her tool kit out of the sealed flap of her cargo pants and made short work of the screws on the vent screen. She had to control the cameras next, keeping them from seeing her as she slid from the tube and landed in a crouch on the floor. Cameras were easy to manage, but also easy to forget. If she let her mind drift, even when she was concentrating on other, more difficult tasks, she would be in trouble.

Dahlia stayed close to the wall and blurred her image just in case she slipped up. The most important thing was the access code. She knew it was changed on a daily basis. This was her favorite thing to do, cracking the access code and opening the vault. Her mind was already humming, feeling how to move the tumblers into place. Even though the vault had an electronic access code keypad, she didn't need to type in the numbers to figure out the right ones. In fact, she didn't dare attempt it since entering more than a couple of tries triggered the alarm. Dahlia simply bypassed the electronic part altogether, and worked directly with the mechanical spring-loaded tumblers.

She stayed very close to the wall, at the best angle to avoid the panning camera, just in case during this phase she forgot in her excitement. The retinal scan was easy enough to bypass, but the code was all-important, and it was her mind against the machine's.

She sat with her back against the wall as she began the hunt for the correct tumbler positions. It was bound to take a little time and with Roman Howard wandering around, she wanted to be in and out as quickly as possible. She had half the positions when the second attack came. A sharp thrust to her brain, piercing jabs scattering through her mind, jarring her out of her concentration. She clapped both hands over her head, pressing hard to relieve the terrible viselike grip. Her stomach lurched.

Dahlia held her mind's grip on the camera. She had to let go of the vault, but the camera was more important to control. She could always start over if she dropped the tumbler positions. The attack was hard and deadly, but because the sender didn't know whom he was attacking, it was unfocused. She received the brunt of it only because she was closer than the GhostWalkers, but they must have felt it as well.

Breathe deeply until it passes. Nicolas sounded gentle, calm. Normal for him. Just his voice seemed to help ease the pain. *We can't retaliate or he'll know for certain someone is here. Right now he's probing. He isn't sure.*

She wanted to answer him, reassure him she was all right, but the pressure in her head combined with controlling the camera was enough work. She hunkered down and went into meditative breathing, waiting for the assault to pass.

It lessened gradually, the pressure easing until she could think again. Immediately she focused on the vault. Roman Howard had absolutely no idea she was in the building, and he certainly didn't know she was opening the vault. He was psychic enough to be uneasy, but he couldn't find an enemy. Still, she needed to get out fast. If his uneasiness continued, he would check the vault.

She worked faster, staying alert as the tumblers dropped into place. She repressed the urge to laugh when she found the last, satisfying position and they lined up perfectly for her. Dahlia worked out the numbers that corresponded to those tumbler positions, and entered them into the digital keypad. Now she could feel the tumblers staying in place without her having to hold them there. She turned her attention to the retinal scan, finding the image of the last scan in the memory of the computer and repeating it. There was a moment of silence. Of expectation. The heavy vault door swung open.

Dahlia moved fast, running toward the row of what looked almost like safety-deposit boxes. Each was large and deep, able to hold most anything a research team needed to leave in safety. She bent to open one nearest the floor. In amongst the stacks of paper and zip drives, she found the precious disks holding the data on stealth torpedoes. There were no identifying marks, but she recognized the strange red circle the professor at Rutgers liked to use on his correspondence.

Dahlia tucked the disks into a Ziploc bag and shoved it inside her tightly woven jumper where she had a hidden pocket. Once it was safe, she arranged everything to look exactly as it had been, closed the vault, and took to the vent. She was going out toward the side entrance where the bushes were close instead of back up toward the roof. It was easier to get through the vents. She simply had to remember to be cautious of the motion sensors.

She had to take a few minutes to orient herself in the maze of vent tunnels before choosing the one she needed that would take her directly to the side entrance facing the narrow street. There was a yard to the back, and dogs were often left loose to guard it at night. The side entrance had less light and only two cameras. Dahlia unscrewed the screen and slipped out of the vent into the office. She could hear the guard talking to someone in the distance. Grateful that she just missed the guard and his dog, she hastily deactivated the alarms at the window and opened it. It was a fair distance to the ground, but she jumped, landing in a crouch close to the wall. She took one step toward the bushes when she heard the door hinges squeak. Men's voice intruded into the night.

Dahlia shrank back against the wall, stilled, and closed her eyes as two men emerged through the side door. Obviously in the middle of an argument, they remained close together, halting just a foot from her. She recognized

Trevor Billings, one of the researchers reputed to be a boy genius. The man Jesse Calhoun had been investigating. He glared at Roman Howard. "I told you not to come here anymore."

Roman shoved Trevor so hard, the smaller man had to grab his glasses to keep them from flying off his nose, and at the same time, he flung out a hand to grab the wall to steady himself. Dahlia could see his fingers only a scant few inches from her shoulder. She stared at them with a kind of sick horror. It seemed impossible that they wouldn't see her, but she concentrated on keeping her image as blurred as possible.

Trevor held up a placating hand as Roman stepped close to him. "We've got a good thing going. You bring me the research, and I develop it, and we can sell it to the highest bidder. You're going to blow it if you keep this up. What's wrong with you? The research was taken and unless we can recover it, we have to focus on the next step."

"Don't talk to me like you're a somebody, Billings. You were nothing, a pissant gofer no one noticed until I brought you the idea and set the entire thing up. My people are the ones taking all the chances while you sit in your little office and get the glory, looking like the genius. We both know you couldn't think your way out of a paper bag."

Dahlia couldn't get past the two men. She was trapped in the dark corner very near the bushes, but light from the streetlamp bathed the path in yellow. They would see her moving and know they weren't alone. She dared not even breathe with Trevor gripping the wall so close to her.

"We lost this one, Roman. I don't understand why it's so important that you'd risk everything. You're *hurting* people. Sooner or later they'll come after us."

Roman smirked at him. "*We're* killing people, Billings. That's an important part of the work and you're too much of a weasel to do it yourself. Get the hell out of here and don't be telling me where I can or can't go. I tell you what to do."

Dahlia was suddenly hit hard with the ferocious violent

energy, the urge to kill. The mass of energy swarmed around Roman, raced to hammer at Dahlia. She felt the rising need as it gained force. She wanted to shout at Trevor Billings to run. He must have seen the promise of death in Roman's eyes because he pulled himself away from the wall and began to edge away, stumbling toward the street.

Roman took a couple of steps after him, but then stopped abruptly and turned back as if he caught sight of something—or someone. She was certain he sensed someone close.

Dahlia froze, pushing her small body hard against the side of the wall, using every ounce of experience she had to control her breathing so that there was nothing to give her away. She kept her image blurred, but Roman Howard was close. So close she could reach out and touch him. He was furious. His anger radiated from him. He turned his head this way and that, sniffing the air, wanting to ferret out his enemy. He paced away from her, about five steps, and the light from the street lamp spilled over him for just an instant as he turned. Dahlia saw the knife blade laid flat against his wrist, the hilt in his closed fist.

Her breath caught in her throat. She pressed closer to the wall, wishing there was a crevice she could crawl into. Not only could she feel his anger, but violent energy poured from his body. Surrounded him. Ate at him until he was mumbling beneath his breath, hissing in retaliation, certain he was being watched and wanting to kill. Air slammed out of his lungs. He *wanted* to kill. Even *needed* to kill something or someone. The craving was so strong she feared for any innocent passersby.

The energy hit her in waves and she could read the ugly truth of Roman Howard's life. Always one step behind his brothers, yet a brilliant man who believed he could outwit everyone. He hated. The emotion boiled and churned in him, poisoning and eating away at him until he could barely control and conceal his actions. Dahlia felt it all, and the energy massed around her, choking her, filling her until the pressure was unbearable. She bit down hard on her wrist, concentrating on the pain, trying to block out the violence of Roman's emotions.

A shadow stepped from the wall not more than six feet from where she was concealed. Roman spun around and froze. Mesmerized, she watched his fingertips stroke the knife hilt.

"Martin, what are you doing here?" Roman cleared his throat and attempted a faint smile. "I thought you were on some big investigation. Louise told me you were in Atlanta."

"I was on my own investigation. I started wondering how anyone could have found out about Dahlia Le Blanc."

"Who? I don't know what you're talking about."

"I wish that were true, Roman, but only a very few people knew about Dahlia. We buried her under layers of flags and not one of those flags was ever raised. That's how I knew whoever went after her didn't find her through the computers, and they couldn't have had personal knowledge of her. Jesse knew where she lived, but it would be ludicrous to think he tortured himself." Martin ran both hands through his hair, dark shadows in his eyes. His face was etched with pain. "Dahlia paid Louise a little visit last night. Jesse's condition wasn't common knowledge, but you knew. How would you know, Roman? You didn't think I'd be talking to Louise so soon after you told me, did you? You let me believe she told you, but she didn't know anything about Jesse and was shocked when I gave her the news."

Roman shrugged. "Who knew they were going to keep it a secret? Why would they? It made sense that Louise would know. A small mistake, but in the end it still won't matter."

"It was enough for me to know what you were doing. Why, Roman?"

Roman's smile was a parody, his teeth bared like a wolf. "You tell me. You're Martin, the almighty. You can never do anything wrong, but I think when they start investigating, they'll see you aren't so innocent."

"You planted evidence to incriminate me."

"Someone has to take the fall. You're too squeaky-clean to be true. How would I ever be a suspect? They won't find a single bug, anything at all to connect me to anything. I didn't know the woman. I've never heard of the woman."

Martin spread his hands out in front of him. "So this was all about jealousy? You wanted to get back at me?"

Roman burst out laughing. It was an ugly sound and the waves of violent energy nearly became a tidal wave washing over her. "Don't flatter yourself. It's about money and power. Of course they chose the golden boy for the experiment, when I had far more ability than you. And of course something went wrong, and they compensated you with a trust to set you up for life. Why you, Martin? We both know I have more natural talent than you do. You lied to them about me. You and Calhoun kept me out of the program."

Dahlia choked back the bile rising in her throat. Her body was trembling, nearly shaking apart. She knew if she didn't expel part of the energy, she would have a seizure. And that meant allowing the two men to know they weren't alone. The research material was burning a hole through her skin, reminding her that she had to protect it at all costs. She was wearing work clothes. Both men would know she'd been recovering something and they would search her body.

She turned her head and focused on the middle of the street where nothing could possibly burn. Flames leapt through the air. The road blackened. Both men turned their heads toward the fiery display.

Roman swore savagely, took a step toward his brother. Martin frowned at the leaping flames, then looked carefully around him, suddenly wary. Suddenly aware Dahlia had to be somewhere close.

"What is it?" Roman demanded.

"How the hell would I know?" Martin asked. "How far are you into this, Roman? What have you done?"

Roman laughed. "*I'm* not into it at all. You forget you're the one they have the evidence against. Are they going to believe I can read minds? That I've been reading Louise's mind for years? I don't think so. They'll blame you, Martin. Louise will even blame you, her golden boy." He stepped closer, his knife hand at his side, concealing the weapon.

"Do you really think I'll let you destroy my reputation and everything I've worked for?" Martin asked.

Dahlia's gaze was on the knife hand. The fingers caressed the hilt. She could feel Roman's rising excitement, the lust for the kill. She stepped away from the wall. Nicolas cursed, his protest loud in her mind.

"He has a knife, Martin, and he intends to use it on you," she said softly.

Both men spun toward her. She stayed in the shadows and kept her image as blurred as possible to prevent either man from seeing the bad shape she was in.

"*You!*" Roman spit on the ground, his eyes narrowed and dangerous. "I should have guessed it was you."

"Are you going to kill both of us with your knife?" she asked. The shaking was worse, rising in direct proportion to Roman's eagerness for violence.

"No one would believe a crazy woman." He took another step toward Martin.

Dahlia sucked in her breath. "Don't!" she said sharply. "Don't get any closer to him. Can't you feel it? Can't you feel the guns trained on you? They'll never let you get close to either one of us. Put the knife down and let the lawyers handle it."

Martin looked around them, a long careful search of their surroundings. "It's them, isn't it? The GhostWalker team. They're out there watching us."

She nodded. "They have a sniper with them, Roman. He's a remarkable shot. Put down the knife. This isn't worth your life."

"You're lying."

"She isn't lying," Martin denied. "You should be able to feel them, Roman, I can. Who's the sniper, Dahlia?"

The violence was building to an appalling level. She felt

her legs turn to rubber and she sat down, frightened at her own weakness. She was only a few feet from Roman. If he chose, he could easily leap on her and stab her, and there was little she could do about it as weak and helpless as she felt. It took all of her concentration to keep from having a seizure. "Nicolas Trevane," she answered.

Roman's head jerked up and he began swearing repetitiously. With each oath, the energy spewing from him swirled around Dahlia, black and ferocious.

Get rid of it. Nicolas sounded calm. Dead calm. Ice-cold calm. She knew immediately he was in hunter mode, and he was locked on target.

I didn't want to distract you.

I don't get distracted. There was complete confidence in his voice.

Dahlia turned her head and once again focused on the street. Fire rained from the sky. White-hot streaks of orange and red fell in a shower and danced over the street, some flames leaping as high as six feet.

Martin looked at the display with a kind of awe. Roman shifted his weight to the balls of his feet, bringing his knife hand low, blade up, as he lunged at his brother. Dahlia saw the impact of the bullet before the sound reached them. Roman's body jerked. Like a rag doll, he was flung forward and fell into Martin, driving him to the ground with his dead weight.

The rush of energy hit her hard and fast, sending her over the edge. She fell to the ground, a seizure taking her, bile choking her, fighting to stay conscious to protect the data she had recovered. It was impossible to stay focused as the energy ate her alive, her temperature soaring and the pressure building and building until there was nowhere for it to go.

Kaden reached her first. Nicolas had been trapped on the rooftop, protecting her and, although he was certain of his shot, he didn't dare take his eyes off his downed target, or even Martin, until Kaden signaled him an all clear. Kaden knelt beside her and put both hands on her shoulders, trying to absorb the energy consuming her. He glanced at Martin who knelt weeping beside his brother. "Are you an anchor?"

Martin hesitated, and then nodded.

"Get the hell over here. Put your hands on her," Kaden ordered.

Martin complied, somewhat in shock as the other GhostWalkers joined them. Gator made the call to Lily to inform the director of the NCIS that the data was recovered and the traitor found. Nicolas rushed to Dahlia's side and gathered her into his arms.

"This is the last time. I swear, never again, Dahlia," he whispered as the convulsion eased and left her staring up at him with wide, dark eyes. "You scare me to death. The only way I'm going to breathe properly again is if you come home with me where I can keep my eye on you around the clock."

"Just get me to some place where the data will be safe until I can give it to the admiral," she whispered.

He brushed a kiss across her forehead. "I'm on it."

TWENTY

"When I asked you to bring me somewhere safe," Dahlia said, "this wasn't what I had in mind." She swam to the edge of the pool and shaded her eyes to look up at him. "And I can't believe you made the director fly out here himself to collect the data. Research, which, by the way, is probably not even going to yield a weapon for them."

"I didn't force him," Nicolas pointed out. "And he could have sent someone else. He wanted to see you."

Dahlia scowled, or pretended to. She was feeling too relaxed and happy to conjure up much of a protest. "He just wanted to meet you and talk about the GhostWalkers. His poor men are struggling through so many problems. Do you really think Lily can help them?"

"She helped us. I told the admiral all they had to do was call her, identify themselves, and she'd bring them into the program. It isn't like it's a deep dark secret that they exist. Lily suspected some time ago that her father had performed the experiment on the girls first, on us, and then on another set of men privately in his laboratories. We haven't uncovered the research on them, but it was only a matter of time. Dr. Whitney was thorough in his research data. He recorded everything. It's in the lab, and Lily will find it. They may as well come in and let her help them."

"I still say you forced the admiral to come here on purpose." She studied his face for a long moment, her gaze moving lovingly over him. "You wanted him to see the contrast in how I was living before, and what I'm doing now, with you," she guessed shrewdly. "You wanted to throw it in his face."

He shrugged easily and shook his head. "I'm going to maintain I didn't force him." He gave her his most expressionless stone face, but it didn't last, turning almost immediately into a smirk. He had made the point in a quiet way, but he knew the admiral had gotten it.

Nicolas stood near his fascinating waterfall, almost hidden among the lush greenery, looking primitive without a stitch on his hard, muscular body. Dahlia sent up a plume of water and pushed off, floating backward away from the edge. She knew he liked watching her, his black gaze drifting over her body, dwelling on every curve and secret hollow. There was always hunger in his gaze, an intense desire he never hid from her. It shook her up inside and she was certain it always would. "Yes you did," she replied. "You told him I couldn't travel and he needed to get the data to a safe place. Basically, you left him no choice."

Nicolas shrugged, in no way perturbed. "We had a good visit." He crouched down beside the edge of the pool and offered her a glass of strawberry lemonade. It was an enticement, pure and simple. Dahlia loved the drink, and he knew she'd eventually swim to the side of the pool and he would be able to devour the sight of her body gliding through the water, her breasts floating free and the occasional inviting temptation of her feminine channel flashing at him as she swam around first. She loved the water and spent a great deal of time swimming naked in the pool. Sometimes he enjoyed just sitting in a chair watching her swim, his body reacting with a hard, painful ache he knew he could assuage at any time.

"Is this a trap?" she asked warily, eyeing the frosted glass.

"Could be." He didn't bother to hide his body's reaction to her. He was hard and thick and throbbing with an urgent desire. But he enjoyed wanting her. He loved what she did to his body, bringing him such complete pleasure. It never mattered where they were or what they were doing, she could move a certain way and the air between them crackled with sexual tension instantly.

Her fascinating mouth curved into a small, enticing smile. "Really? I do so love your little traps. I've been here nearly two weeks."

"Yes, my prisoner. I've got you where I want you." He took a sip of the strawberry lemonade and ran his tongue over his bottom lip to catch every drop. "And I don't intend to let you go."

"That's so not fair! You know I'm addicted to that lemonade."

"It's ice-cold, just the way you like it too," he tempted her. He took another slow swallow, allowed icy droplets that beaded on the glass to run down his skin. Her gaze followed the small drops, her black eyes suddenly blazing with heat.

"You know what I think?" she asked. "I think you're trying to make me forget I've been living in your house for nearly two weeks and doing nothing but playing." She ran to her heart's content, all along the small narrow paths winding through the mountainous property. She spent hours swimming in the pool, feeling incredibly decadent. They worked out together in his gym and sparred in his dojo. And they made love everywhere. Wherever he wanted, or she wanted. Or when emotions were so intense they had to be indulged. Sometimes it was a dark and ravenous hunger and sometimes it was unbearably tender and gentle.

"I think you're right," he acknowledged without the

least bit of remorse. "You've been so worried you couldn't have a life with me, but here you are and we've done fine."

She laughed. The sound pleased him, turning him inside out, the way it always did. The air crackled. He could hear the sound mingle with her laugh, and the urge in him to have her under him, crying out his name, grew stronger. They found they fed each other sexual energy and they learned to allow it to flow over them and through them without fighting it. Utilizing it. Enjoying it.

"I think you're leading me somewhere, Nicolas."

"Are you accusing me of having ulterior motives?"

Dahlia swam closer. The tips of her breasts swayed enticingly. She looked like an exotic water nymph to him, a siren calling continually. Nicolas loved to answer the call. She was calling to him now, with every movement of her body. Dahlia wasn't shy, and she wasn't in the least inhibited about lovemaking. She enjoyed his body every bit as much as he enjoyed hers and she let him know.

He set the glass on the edge of the pool, just out of her reach. She took the bait, holding out a hand to him so he could pull her out of the water. It poured off her body, leaving behind little beads. She lay on her stomach on the thick mat he always left out for her to sun on, reaching for her drink. The action stretched her body, gave him a pleasant view of the round side of her breast and a perfect view of the inviting curve of her bottom. He leaned down lazily and lapped at the water pooling in the small of her back. His hand wandered over the feminine slope of her bottom.

Dahlia smiled. "I love this lemonade." She shivered under his touch. His tongue dipped into the dimples on her back, his mouth wandered lower. "Hey!" It was a half-hearted protest as his teeth nipped, but she lay still, absorbing the feel of his mouth and hands as he leisurely explored her body, his teeth giving little love bites and his tongue licking along her skin. She closed her eyes and laid her head on her arm, fingers curled around the glass of lemonade.

Nicolas massaged her legs, his fingers kneading her

muscles. The sun beat down on her body and the wind touched her gently, adding to the bliss of the moment.

"Turn over, *kiciciyapi mitawa*." Nicolas's voice had the husky note in it, the one she was so familiar with when he called her his heart. That single note could turn her entire body to instant liquid heat.

She kept her eyes closed. "If I turn over, you're going to have your wicked way with me. I rather like lying here, knowing how much you want me."

He leaned over her, kissed the nape of her neck, blazed a trail of kisses along her spine. "I'm going to have my wicked way with you no matter what."

"Are you now?" She shifted, a slow, lazy roll over with his body over hers so that her skin rubbed against his skin. The ache in her breasts grew. The throbbing between her legs became more insistent. His shoulders were wide, blocking out the sun, his eyes black with hunger. She traced his strong jaw with loving fingers. "I have no say in this at all?"

"None," he declared. "This is all mine." His face was close to hers, his warm breath teasing her skin. He kissed her, a long, hard kiss that told her his slow, leisurely manner was a façade. He was boiling inside, a volcanic eruption imminent. Deliberately, Dahlia trailed her fingertips over his belly. She smiled as she felt the reaction, his muscles tightening, the long thick length of him hardening even more against her thigh.

He pushed her hands away from him, took her glass of lemonade from her, tilting the glass so that the ice-cold contents splashed on her stomach and raced to her belly button. Immediately he followed the path of the liquid, his tongue swirling over her bare skin, lapping at the underside of her breast, along her ribs, teasing her stomach and navel until her hips writhed beneath him.

His arm clamped over her thighs. "Don't move. I just want to indulge myself."

Dahlia lay back, her arms stretched over her head, her body open to his exploration. She loved him in this mood. "Go ahead, who am I to stop your fun."

He pulled her thighs apart and pushed his hand into her heat. He was a little rough, his hands hard as they massaged her thighs and his fingers pushed through her wet folds, but her body and her heart always wanted more.

She could taste her own sexual excitement, lying there open to him in the sun, an offering to him as his tongue made a foray lower, teasing her, taunting her, claiming her body for his own. He always made her feel as if she belonged to him. As if he belonged to her. She shivered as his tongue plunged deep and he held her helpless under his larger, stronger body. He always made her feel safe and excited rather than vulnerable.

He lapped at her, licking her as if she were filled with honey and he needed every drop just to live. A sound escaped her throat. She tried to push into his hungry mouth, but his arm was clamped hard around her thighs, making it impossible. His teeth scraped at the tender flesh just inside her thigh. He lifted her hips, dragged her to him, allowing his sexual appetite to increase. The energy flowed around them, massed between them.

Dahlia recognized it, embraced it, allowing it to take her over, swamp her with the same driving obsession of hunger. Her breasts ached until she cupped them, wanting to relieve the ache. Instantly he pulled her hands away from her body and took possession of her breasts, claiming her for his own. He suckled strongly, the rhythm in time with his fingers as they drove in and out of her, going deep, pushing her needs higher and higher.

Excitement flushed her body, made her so wet and welcoming she could barely keep from screaming. Her fingers tangled in his hair and she tried to tug, to bring him over her, to make him enter her. "I want you so much, Nicolas, hurry up."

Her breathless gasps only fueled the fire raging in him. Elusive Dahlia. She refused to commit to him. It made him crazy sometimes. He wanted to bind her to him, even if all he had was the sexual firestorm neither could ever sufficiently put out. She moved under him like so much heated silk. She tasted of honey and strawberry. She matched his every sexual hunger, never denied him anything. Yet he always felt her slipping away from him.

He lifted his head to look at her face. The sexual need was etched there, just as he knew it was on his face. "Marry me, Dahlia. Stay with me forever."

She stilled beneath his hands, his mouth. He couldn't believe the plea had slipped out when he knew she wasn't ready. He lowered his mouth to her breast, lapping at her nipple, suckling there, while his fingers pushed deeper into her body.

Dahlia's gaze was on the flames dancing around the pool. They tried to save their hottest lovemaking for outdoors, near the water where they knew it was safer. "Are you certain, Nicolas?"

He went just as still, lifting his head to look down at her. Shocked. Hope was a terrible thing, pushing its way into his heart and soul. "You know I love you, Dahlia. I never want to be without you."

"What if we can't ever have a family?" She pushed her hips against his plunging fingers, wanting him inside of her. Desperate for his invasion.

"We'll be our own family." His heart was pounding, his body nearly exploding.

She squirmed against his hand. "Once you're inside me, I'll give you my answer."

He didn't wait. There was no waiting, if he didn't take her right then, he might lose all control. He caught her hips and dragged her to him, her legs around him, so that he could plunge into her tight, wet channel. He drove in deep and hard, his hands clamped on her ankles, forcing her legs to wrap around his waist. There was little give in the mat and he could lever himself above her, thrusting with long, deep strokes. He was instantly lost in the inferno of her body. Sanity always went out the window when he was thrusting into her, when she was lifting her hips to meet the impact of his, when she opened herself more, determined to take all of him.

He loved her like this, her face turned up to his, her breasts swaying with the jolting impact of their union. She was so beautiful. So real. Her muscles clenched around him, squeezing and gripping until he thought he'd go out of his mind. He heard his mind screaming at her, chanting over and over. *Say yes, say you want me the same way*. He couldn't speak, couldn't get a word out when she was milking his body of every drop of pleasure from his toes to the top of his head.

Dahlia's body moved in perfect rhythm with his. He surrounded her, battered at her, loved her. She craved him in the same way he craved her. Not just his body, as beautiful as it was, but the two sides of his nature, wild and rough and gentle and tender. He was rough now, his hands hard, fingers biting into her as the energy swelled with the ferocity of their lovemaking. She matched him, her nails biting deep, her cries for more, always more. She drove him with the same wild hunger as he drove her.

She felt her climax building and building, pushing past pleasure until it was close to pain. Then she was gripping him hard, taking him with her over the edge so they tumbled together. She screamed her answer, the breath exploding out of her as her body rocked with her orgasm. Sparks showered down over the pool, a spectacular display of fireworks. The embers fell hissing into the water. They lay together in silence listening to the crackle of the dancing flames and just smiled at one another.

When he could breathe again, when his heart stopped pounding, Nicolas leaned down to press a kiss into her navel. "You said yes." He whispered the words against her belly, not looking at her. Just waiting.

Her fingers clutched his hair. "Surely you aren't going to hold me to it when you were clearly using unethical means of persuasion." There was teasing laughter in her voice. Contentment. Purring.

Nicolas kissed his way up to her breast. "Of course I am. I'm that kind of man."

"Well then, I guess you're stuck with me."

Nicolas kept his head down. He didn't dare look at her when his heart was overwhelmed with joy. Emotions with Dahlia were always amplified. Always intense. "I guess I am." His voice was husky, but it worked. "I love you, Dahlia. You won't be sorry."

Her laughter vibrated around him. "I'm not worried about me."

He kissed her because he had to. They shared the last of the lemonade and lay side by side, relaxing in the sun. He kept his hand on her. "I thought we could visit Lily next week. She's been so anxious, and I hate to keep putting her off." He made it casual, but he felt her stiffen beneath his palm.

"I don't know." That was all she said, but he heard the fear in her voice.

"Ryland said if we don't go there soon, Lily and Ryland will be coming here. It means so much to her, Dahlia, and she can start you on all the exercises she has us doing daily to strengthen our barriers."

"You can teach me the exercises," she pointed out.

"True, but she can come up with ones specifically designed to keep energy at bay." He had no idea if Lily could really do that, but he thought there was a good chance that she could.

"All right. I'll go. But if I burn down her house and disgrace you in front of your friend Ryland and all the Ghost-Walkers, you still have to marry me."

She had her face turned away from him, but he knew, in spite of her teasing tone, she was voicing a real fear.

He moved over the top of her again, pinning her small, fragile body beneath him. Framing her face with his hands, he took possession of her mouth. He could never get enough of kissing her. His tongue forced her lips apart and swept inside, staking his claim, pouring his love into her mouth, down her throat, into her body. "That's a promise," he agreed sincerely.

* * *

"I can't do this, Nicolas," Dahlia said.

She was so pale Nicolas was certain she was going to faint. He brought the car to a halt just outside the gates to the huge estate and leaned out the window to key in the proper code.

Dahlia had one hand on the door handle, ready to jump. She looked at him, her eyes huge. "Really, Nicolas, I can't. Let's go before someone sees we're here."

Nicolas waved to the security camera, knowing Arly, Lily's security man, would have already spotted them, identified them, and taken down the license number on the car. The gates swung open slowly, and Dahlia held her breath until he thought she was going to pass out.

"I've never seen you like this, Dahlia." He put his hand over hers to calm her. "Lily has waited and waited to meet you. She was going to come to us, and she would have, but you said you wanted to come back here, to see what you could remember." He kept his voice very soothing.

"I know. I just never thought I'd feel this way." She caught at his fingers and squeezed hard. "I can barely breathe."

Dahlia looked around her at the lush grounds with rolling lawns and flowers of every color rioting for space. She had believed she would remember the house, the grounds, yet she didn't remember any of it. She could only sit, trembling, waiting to see Lily. Waiting to believe Lily was real and not a figment of her childhood imagination, born out of desperation and need for one person to love her in her life. If Lily rejected her, turned away from her, Dahlia wasn't certain she would survive it.

As the car moved up the long drive, she could see a woman standing on the steps of the huge, sprawling mansion. The house belonged in Europe with its enormous design and many wings. Dahlia watched as the woman shaded her eyes and clutched at the man standing close to her. He put his arm around her.

"That's Lily, isn't it?" Lily. She was beautiful and very

real. Dahlia hardly recognized her own voice. She held Nicolas's hand tighter.

"Yes, with her husband, Ryland." Nicolas wanted to gather Dahlia in his arms and hold her to him. She was trembling with excitement, gripping his hand and he could see her pulse pounding frantically in her neck. She was very pale, her eyes enormous, almost too big for her face. "*Tekihila*, my love, she'll love you. How could she not?" Dahlia still didn't believe herself lovable. He could see the hesitation in her gaze every time she looked at him. Her confidence in their relationship had grown over the two weeks he'd kept her to himself at his home, but coming to Lily's house had shaken her.

He stopped the car, barely getting it in park before Lily rushed down the stairs toward them.

"She's limping," Dahlia said.

"An accident, when she was a child," Nicolas answered. "During an experiment."

It was the right thing to say to propel Dahlia out of the car and into Lily's arms. Nicolas slipped from the car and took Ryland's outstretched hand. Ryland tugged and gave him a warrior's embrace, releasing him abruptly.

"She's been on pins and needles all morning," Ryland reported. "I've never seen her like this. She even gave the staff orders left and right. That's never done."

"Dahlia's the same. I didn't think we'd make it here. She's a bundle of nerves. She's very afraid she might hurt someone or at the least, start a fire."

"Believe me, Lily could care less. I think Dahlia's like a long-lost sister to her."

"Dahlia feels the same way," Nicolas said. "Any news on Trevor Billings? Has the NCIS finished their investigation? The admiral came out a couple of weeks ago, but we haven't heard since."

Ryland shook his head. "Not completely. Billings has been arrested, and, of course, banned from Lombard Inc. Lombard is denying any knowledge of the things he was doing and they're still investigating. Their lawyers dropped him like a hot potato. They want the company to come out of this squeaky-clean."

"It's possible they didn't know anything at all about what he was doing," Nicolas pointed out.

"Possible, but not probable that someone at the top didn't have a clue," Ryland said. "In any case, it isn't our problem." He put his arm around Lily, a signal for an introduction.

Lily pulled herself out of Dahlia's arms, tears running down her face. "Dahlia, this is my husband, Ryland Miller. He's a GhostWalker as well."

Ryland ignored Dahlia's outstretched hand and pulled her into his arms, giving her a hard, welcoming hug, completely ignoring her slight hesitation. "It's great to finally meet the woman who conquered Nicolas."

That made Dahlia laugh. "Is that what I've done?"

"He says so," Ryland said, gently wiping the tears from Lily's face and leaning in to kiss the corner of her mouth.

That small gesture won Dahlia's heart. She couldn't stop staring at Lily, at the beloved face, the eyes she remembered. And Lily was looking at her the same way.

Nicolas swept his arm around Dahlia's waist. "You know you have."

"Are you ready to go in the house, Dahlia?" Lily asked uncertainly. "I don't want you to do anything you're uncomfortable with. We're very good at guarding emotions, so we can keep you from overload, but facing the house may be too much."

Dahlia shook her head. "I thought I'd remember so much more. Nothing looks familiar to me."

Lily took Dahlia's hand. "The room will. The moment I found his hidden laboratory, I recognized our rooms. I hadn't even remembered until that moment. I don't want you to feel alone and violated and confused the way I did. I want to be with you, if you don't mind."

"I came to see you, Lily. I came to terms with my past a long time ago." Dahlia wasn't certain if that were completely true. She wanted it to be. Now that Lily was standing in front of her, she wasn't certain she wanted to confront her past. She had a future. She still had one foot out the door, and thought of her relationship with Nicolas as tentative, but she knew he was fully committed and would do his best to help her. She thought having Nicolas would be enough. Now she wanted a family. She wanted to be part of something, and the GhostWalkers were welcoming her, treating her as a valued member. And there was Lily. Wonderful Lily.

"Have you spoken to Jesse Calhoun?" Lily asked as they turned to go into the house together.

Dahlia ignored the sudden tripping of her heart. "Yes, several times. He's very upbeat. He told me he's always written songs and plans to continue with that. He mentioned something about owning a radio station in his hometown. He's going back there as soon as the hospital allows him to go. He didn't tell me, but the director said he wouldn't walk again."

"I've spoken with him several times, and I've already begun working with him on building barriers in his mind." Lily sighed. "It's such a tragedy. Jesse is a good man. Ryland and I spent a great deal of time with him. He just doesn't let anything get him down. I know he'll come through this, but it's sad."

"The man I feel sorry for is Martin Howard," Dahlia said. "He loved his brother. I saw it on his face. I think he might have let his brother kill him."

Nicolas pressed a kiss to her temple. Dahlia had been so close to Roman Howard that his heart had been in his throat. He hadn't dared to take his eye from the target, and there'd been no way to protect her from the raging violent energy that had surrounded her. He never wanted to feel that helpless again. "I wasn't going to let that happen," he said matter-of-factly, pushing away the memory of her convulsions and his fear of what kind of damage her physical response to violence might occur.

They walked through the enormous, intricately carved oak door into the entryway of the house. Dahlia found her mouth was dry. An older woman stood uncertainly, wringing her hands together and smiling, although she looked suspiciously close to tears. "Dahlia, this is Rosa. She's been a mother to me all these years and keeps the house running," Lily said.

Dahlia didn't recognize the woman at all, but the name stirred memories. Of a nurse named Rosa who always took care of Lily. Milly had stayed with Dahlia just as Rosa had opted to stay with Lily. "I'm so pleased to meet you," she murmured around the lump in her throat. She couldn't quite decide how she felt. Her emotions were welling up out of nowhere, struggling to be recognized, but it was the last thing Dahlia wanted. She was *not* going to set fire to Lily's house.

"It's good you've come back to us, Miss Dahlia," Rosa greeted.

The voice was in her head. She remembered it calling to Lily, pulling her away from Dahlia in the middle of the night. She remembered the pain in her head, nearly splitting it open, the shards of glass being driven into her skull. At once her temperature began to rise and the pressure in her chest increased. Dahlia halted. "Maybe this isn't such a good idea. It could be dangerous."

"This house belongs to all of us, Dahlia," Lily said firmly. "It's stood up to all of our various problems and it can stand up to yours. Won't it, Rosa?"

"Of course. Can I offer you anything to eat or drink?" Rosa asked.

Dahlia shook her head. If she tried to eat, she might get sick.

Lily seemed to know how she was feeling. They just wanted it over. She led Dahlia and Nicolas to the room that had been her father's office. The door was securely locked. "I don't let anyone come in here," Lily explained. "There are too many sensitive documents." She approached a tall, beautiful clock and opened the glass door.

"If this is too difficult, Lily," Dahlia began.

"No, I want you to see. It helps that there were several

of us. We started together. I found you, and together, we'll find the others." The clock revealed a hidden door. It slid open and revealed another door in the floor itself.

Dahlia's heart was pounding out of control. For a moment she couldn't move. Lily started down the stairs, calling back to her. "I can help you shield yourself from the amounts of energy you draw, not all, but it should allow you to be in public, maybe go to a show once in a while or shop for clothes when people are in the store with you."

Nicolas reached for Dahlia's hand, pulled her tightly against him, ready to take her out of the house the instant she indicated it was too much for her.

With Nicolas touching her, Dahlia's emotions could be kept in check. "How? I've worked all my life to control it, Lily," she asked, wanting to believe, but not daring to. "All of you do seem to have such control." She didn't set a foot on the stairs, but watched Ryland follow his wife down.

"Everyone suffers headaches, and other physical repercussions when they use their talents, but you're the first energy magnet," Lily replied. "I didn't realize I'd been experimented on, and I thought my father had provided this house with its massive walls and soundproofing to protect me. Of course, he was protecting his experiments for the most part." She stopped on the bottom stair and looked back up at Dahlia.

"It must have been terrible for you to discover the truth," Dahlia sympathized. She felt physically ill at the thought of Lily finding the tapes of their terrible childhood. Nicolas had told her how Lily had gone looking for a way to help save the GhostWalkers and found the evidence of her father's betrayal. She felt physically ill at the thought of joining Lily in viewing those tapes.

"You don't have to do this," Nicolas reminded.

Dahlia took a deep breath. She did have to do this. Dr. Peter Whitney was the monster in her nightmares. She'd believed she might be crazy because she had such vivid impressions of this laboratory, yet she'd been told repeatedly it didn't exist. But most of all, she had to go see her past because Lily was grounded there. She wanted Lily in her life. She wanted to claim her as family. And she wanted to help Lily find the other women Whitney had experimented on. She couldn't bear to think they were out there somewhere in the world, alone, feeling as if they might be insane. It had started in the underground laboratory and she needed to confront it. She put her foot on the narrow, steep stair, and made her way down.

She stared at the one-way expanse of glass. At the door leading to the small dormitory rooms. Her hand went to her throat protectively. "It is real. I'm not crazy."

Lily wrapped her arms around Dahlia. "No, of course you're not crazy. I've got all the tapes of our childhood. I've got investigators looking for the other girls as well. I think I may have found one. We're not certain yet, but it's a possibility. I'll show you everything, Dahlia."

"Do you remember the other girls? I've been trying to remember them. Flame, with her red, red hair. She's very vivid in my memory."

"Iris," Lily confirmed. "And there was Tansy. She was very quiet and introverted."

"That's right." Relief was flooding through her. She did remember the other children. Girls, all of them with their own nurse. "There was the baby, Jonquille. She was so tiny. And Laurel. Who else?"

"Wasn't there a Rose? I remember her laughing."

Dahlia nodded. There wasn't much laughter in the laboratory. She should have remembered Rose. "I know there are others."

"We'll think of them together," Lily consoled. "We'll find all their tapes, and we'll find them."

They looked at one another and smiled in understanding. Lily held out her hand. Dahlia took it. "I'm so glad you've come. Ryland is wonderful. I love him so much, but I felt alone sometimes. You make that go away."

"That's exactly how I feel," Dahlia admitted. "Is this where Dr. Whitney brought Jesse and the others when he experimented on them?"

Lily nodded. "He didn't want Colonel Higgens to know about them. He suspected Higgens was trying to kill the GhostWalkers, and he wanted to make certain his experiment was carried on."

"Basically," Ryland said, "Dr. Whitney used my group as a decoy to keep Higgens from knowing about his other group. He worked here at this laboratory and the men used the tunnels to get in and out."

"So if you all died," Dahlia reached for Nicolas, "he'd still have someone to continue his research on." She bit back the rest of her thoughts when she saw Lily's face. "I'm sorry, I know you must have loved him."

Lily leaned against Ryland for comfort. "I think of him as two men. The monster who did all this to us, and to the men, and the man who was my father."

"Have you found his research on Calhoun and the others?" Nicolas asked.

Lily nodded. "A couple of days ago. I haven't gone over it, but once I do, I should be able to find all the problems and start working up a program for them." She turned to Dahlia. "Just as I will for you."

Dahlia looked up at Nicolas—her rock, her anchor. The man that had provided a life and now a family for her. She wrapped her arms around his neck, her first real spontaneous demonstration of affection in front of others. "Thank you. Thank you for giving me back my life."

He kissed her, uncaring that Ryland had a silly grin on his face and that Lily was looking too pleased with herself. "I love you, Dahlia Le Blanc. I always will."

Her black, haunting gaze drifted over his face. "It's a good thing, because I love you very much, Nicolas Trevane, and if you trifle with my feelings, you're playing with fire. Literally."